POKÉMON

POCKET COMICS CLASSIC

STORY & ART BY
SANTA HARUKAZE

SLOWKING KIRLIA: Pun King

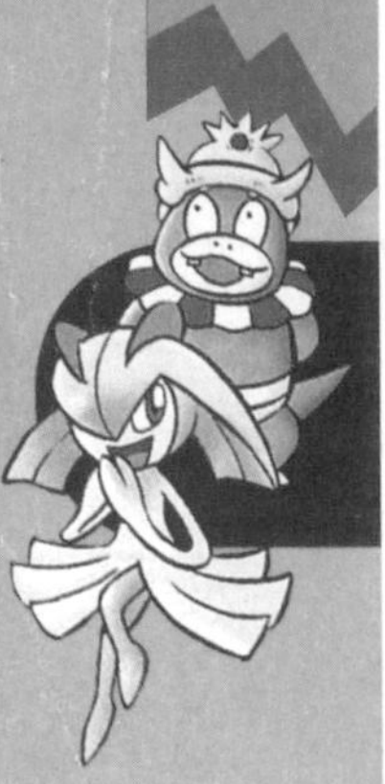

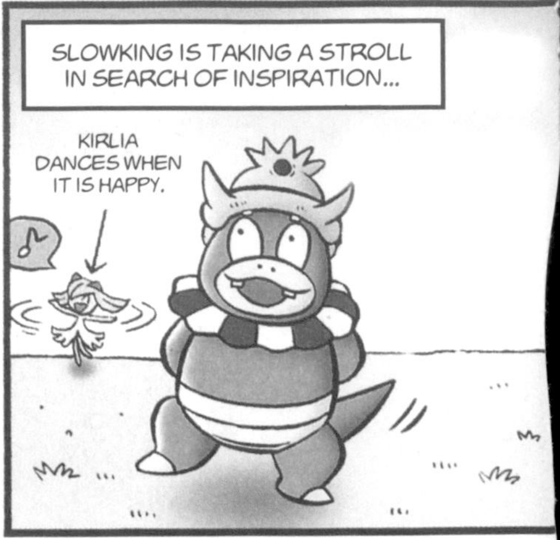
SLOWKING IS TAKING A STROLL IN SEARCH OF INSPIRATION...
KIRLIA DANCES WHEN IT IS HAPPY.

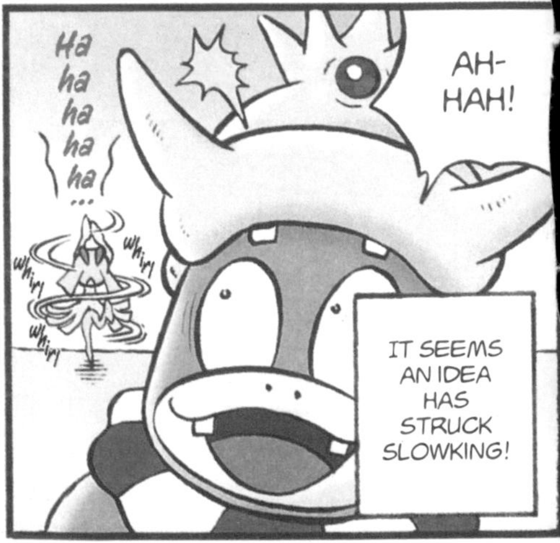
Ha ha ha ha ha...
AH-HAH!
whirl
whirl
whirl
IT SEEMS AN IDEA HAS STRUCK SLOWKING!

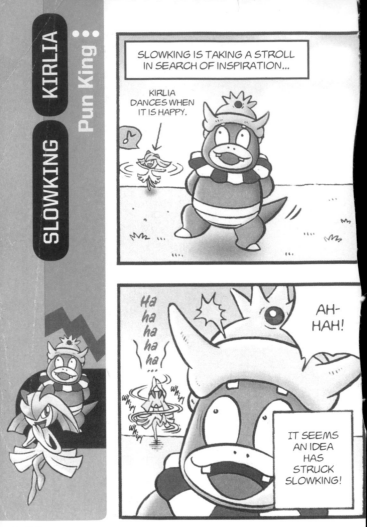

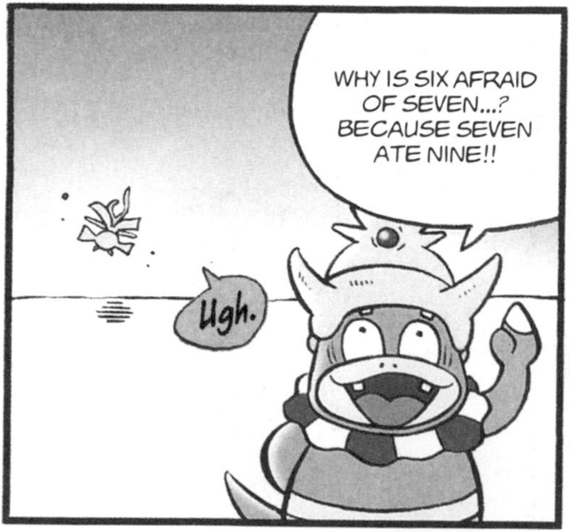
WHY IS SIX AFRAID OF SEVEN...? BECAUSE SEVEN ATE NINE!!
Ugh.

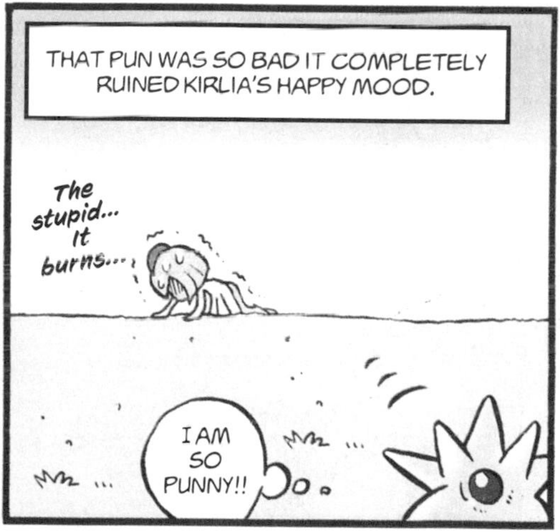
THAT PUN WAS SO BAD IT COMPLETELY RUINED KIRLIA'S HAPPY MOOD.
The stupid... It burns...
I AM SO PUNNY!!

SLOWKING

When its head was bitten, toxins entered Slowking's head and unlocked an extraordinary power. However, it apparently forgets everything it has learned if the Shellder on its head comes off.

KIRLIA

It has the power to see into the future. It also dances happily on sunny mornings.

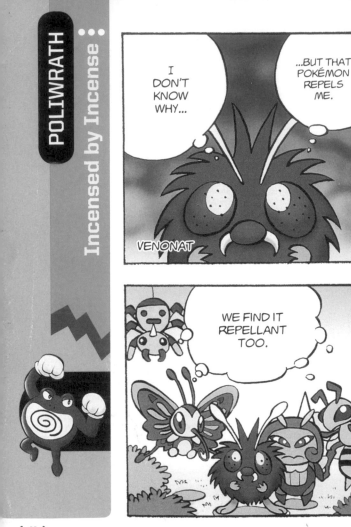

POLIWRATH

Incensed by Incense...

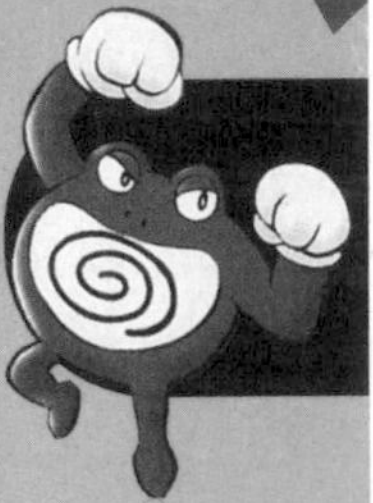

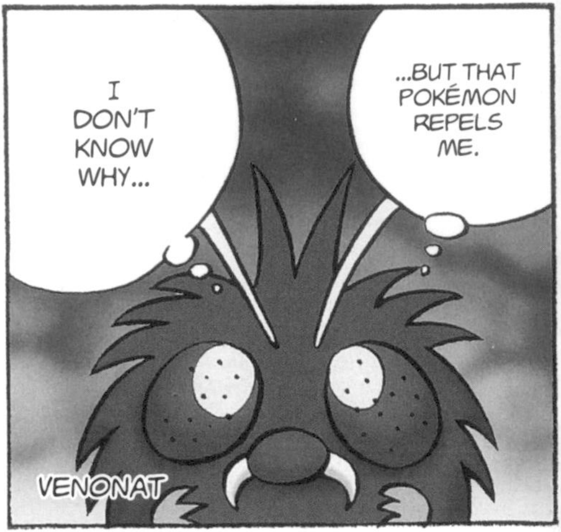
I DON'T KNOW WHY...
...BUT THAT POKÉMON REPELS ME.
VENONAT

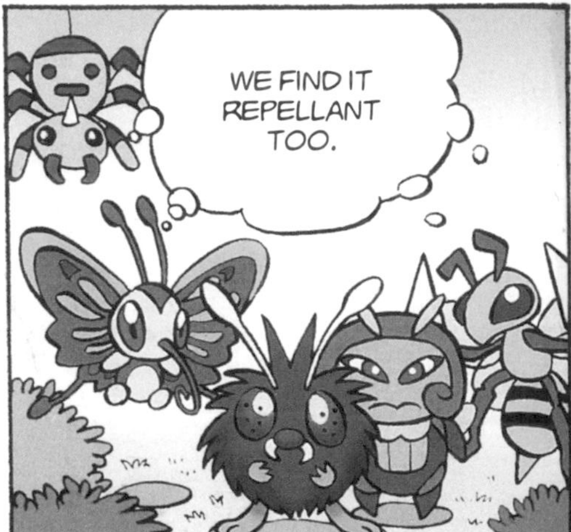
WE FIND IT REPELLANT TOO.

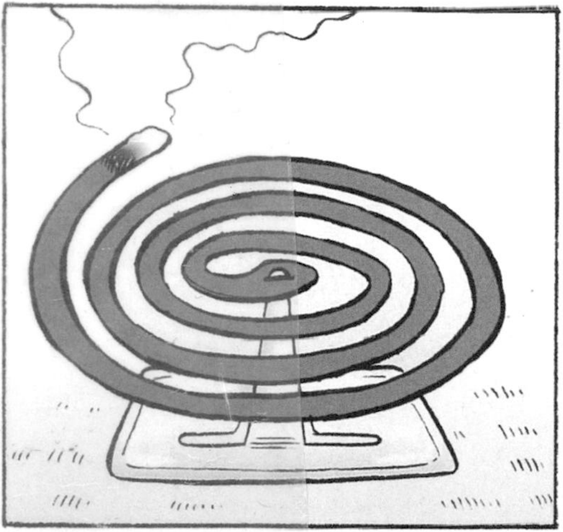

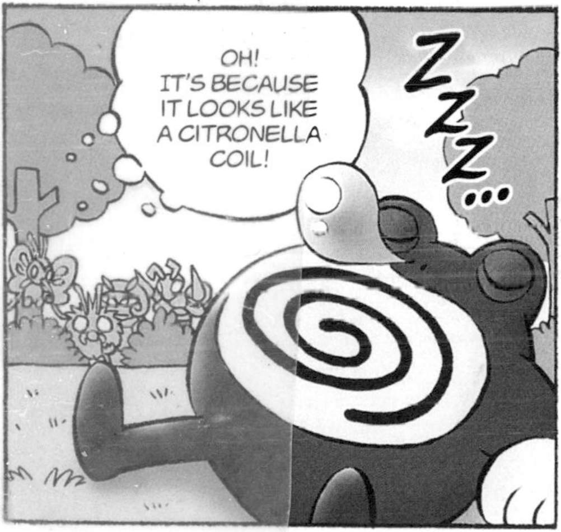

OH! IT'S BECAUSE IT LOOKS LIKE A CITRONELLA COIL!
ZZZ...

POLIWRATH

An adept swimmer at both the front crawl and breast stroke. It can even overtake champion swimmers. Its highly developed, brawny muscles never grow fatigued, however much it exercises. It can easily cross even the largest lakes.

SNUBBULL BLISSEY

Ugly Mug...

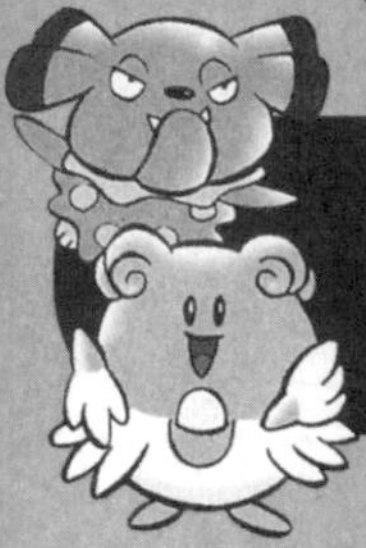

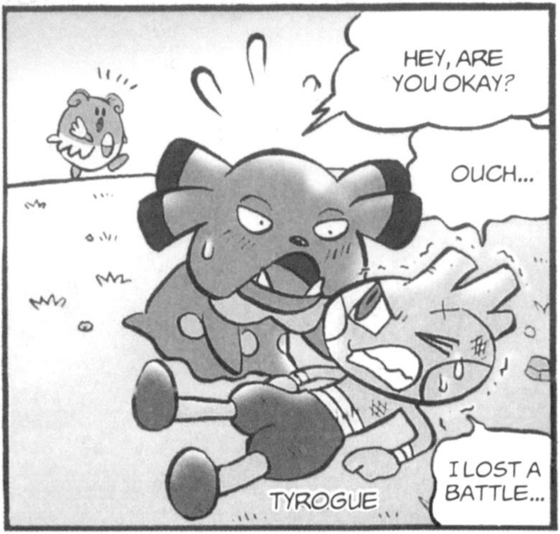
HEY, ARE YOU OKAY?
OUCH...
I LOST A BATTLE...
TYROGUE

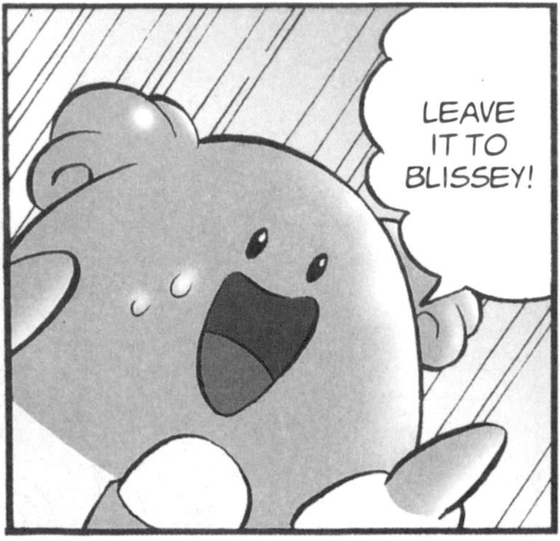
LEAVE IT TO BLISSEY!

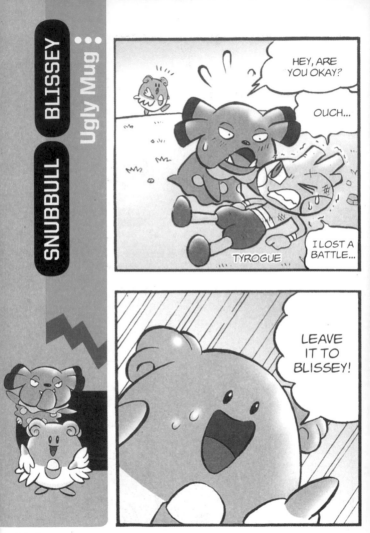

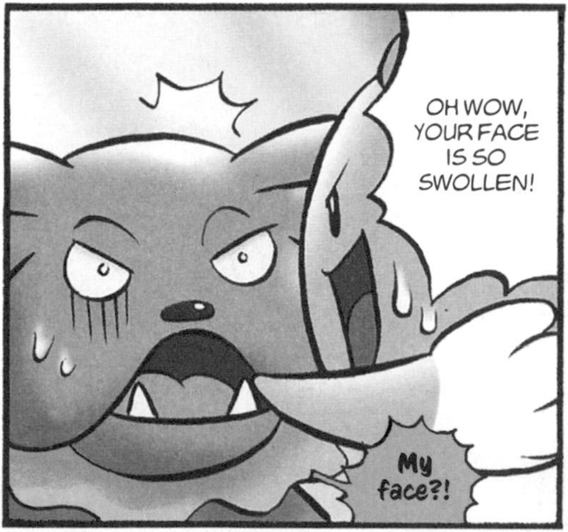
OH WOW, YOUR FACE IS SO SWOLLEN!
My face?!

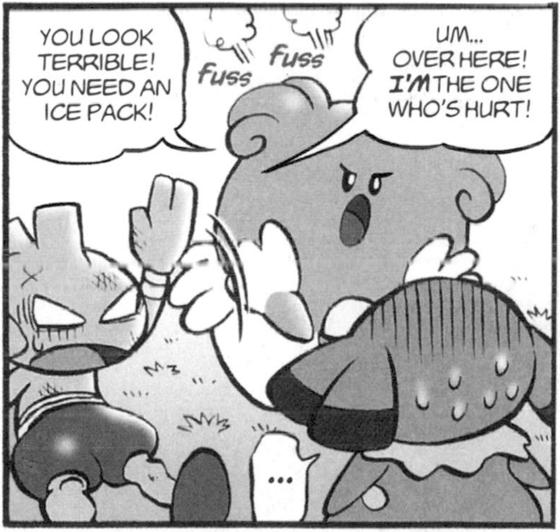
YOU LOOK TERRIBLE! YOU NEED AN ICE PACK!
fuss
fuss
UM... OVER HERE! I'M THE ONE WHO'S HURT!
...

SNUBBULL

It has an active, playful nature. Although it looks frightening, it is actually kind and affectionate.

BLISSEY

If it senses sadness with its fluffy fur, it will rush over to the sad person, however far away, to share an egg of happiness that brings a smile to any face.

SPOINK: Sleep Bouncing

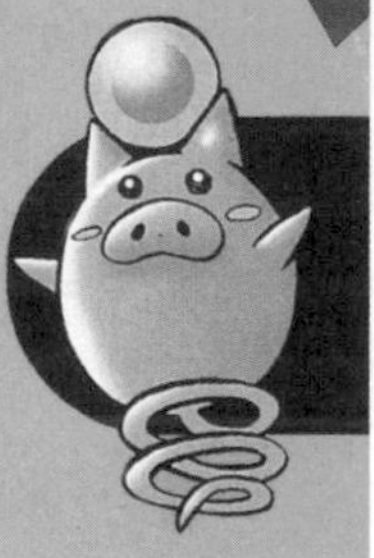

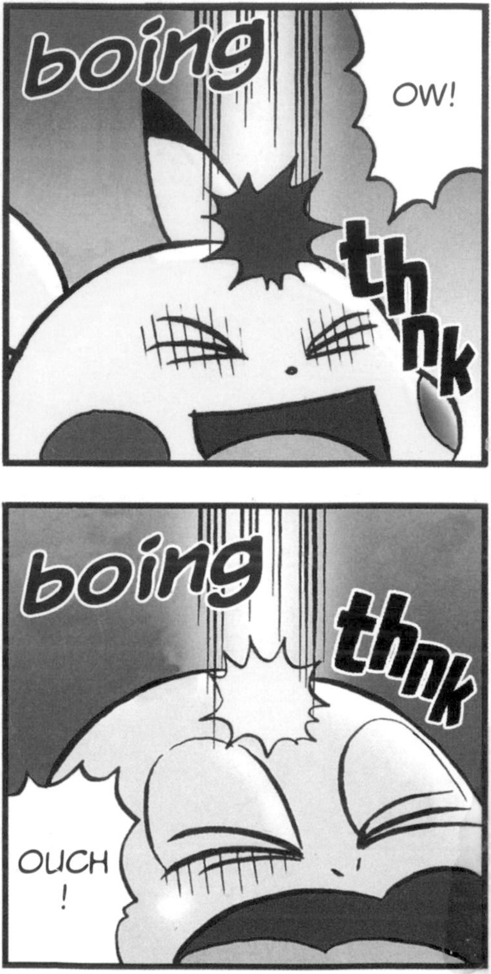
boing
OW!
thnk
boing
thnk
OUCH
!

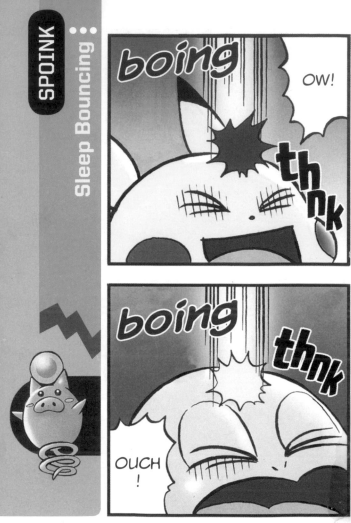

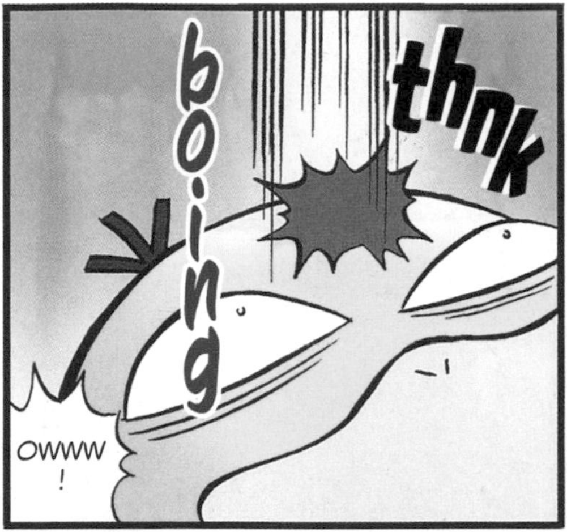
boing
thnk
OWWW!

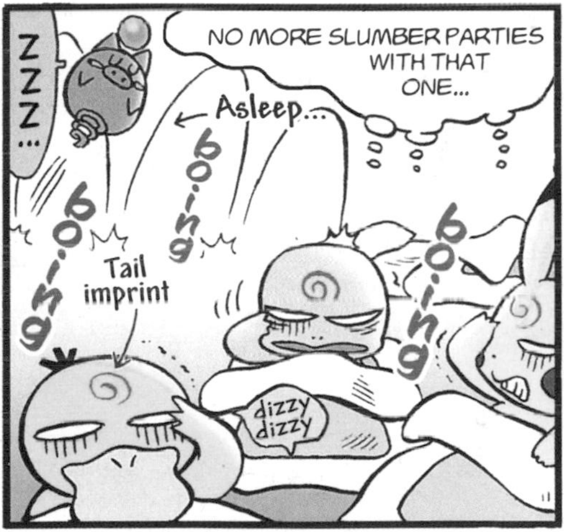
ZZZ...
NO MORE SLUMBER PARTIES WITH THAT ONE...
Asleep...
boing
boing
Tail imprint
boing
dizzy dizzy

SPOINK

A Pokémon who manipulates psychic power at will. It doesn't stop bouncing even when it is asleep. It apparently dies if it stops bouncing about. It carries a pearl from Clamperl on its head. The pearl functions to amplify this Pokémon's psychokinetic powers. It loves eating mushrooms that grow underground.

SWELLOW

No Three-Second Rule

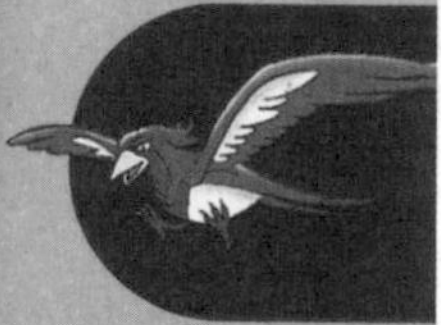

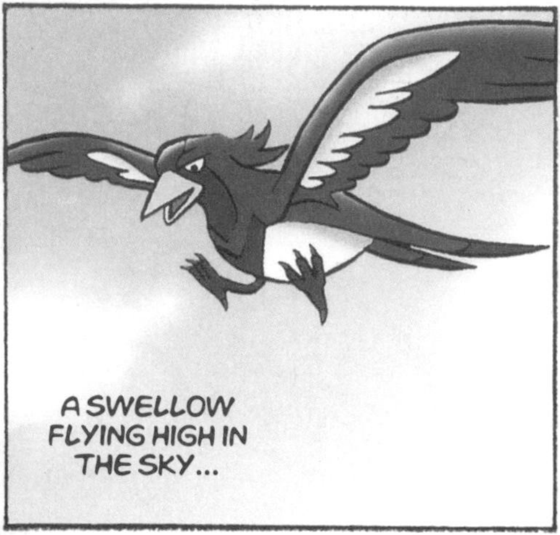
A SWELLOW FLYING HIGH IN THE SKY...

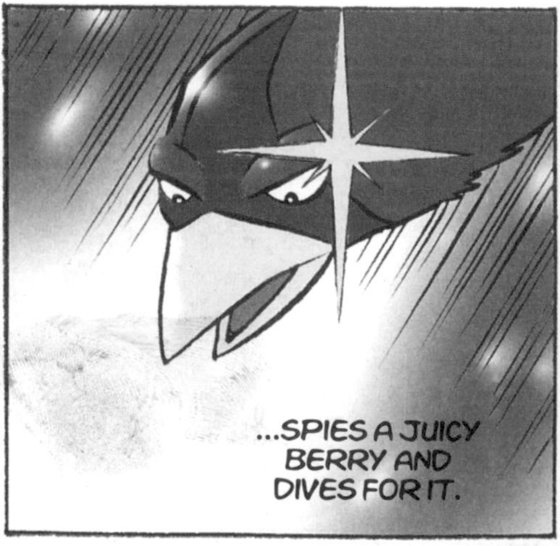
...SPIES A JUICY BERRY AND DIVES FOR IT.

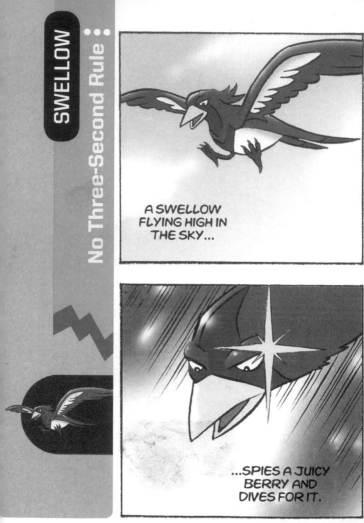

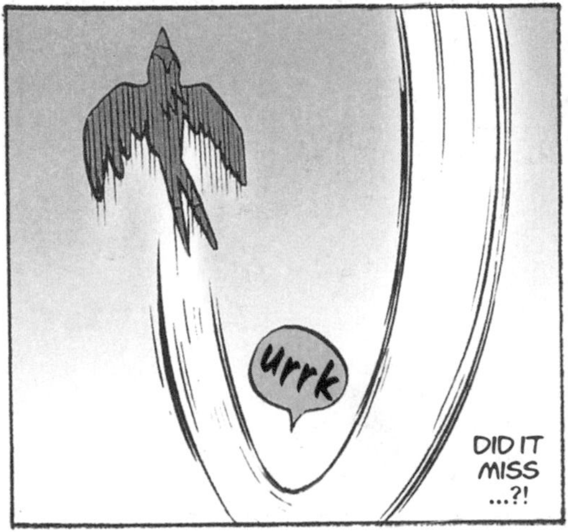
urrk
DID IT MISS ...?!

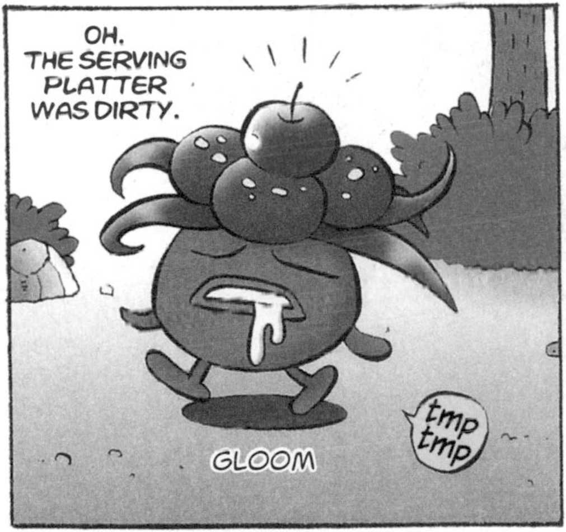
OH. THE SERVING PLATTER WAS DIRTY.
GLOOM
tmp tmp

SWELLOW

It flies high above our heads, making graceful arcs in the sky. This Pokémon dives at a steep angle as soon as it spots its prey. The hapless prey is tightly grasped by Swellow's clawed feet, preventing escape. Swellow is very conscientious about the upkeep of its glossy wings. Once two Swellow are gathered, they diligently take care of cleaning each other's wings.

MEOWTH

Meowth Is Punny Too...

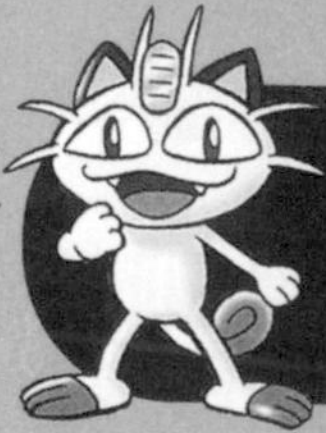

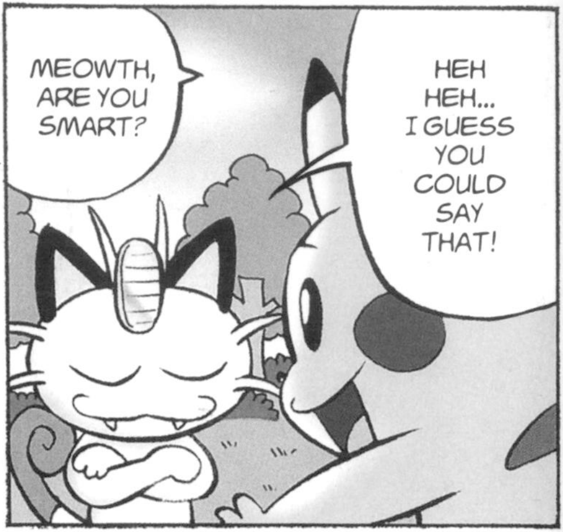
MEOWTH, ARE YOU SMART?
HEH HEH... I GUESS YOU COULD SAY THAT!

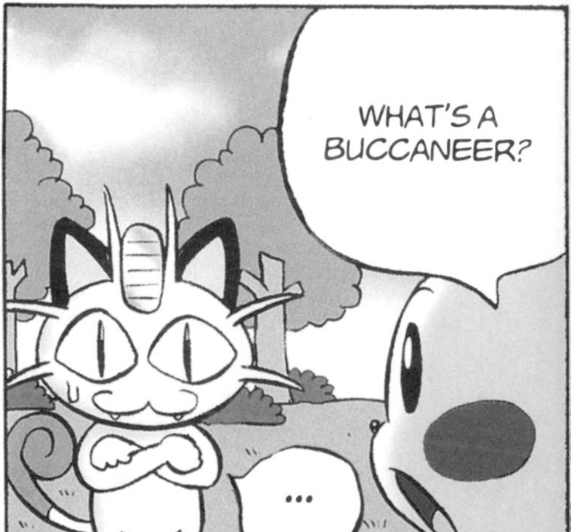
WHAT'S A BUCCANEER?
...

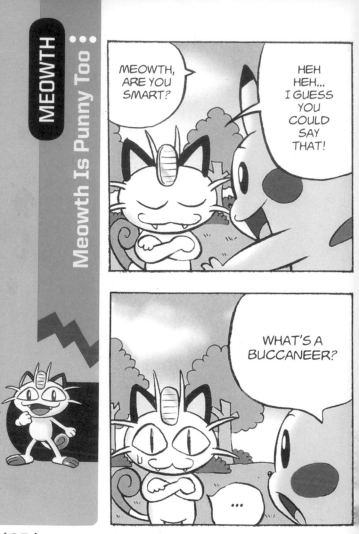

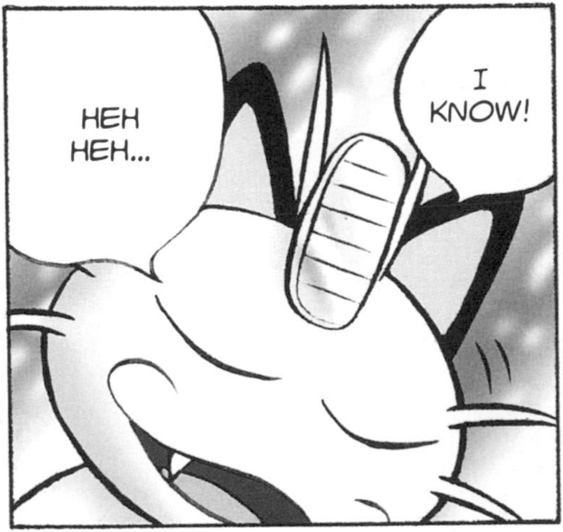
HEH HEH...
I KNOW!

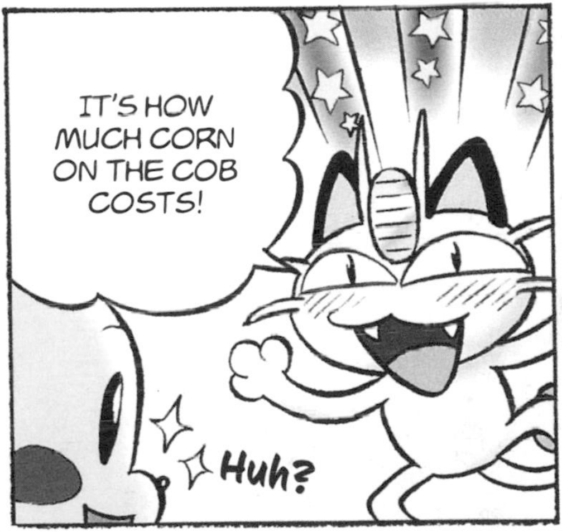
IT'S HOW MUCH CORN ON THE COB COSTS!
Huh?

MEOWTH

All it does is sleep during the daytime. At night, it patrols its territory with its eyes aglow. It withdraws its sharp claws into its paws to silently sneak about. For some reason, this Pokémon loves to collect shiny coins that glitter with light.

HYPNO

Swap Meet...

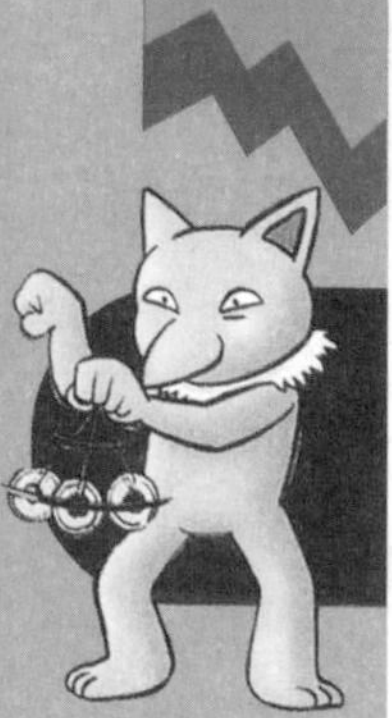

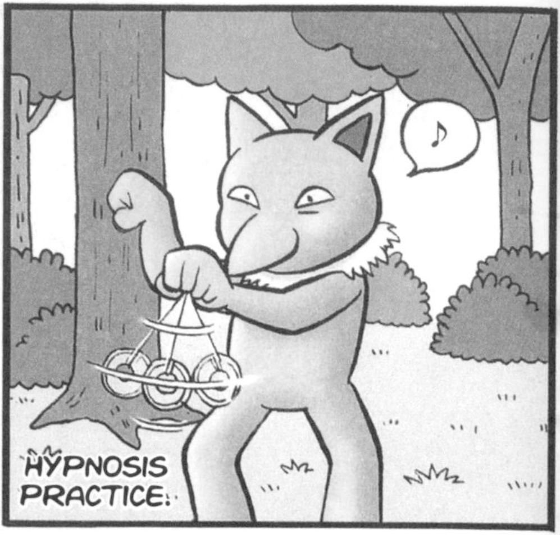
♪
HYPNOSIS PRACTICE.

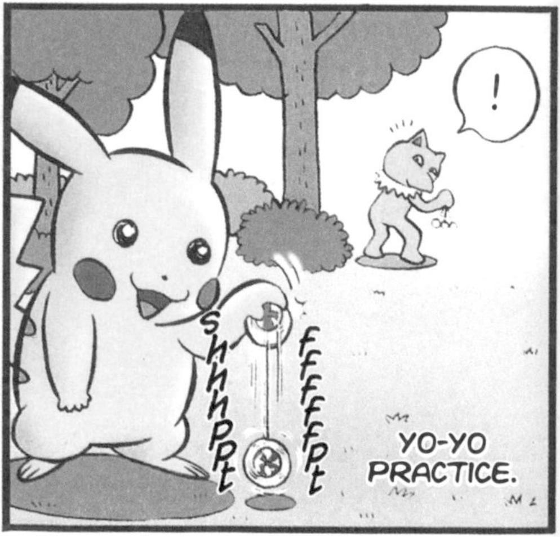
!
shhhppt
ffffffpt
YO-YO PRACTICE.

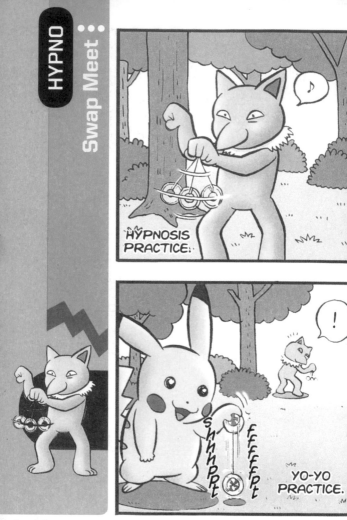

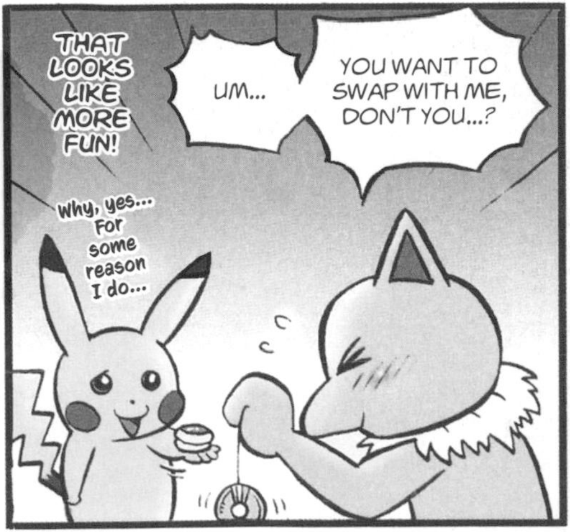
THAT LOOKS LIKE MORE FUN!
UM...
YOU WANT TO SWAP WITH ME, DON'T YOU...?
Why, yes... For some reason I do...

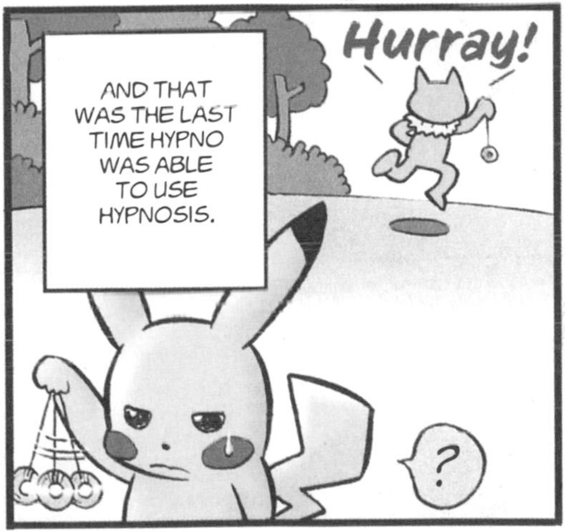
AND THAT WAS THE LAST TIME HYPNO WAS ABLE TO USE HYPNOSIS.
Hurray!
?

HYPNO

It holds a pendulum in its hand. The arcing movement and glitter of the pendulum lull the foe into a deep state of hypnosis. While this Pokémon searches for prey, it polishes its pendulum. Avoid eye contact if you come across one. It will try to put you to sleep by using its pendulum.

MUK GRIMER

Incensed by Incense

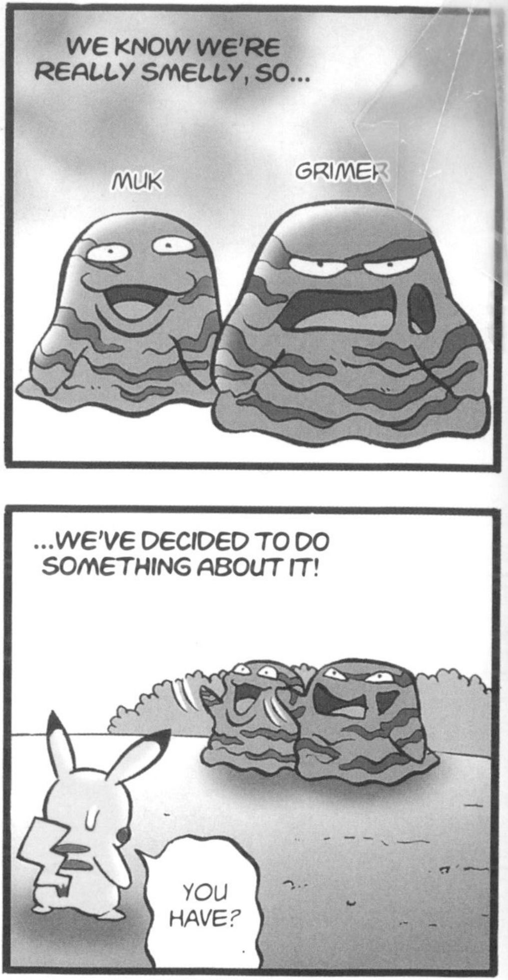
WE KNOW WE'RE REALLY SMELLY, SO...
MUK
GRIMER
...WE'VE DECIDED TO DO SOMETHING ABOUT IT!
YOU HAVE?

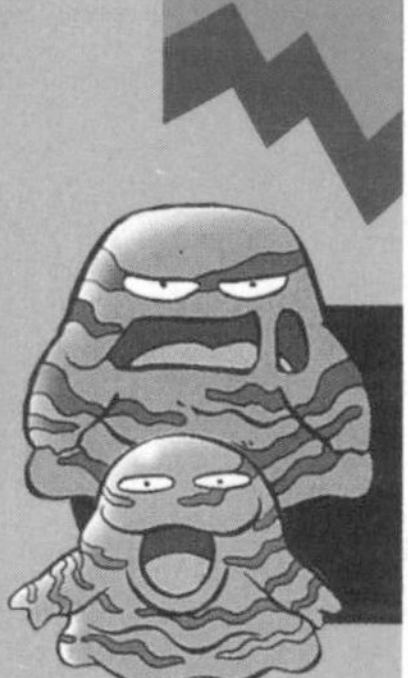

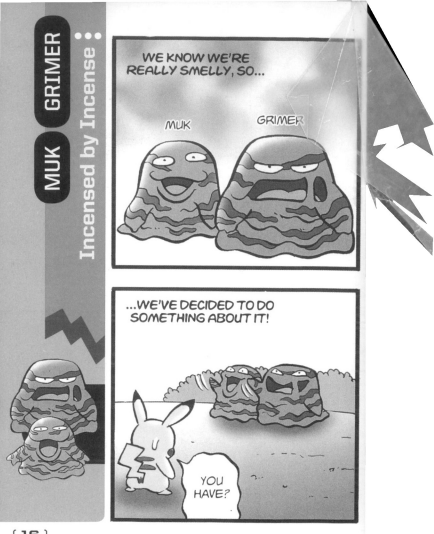

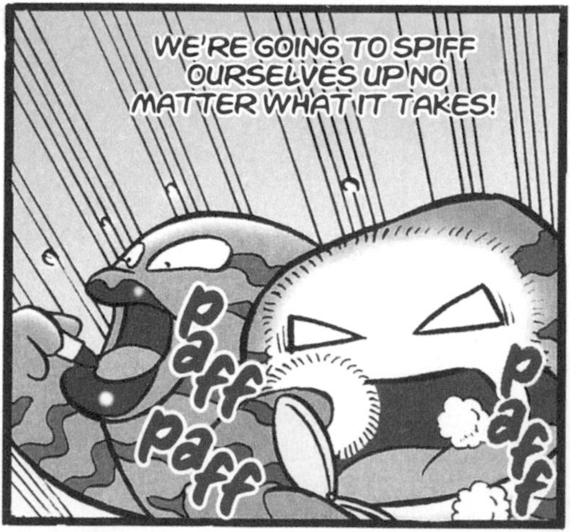
WE'RE GOING TO SPIFF OURSELVES UP NO MATTER WHAT IT TAKES!
paff paff
paff

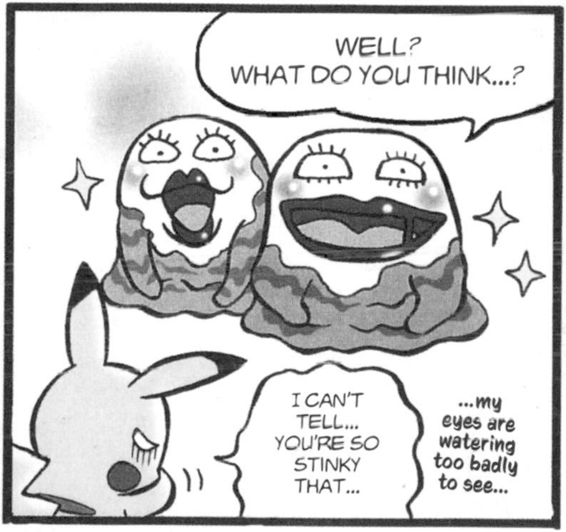
WELL? WHAT DO YOU THINK...?
I CAN'T TELL... YOU'RE SO STINKY THAT...
...my eyes are watering too badly to see...

MUK

It prefers warm and humid habitats. It is usually undetectable because it blends in with the ground. In the summertime, the toxic substances in its body intensify, making Muk reek like putrid kitchen garbage.

GRIMER

Born from polluted sludge in the sea, its favorite food is anything filthy.

MAROWAK

Meet Swap

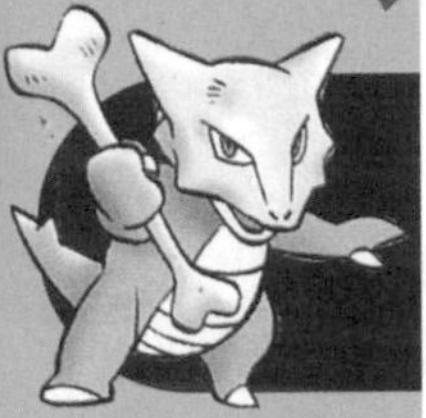

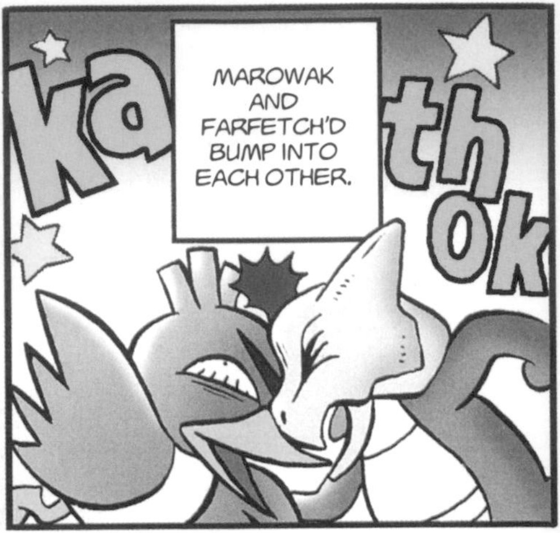
ka
th
ok
MAROWAK AND FARFETCH'D BUMP INTO EACH OTHER.

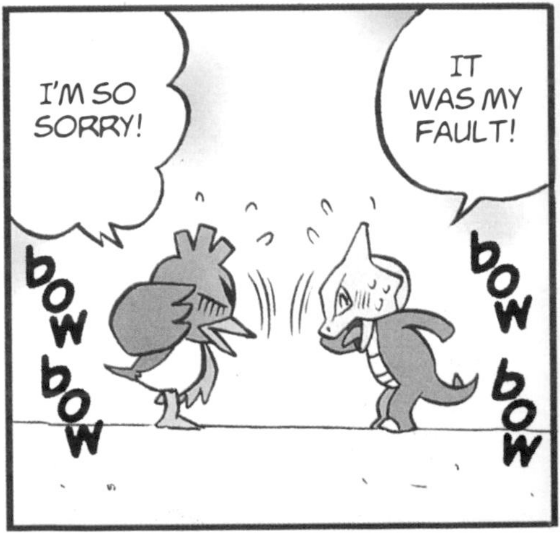
I'M SO SORRY!
bow bow
bow bow
IT WAS MY FAULT!
bow bow
bow bow

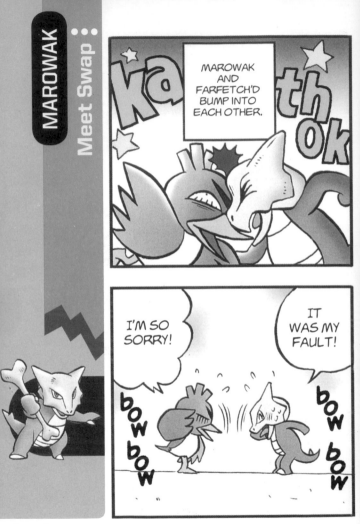

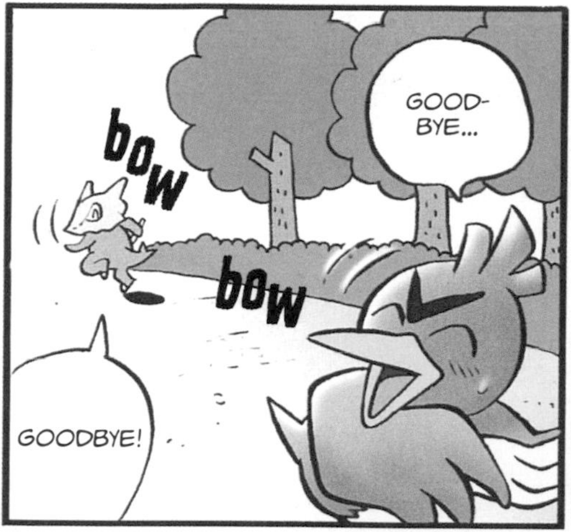
bow
bow
GOOD-BYE...
GOODBYE!

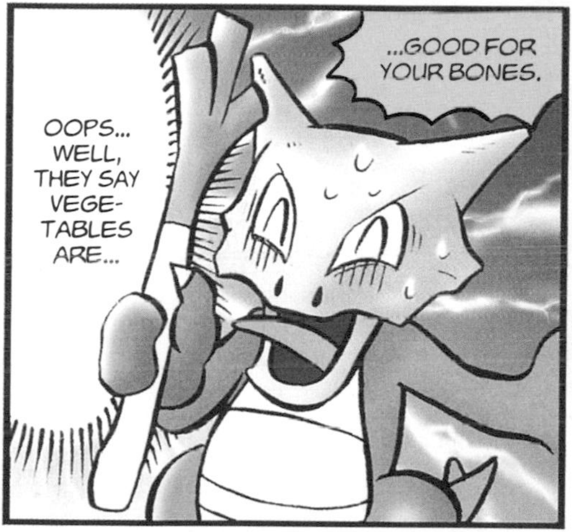
OOPS... WELL, THEY SAY VEGE-TABLES ARE...
...GOOD FOR YOUR BONES.

MAROWAK

It is the evolved form of a Cubone that has overcome its sadness at the loss of its mother and grown tough. This Pokémon's tempered and hardened spirit is not easily broken. It was originally a small and weak Pokémon, but it has become rough and aggressive and uses bones as weapons. It throws the bone skillfully like a boomerang to KO targets.

DODUO DODRIO
Third Wheel

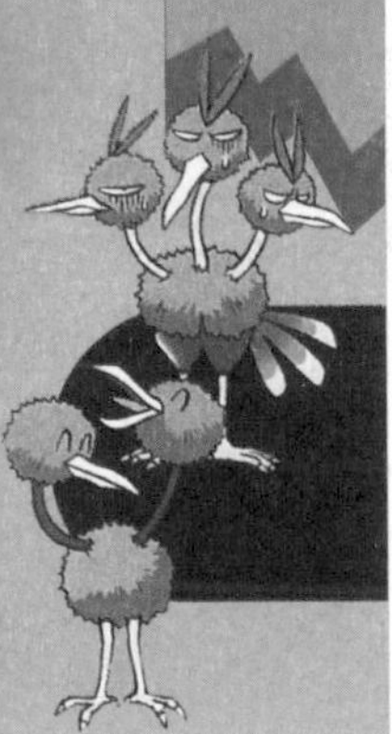

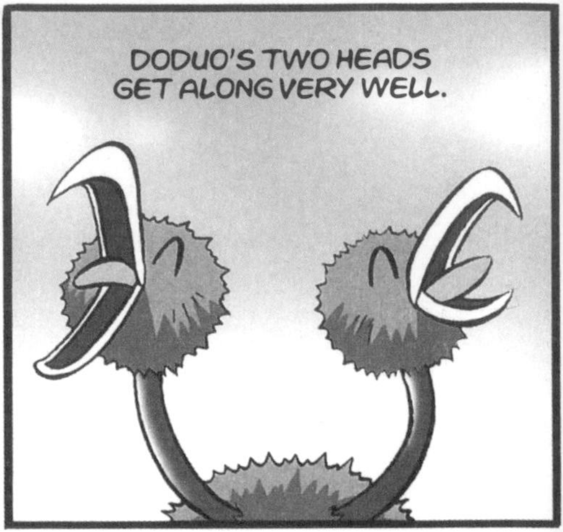
DODUO'S TWO HEADS GET ALONG VERY WELL.

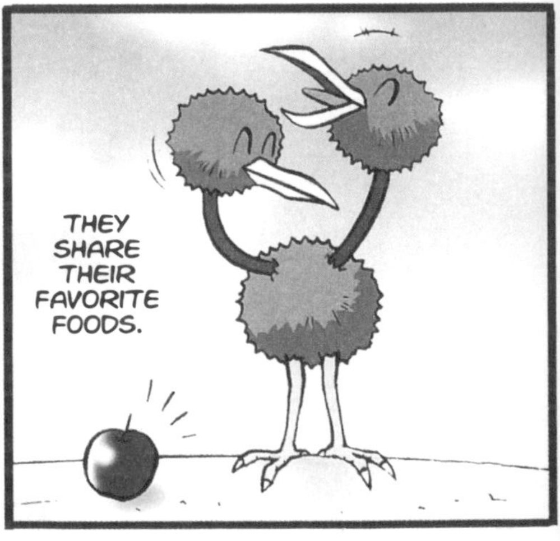
THEY SHARE THEIR FAVORITE FOODS.

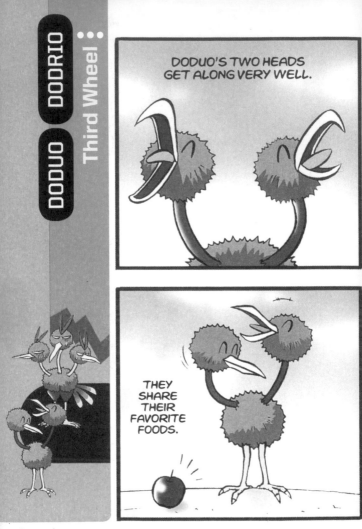

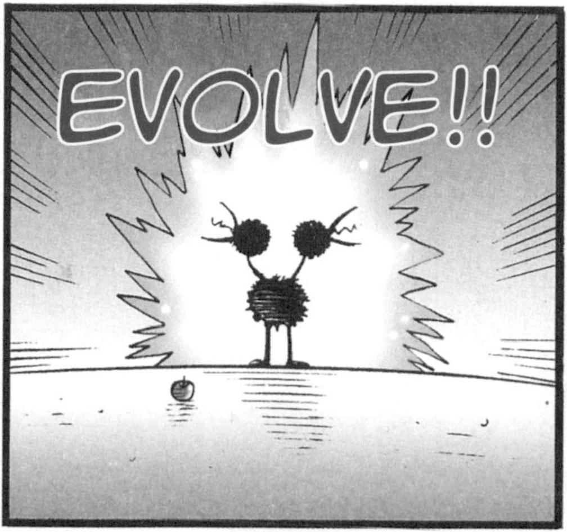
EVOLVE!!

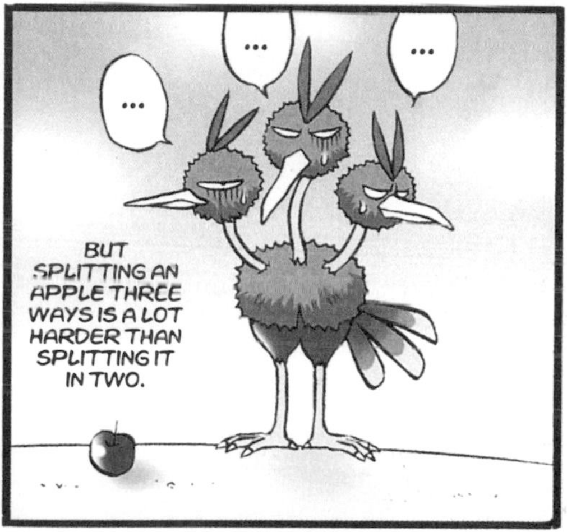
...
...
...
BUT SPLITTING AN APPLE THREE WAYS IS A LOT HARDER THAN SPLITTING IT IN TWO.

DODUO

The Twin Bird Pokémon. Even while eating or sleeping, one of the heads remains always vigilant for any sign of danger.

DODRIO

The Triple Bird Pokémon. The three heads express joy, sorrow and anger.

CHIKORITA SWINUB

Smells Like Trouble

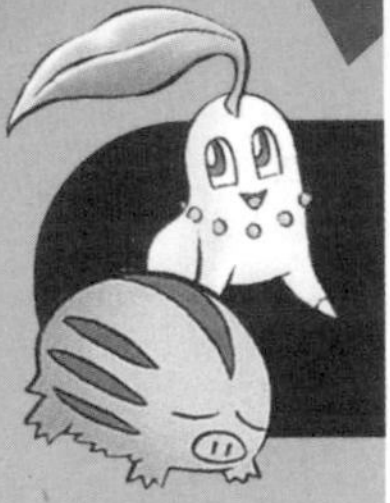

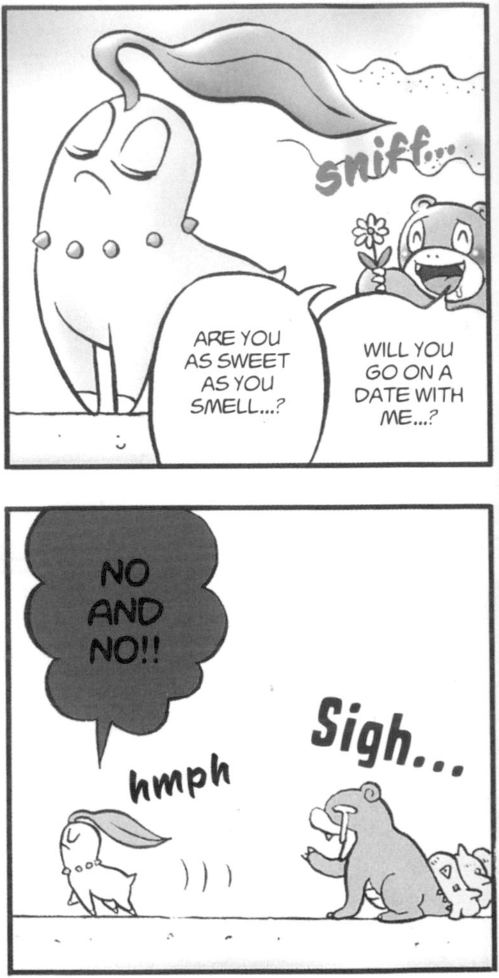
sniff...
ARE YOU AS SWEET AS YOU SMELL...?
WILL YOU GO ON A DATE WITH ME...?
NO AND NO!!
hmph
Sigh...

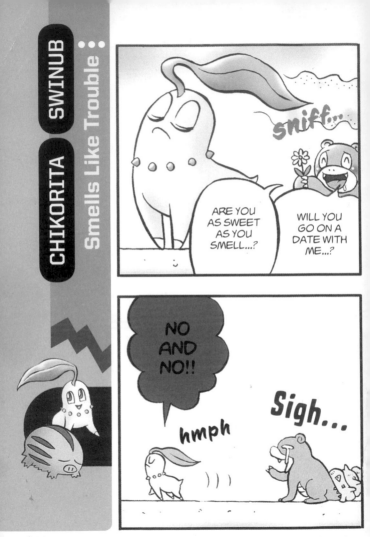

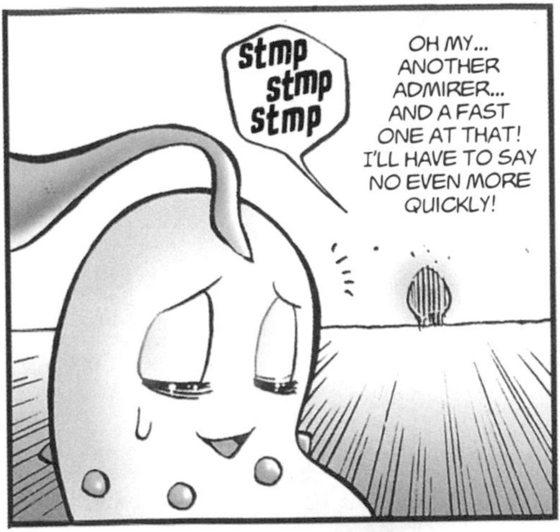
stmp stmp stmp
OH MY... ANOTHER ADMIRER... AND A FAST ONE AT THAT! I'LL HAVE TO SAY NO EVEN MORE QUICKLY!

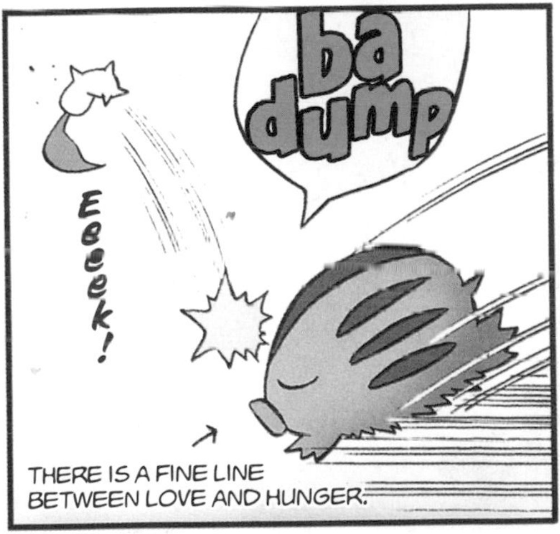
ba dump
Eeeek!
THERE IS A FINE LINE BETWEEN LOVE AND HUNGER.

CHIKORITA

In battle, it waves its leaf around to keep the foe at bay. However, a sweet fragrance also wafts from the leaf, becalming the battling Pokémon and creating a cozy, friendly atmosphere all around.

SWINUB

If it smells something enticing, it dashes off to find the source of the aroma. It roots for food by rubbing its snout against the ground.

BUTTERFREE WYNAUT

Scents of Preservation

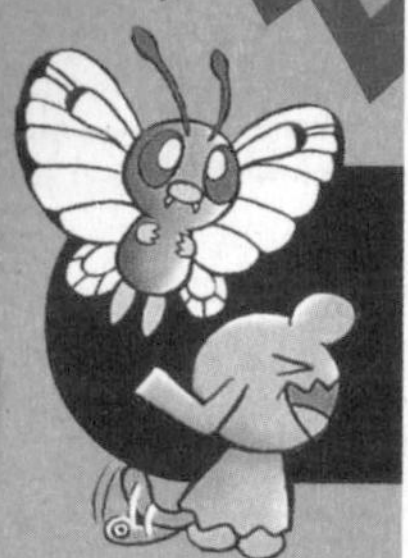

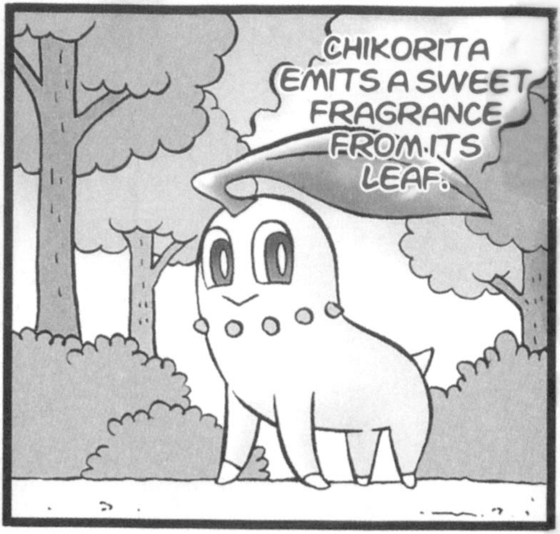
CHIKORITA EMITS A SWEET FRAGRANCE FROM ITS LEAF.

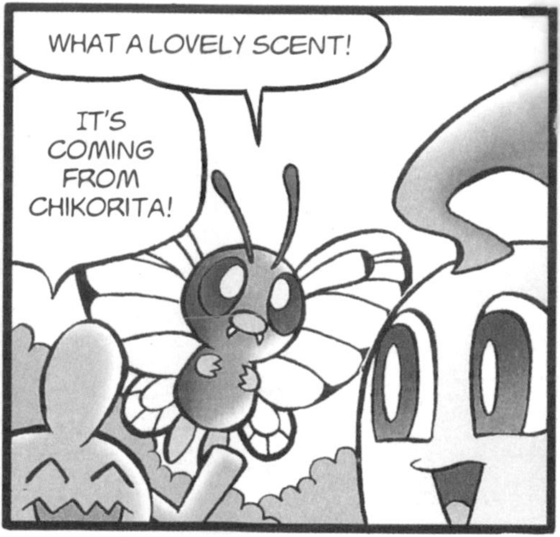
WHAT A LOVELY SCENT!
IT'S COMING FROM CHIKORITA!

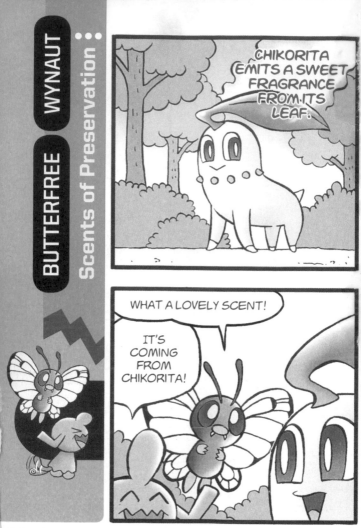

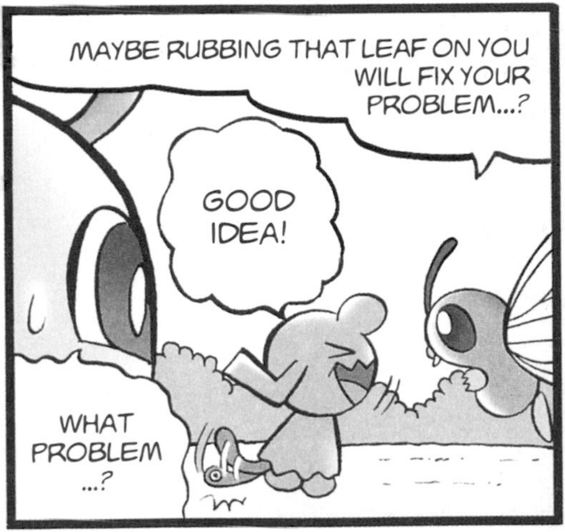
MAYBE RUBBING THAT LEAF ON YOU WILL FIX YOUR PROBLEM...?
GOOD IDEA!
WHAT PROBLEM ...?

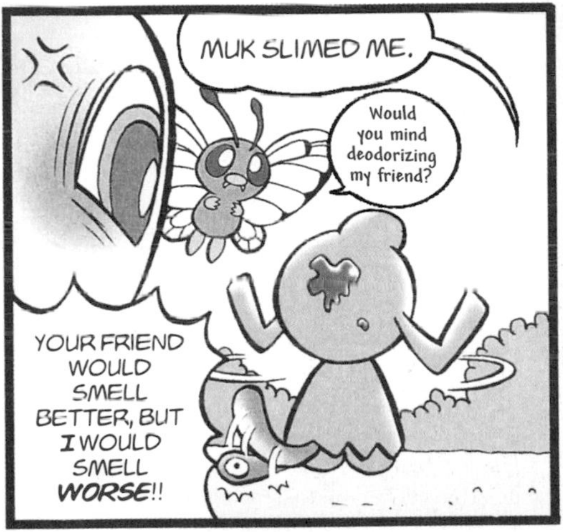
MUK SLIMED ME.
Would you mind deodorizing my friend?
YOUR FRIEND WOULD SMELL BETTER, BUT I WOULD SMELL WORSE!!

BUTTERFREE

It has a superior ability to search for delicious honey from flowers. It can seek, extract and carry honey from flowers blooming over six miles away.

WYNAUT

It loves to eat sweet fruits. It cleverly picks fruits using its earlike arms. They gather in fruit gardens, drawn by the fragrance.

BULBASAUR SQUIRTLE
Clean Up Your Act

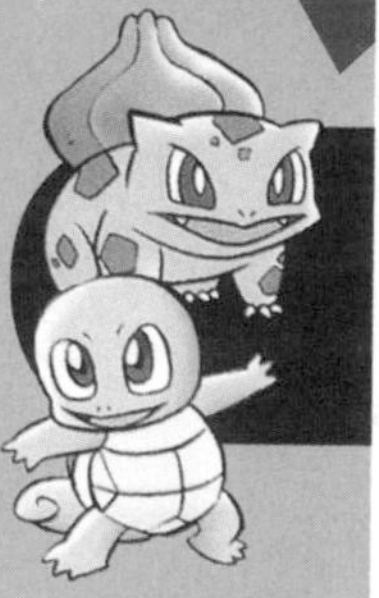

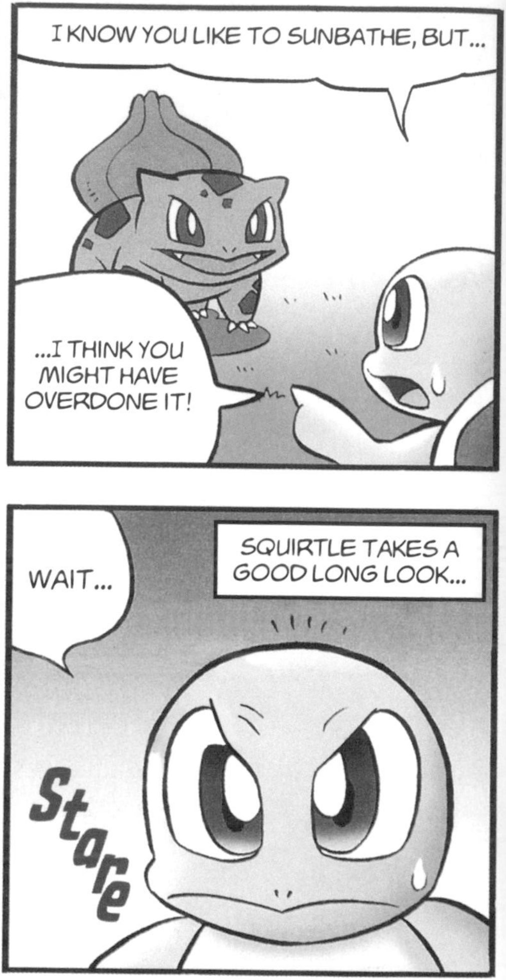
I KNOW YOU LIKE TO SUNBATHE, BUT...
...I THINK YOU MIGHT HAVE OVERDONE IT!
WAIT...
SQUIRTLE TAKES A GOOD LONG LOOK...
Stare

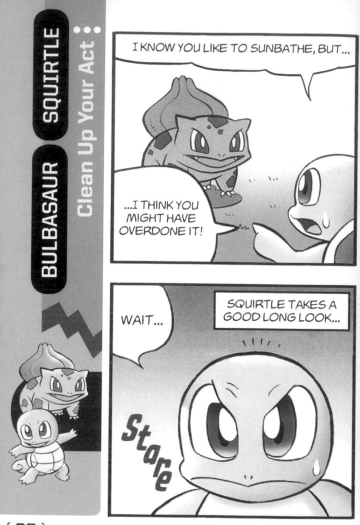

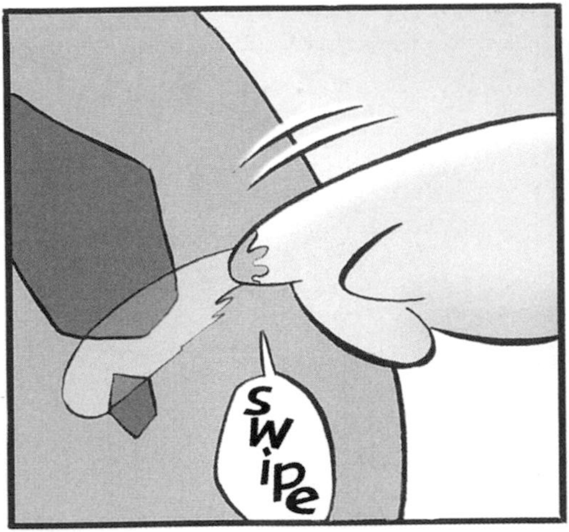
SWiPe

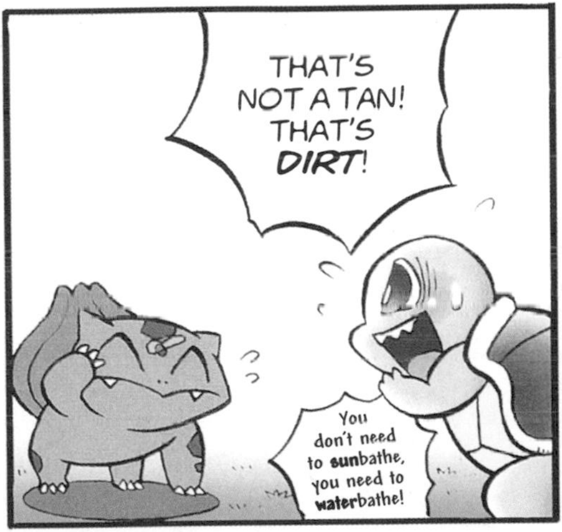
THAT'S NOT A TAN! THAT'S DIRT!
You don't need to sunbathe, you need to waterbathe!

BULBASAUR

It carries a seed on its back right from birth. As it grows older, the seed also grows larger. Bulbasaur can be seen napping in bright sunlight.

SQUIRTLE

Its shell is not just for protection. Its rounded shape and the grooves on its surface minimize resistance in water, enabling Squirtle to swim at high speeds.

LOMBRE

Time to Move On...

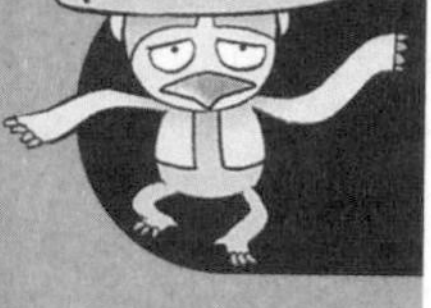

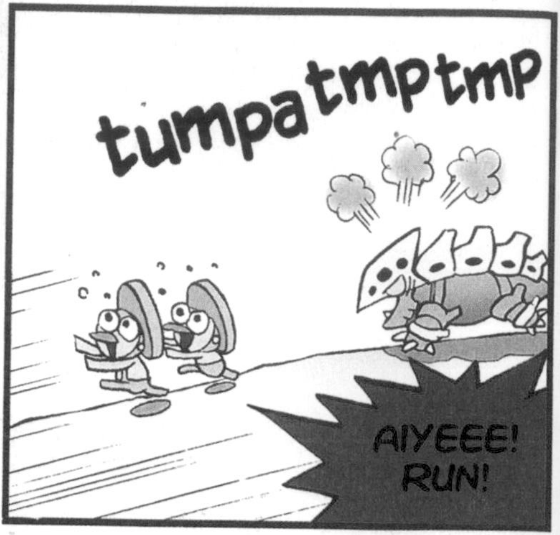
tumpa tmp tmp
AIYEEE! RUN!

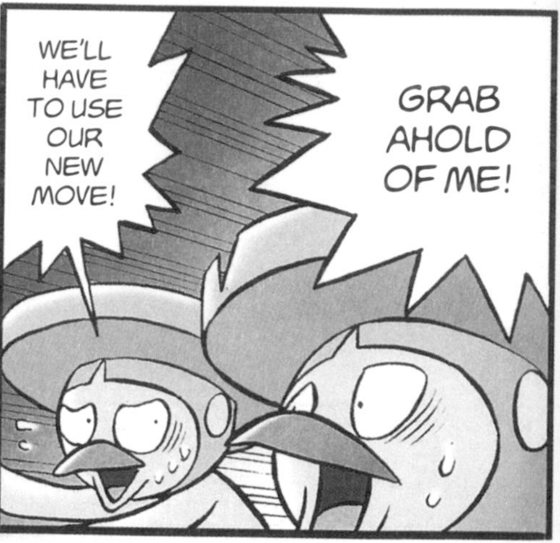
WE'LL HAVE TO USE OUR NEW MOVE!
GRAB AHOLD OF ME!

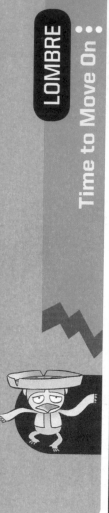

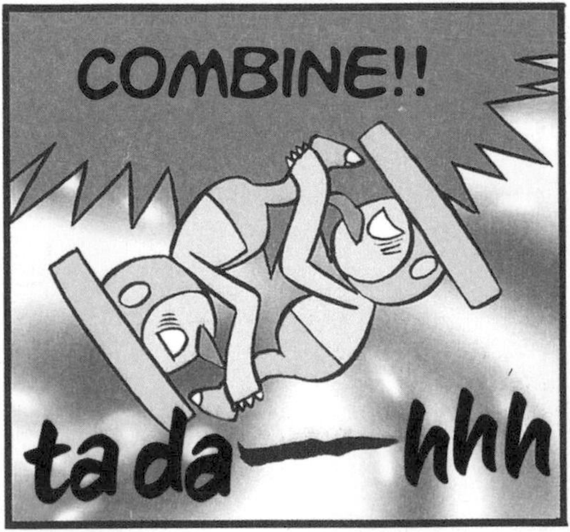
COMBINE!!
ta da——hhh

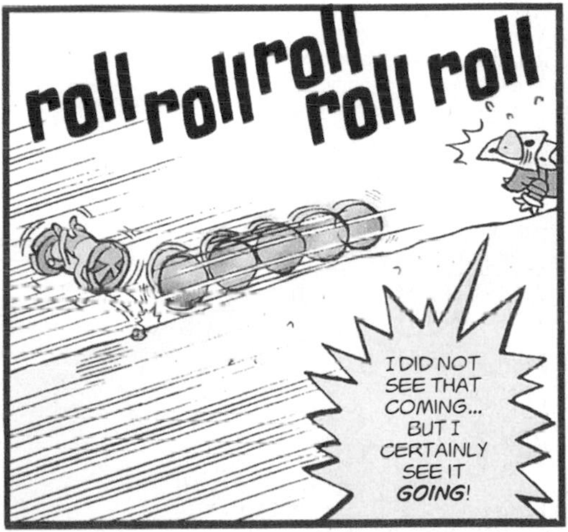
roll roll roll roll roll
I DID NOT SEE THAT COMING... BUT I CERTAINLY SEE IT *GOING*!

LOMBRE

It lives at the water's edge where it's sunny. In the evening, it takes great delight in popping out of rivers and startling people. It feeds on aquatic moss that grows on rocks in the riverbed. When this Pokémon spots anglers, it tugs on their fishing lines from beneath the surface and enjoys their consternation.

CORSOLA KINGLER

Top-Heavy

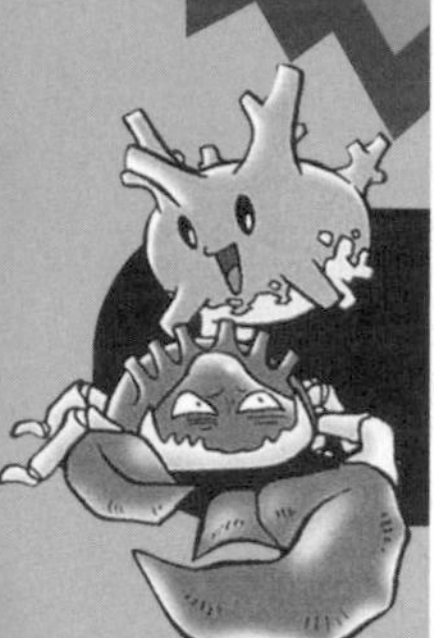

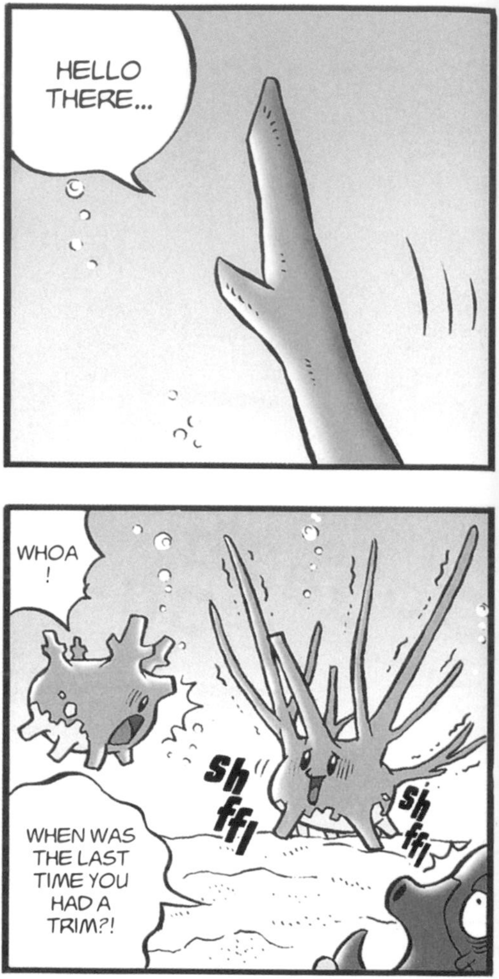
HELLO THERE...
WHOA!
WHEN WAS THE LAST TIME YOU HAD A TRIM?!
Shffl
Shffl

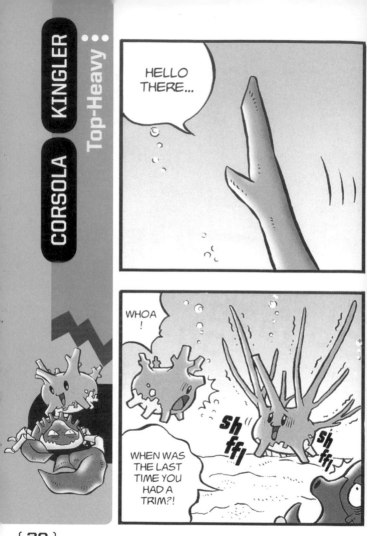

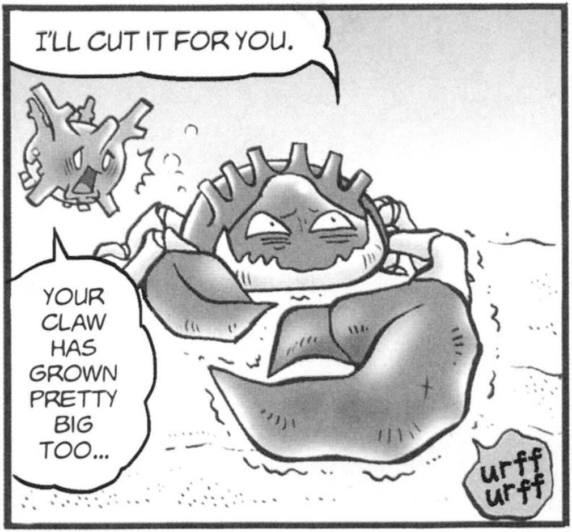
I'LL CUT IT FOR YOU.
YOUR CLAW HAS GROWN PRETTY BIG TOO...
urff urff

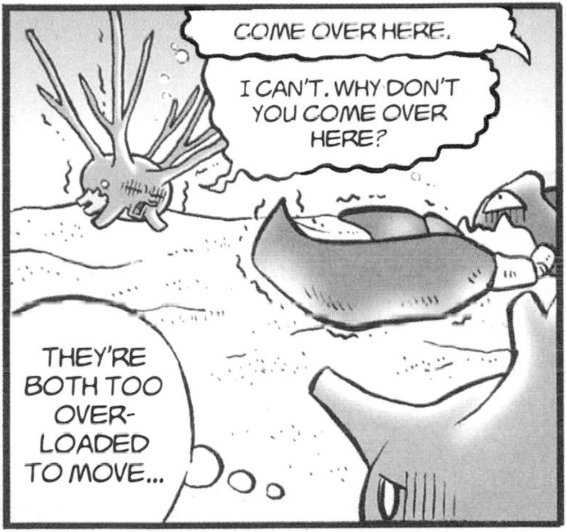
COME OVER HERE.
I CAN'T. WHY DON'T YOU COME OVER HERE?
THEY'RE BOTH TOO OVER-LOADED TO MOVE...

CORSOLA

It continuously sheds and grows. The tip of its head is prized as a treasure for its beauty. Corsola live in warm southern seas.

KINGLER

It waves its huge, oversized claw in the air to communicate with others. But since the claw is so heavy, this Pokémon quickly tires.

TOTODILE SEAKING

Fishing for Compliments...

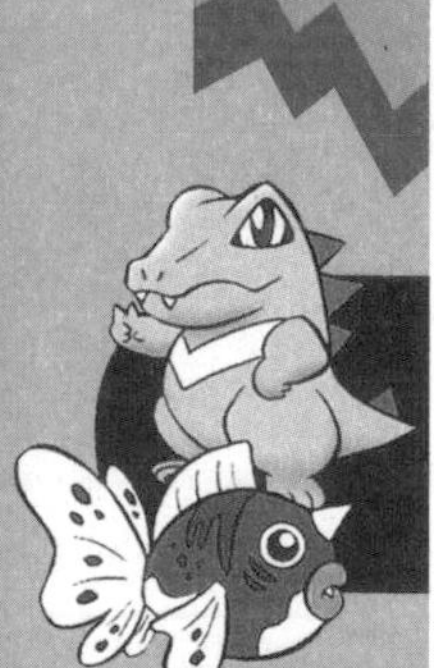

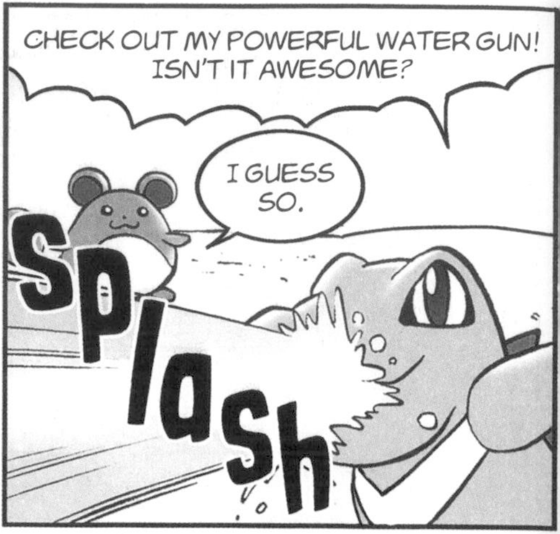
CHECK OUT MY POWERFUL WATER GUN! ISN'T IT AWESOME?
I GUESS SO.
SPLASH

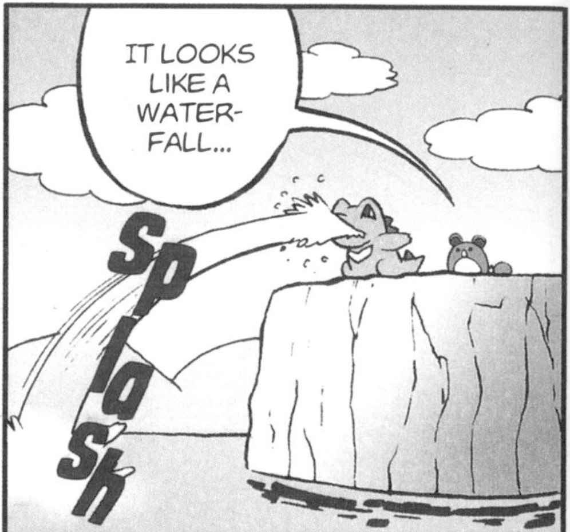
IT LOOKS LIKE A WATER-FALL...
SPLASH

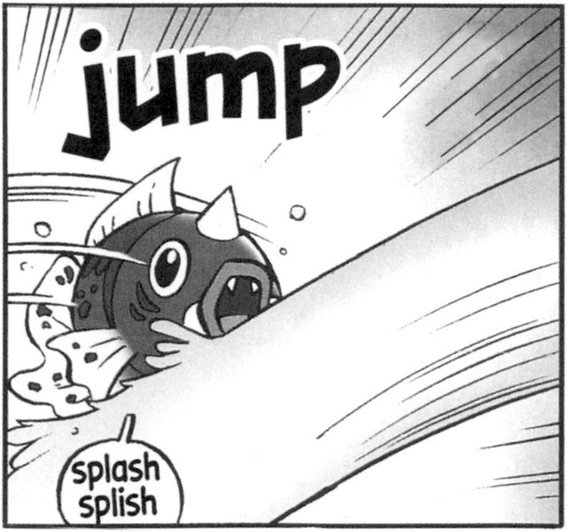
jump
splash splish

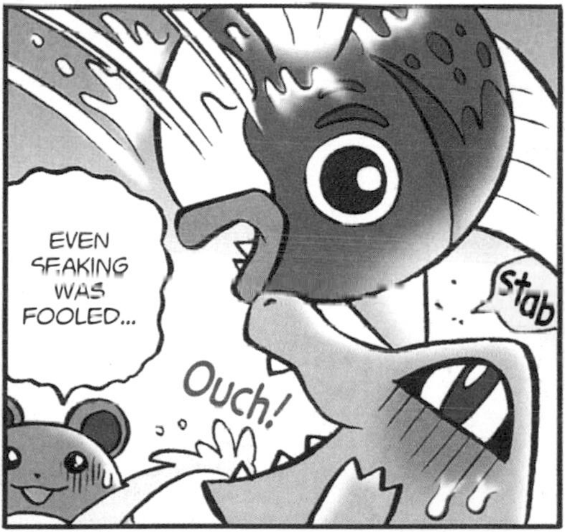
EVEN SEAKING WAS FOOLED...
Stab
Ouch!

TOTODILE

Its well-developed jaws are powerful and capable of crushing anything. It won't hesitate to take a bite out of anything that moves.

SEAKING

It bores a hole in a boulder to make its nest. In the autumn spawning season, this Pokémon can be seen swimming powerfully up rivers and creeks.

CHIMECHO
Chime In!

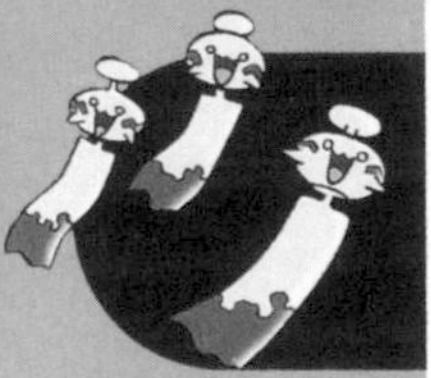

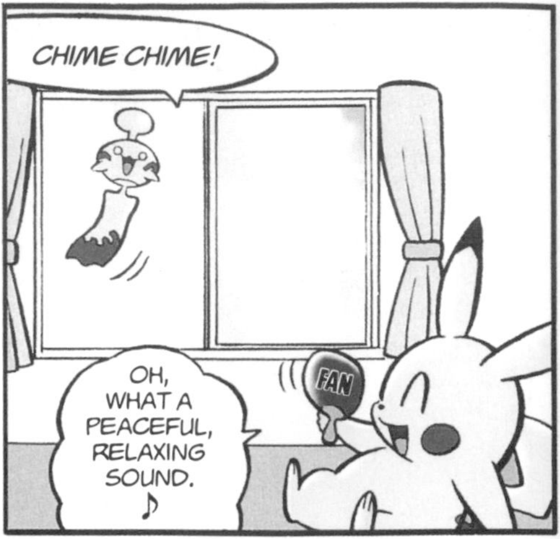
CHIME CHIME!
OH, WHAT A PEACEFUL, RELAXING SOUND. ♪
FAN

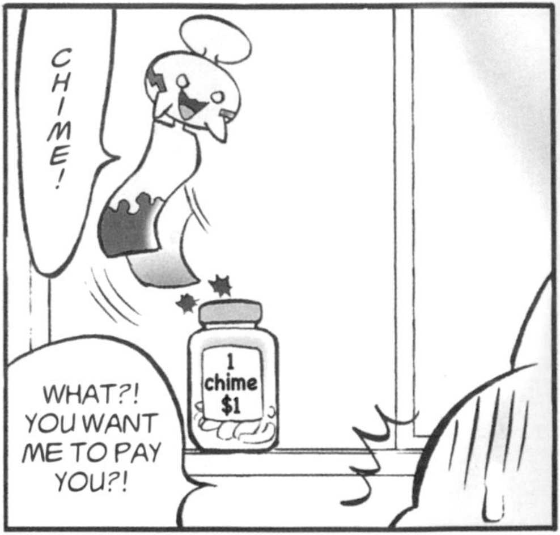
CHIME!
1 chime $1
WHAT?! YOU WANT ME TO PAY YOU?!

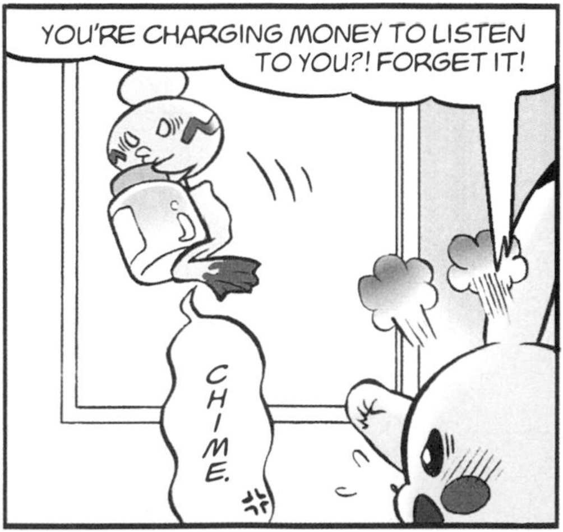
YOU'RE CHARGING MONEY TO LISTEN TO YOU?! FORGET IT!
CHIME.

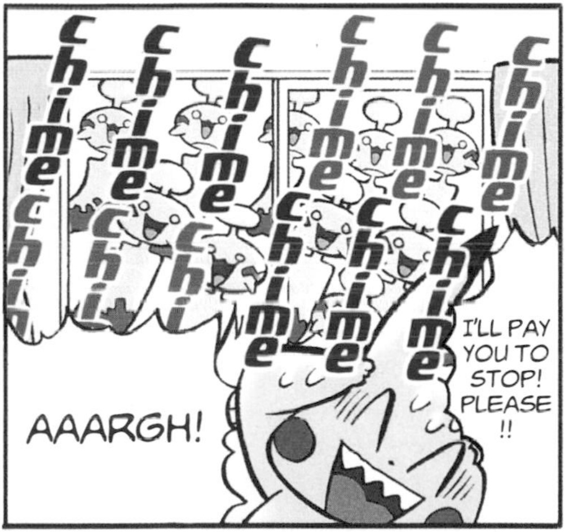
chime
chime
chime
chime
chime
chime
chi
chi
chi
chime
chime
chime
I'LL PAY YOU TO STOP! PLEASE !!
AAARGH!

CHIMECHO

It flies about very actively when the hot season arrives. In high winds, Chimecho lets out its cry as it hangs from a tree branch or the eaves of a building using a suction cup on its head. Chimecho communicate among themselves using seven different and distinguishing cries. They travel by riding on winds.

CROBAT

A Soft Landing

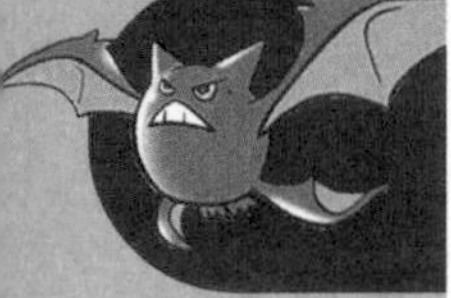

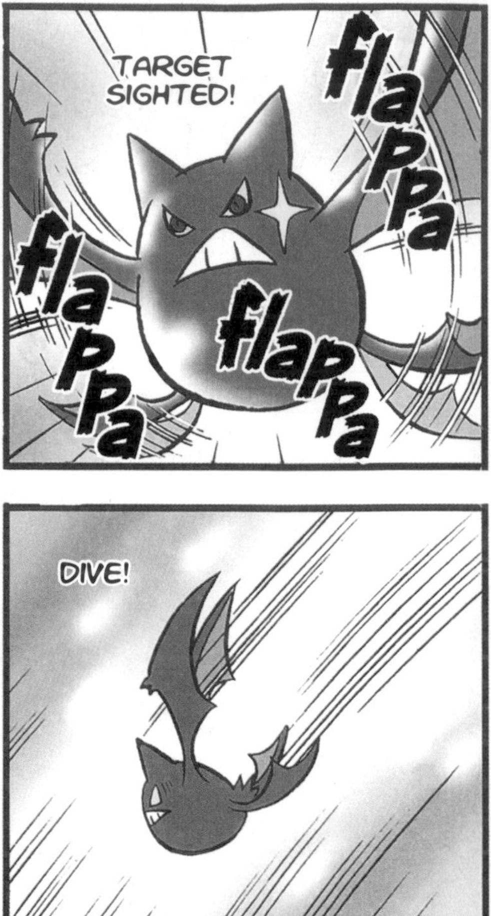
TARGET SIGHTED!
flappa
flappa
flappa
DIVE!

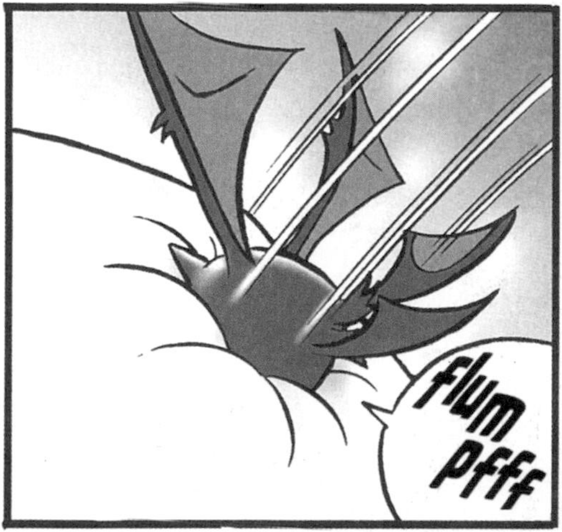
flum
pfff

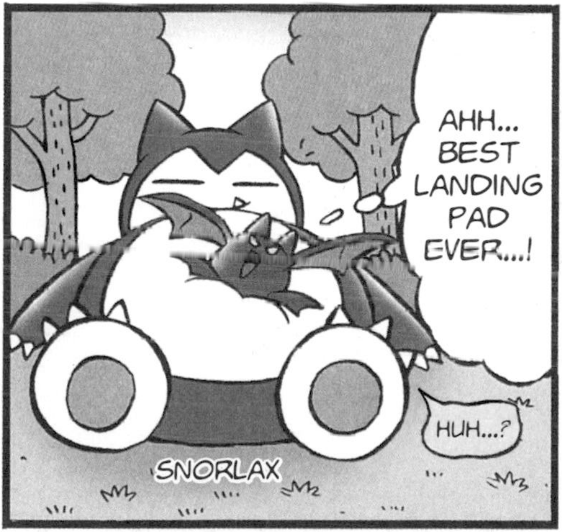
AHH... BEST LANDING PAD EVER...!
HUH...?
SNORLAX

CROBAT

Over the course of evolution, its hind legs turned into wings. By alternately resting its front and rear wings, it can fly all day without having to stop. The development of wings on its legs enables it to fly fast but also makes it tough to stop and rest. It flies silently through the dark on its four wings.

MEDITITE SNORLAX
Yoga Training 1

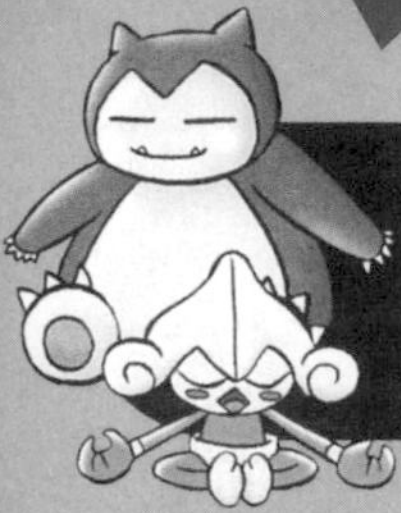

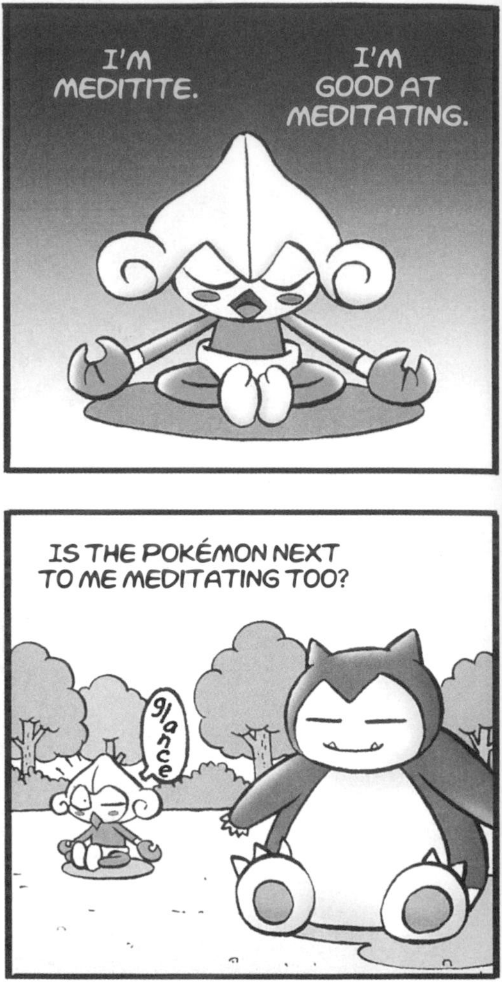
I'M MEDITITE.
I'M GOOD AT MEDITATING.
IS THE POKÉMON NEXT TO ME MEDITATING TOO?
glance

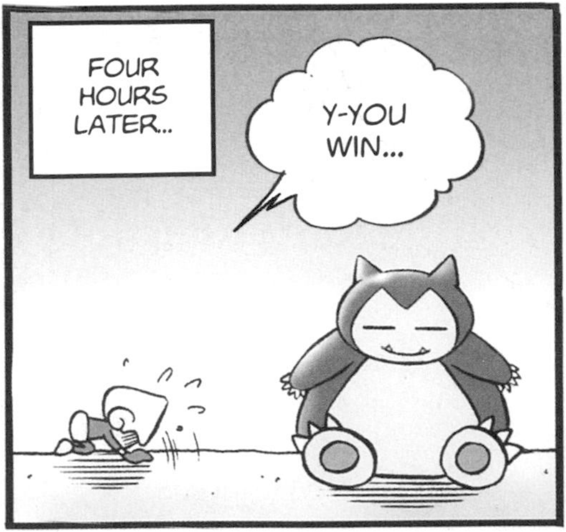
FOUR HOURS LATER...
Y-YOU WIN...

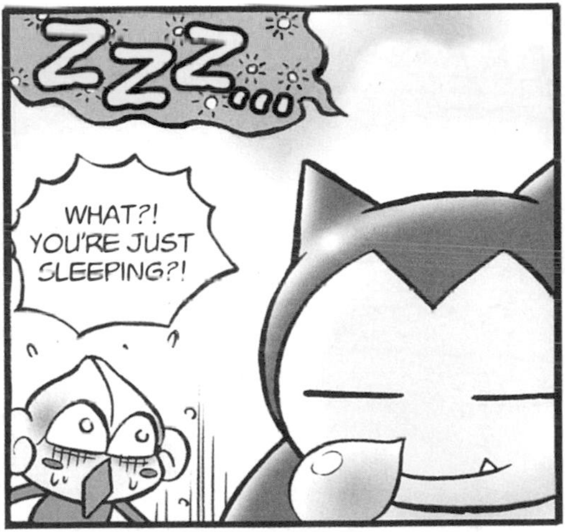
ZZZooo
WHAT?! YOU'RE JUST SLEEPING?!

MEDITITE

It continually meditates for hours every day. As a result of rigorous and dedicated yoga training, it has tempered its spiritual power so much it can fly.

SNORLAX

Very lazy. Just eats and sleeps. It is not satisfied unless it eats over 880 pounds of food every day. When it is done eating, it goes promptly to sleep.

BELLOSSOM GLOOM

Time for Reflection

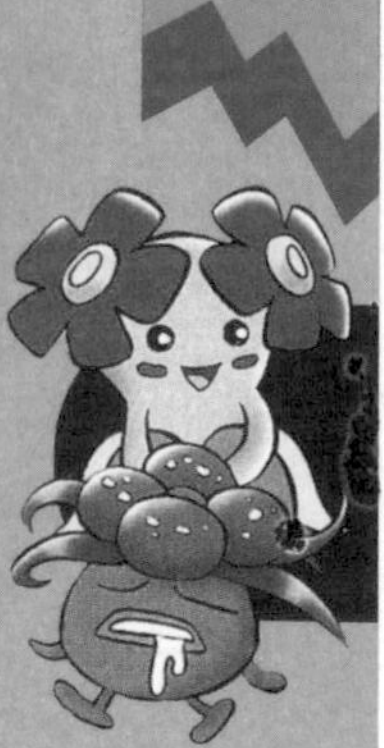

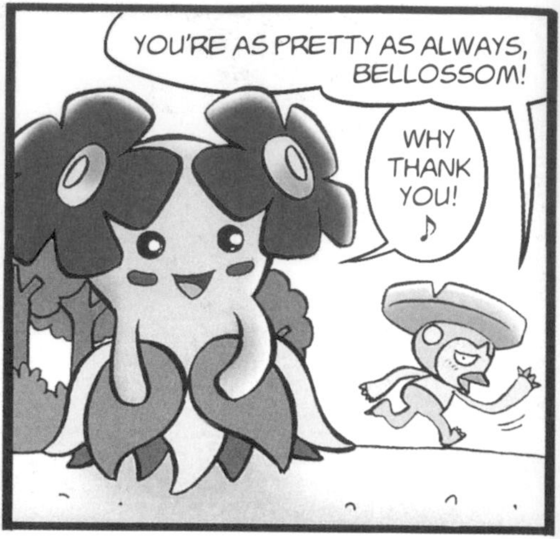
YOU'RE AS PRETTY AS ALWAYS, BELLOSSOM!
WHY THANK YOU! ♪

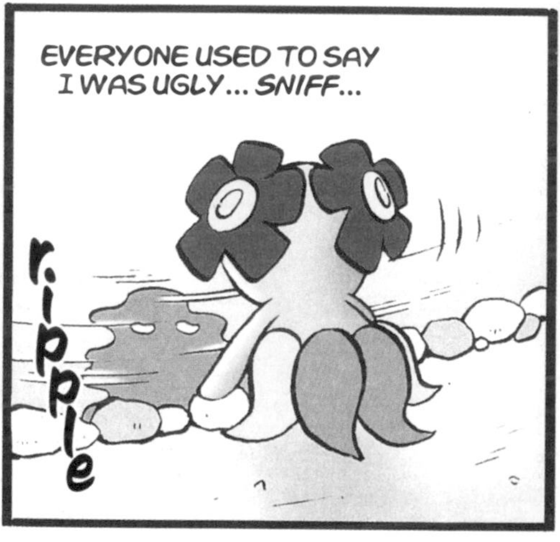
EVERYONE USED TO SAY I WAS UGLY... SNIFF...
ripple

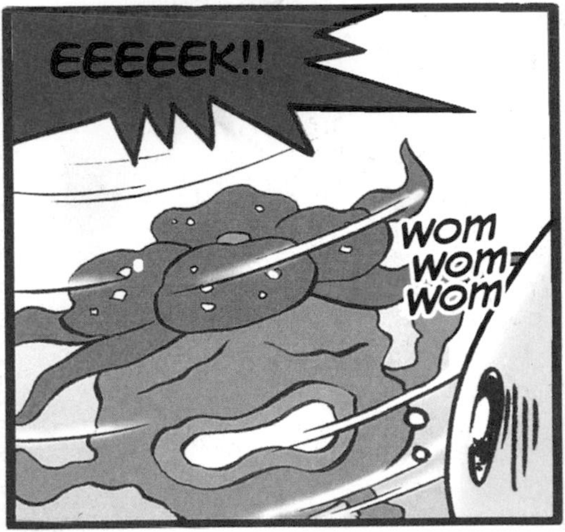
EEEEEK!!
wom wom wom

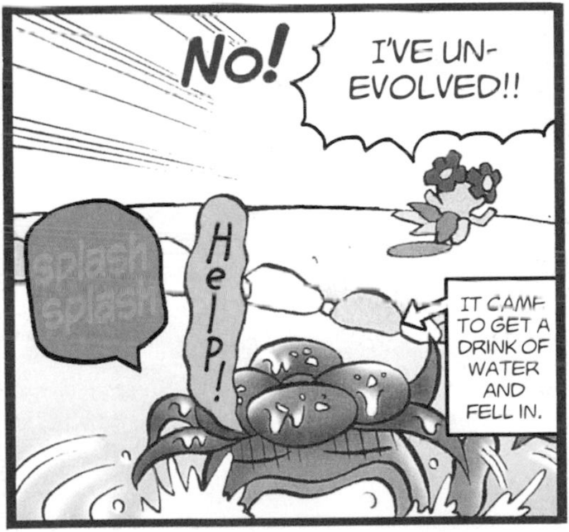
No!
I'VE UN-EVOLVED!!
splash splash
Help!
IT CAME TO GET A DRINK OF WATER AND FELL IN.

BELLOSSOM

It is plentiful in the tropics. A Bellossom grows flowers more beautifully if it evolves from a smelly Gloom—the stinkier the better.

GLOOM

A horribly noxious honey drools from its mouth. One whiff of the honey can result in memory loss.

FARFETCH'D

Souper Soaker

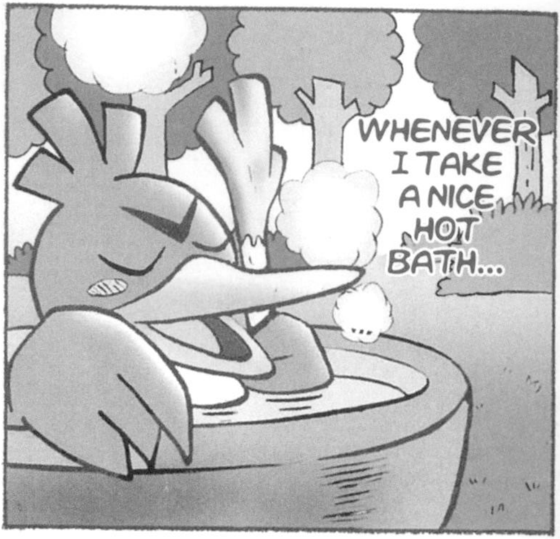
WHENEVER I TAKE A NICE HOT BATH...

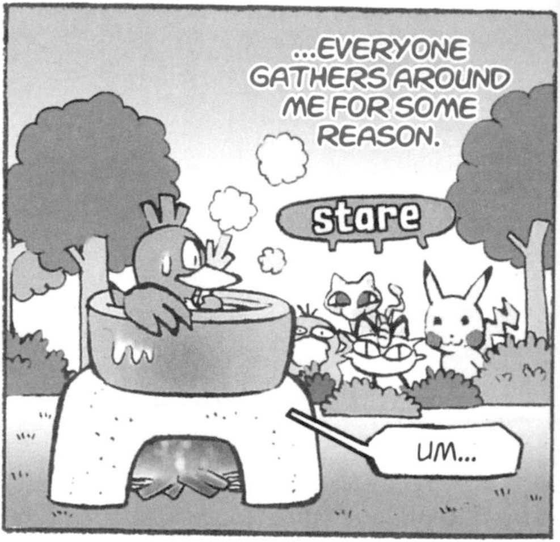
...EVERYONE GATHERS AROUND ME FOR SOME REASON.
stare
UM...

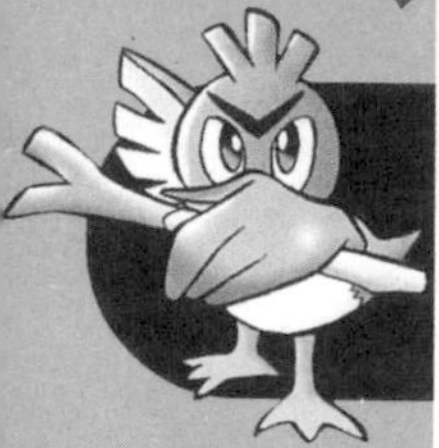

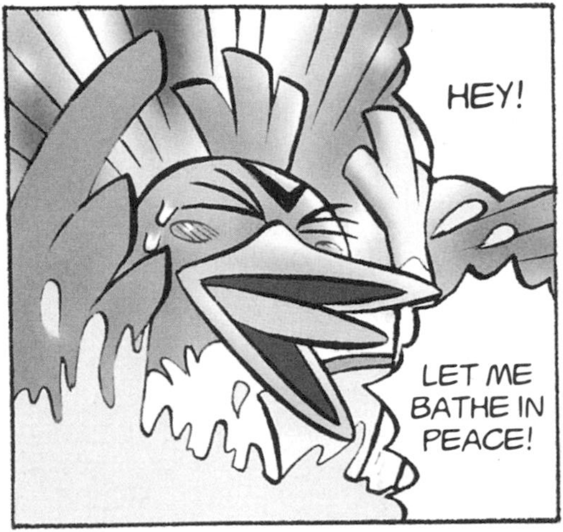
HEY!
LET ME BATHE IN PEACE!

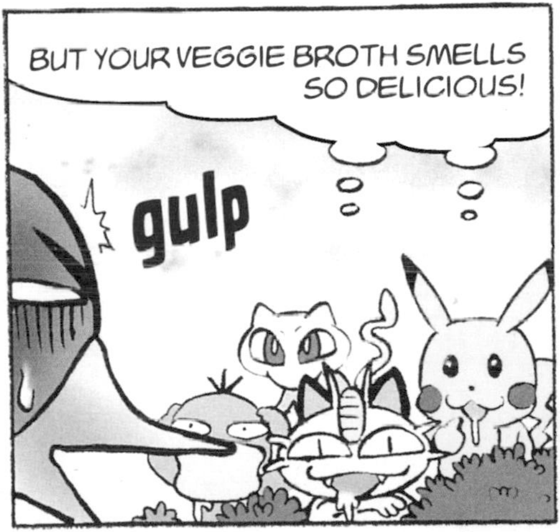
BUT YOUR VEGGIE BROTH SMELLS SO DELICIOUS!
gulp

FARFETCH'D

It always walks about with a plant stalk clamped in its beak. The stalk is used for building its nest. The stalk can also be a weapon and is used like a sword to cut all sorts of things. Apparently, there are good sticks and bad sticks. This Pokémon has been known to fight with others over sticks.

ABRA

Yoga Training 2

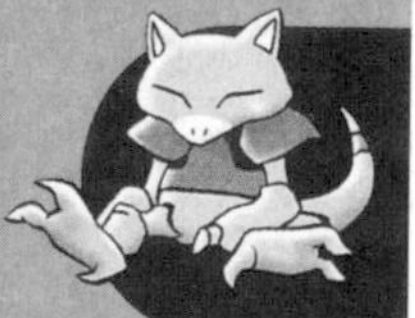

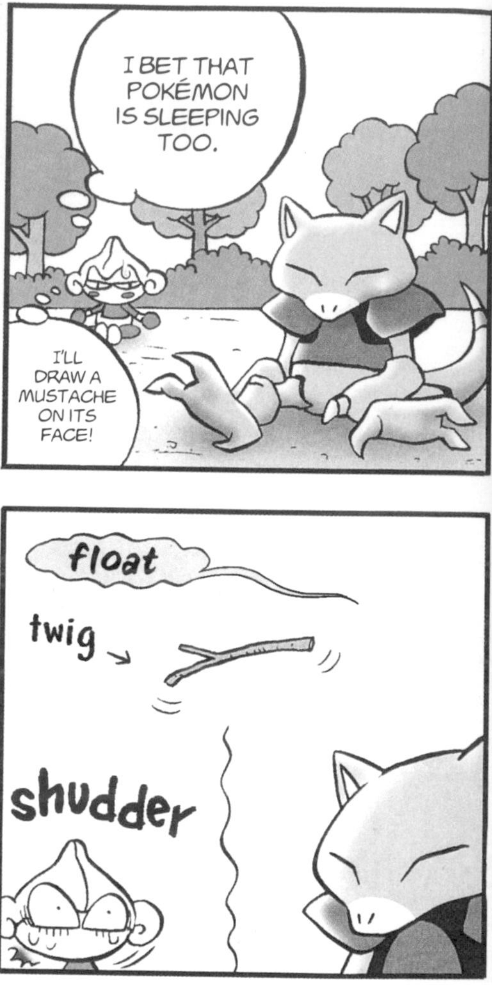
I BET THAT POKÉMON IS SLEEPING TOO.
I'LL DRAW A MUSTACHE ON ITS FACE!
float
twig
shudder

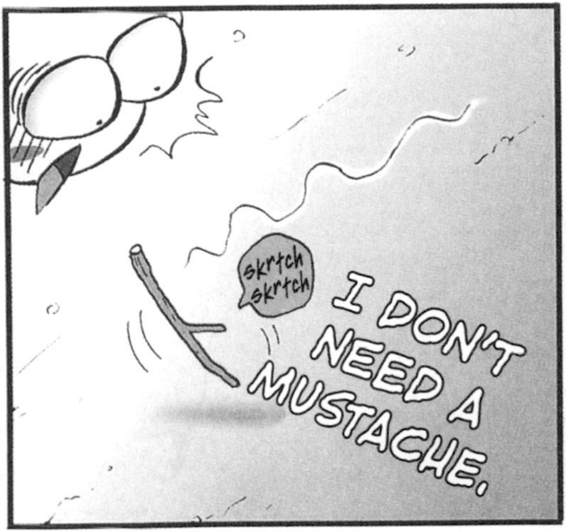
skrtch skrtch
I DON'T NEED A MUSTACHE.

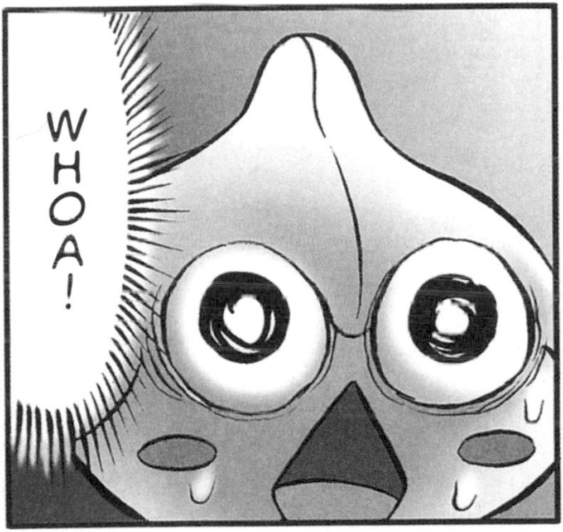
WHOA!

ABRA

It uses a variety of extrasensory powers even while asleep. However, it can sense the presence of foes even while it is sleeping. In such a situation, this Pokémon immediately teleports to safety. Abra needs to sleep for 18 hours a day. If it doesn't, this Pokémon loses its capacity to use telekinetic powers.

GRANBULL BELLSPROUT
Fangs for Nothing

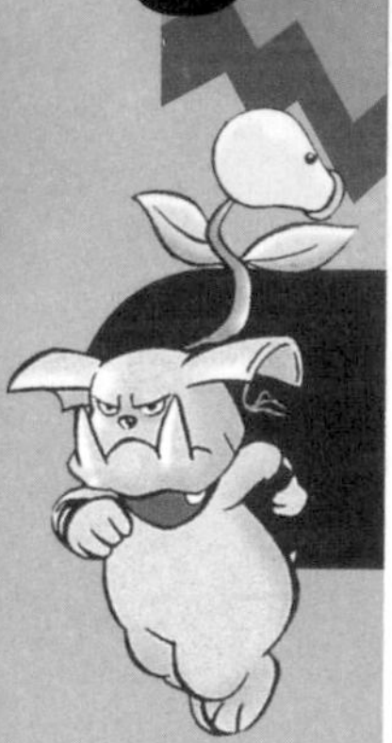

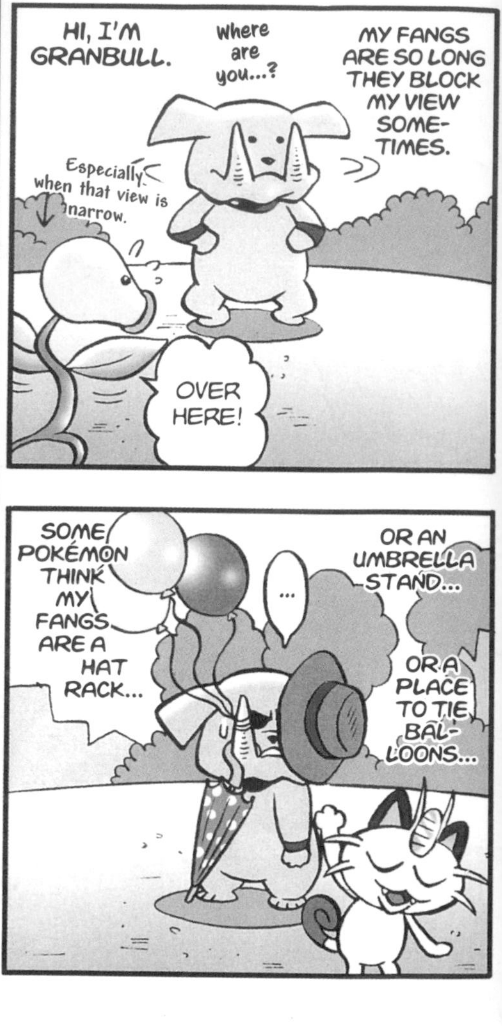
HI, I'M GRANBULL.
Where are you...?
MY FANGS ARE SO LONG THEY BLOCK MY VIEW SOMETIMES.
Especially when that view is narrow.
OVER HERE!
SOME POKÉMON THINK MY FANGS ARE A HAT RACK...
...
OR AN UMBRELLA STAND...
OR A PLACE TO TIE BALLOONS...

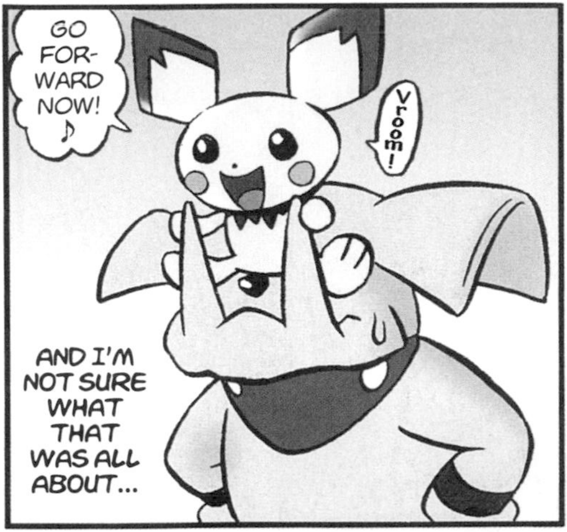
GO FOR-WARD NOW! ♪
Vroom!
AND I'M NOT SURE WHAT THAT WAS ALL ABOUT...

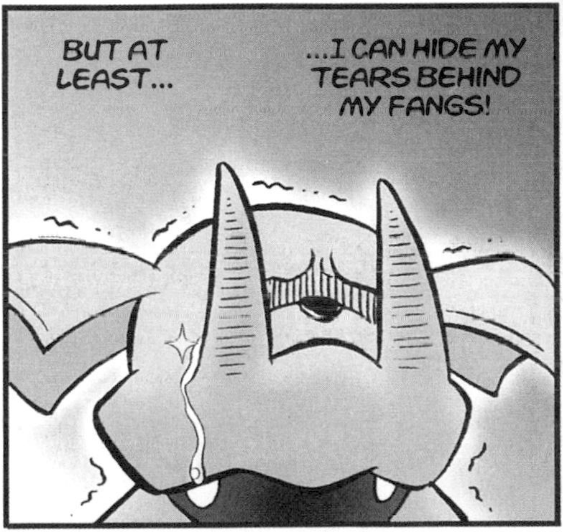
BUT AT LEAST...
...I CAN HIDE MY TEARS BEHIND MY FANGS!

GRANBULL

It is actually timid and easily spooked. Because its fangs are too heavy, it always keeps its head tilted down.

BELLSPROUT

Its thin and flexible body lets it bend and sway to avoid any attack. It is a carnivorous Pokémon that traps and eats bugs.

DRAGONAIR
A Lofty Dream

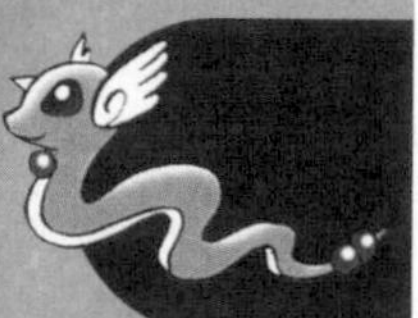

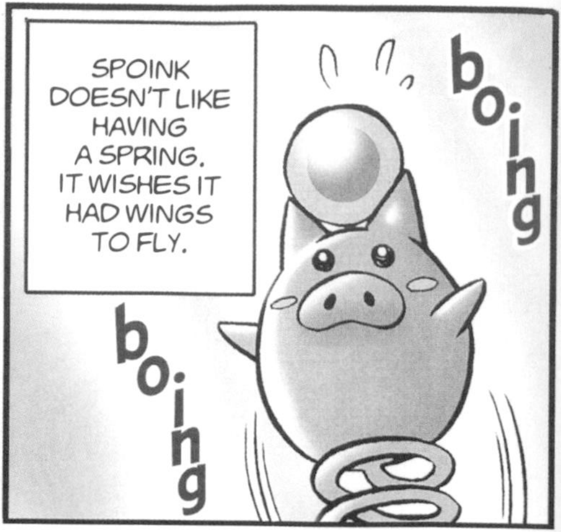
SPOINK DOESN'T LIKE HAVING A SPRING. IT WISHES IT HAD WINGS TO FLY.
boing
boing

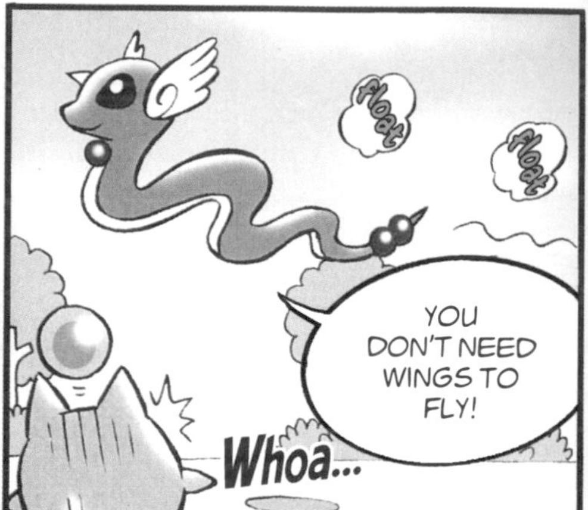
float
float
YOU DON'T NEED WINGS TO FLY!
Whoa...

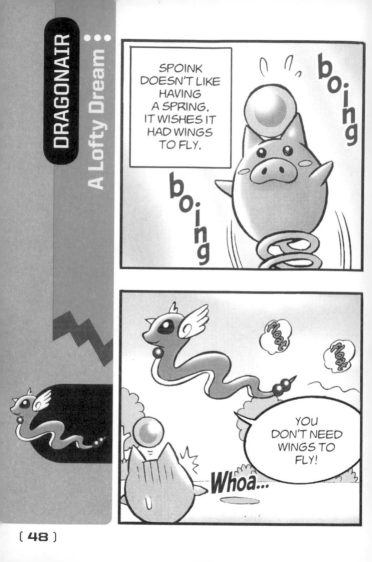

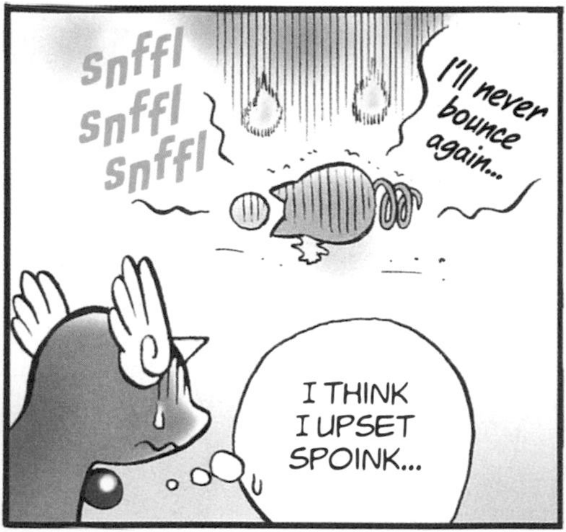
Snffl
Snffl
Snffl
I'll never bounce again...
I THINK I UPSET SPOINK...

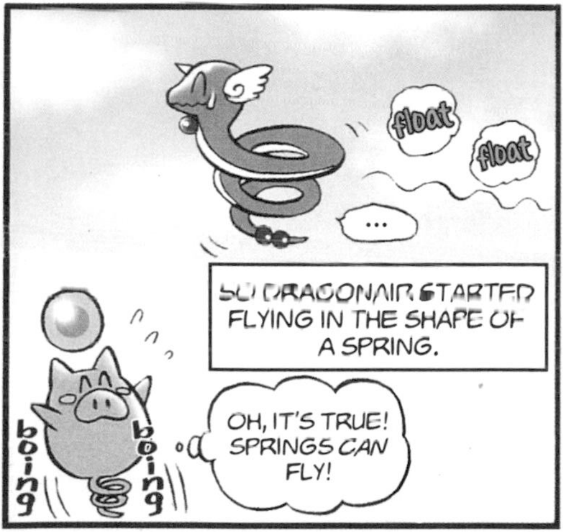
float
float
...
SO DRAGONAIR STARTED FLYING IN THE SHAPE OF A SPRING.
boing
boing
OH, IT'S TRUE! SPRINGS CAN FLY!

DRAGONAIR

It is said to live in seas and lakes. Even though it has no wings, it has been seen flying occasionally. A Dragonair stores an enormous amount of energy inside its body. It is said to alter the weather around it by releasing energy from the crystals on its neck and tail.

HITMONLEE

It's a Stretch

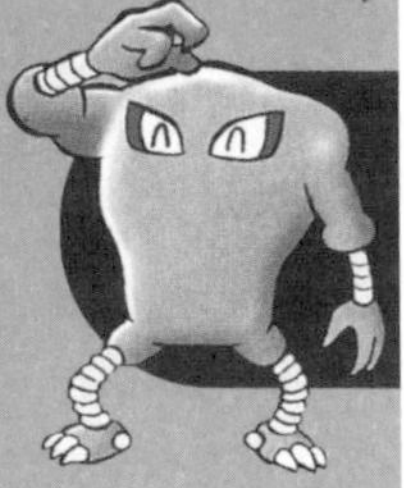

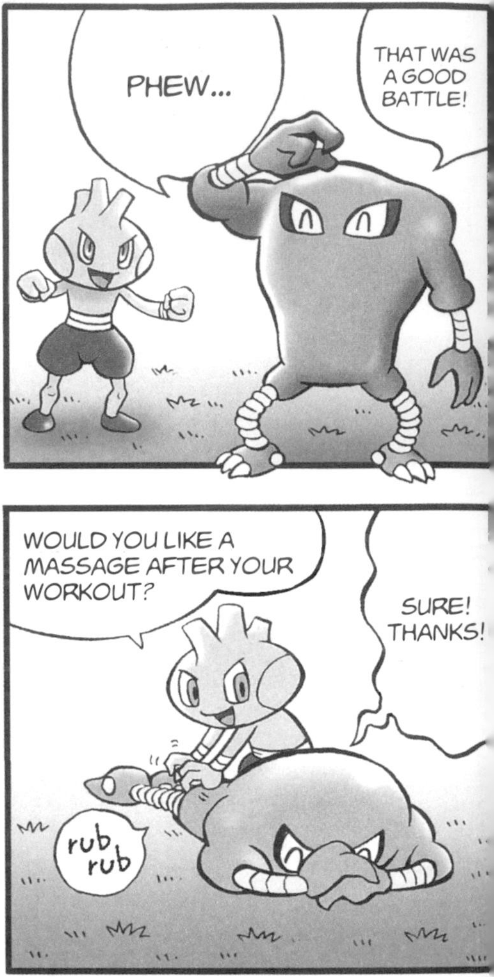
PHEW...
THAT WAS A GOOD BATTLE!
WOULD YOU LIKE A MASSAGE AFTER YOUR WORKOUT?
SURE! THANKS!
rub rub

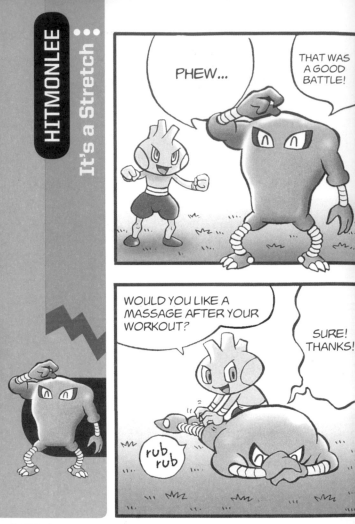

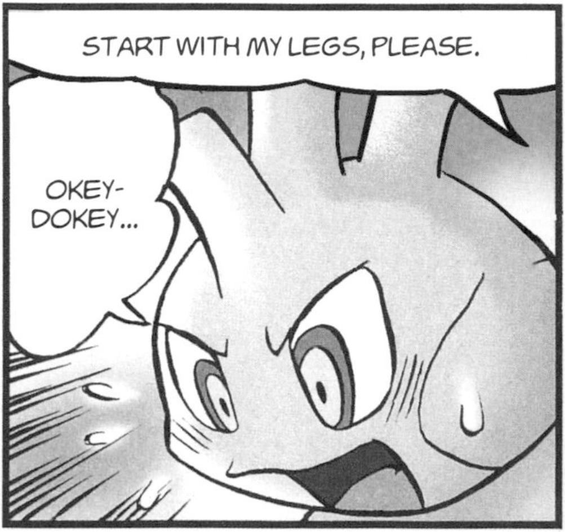
START WITH MY LEGS, PLEASE.
OKEY-DOKEY...

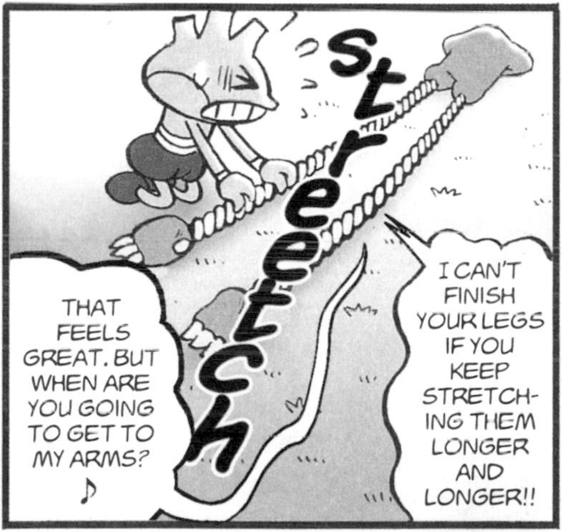
stretch
THAT FEELS GREAT. BUT WHEN ARE YOU GOING TO GET TO MY ARMS? ♪
I CAN'T FINISH YOUR LEGS IF YOU KEEP STRETCH-ING THEM LONGER AND LONGER!!

HITMONLEE

Its legs freely contract and stretch. Using these springlike legs, it bowls over foes with devastating kicks. When kicking, the sole of its foot turns as hard as a diamond on impact and destroys its enemy. After battle, it rubs down its legs and loosens the muscles to overcome fatigue.

TYROGUE MACHAMP
Give Me a Hand

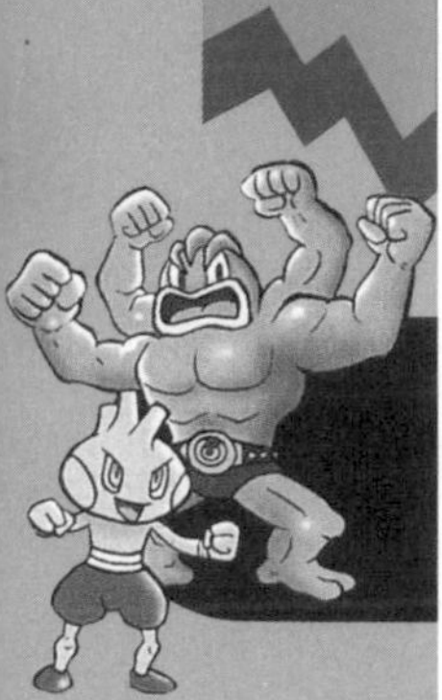

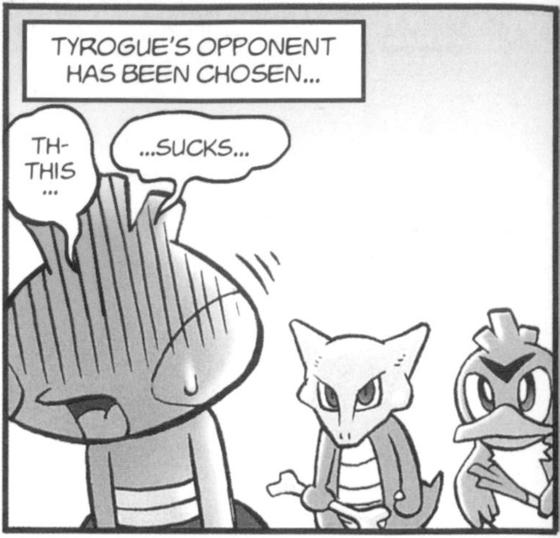
TYROGUE'S OPPONENT HAS BEEN CHOSEN...
TH-THIS...
...SUCKS...

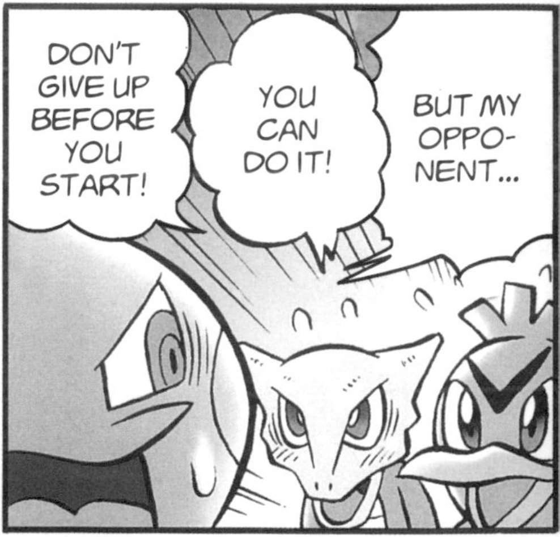
DON'T GIVE UP BEFORE YOU START!
YOU CAN DO IT!
BUT MY OPPONENT...

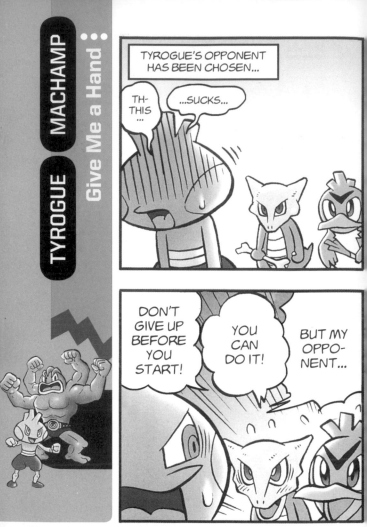

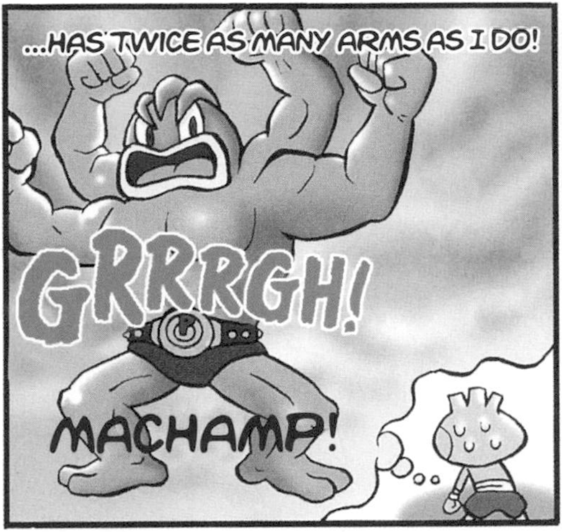
...HAS TWICE AS MANY ARMS AS I DO!
GRRRGH!
MACHAMP!

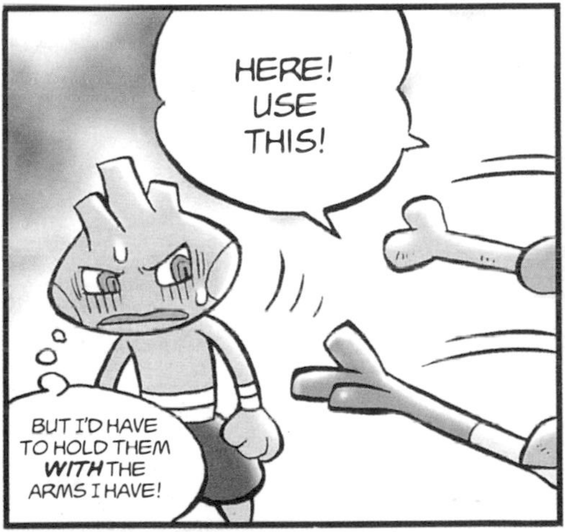
HERE! USE THIS!
BUT I'D HAVE TO HOLD THEM WITH THE ARMS I HAVE!

TYROGUE

It is always bursting with energy. To make itself stronger, it keeps on fighting even if it loses.

MACHAMP

Its four ruggedly developed arms can launch a flurry of 1,000 punches in just two seconds. Machamp is known as the Pokémon that has mastered every kind of martial art.

PHANPY
Comedy Duo

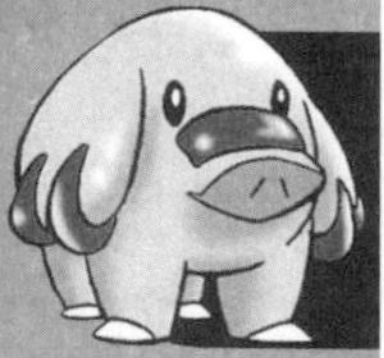

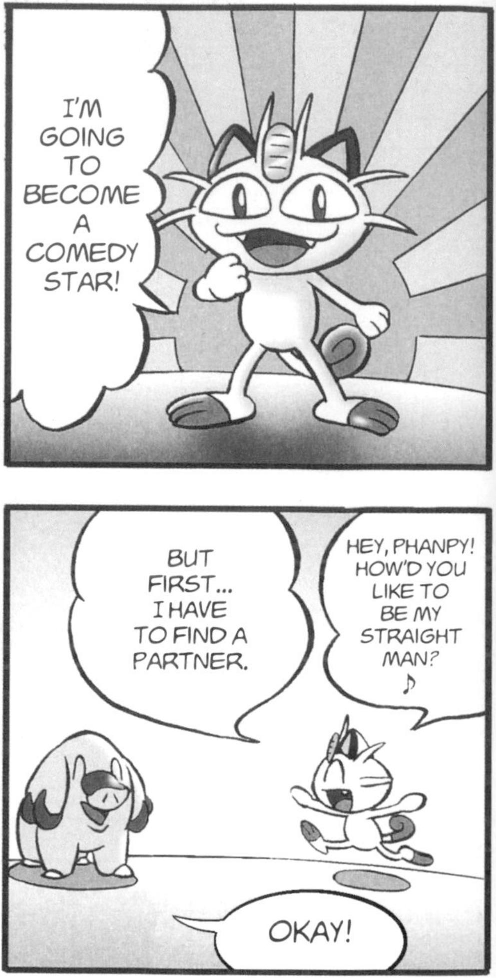
I'M GOING TO BECOME A COMEDY STAR!
BUT FIRST... I HAVE TO FIND A PARTNER.
HEY, PHANPY! HOW'D YOU LIKE TO BE MY STRAIGHT MAN? ♪
OKAY!

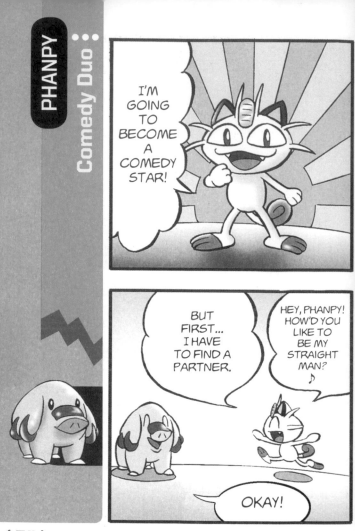

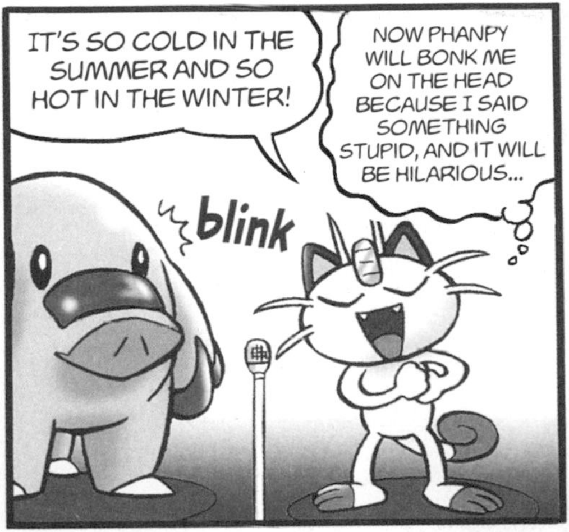
IT'S SO COLD IN THE SUMMER AND SO HOT IN THE WINTER!
NOW PHANPY WILL BONK ME ON THE HEAD BECAUSE I SAID SOMETHING STUPID, AND IT WILL BE HILARIOUS...
blink

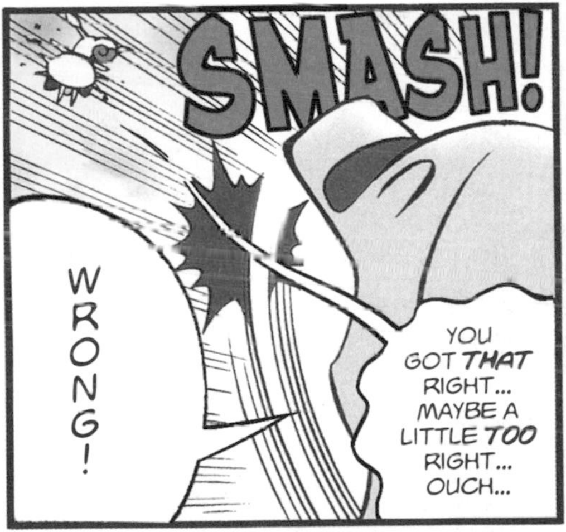
SMASH!
WRONG!
YOU GOT THAT RIGHT... MAYBE A LITTLE TOO RIGHT... OUCH...

PHANPY

For its nest, it digs a vertical pit in the ground at the edge of a river. When it becomes hot, it flaps its ears busily to cool down. Even the young are very strong. As a sign of affection, it will bump another Pokémon with its snout. However, it is so strong it may send it flying.

DUGTRIO

All for One or One for All?

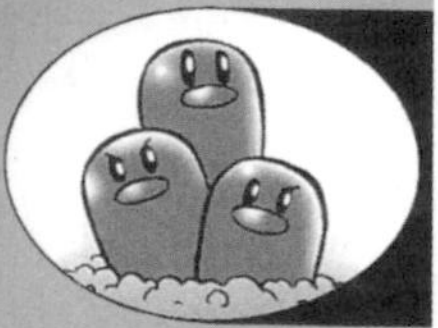

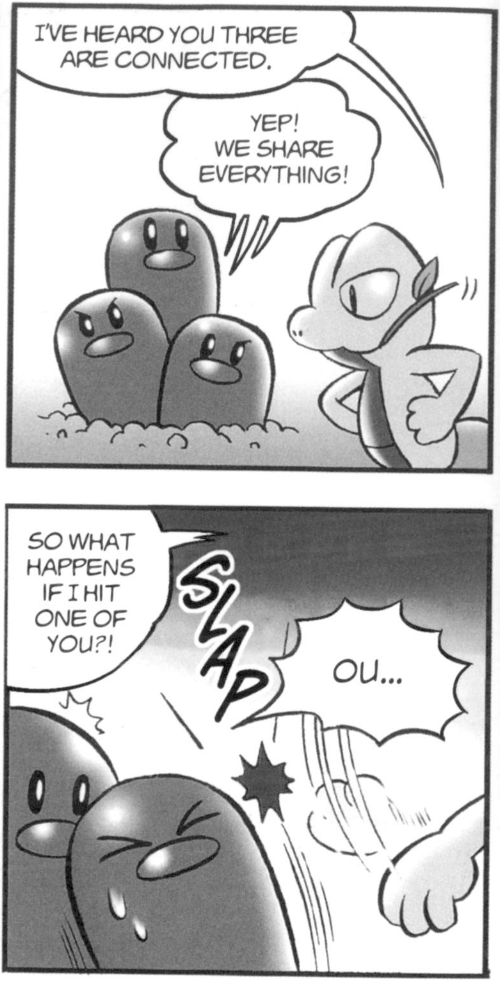
I'VE HEARD YOU THREE ARE CONNECTED.
YEP! WE SHARE EVERYTHING!
SO WHAT HAPPENS IF I HIT ONE OF YOU?!
SLAP
OU...

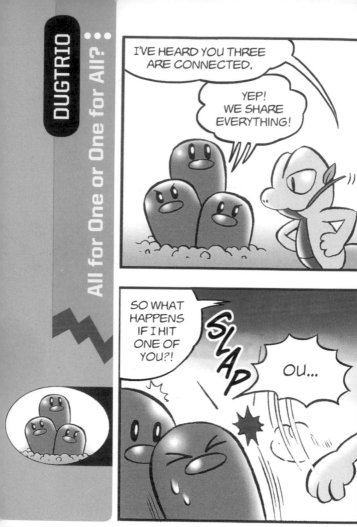

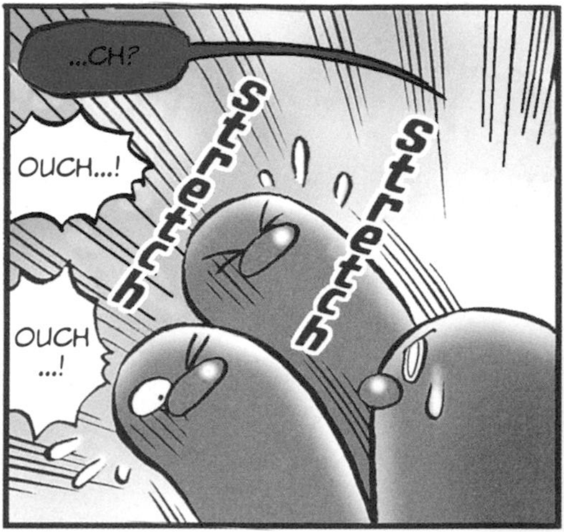
...CH?
OUCH...!
Stretch
Stretch
OUCH ...!

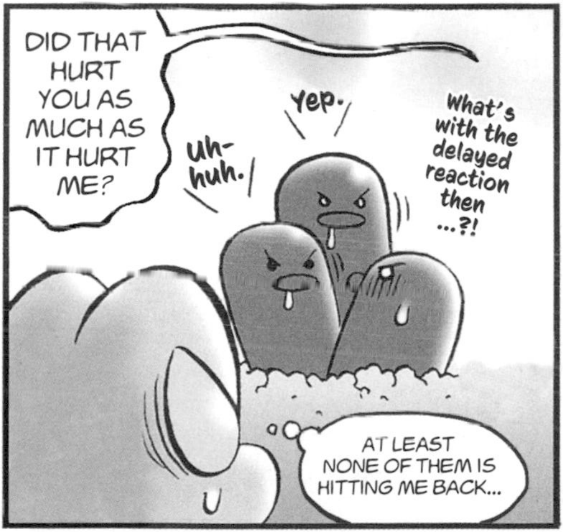
DID THAT HURT YOU AS MUCH AS IT HURT ME?
Uh-huh.
Yep.
What's with the delayed reaction then ...?!
AT LEAST NONE OF THEM IS HITTING ME BACK...

DUGTRIO

A team of Diglett triplets. Because the triplets originally split from one body, they think exactly alike. Dugtrio triggers huge earthquakes by burrowing 60 miles underground.

LEDIAN VOLBEAT
The Forest for the Trees

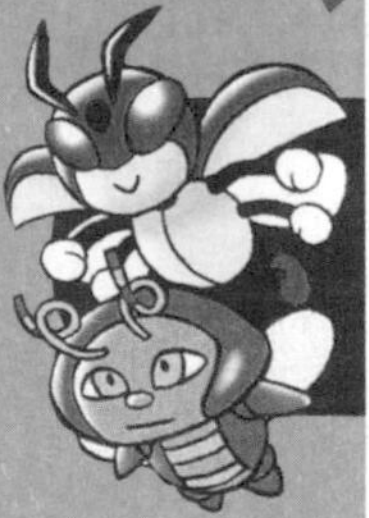

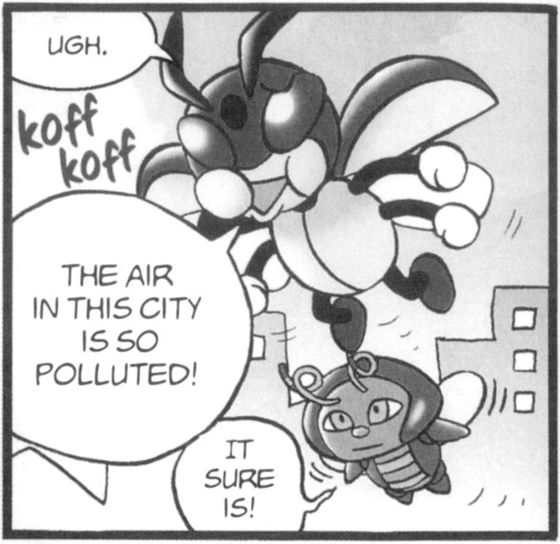
UGH.
koff koff
THE AIR IN THIS CITY IS SO POLLUTED!
IT SURE IS!

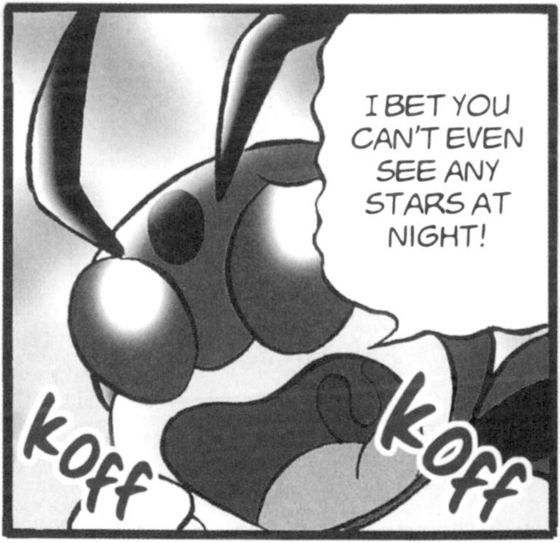
I BET YOU CAN'T EVEN SEE ANY STARS AT NIGHT!
koff
koff

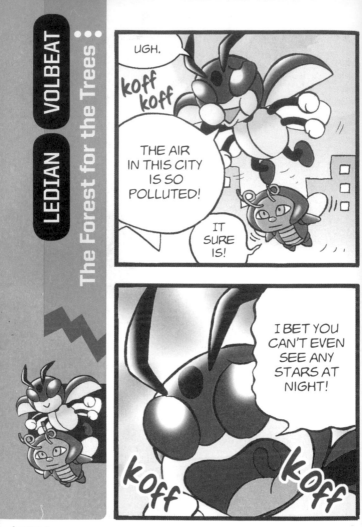

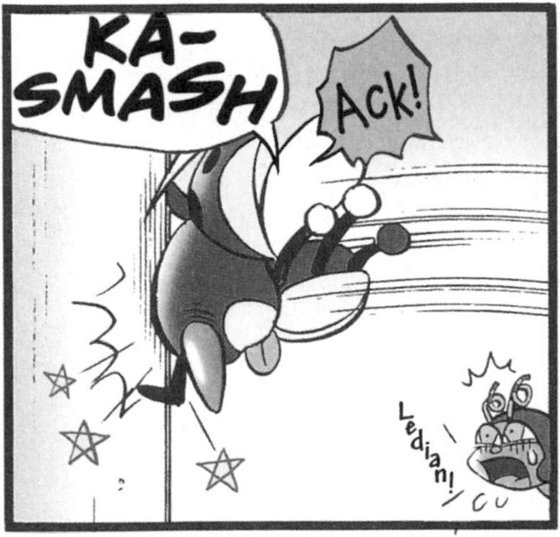
KA-
SMASH
Ack!
Ledian!

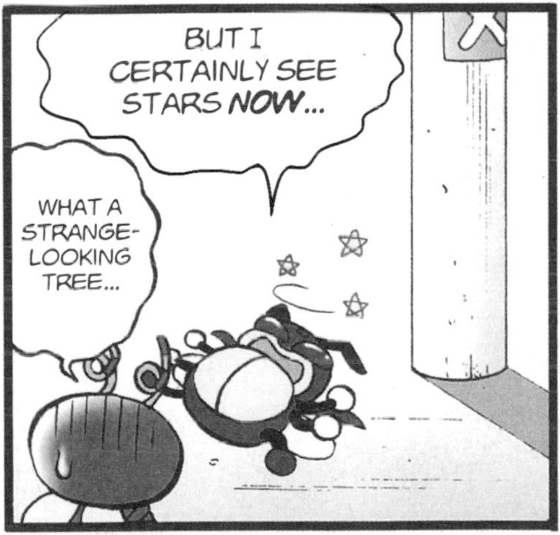
BUT I CERTAINLY SEE STARS ***NOW***...
WHAT A STRANGE-LOOKING TREE...

LEDIAN

It is said that in lands with clean air, where the stars fill the sky, there live Ledian in countless numbers. There is good reason for this—the Pokémon uses the light of the stars as an energy source.

VOLBEAT

It communicates with others by lighting up its rear at night. It lives around clean ponds. It moves its nest if the pond water becomes dirty.

SWABLU VAPOREON
Squeaky Clean:

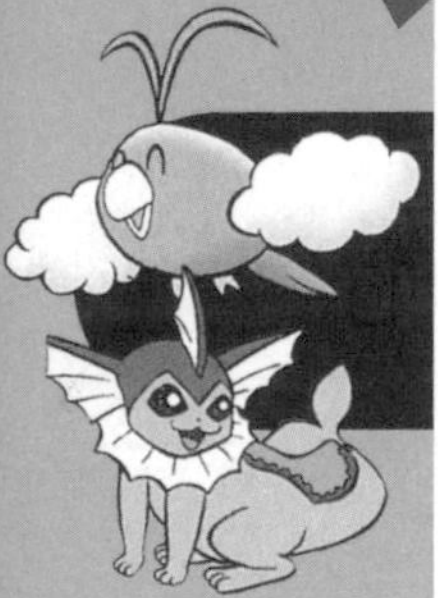

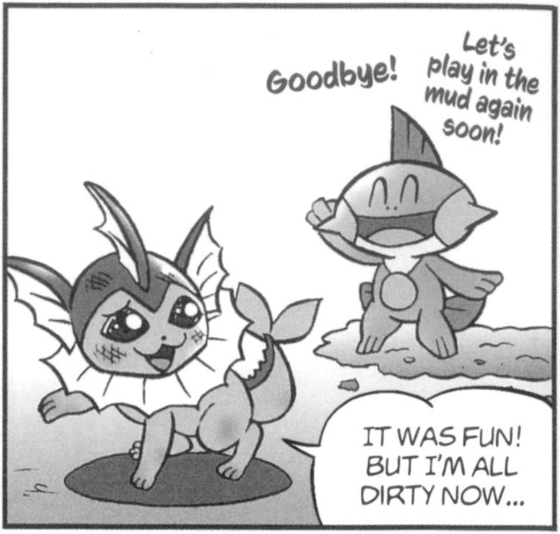
Goodbye!
Let's play in the mud again soon!
IT WAS FUN! BUT I'M ALL DIRTY NOW...

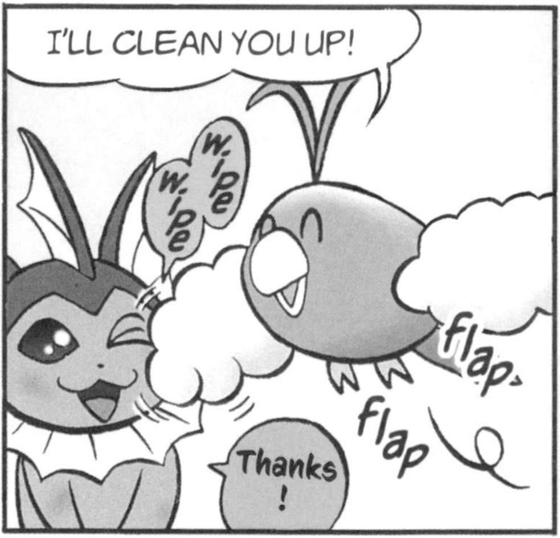
I'LL CLEAN YOU UP!
wipe
wipe
flap
flap
Thanks!

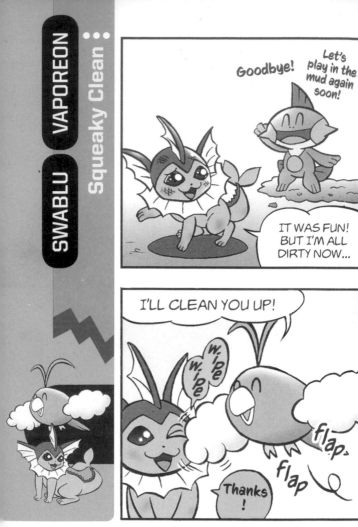

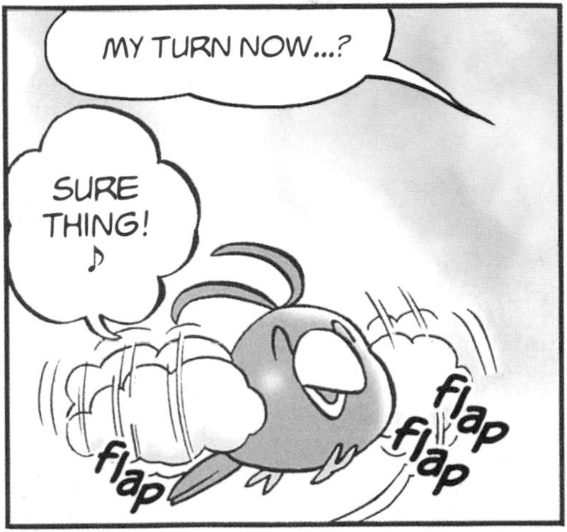
MY TURN NOW...?
SURE THING! ♪
flap
flap
flap

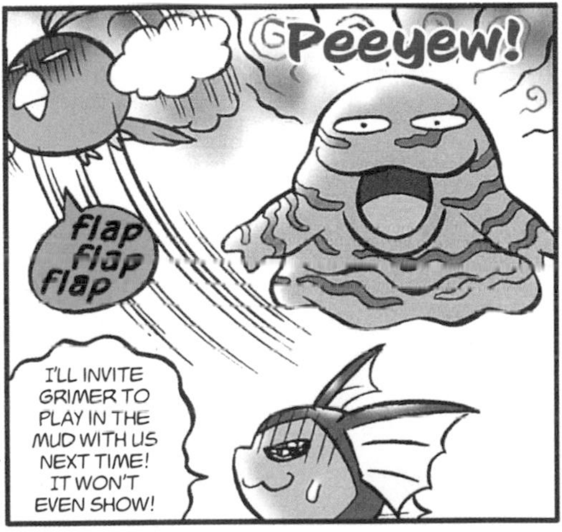
Peeyew!
flap flap flap
I'LL INVITE GRIMER TO PLAY IN THE MUD WITH US NEXT TIME! IT WON'T EVEN SHOW!

SWABLU

It loves to make things clean. If it spots something dirty, it will wipe and polish with its cottony wings. If its wings become dirty, this Pokémon finds a stream and takes a shower.

VAPOREON

It underwent a spontaneous mutation and grew fins and gills that allow it to live underwater. This Pokémon has the talent to freely control water.

SHEDINJA MEDICHAM

Molted Carapace

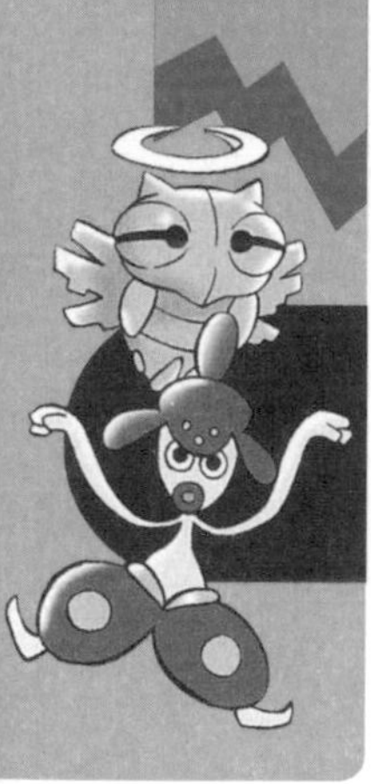

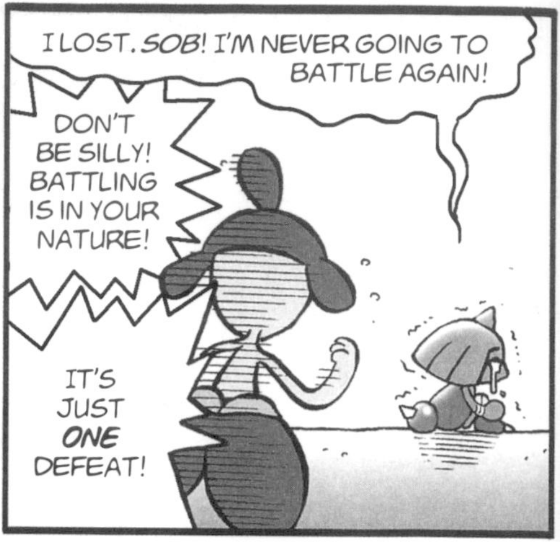
I LOST. *SOB*! I'M NEVER GOING TO BATTLE AGAIN!
DON'T BE SILLY! BATTLING IS IN YOUR NATURE!
IT'S JUST ***ONE*** DEFEAT!

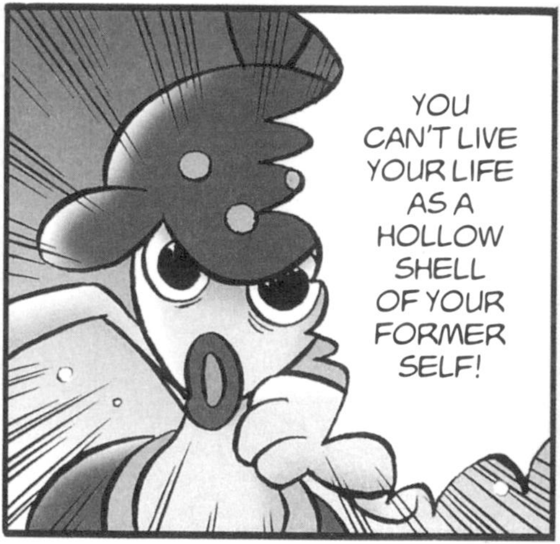
YOU CAN'T LIVE YOUR LIFE AS A HOLLOW SHELL OF YOUR FORMER SELF!

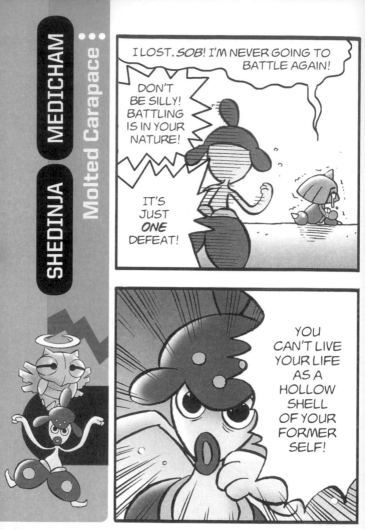

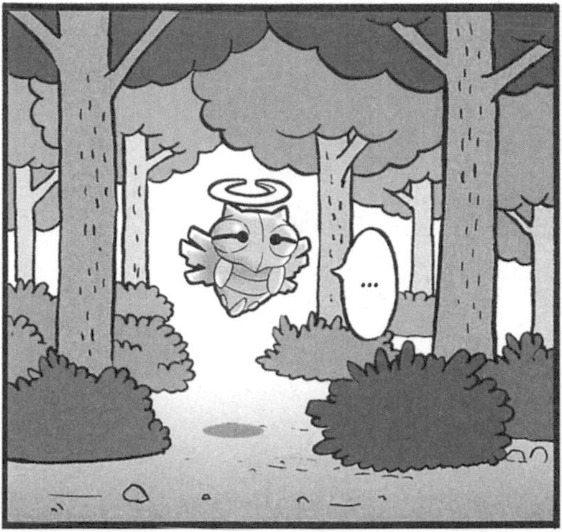
...

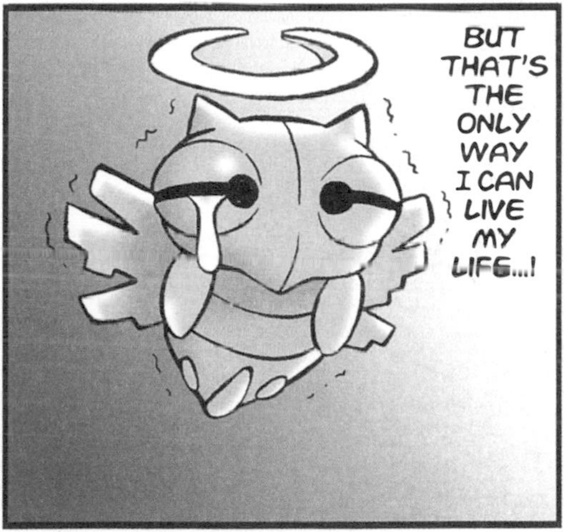
BUT THAT'S THE ONLY WAY I CAN LIVE MY LIFE...!

SHEDINJA

A peculiar Pokémon that floats in the air even though its wings remain completely still. This bizarre Pokémon is entirely immobile—it doesn't even breathe.

MEDICHAM

It battles with elegant, dance-like movements. This Pokémon is known to meditate for a whole month without eating.

SWALOT GULPIN
Where Does It Hurt?

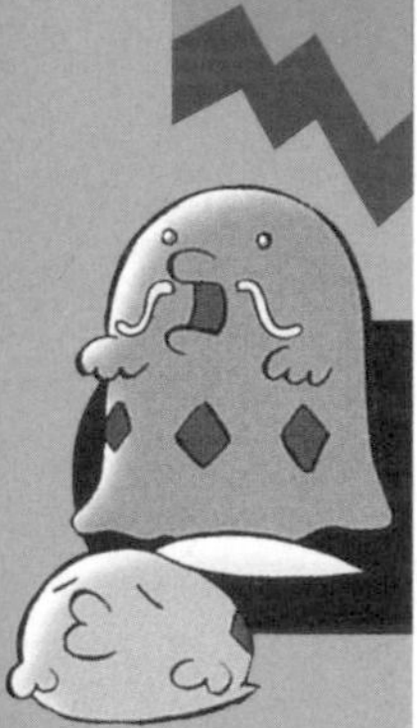

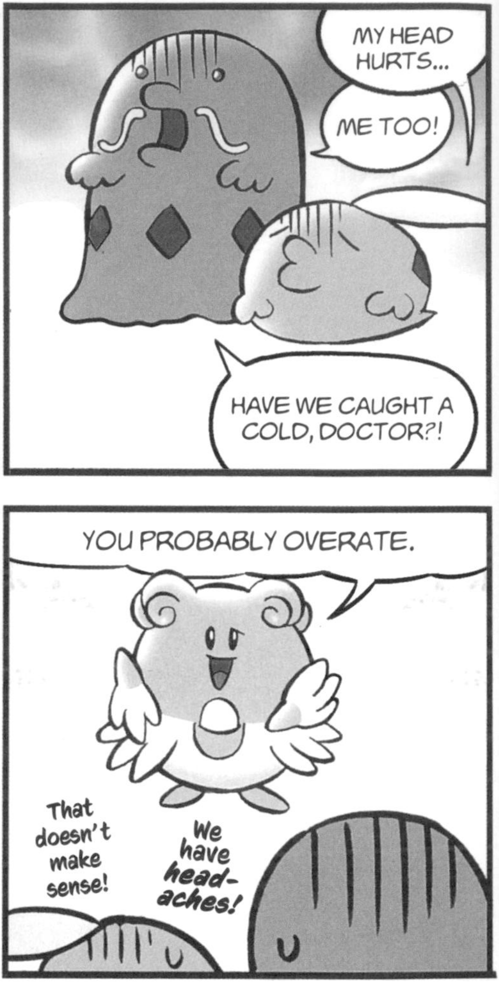
MY HEAD HURTS...
ME TOO!
HAVE WE CAUGHT A COLD, DOCTOR?!
YOU PROBABLY OVERATE.
That doesn't make sense!
We have head-aches!

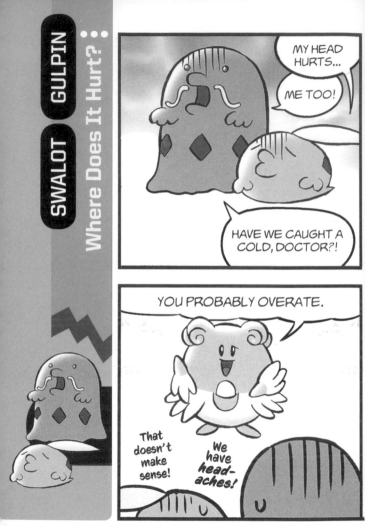

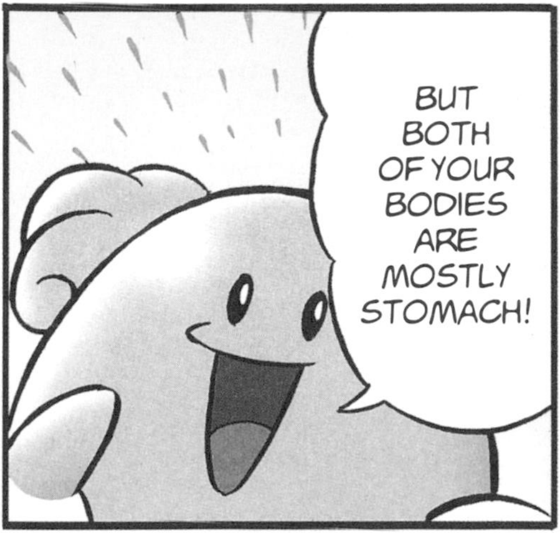
BUT BOTH OF YOUR BODIES ARE MOSTLY STOMACH!

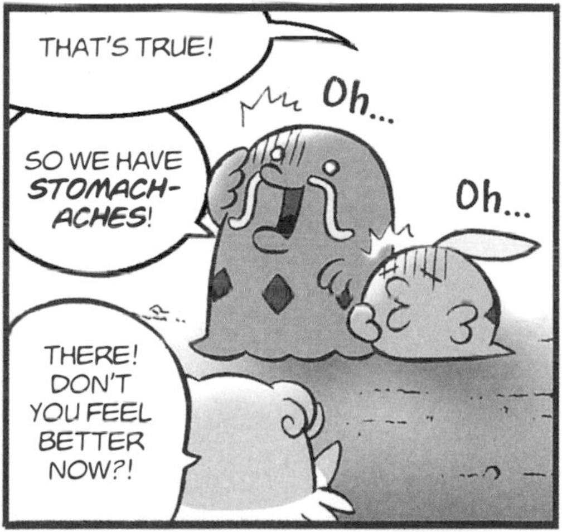
THAT'S TRUE!
Oh...
SO WE HAVE *STOMACH-ACHES*!
Oh...
THERE! DON'T YOU FEEL BETTER NOW?!

SWALOT

It swallows anything whole. Its special enzymes can dissolve anything. The one thing in the whole world a Swalot can't digest is its own stomach.

GULPIN

Almost all of its body is its stomach. Its harsh digestive juices quickly dissolve anything it swallows. It can swallow something its own size.

DUSKULL SUNFLORA

Opposites Don't Attract

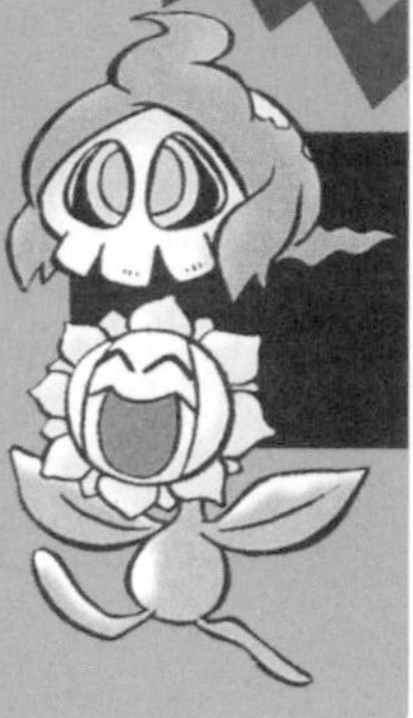

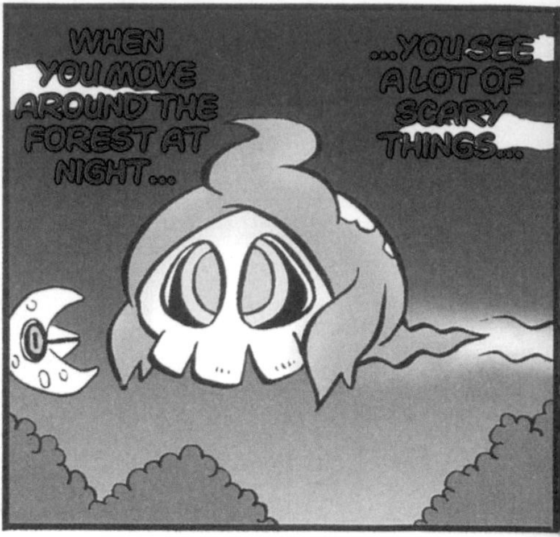
WHEN YOU MOVE AROUND THE FOREST AT NIGHT...
...YOU SEE A LOT OF SCARY THINGS...

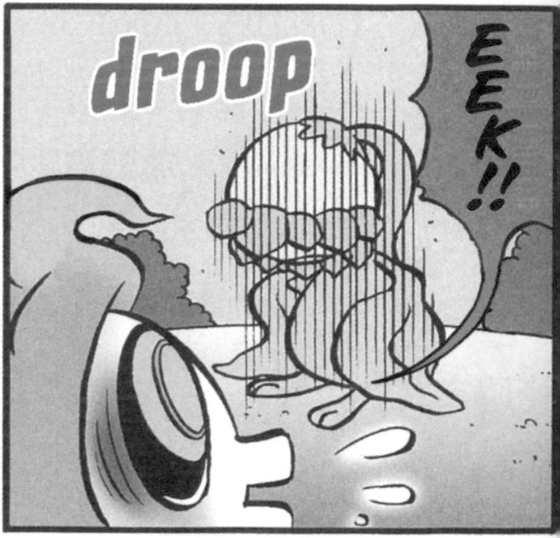
droop
EEK!!

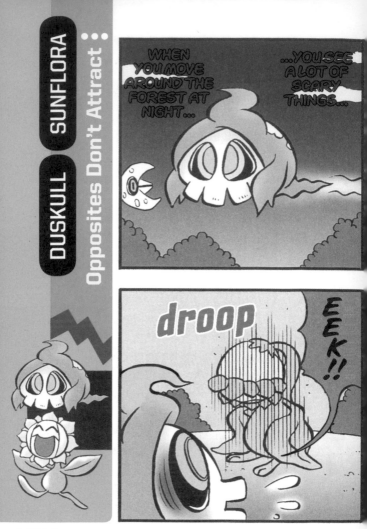

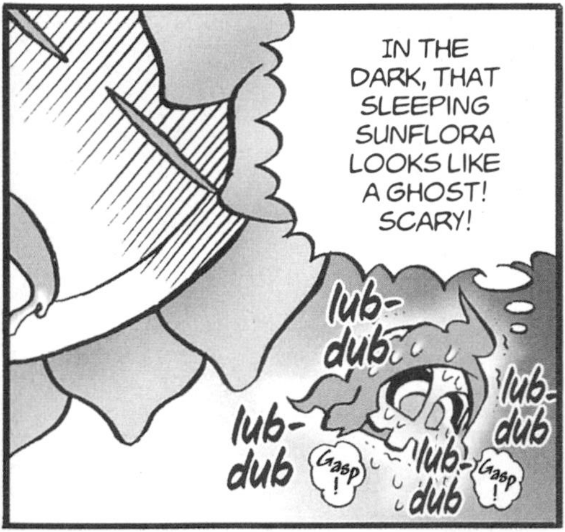
IN THE DARK, THAT SLEEPING SUNFLORA LOOKS LIKE A GHOST! SCARY!
lub-dub
lub-dub
lub-dub
lub-dub
Gasp!
Gasp!

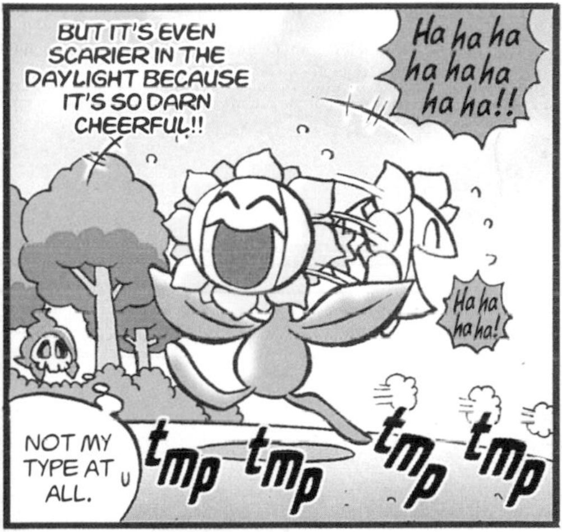
BUT IT'S EVEN SCARIER IN THE DAYLIGHT BECAUSE IT'S SO DARN CHEERFUL!!
Ha ha ha ha ha ha ha ha!!
Ha ha ha ha!
NOT MY TYPE AT ALL.
tmp tmp tmp tmp

DUSKULL

It wanders lost in the deep darkness of midnight. A glare from its single scarlet eye makes even burly grown-ups freeze in utter fear.

SUNFLORA

It converts sunlight into energy. In the daytime, it rushes about in a hectic manner, but it comes to a complete stop when the sun sets.

VIGOROTH
Sleepless Fights

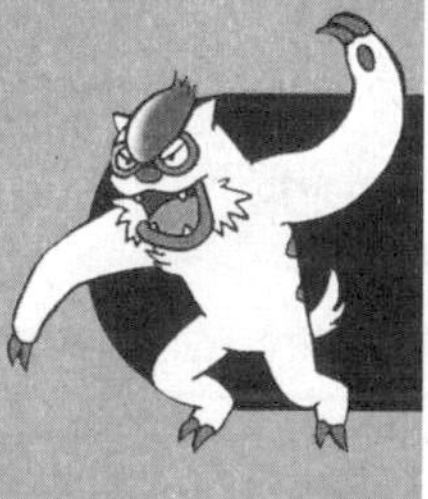

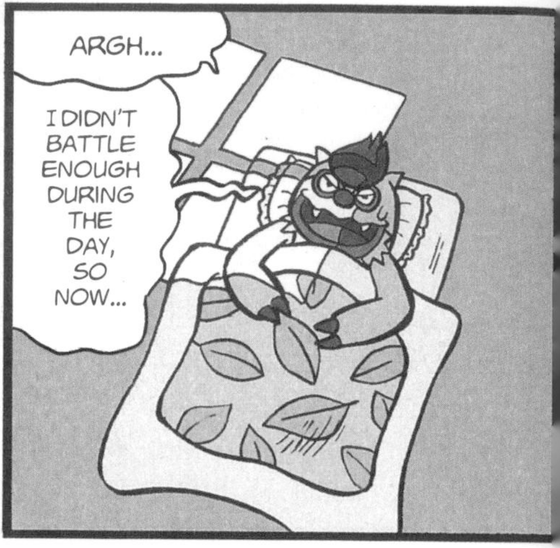
ARGH...
I DIDN'T BATTLE ENOUGH DURING THE DAY, SO NOW...

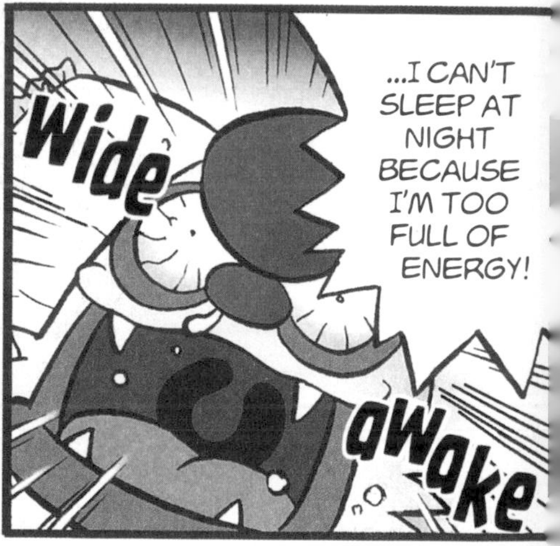
wide
...I CAN'T SLEEP AT NIGHT BECAUSE I'M TOO FULL OF ENERGY!
awake

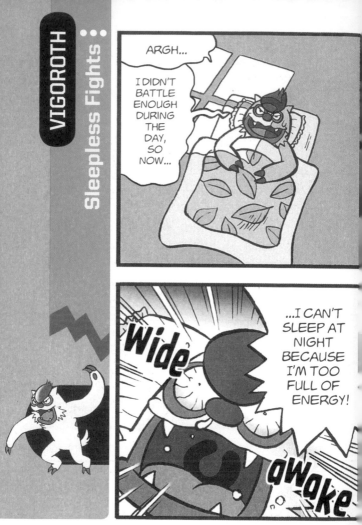

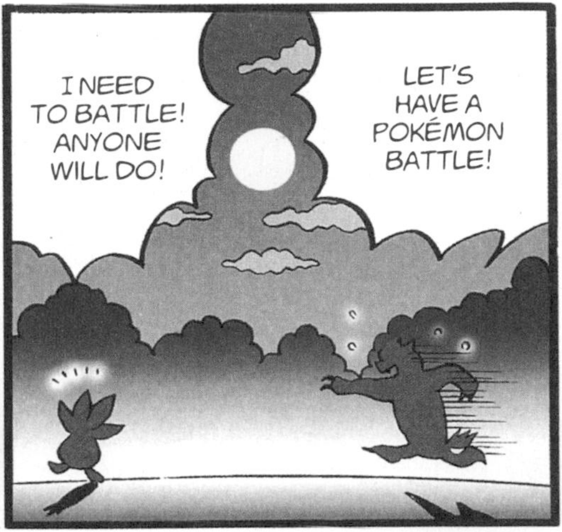
I NEED TO BATTLE! ANYONE WILL DO!
LET'S HAVE A POKÉMON BATTLE!

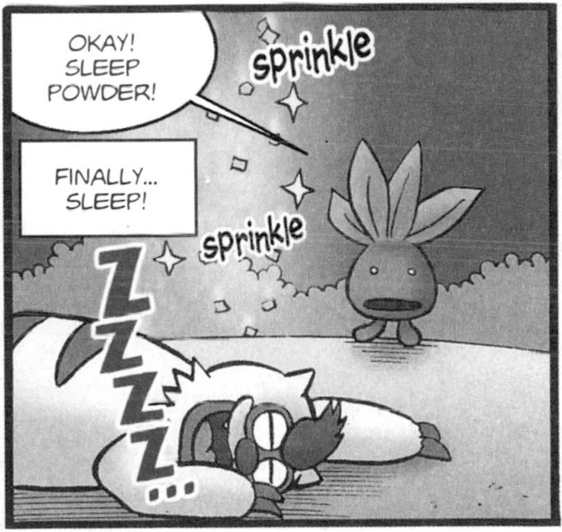
OKAY! SLEEP POWDER!
sprinkle
FINALLY... SLEEP!
sprinkle
ZZZZ...

VIGOROTH

It evolves from Slakoth. It is always hungry because it won't stop rampaging. It can't keep still because its blood boils with energy. It runs through the fields and mountains all day to calm itself. If it doesn't, it can't sleep at night.

MACHOKE MACHOP
Belt It Out

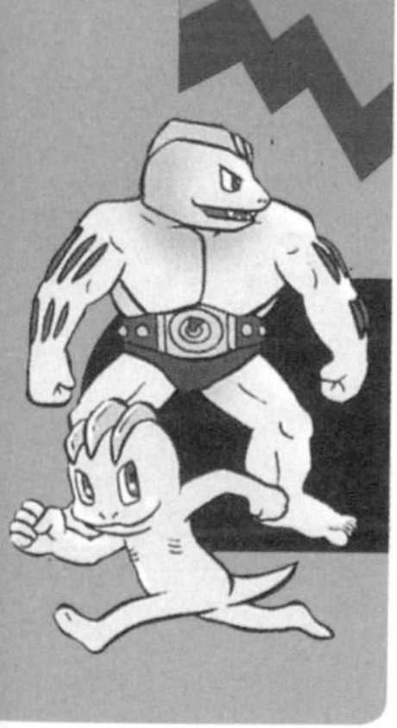

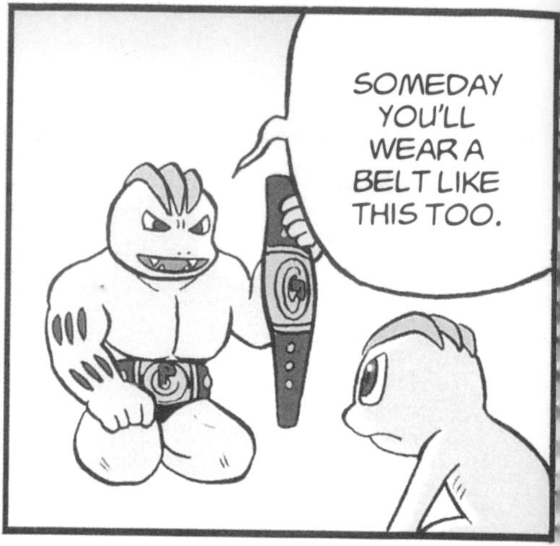
SOMEDAY YOU'LL WEAR A BELT LIKE THIS TOO.

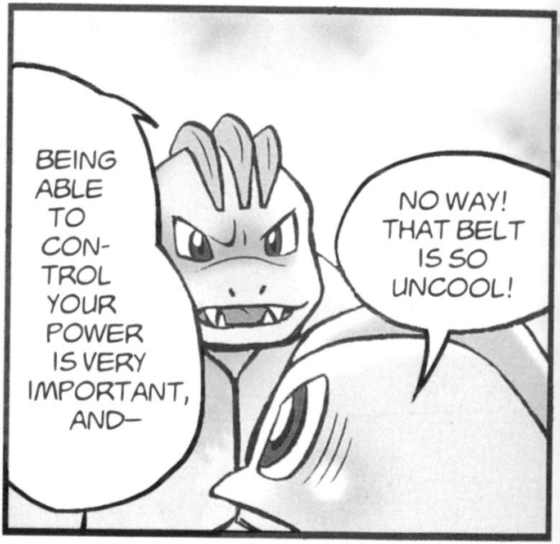
BEING ABLE TO CON-TROL YOUR POWER IS VERY IMPORTANT, AND—
NO WAY! THAT BELT IS SO UNCOOL!

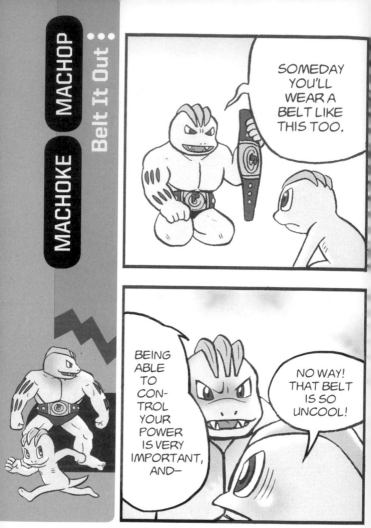

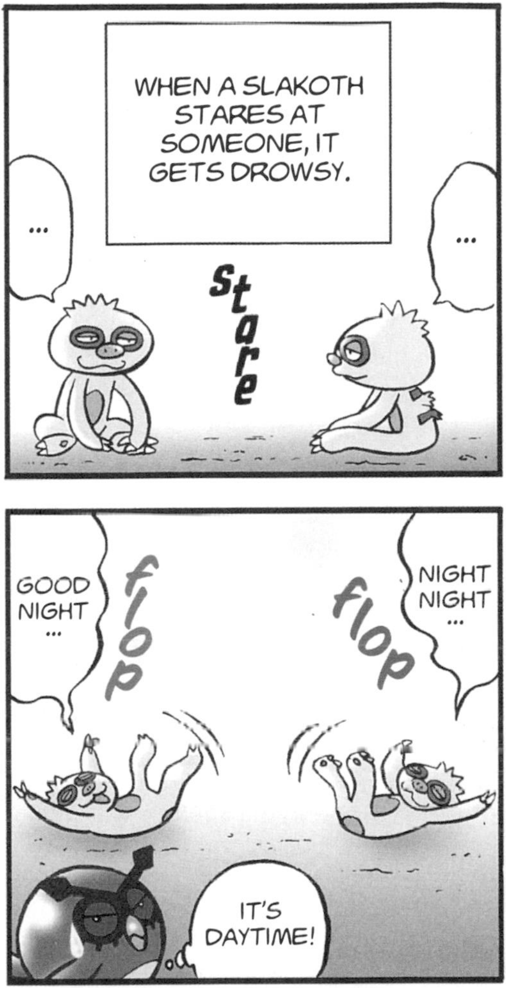
WHEN A SLAKOTH STARES AT SOMEONE, IT GETS DROWSY.
...
...
stare
GOOD NIGHT ...
flop
flop
NIGHT NIGHT ...
IT'S DAYTIME!

SLAKOTH

It sleeps for 20 hours every day. Making those that see it drowsy is one of its talents. Because it moves so little, this Pokémon's sole daily meal consists of just three leaves. It doesn't change its nest its entire life, but it sometimes travels great distances by swimming in rivers.

EXPLOUD

Notification...

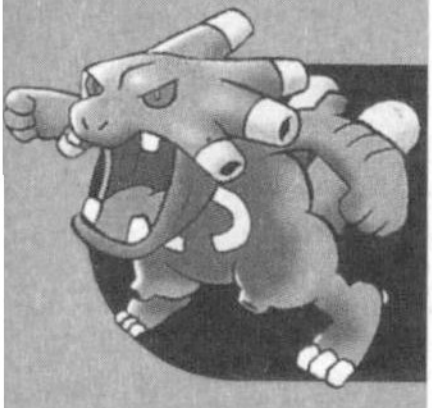

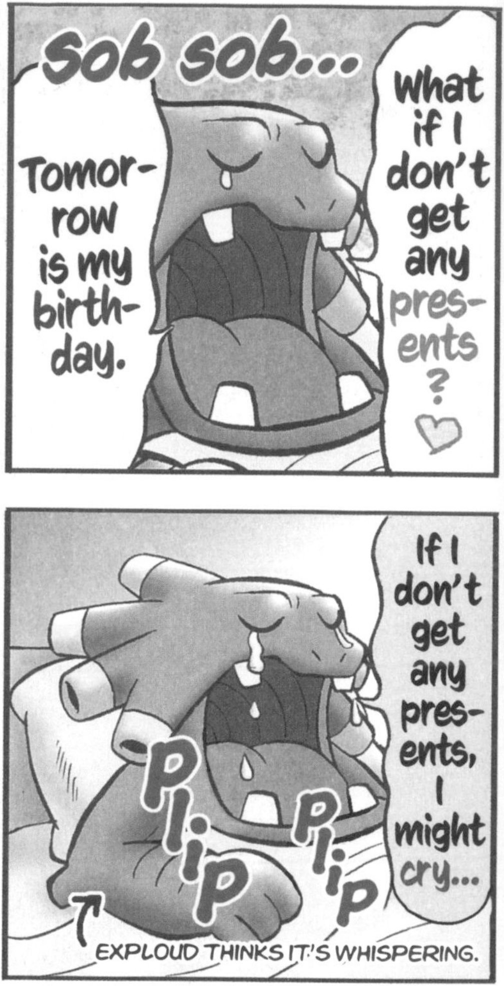
Sob sob...
Tomorrow is my birthday.
What if I don't get any presents?
If I don't get any presents, I might cry...
Plip
Plip
EXPLOUD THINKS IT'S WHISPERING.

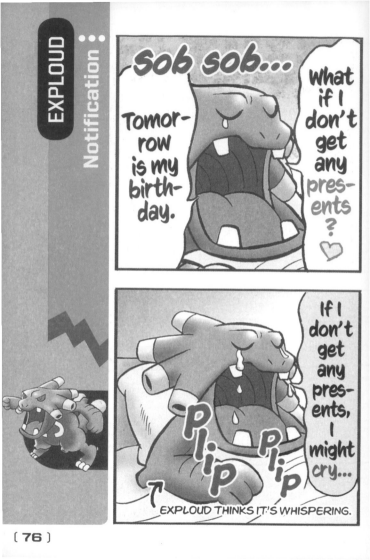

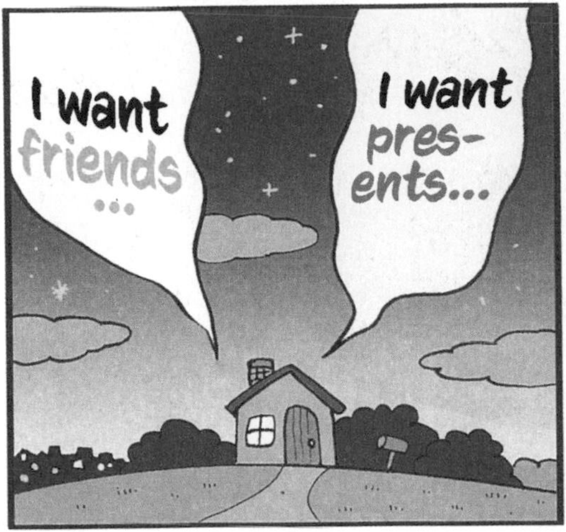
I want friends...
I want pres-ents...

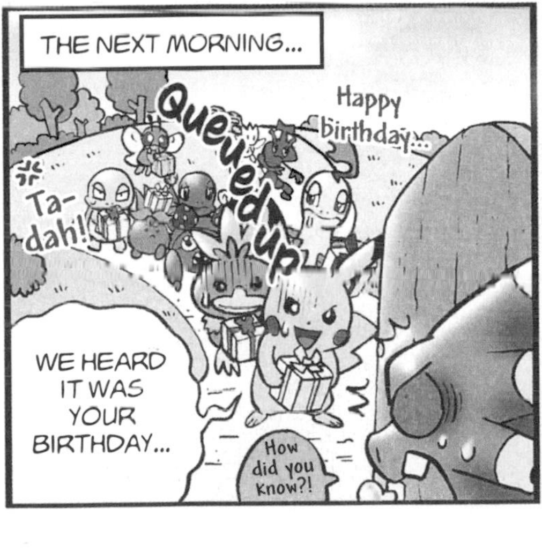
THE NEXT MORNING...
Queued up
Happy birthday...
Ta-dah!
WE HEARD IT WAS YOUR BIRTHDAY...
How did you know?!

EXPLOUD

It has sound-generating organs all over its body. Its howls can be heard over six miles away. It communicates with others by adjusting the tone and volume of the cries it emits. It triggers earthquakes with the tremor it creates by bellowing.

GRUMPIG FLYGON

Dancing Fool

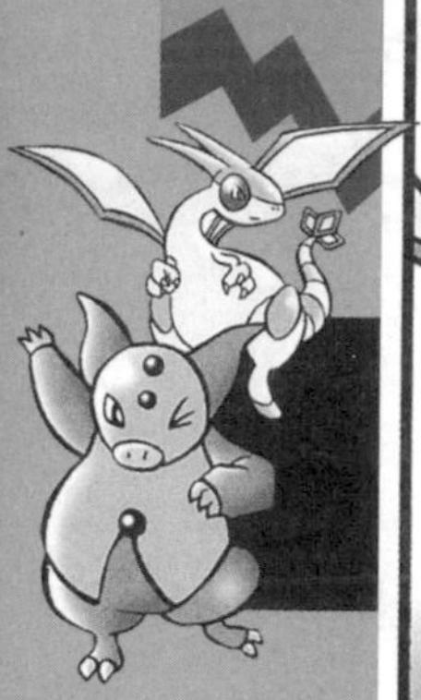

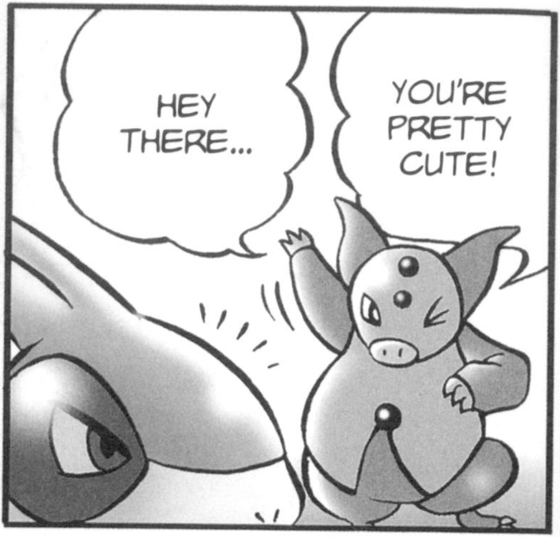
HEY THERE...
YOU'RE PRETTY CUTE!

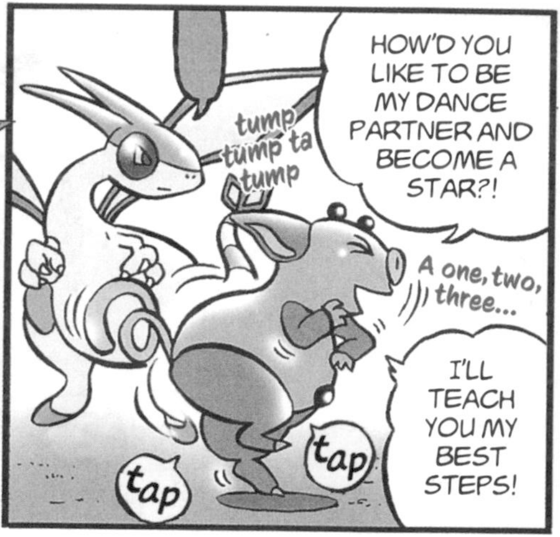
HOW'D YOU LIKE TO BE MY DANCE PARTNER AND BECOME A STAR?!
tump tump ta tump
A one, two, three...
I'LL TEACH YOU MY BEST STEPS!
tap
tap

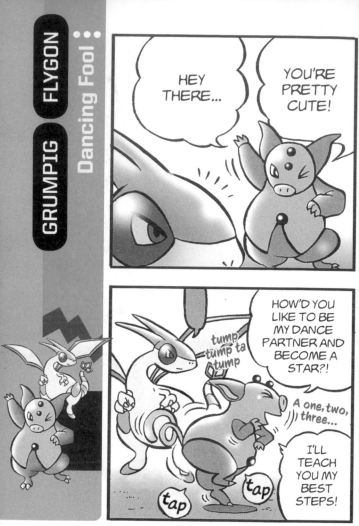

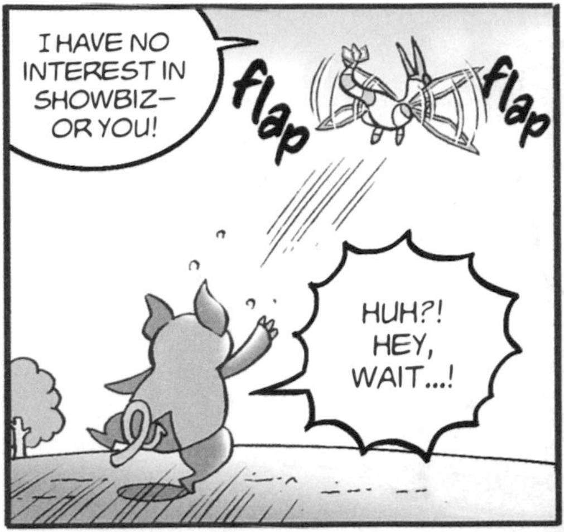
I HAVE NO INTEREST IN SHOWBIZ— OR YOU!
flap
flap
HUH?! HEY, WAIT...!

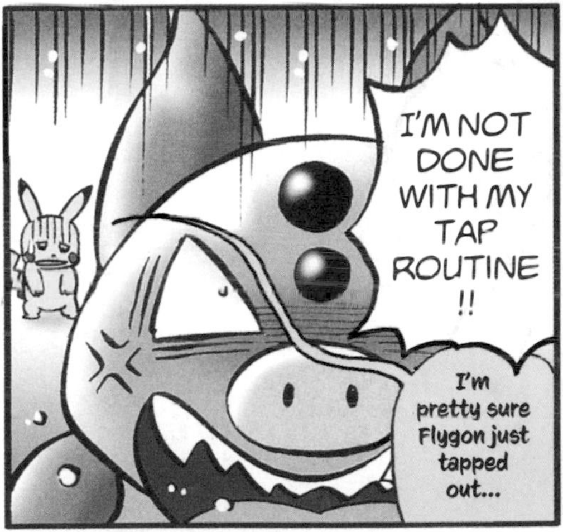
I'M NOT DONE WITH MY TAP ROUTINE !!
I'm pretty sure Flygon just tapped out...

GRUMPIG

It stores power in the black pearls on its forehead. When it uses psychic power, it performs an odd dance step. Its type of dancing became hugely popular overseas.

FLYGON

It is nicknamed "the elemental spirit of the desert." It hides itself by kicking up desert sand with its wings. Red covers shield its eyes from sand.

JIRACHI NUZLEAF

Be Careful What You Wish For!

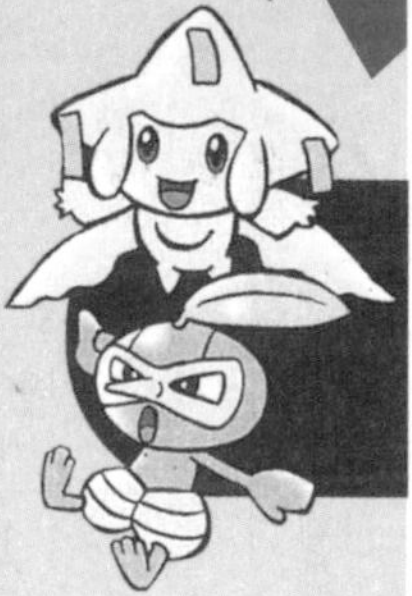

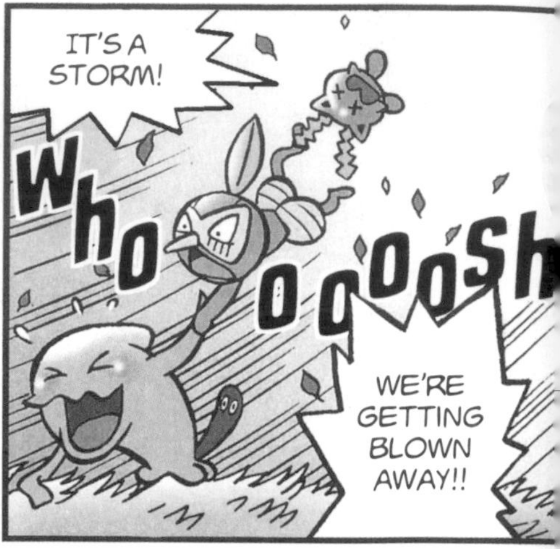
IT'S A STORM!
WHOOOOOOSH
WE'RE GETTING BLOWN AWAY!!

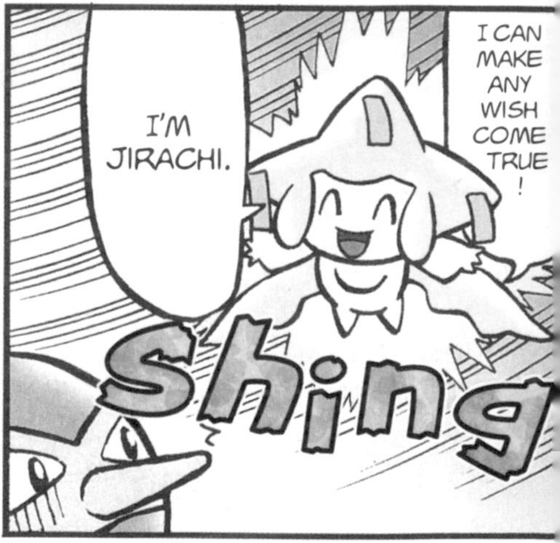
I'M JIRACHI.
I CAN MAKE ANY WISH COME TRUE!
Shing

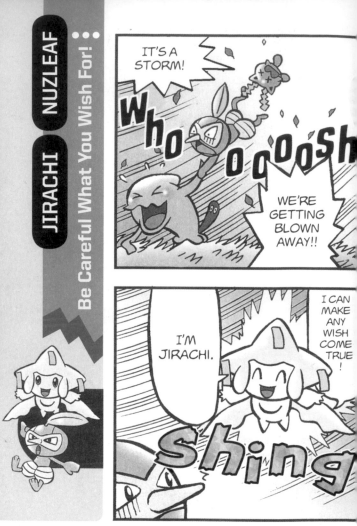

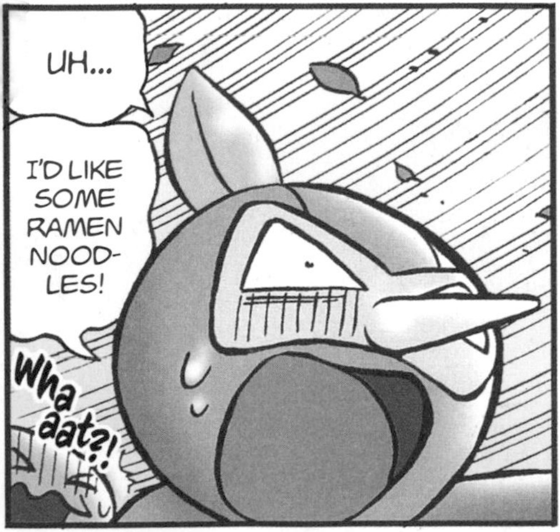
UH...
I'D LIKE SOME RAMEN NOOD-LES!
Whaaat?!

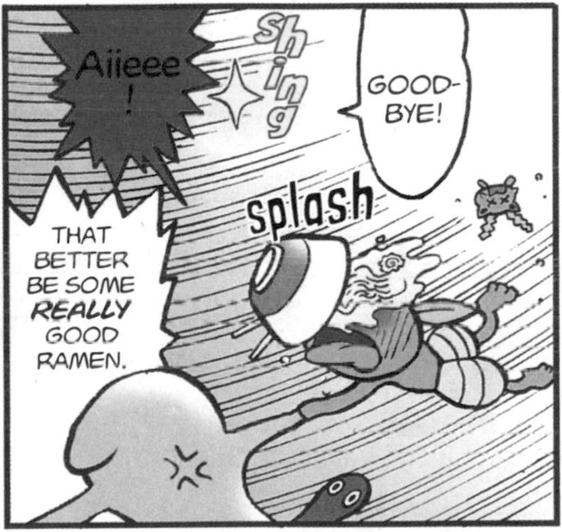
GOOD-BYE!
Shing
Aiieee!
splash
THAT BETTER BE SOME REALLY GOOD RAMEN.

JIRACHI

It is said to make any wish come true. It is only awake for seven days out of a thousand years.

NUZLEAF

A forest-dwelling Pokémon skilled at climbing trees. It lives in holes bored in large trees. Its long and pointed nose is its weak point—it loses power if its nose is gripped.

ELEKID CUBONE
Stand by Me...

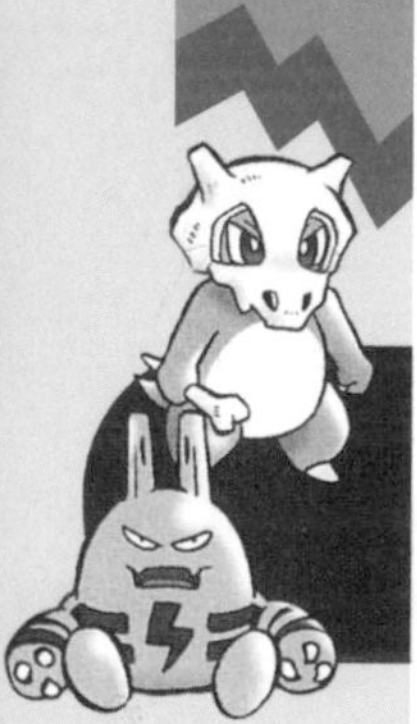

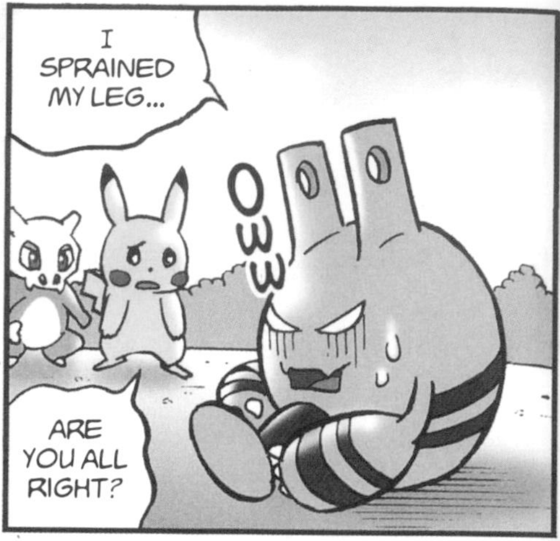
I SPRAINED MY LEG...
OWW
ARE YOU ALL RIGHT?

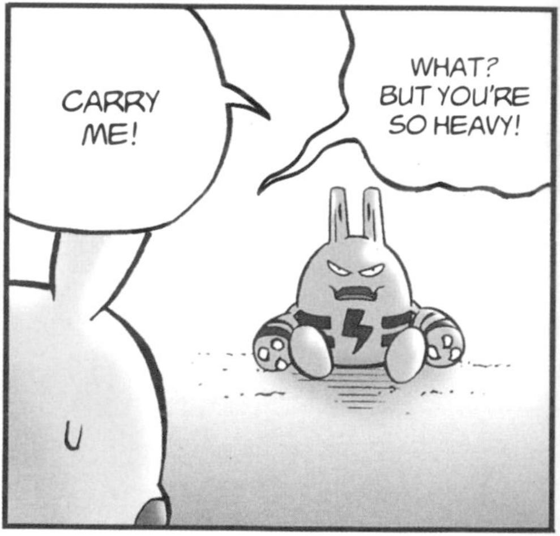
CARRY ME!
WHAT? BUT YOU'RE SO HEAVY!

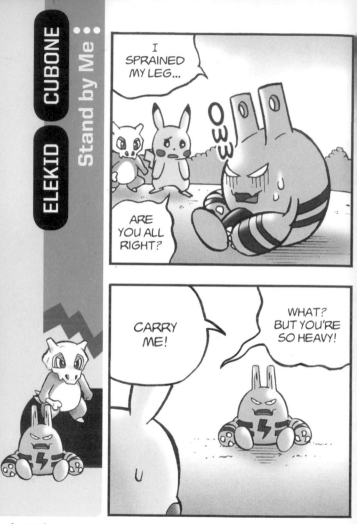

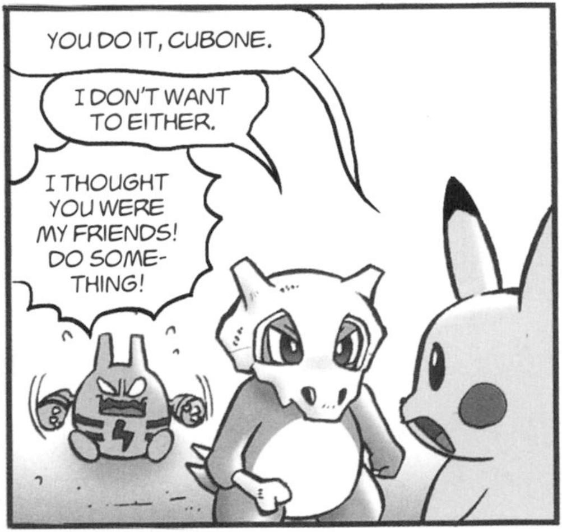
YOU DO IT, CUBONE.
I DON'T WANT TO EITHER.
I THOUGHT YOU WERE MY FRIENDS! DO SOME-THING!

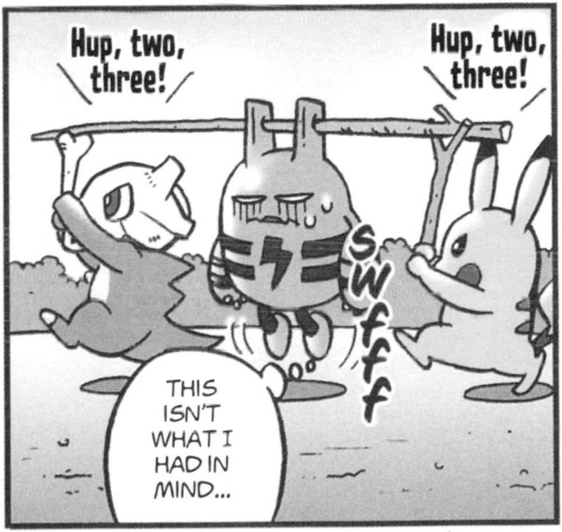
Hup, two, three!
Hup, two, three!
SWFFF
THIS ISN'T WHAT I HAD IN MIND...

ELEKID

It stores electricity in its body. If it discharges all of its built-up electricity, this Pokémon begins swinging its arms in circles to recharge itself.

CUBONE

It wears the skull of its dead mother on its head. When it becomes lonesome, it is said to cry loudly.

WARTORTLE

X Marks the Spot

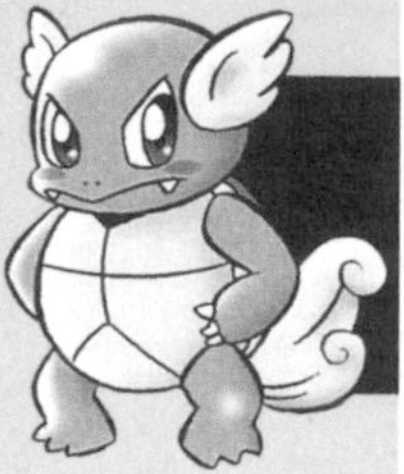

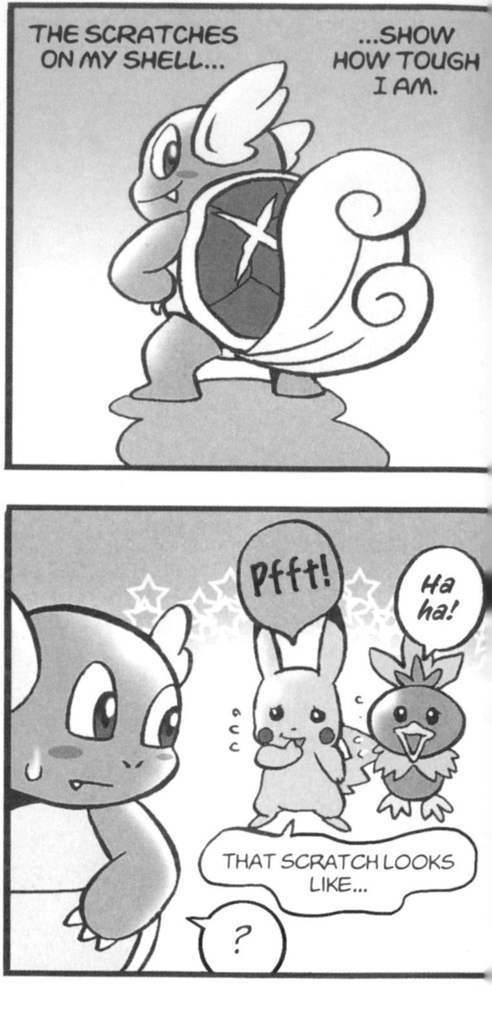
THE SCRATCHES ON MY SHELL...
...SHOW HOW TOUGH I AM.
Pfft!
Ha ha!
THAT SCRATCH LOOKS LIKE...
?

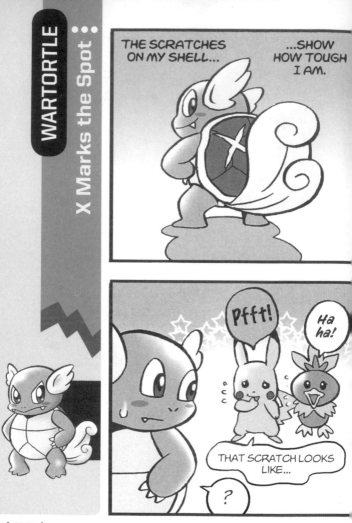

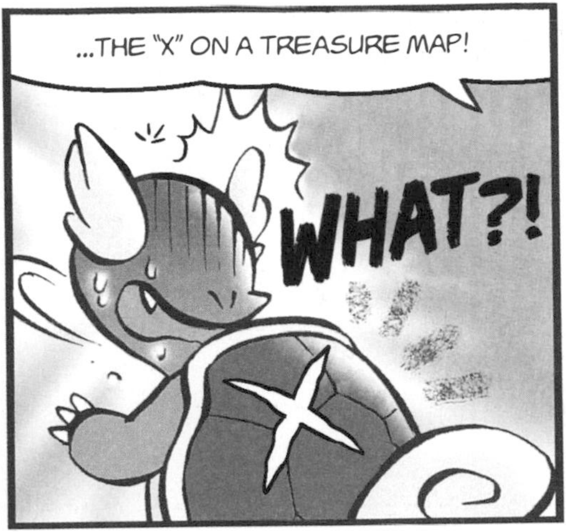
...THE "X" ON A TREASURE MAP!
WHAT?!

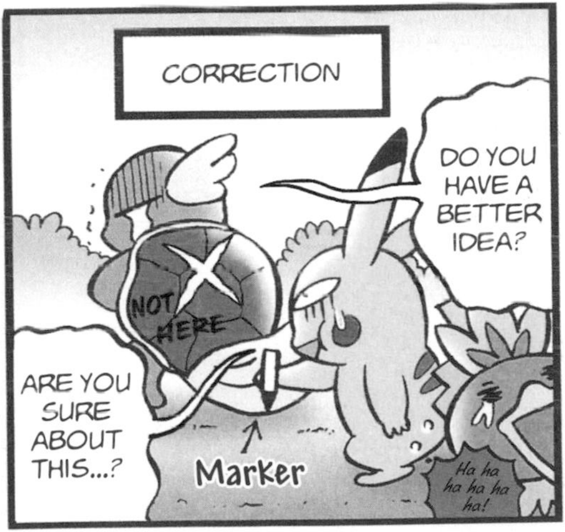
CORRECTION
DO YOU HAVE A BETTER IDEA?
NOT HERE
ARE YOU SURE ABOUT THIS...?
Marker
Ha ha ha ha ha ha!

WARTORTLE

It is recognized as a symbol of longevity. It often hides in water to stalk unwary prey. For fast swimming, it moves its ears to maintain balance. Its tail is large and is covered with a rich, thick fur. The tail becomes increasingly deeper in color as the Wartortle ages. The scratches on its shell are evidence of this Pokémon's toughness as a battler.

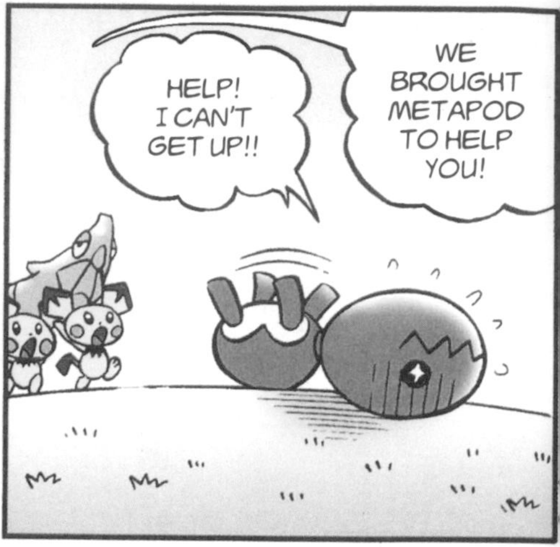
HELP! I CAN'T GET UP!!
WE BROUGHT METAPOD TO HELP YOU!

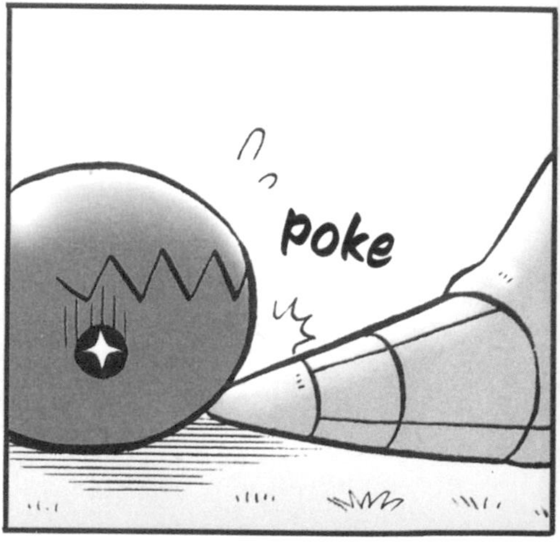
poke

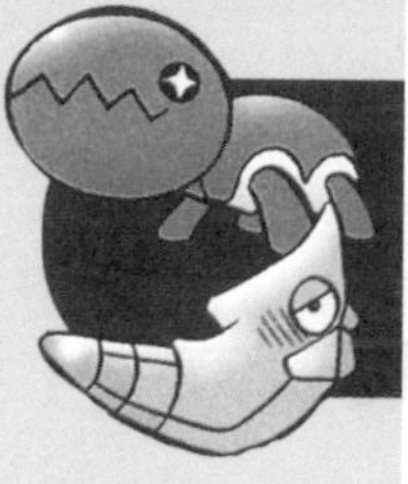

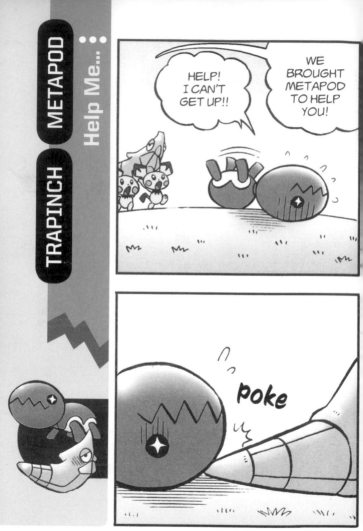

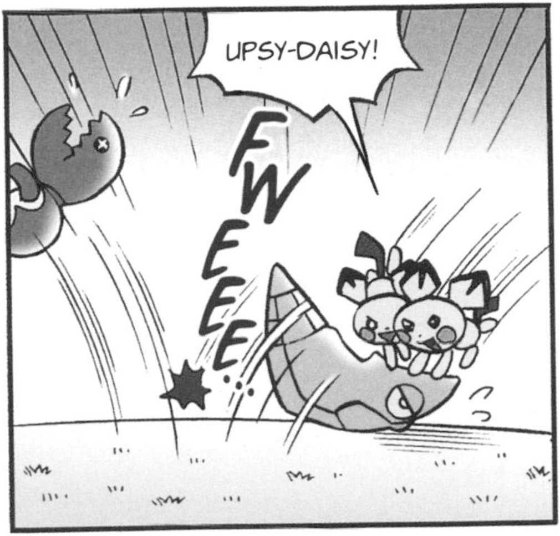
UPSY-DAISY!
FWEEE...

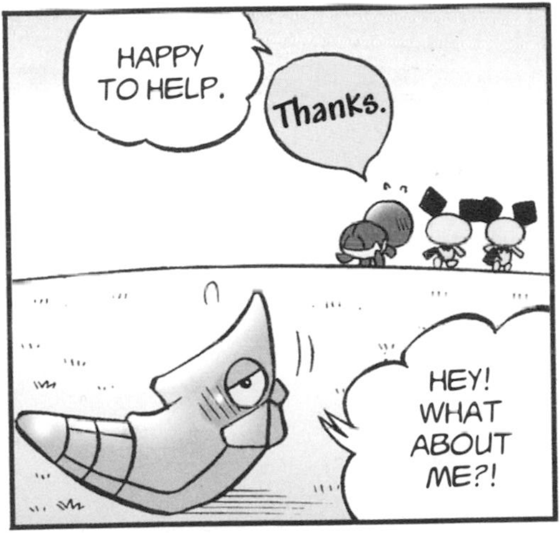
HAPPY TO HELP.
Thanks.
HEY! WHAT ABOUT ME?!

TRAPINCH

Its big jaws crunch through boulders. Because its head is so big, it has a hard time getting back upright if it tips over onto its back.

METAPOD

The shell covering this Pokémon's body is as hard as an iron slab. Metapod does not move very much. It stays still because it is preparing for evolution inside its hard shell.

AGGRON LARVITAR
Home Sweet Mountain

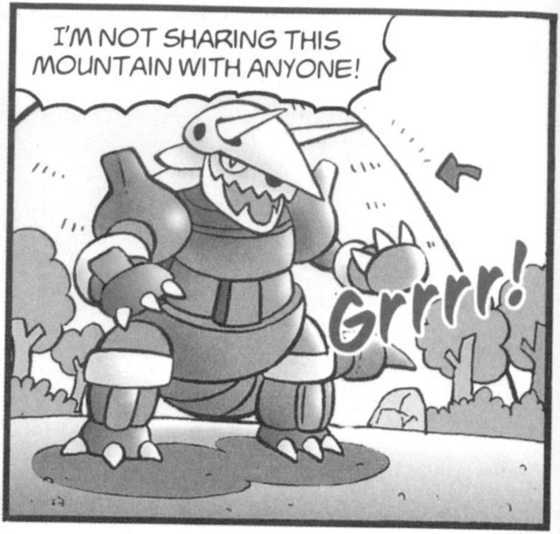

I'M NOT SHARING THIS MOUNTAIN WITH ANYONE!
Grrrrr!

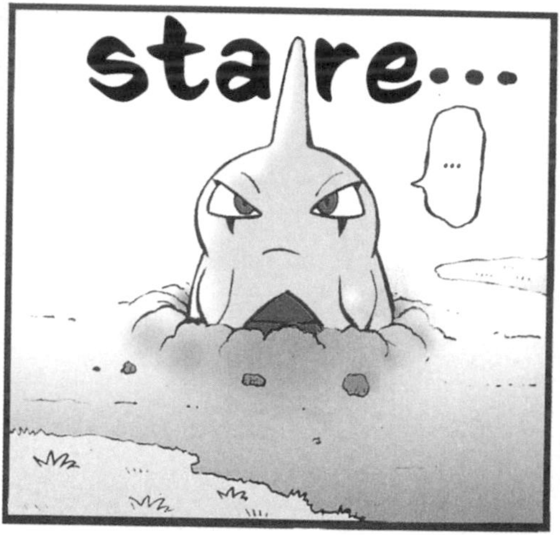

stare...
...

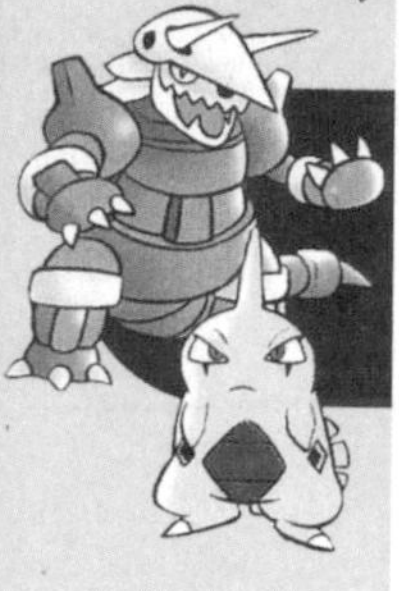

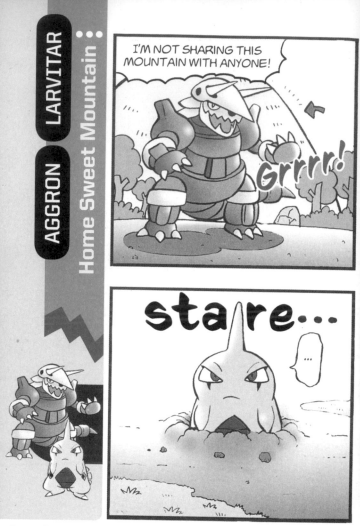

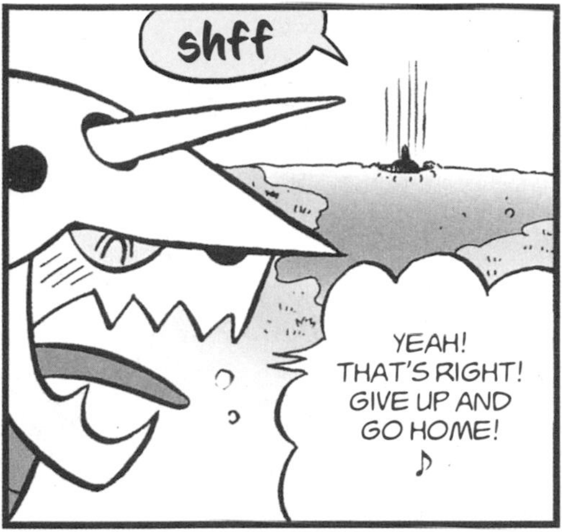
shff
YEAH! THAT'S RIGHT! GIVE UP AND GO HOME! ♪

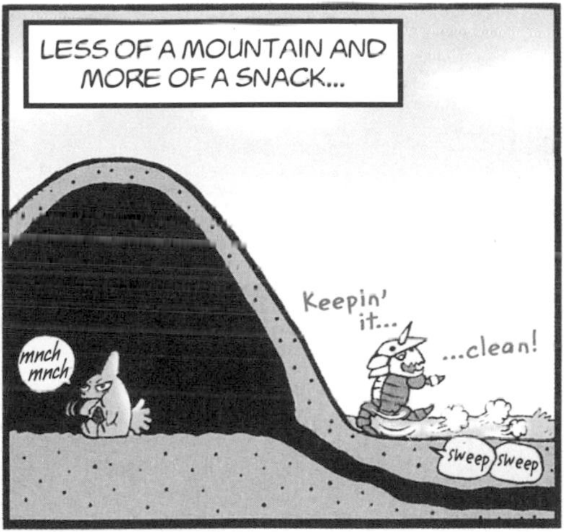
LESS OF A MOUNTAIN AND MORE OF A SNACK...
mnch mnch
Keepin' it...
...clean!
sweep sweep

AGGRON

It claims a large mountain as its sole territory. It mercilessly beats up anything that violates its space. If its mountain is ravaged by a landslide or a fire, this Pokémon will haul topsoil to the area, plant trees and beautifully restore its territory.

LARVITAR

It is born deep underground. It can't emerge until it has entirely consumed the soil around it.

TORCHIC COMBUSKEN
Sudden Evolution

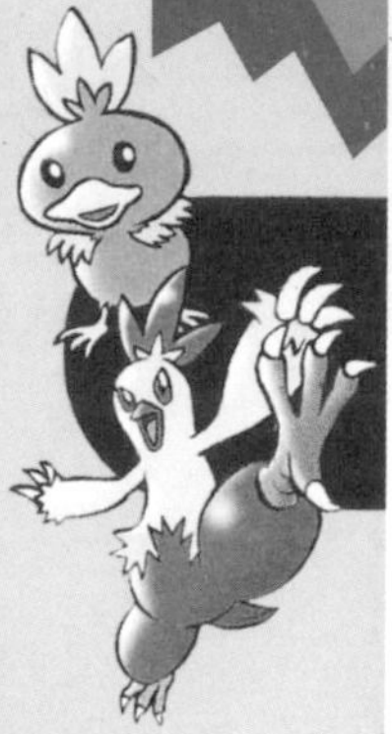

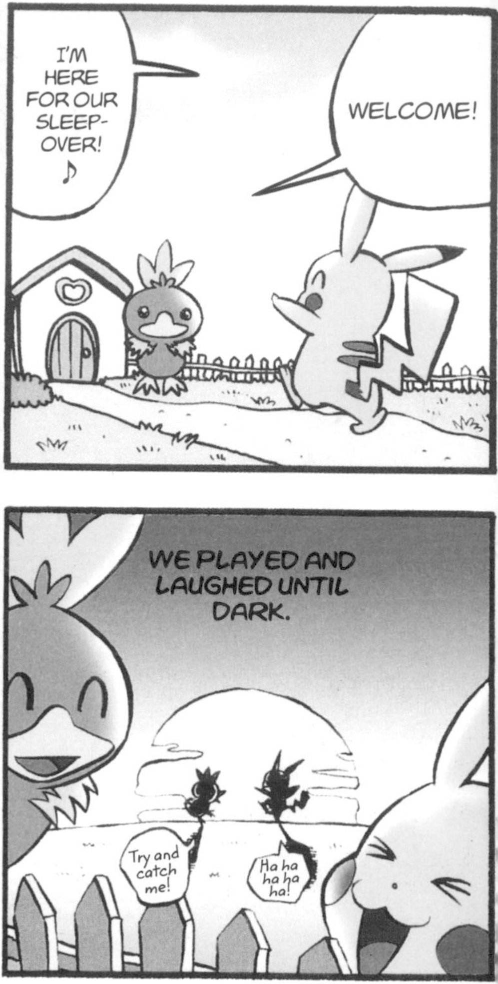
I'M HERE FOR OUR SLEEP-OVER! ♪
WELCOME!
WE PLAYED AND LAUGHED UNTIL DARK.
Try and catch me!
Ha ha ha ha ha!

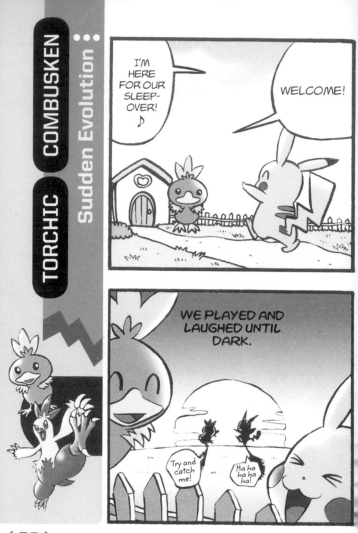

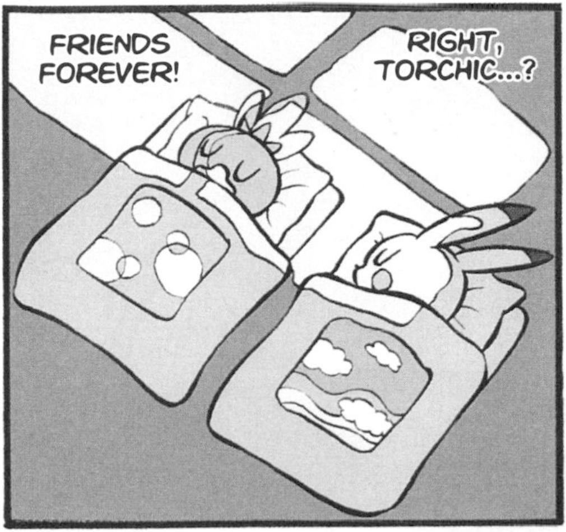
FRIENDS FOREVER!
RIGHT, TORCHIC...?

TORCHIC

It has a flame sac inside its belly that perpetually burns. If attacked, it strikes back by spitting balls of fire it forms in its stomach.

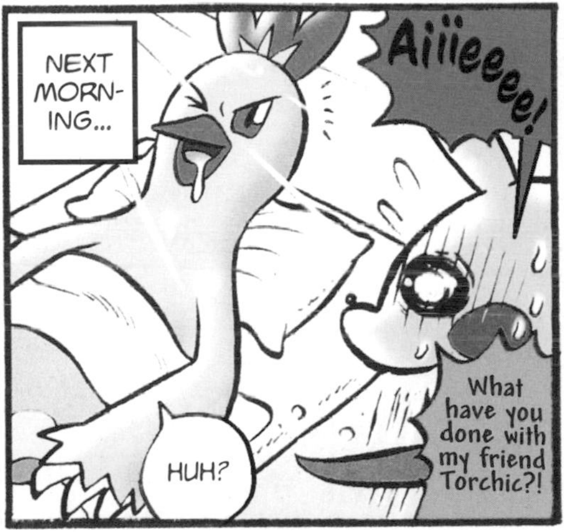
NEXT MORN-ING...
Aiiieeeee!
HUH?
What have you done with my friend Torchic?!

COMBUSKEN

Torchic evolves into Combusken. Combusken boosts its concentration by emitting harsh cries. Its strong fighting instinct compels it to keep up its offensive until the opponent gives up.

SMOOCHUM JYNX
Beware of the Kiss

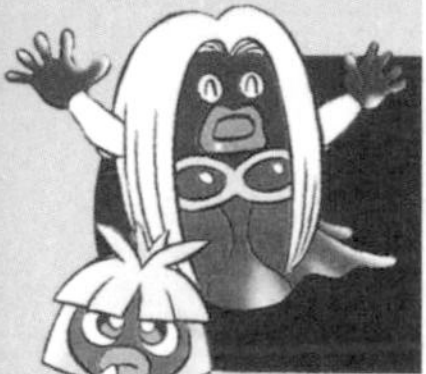

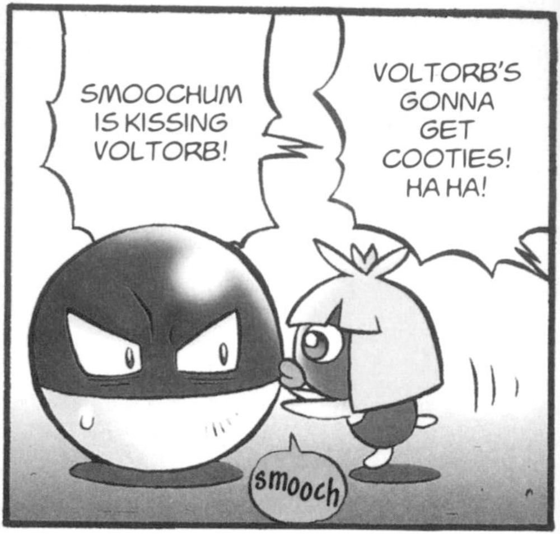
SMOOCHUM IS KISSING VOLTORB!
VOLTORB'S GONNA GET COOTIES! HA HA!
smooch

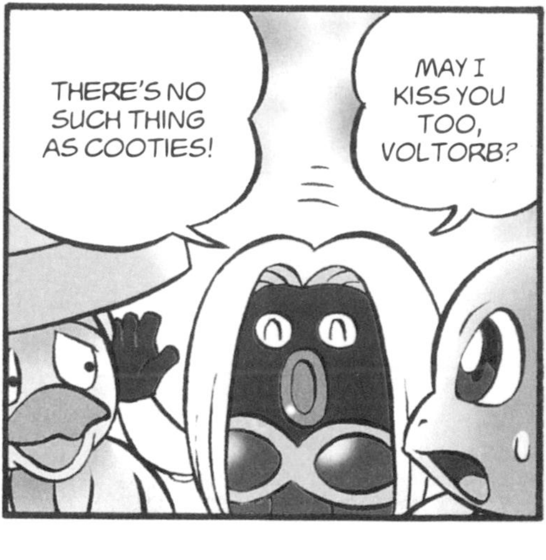
THERE'S NO SUCH THING AS COOTIES!
MAY I KISS YOU TOO, VOLTORB?

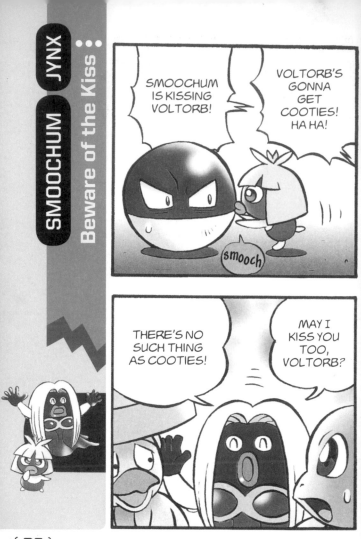

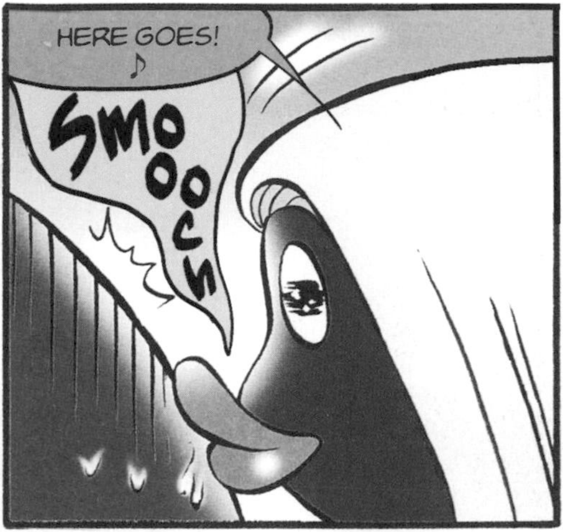
HERE GOES! ♪
SMOOOCH

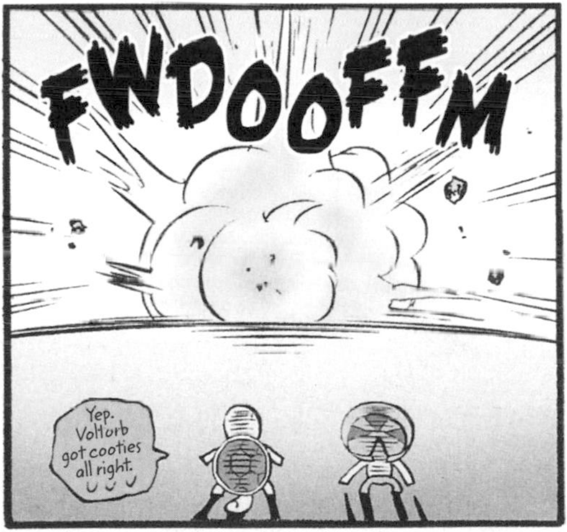
FWDOOFFM
Yep. Voltorb got cooties all right.

SMOOCHUM

Its lips are the most sensitive part of its body. It uses its lips first to examine things. It always rocks its head slowly backwards and forwards.

JYNX

It moves gracefully, like a dancer.

DROWZEE

Sweet Dreams

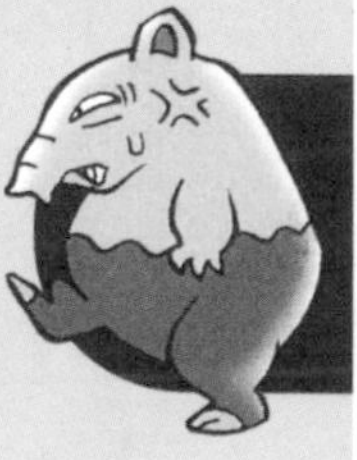

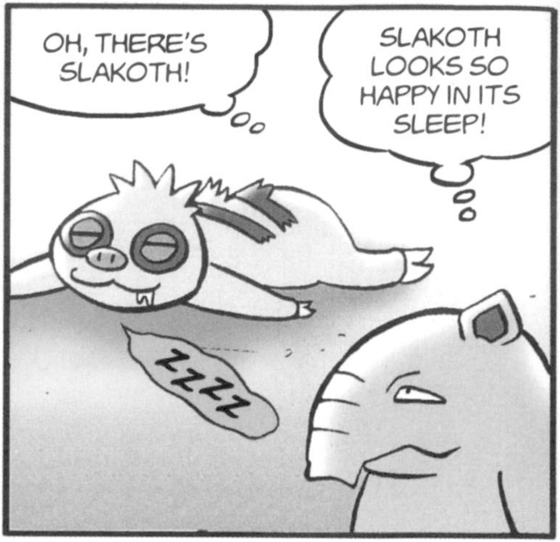
OH, THERE'S SLAKOTH!
SLAKOTH LOOKS SO HAPPY IN ITS SLEEP!
ZZZZ

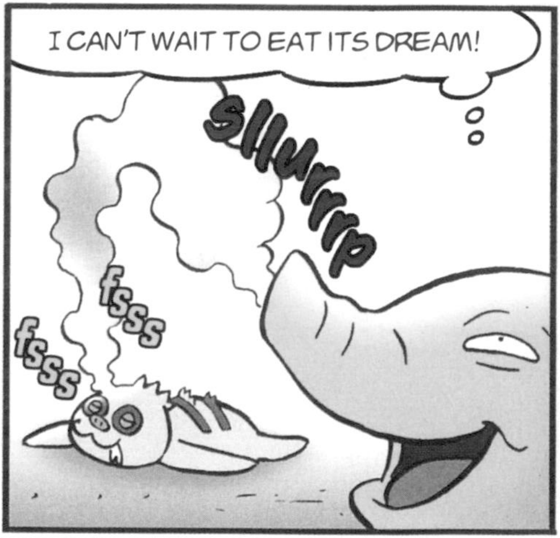
I CAN'T WAIT TO EAT ITS DREAM!
Sllurrrp
fsss
fsss

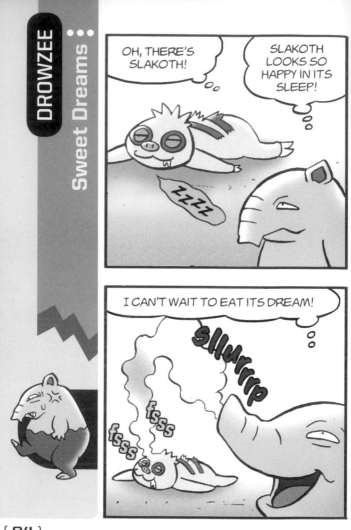

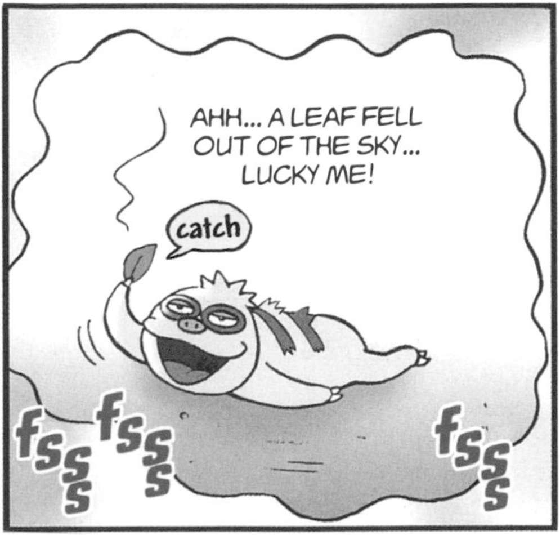
AHH... A LEAF FELL OUT OF THE SKY... LUCKY ME!
catch
fsss
fsss
fsss

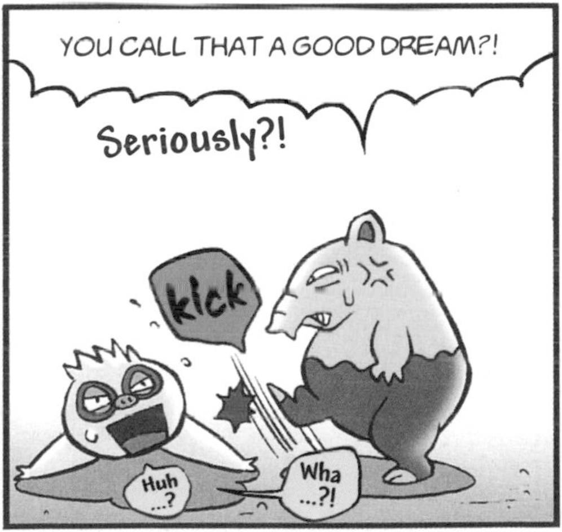
YOU CALL THAT A GOOD DREAM?!
Seriously?!
kick
Huh ...?
Wha ...?!

DROWZEE

A descendant of the legendary *baku*, a creature said to eat dreams. If your nose becomes itchy while you are sleeping, it's a sure sign that a Drowzee is standing above your pillow and trying to eat your dream through your nostrils. If you sleep by it all the time, it will sometimes show you dreams it has eaten in the past.

SMEARGLE DELCATTY

A Blank Canvas

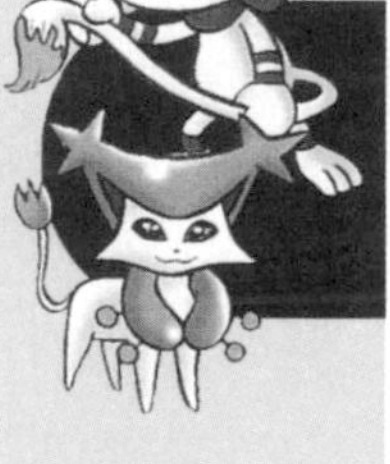

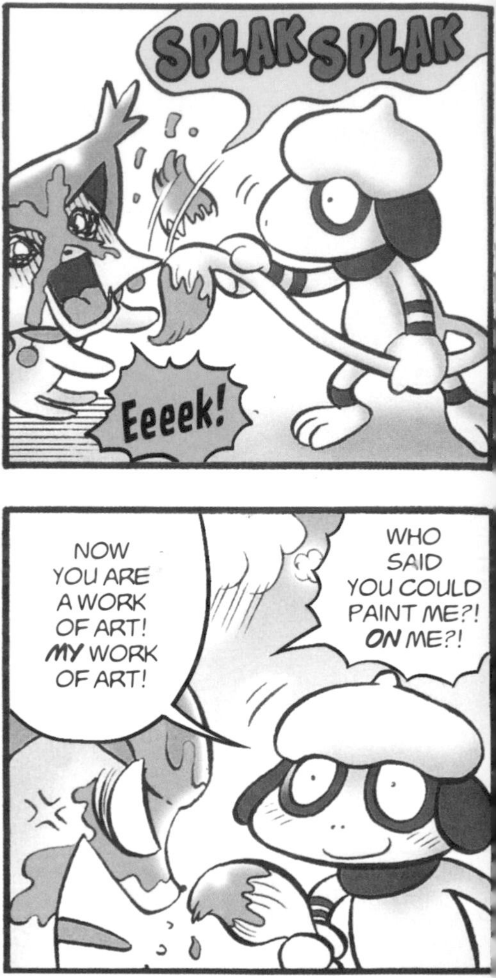
SPLAKSPLAK
Eeeek!
NOW YOU ARE A WORK OF ART! *MY* WORK OF ART!
WHO SAID YOU COULD PAINT ME?! *ON* ME?!

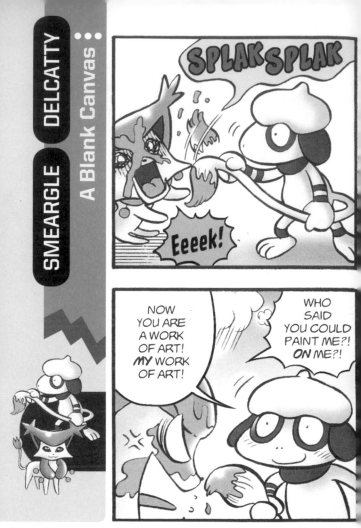

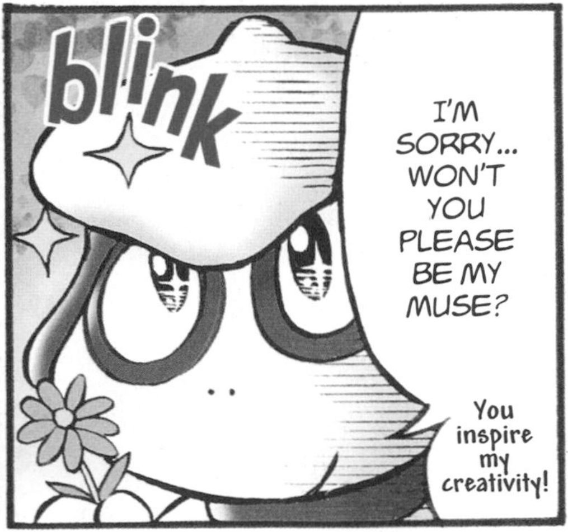
blink
I'M SORRY... WON'T YOU PLEASE BE MY MUSE?
You inspire my creativity!

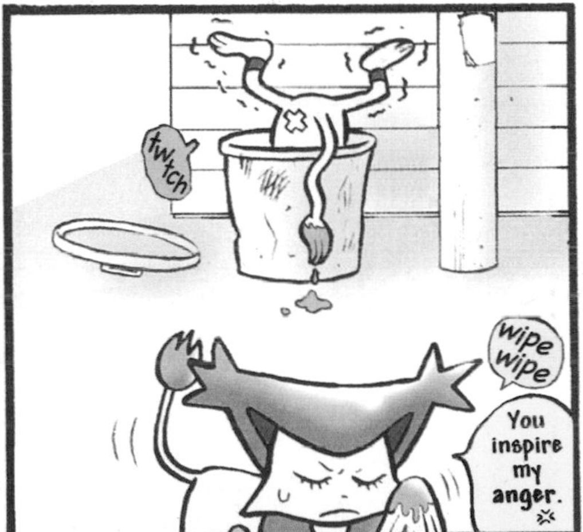
twitch
wipe wipe
You inspire my anger.

SMEARGLE

It marks the boundaries of its territory using a body fluid that leaks out of the tip of its tail. Over 5,000 different marks left by this Pokémon have been found.

DELCATTY

Rather than keeping a permanent lair, it habitually seeks comfortable spots and sleeps there. It is nocturnal and becomes active at dusk.

SEALEO SPHEAL QWILFISH

Having a Ball...

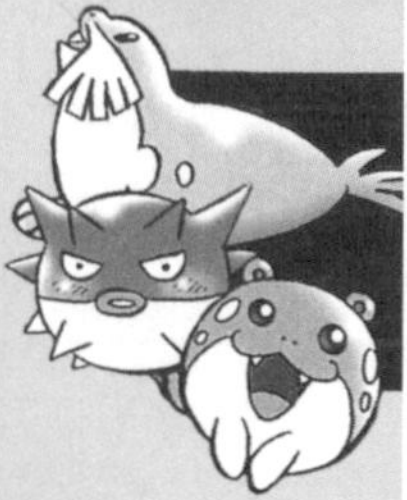

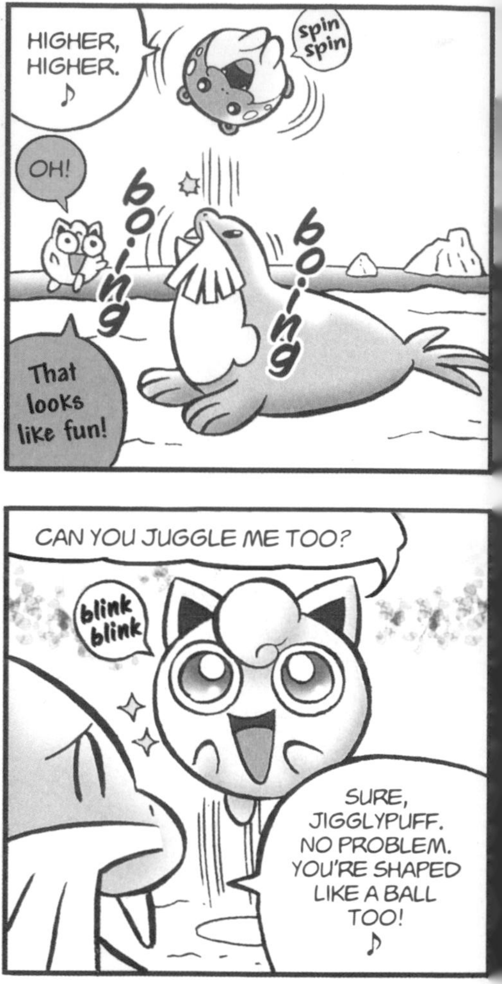
HIGHER, HIGHER. ♪
spin spin
OH!
boing
boing
That looks like fun!
CAN YOU JUGGLE ME TOO?
blink blink
SURE, JIGGLYPUFF. NO PROBLEM. YOU'RE SHAPED LIKE A BALL TOO! ♪

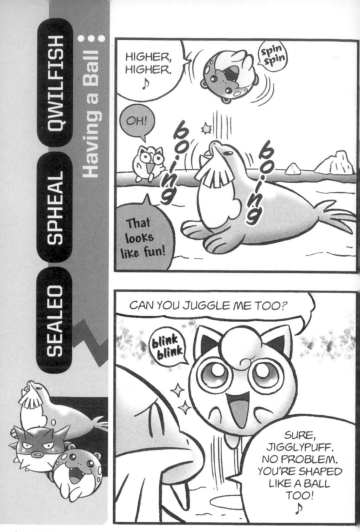

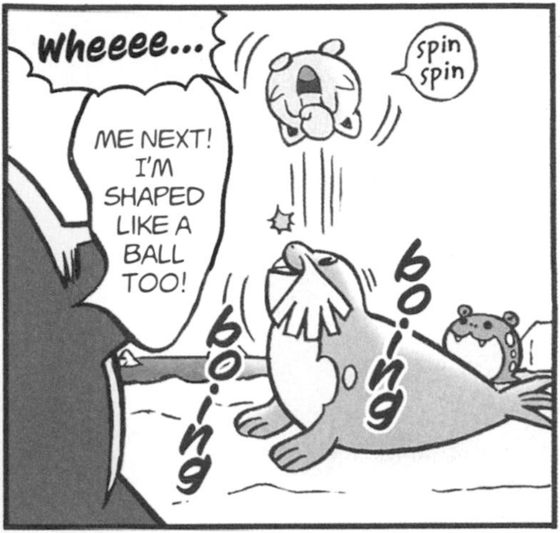
Wheeee...
spin spin
ME NEXT! I'M SHAPED LIKE A BALL TOO!
bo·i·ng
bo·i·ng

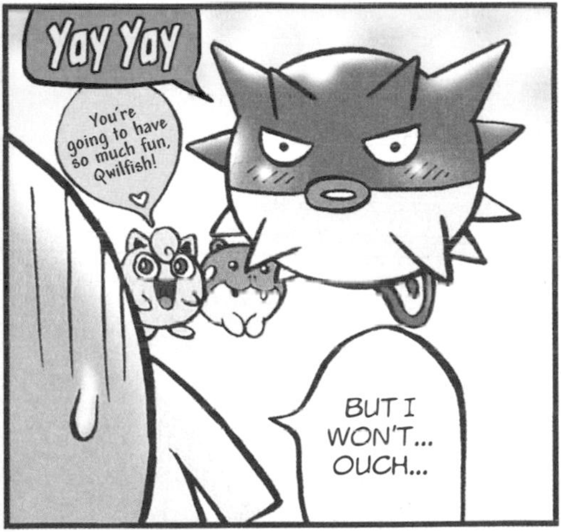
Yay Yay
You're going to have so much fun, Qwilfish!
BUT I WON'T... OUCH...

SEALEO

It has the habit of always juggling on the tip of its nose anything it sees for the first time. It plays by spinning Spheal on its nose.

SPHEAL

It gets around much faster rolling than walking. It is completely covered with plushy fur.

QWILFISH

This Pokémon uses the pressure of the water it swallows to suddenly shoot toxic quills from all over its body.

ARBOK

Picture Perfect

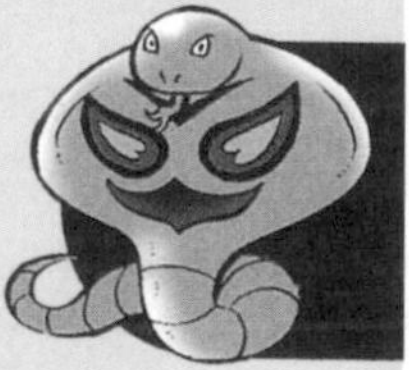

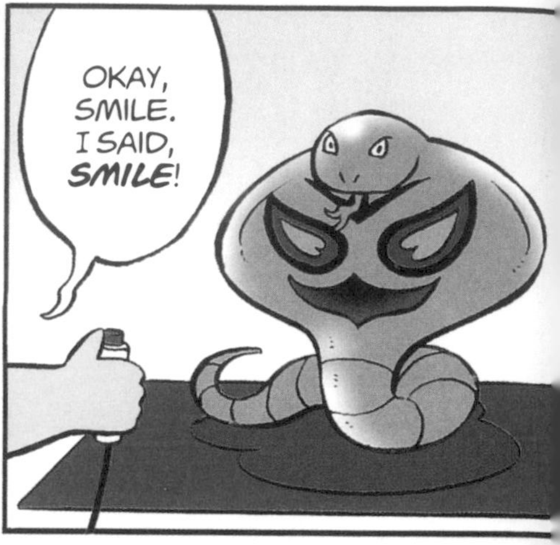
OKAY, SMILE. I SAID, *SMILE*!

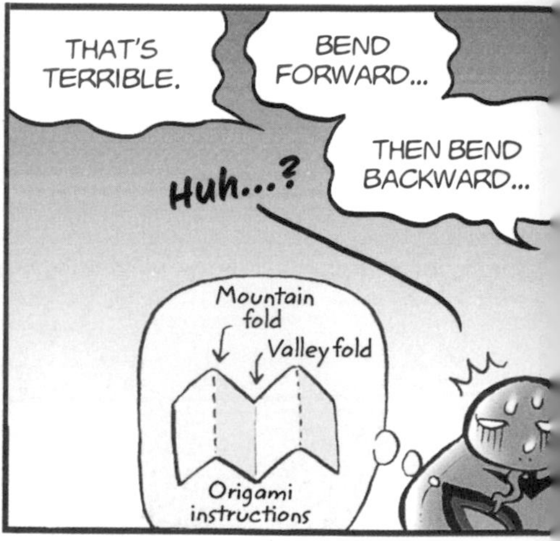
THAT'S TERRIBLE.
BEND FORWARD...
THEN BEND BACKWARD...
Huh...?
Mountain fold
Valley fold
Origami instructions

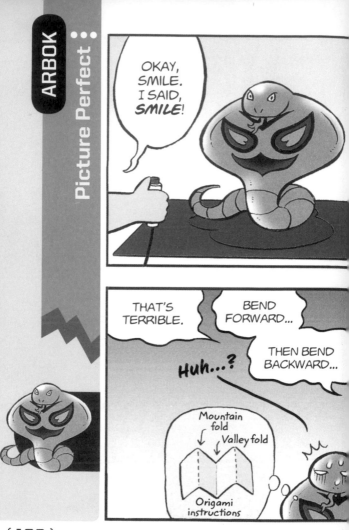

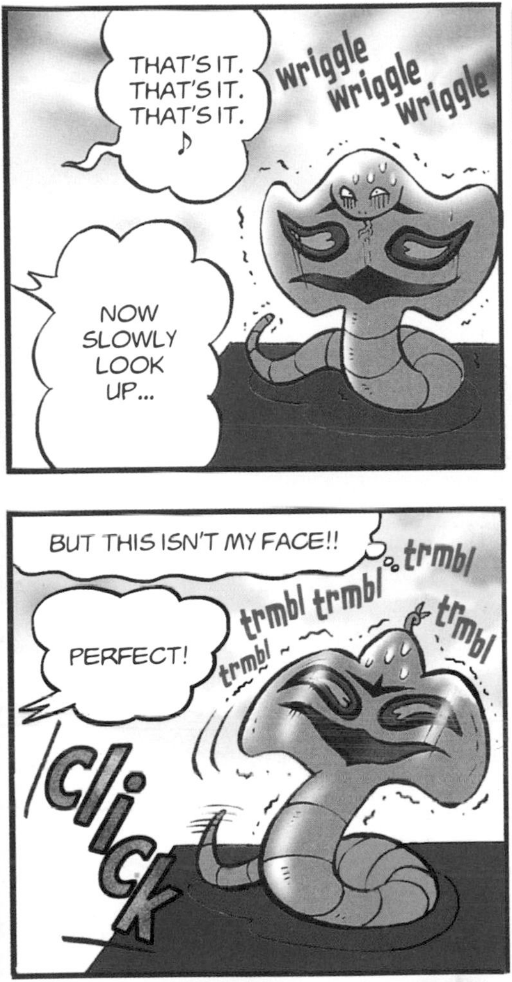
THAT'S IT. THAT'S IT. THAT'S IT. ♪
wriggle wriggle wriggle
NOW SLOWLY LOOK UP...
BUT THIS ISN'T MY FACE!!
trmbl
PERFECT!
trmbl trmbl
trmbl
trmbl
click

ARBOK

Transfixing prey with the face-like pattern on its belly, it binds and poisons the frightened victim. This Pokémon has a terrifically strong constricting power. It can even flatten steel oil drums. Once it wraps its body around its foe, escape is impossible.

HAUNTER

Mix and Match

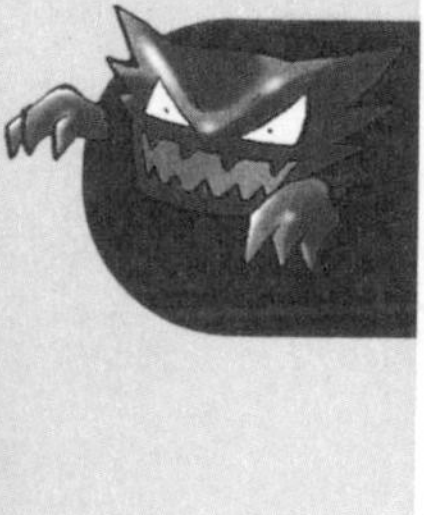

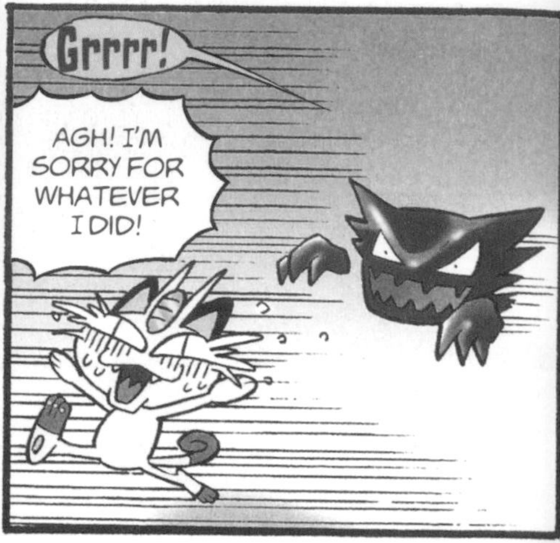
Grrrr!
AGH! I'M SORRY FOR WHATEVER I DID!

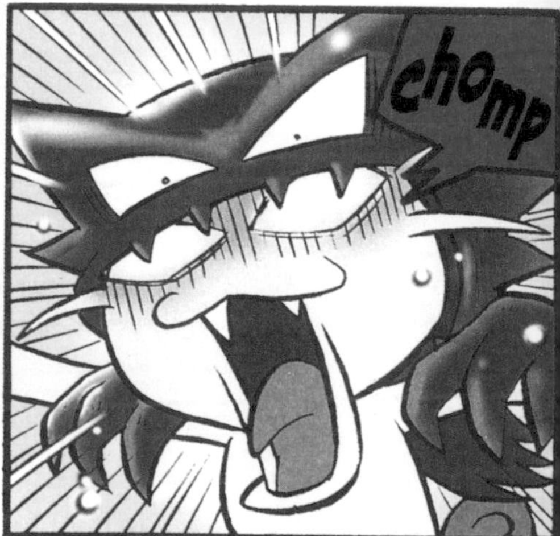
chomp

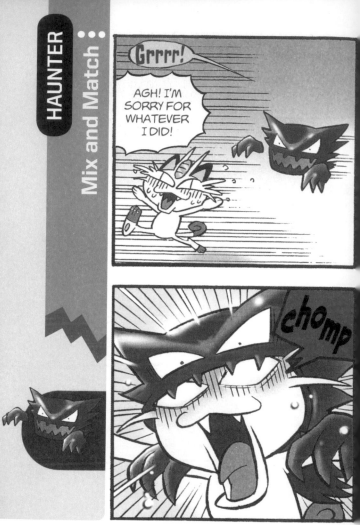

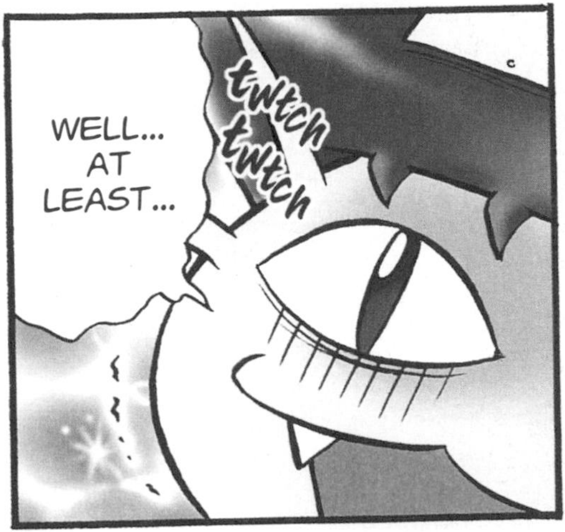
WELL... AT LEAST...
twtch twtch

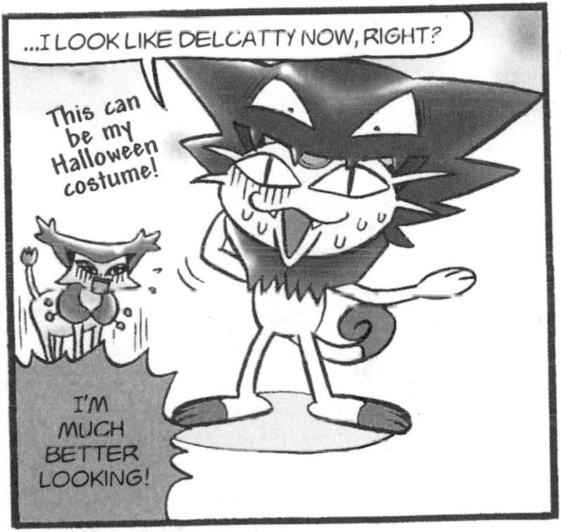
...I LOOK LIKE DELCATTY NOW, RIGHT?
This can be my Halloween costume!
I'M MUCH BETTER LOOKING!

HAUNTER

If you get the feeling of being watched in the darkness when nobody is around, Haunter is there. If one beckons you, you must never approach it. This Pokémon will try to lick you with its tongue and steal your life away.

SUDOWOODO MR. MIME

One, Two, Tree!

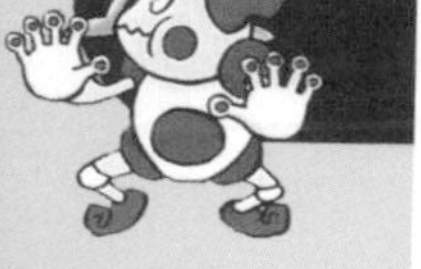

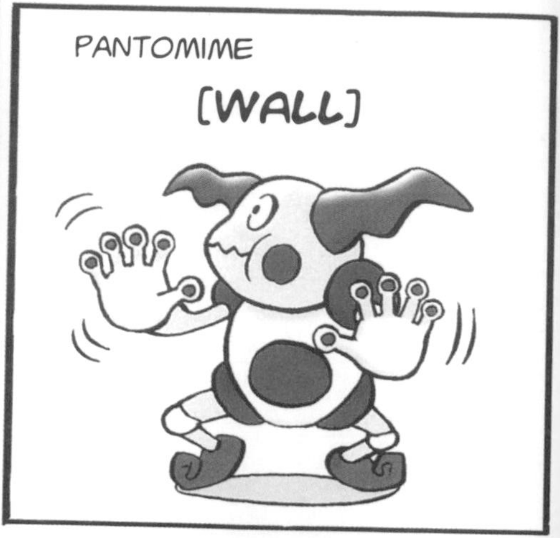
PANTOMIME
[WALL]

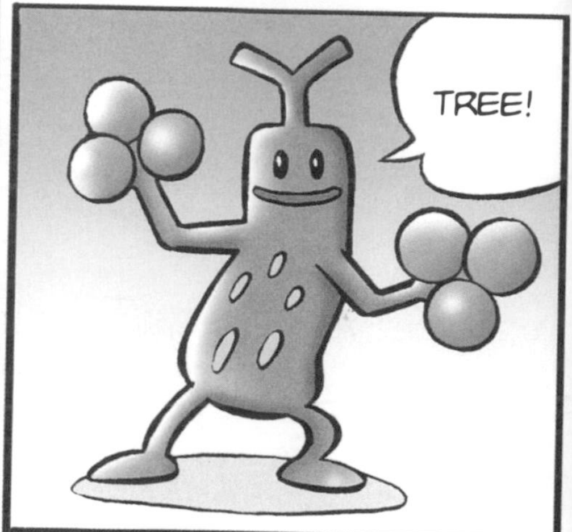
TREE!

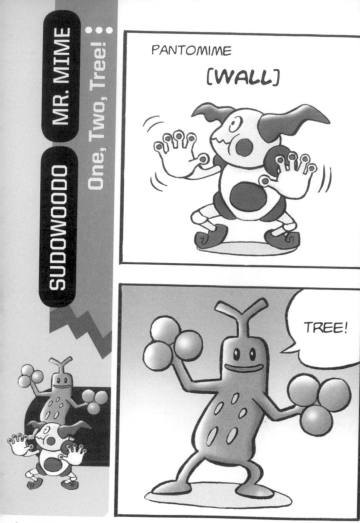

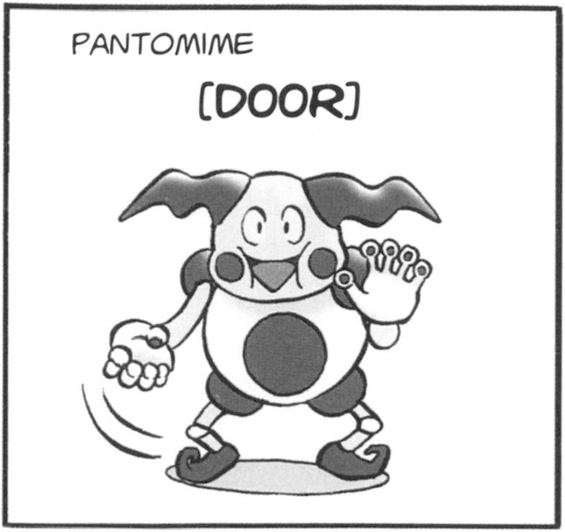
PANTOMIME
[DOOR]

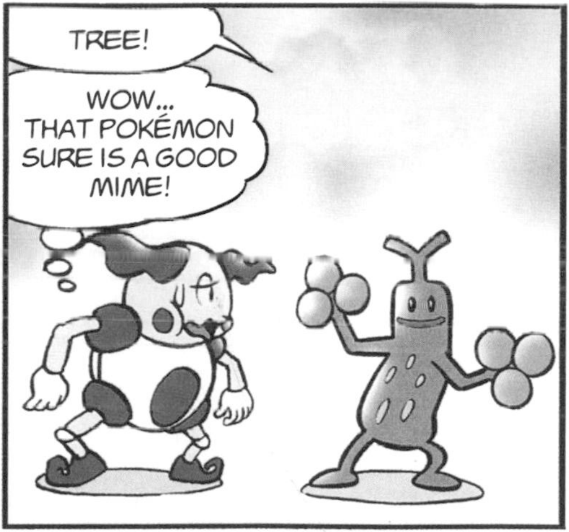
TREE!
WOW... THAT POKÉMON SURE IS A GOOD MIME!

SUDOWOODO

It disguises itself as a tree to avoid attack. However, because its forelegs remain green throughout the year, the Pokémon is easily identified as being fake during the winter.

MR. MIME

A skilled mime from birth. Its fingertips emit a peculiar force field that hardens air to create an actual wall.

ALAKAZAM

IQ, Your Q...

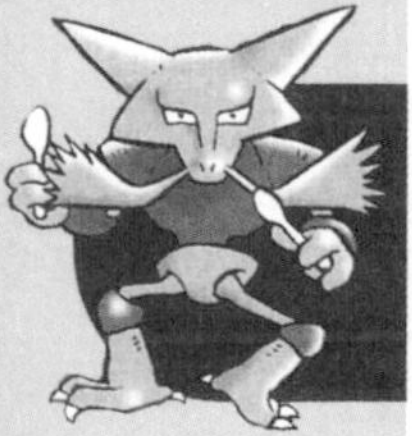

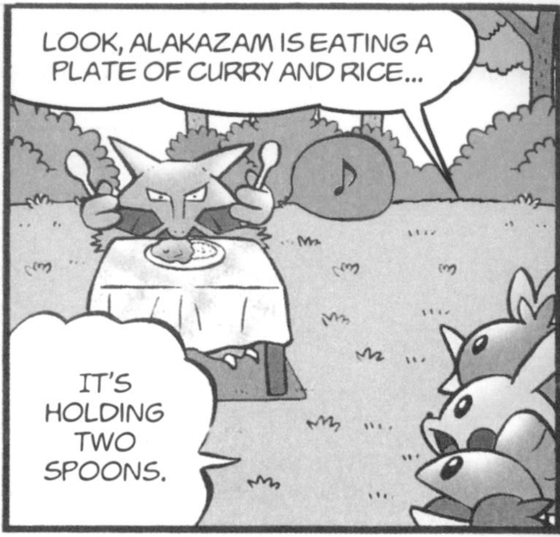

LOOK, ALAKAZAM IS EATING A PLATE OF CURRY AND RICE...
IT'S HOLDING TWO SPOONS.

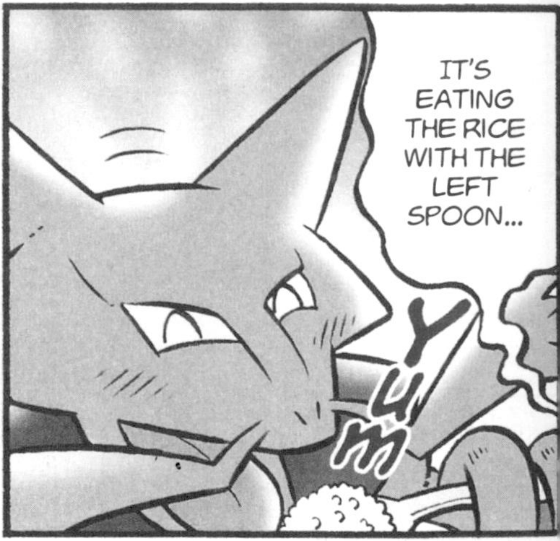

IT'S EATING THE RICE WITH THE LEFT SPOON...
YUM

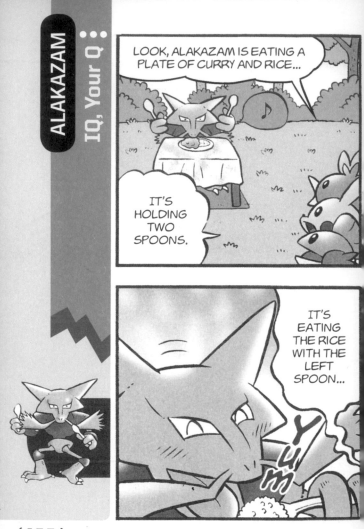

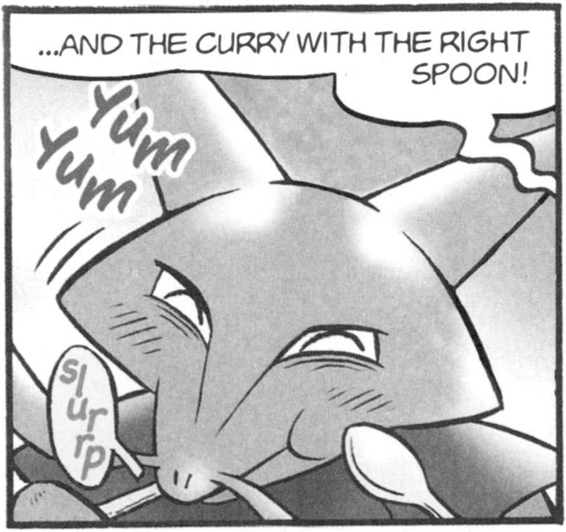
...AND THE CURRY WITH THE RIGHT SPOON!
Yum Yum
slurp

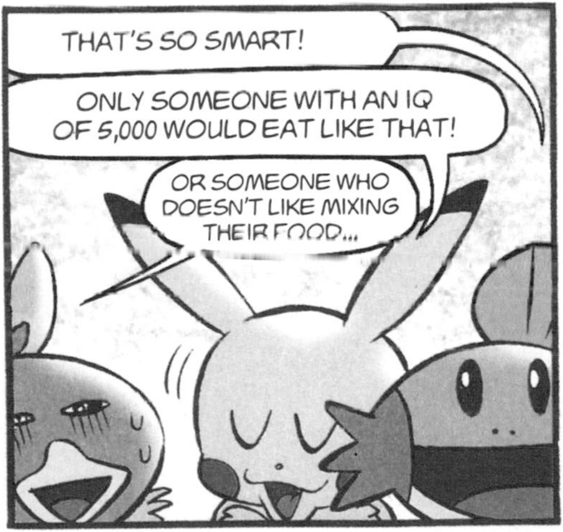
THAT'S SO SMART!
ONLY SOMEONE WITH AN IQ OF 5,000 WOULD EAT LIKE THAT!
OR SOMEONE WHO DOESN'T LIKE MIXING THEIR FOOD...

ALAKAZAM

A Pokémon that uses psychic power to defeat foes. It has an IQ of 5,000 and has a comprehensive memory of everything that has ever happened. Alakazam's muscles are very weak, so it does not rely on physical attacks. It holds up its heavy head using its psychokinetic power.

MY JAW IS SO HEAVY IT WEARS ME OUT.

I need to take a load off.

PHEW.

MAY I HAVE SECONDS?

?!

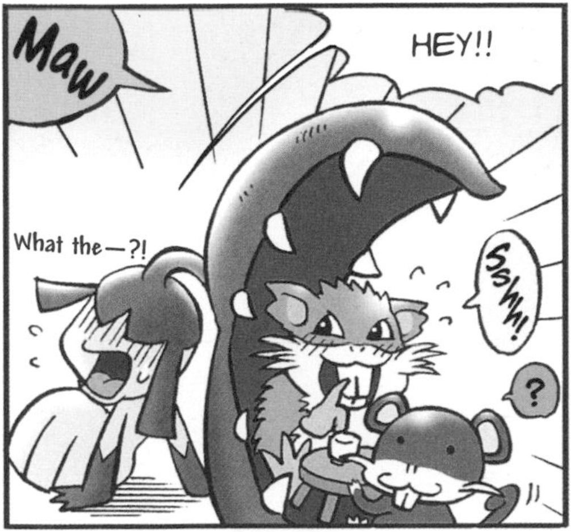
Maw
HEY!!
What the—?!
Sshh!
?

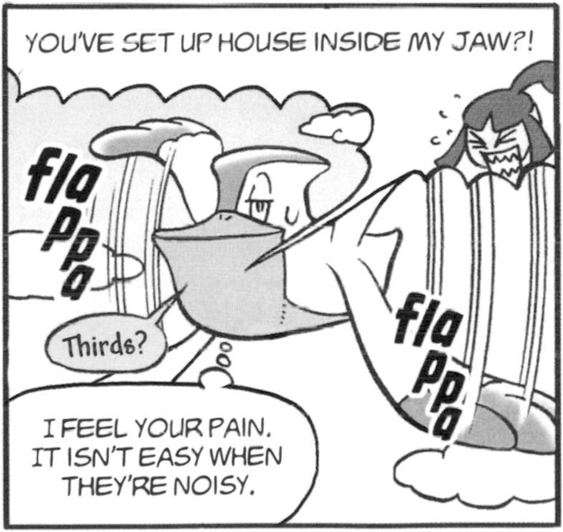
YOU'VE SET UP HOUSE INSIDE MY JAW?!
flappa
flappa
Thirds?
I FEEL YOUR PAIN. IT ISN'T EASY WHEN THEY'RE NOISY.

MAWILE

It uses its docile-looking face to lull foes into complacency, then bites with its huge, relentless jaws.

RATICATE

Its sturdy fangs grow steadily. To keep them ground down, it gnaws on rocks and logs.

RATTATA

It will make its nest anywhere.

LOUDRED • SKITTY
A Real Mouthful

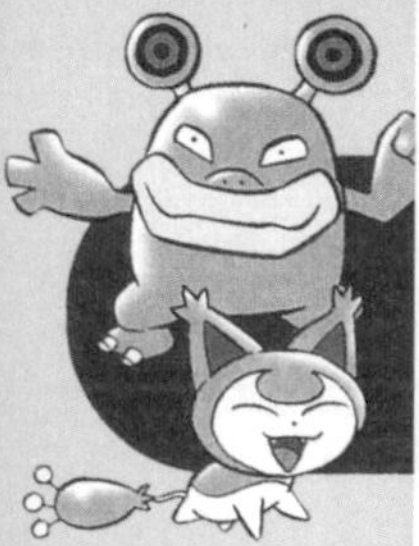

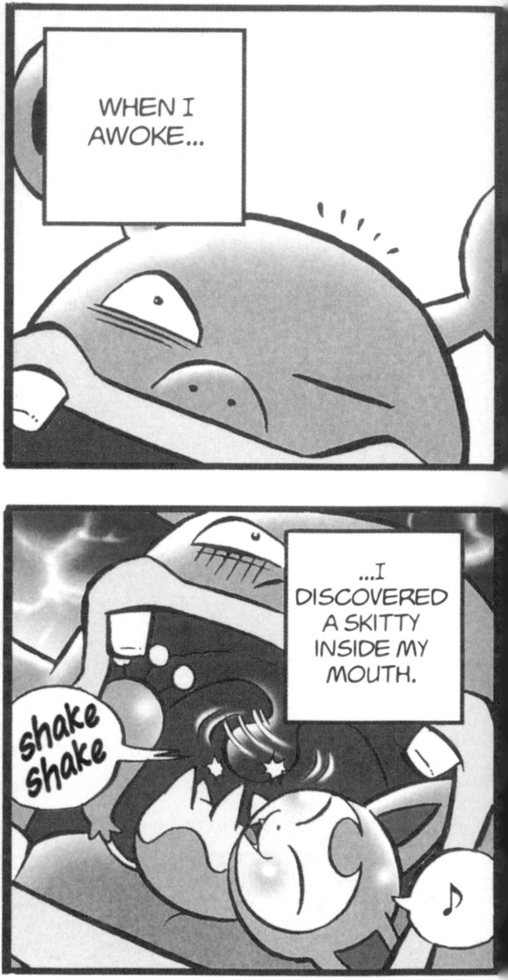
WHEN I AWOKE...
...I DISCOVERED A SKITTY INSIDE MY MOUTH.
shake shake
♪

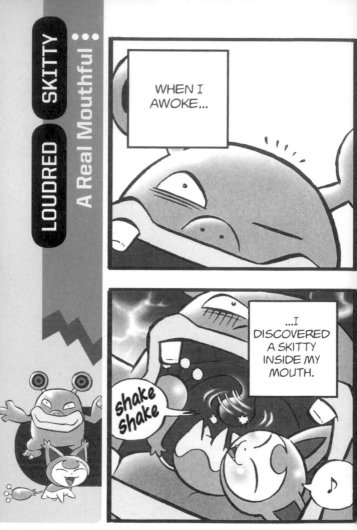

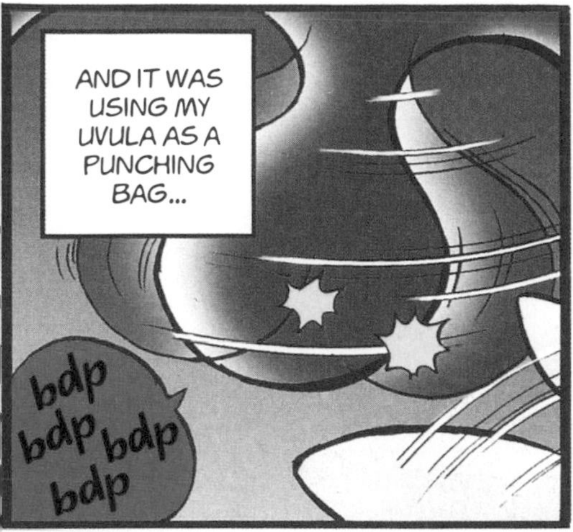
AND IT WAS USING MY UVULA AS A PUNCHING BAG...
bdp bdp bdp bdp

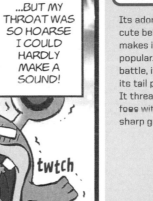

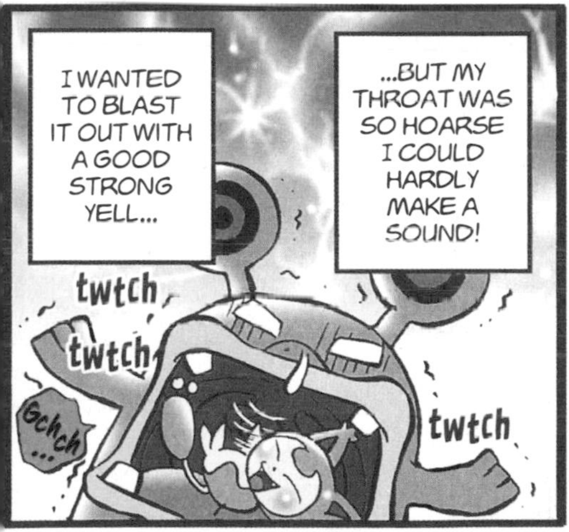
I WANTED TO BLAST IT OUT WITH A GOOD STRONG YELL...
...BUT MY THROAT WAS SO HOARSE I COULD HARDLY MAKE A SOUND!
twtch
twtch
Gchch...
twtch

LOUDRED

It shouts while stamping its feet. After it finishes shouting, this Pokémon becomes incapable of hearing anything for a while. This is considered to be a weak point.

SKITTY

Its adorably cute behavior makes it highly popular. In battle, it makes its tail puff out. It threatens foes with a sharp growl.

SHROOMISH ODDISH
Dry Up

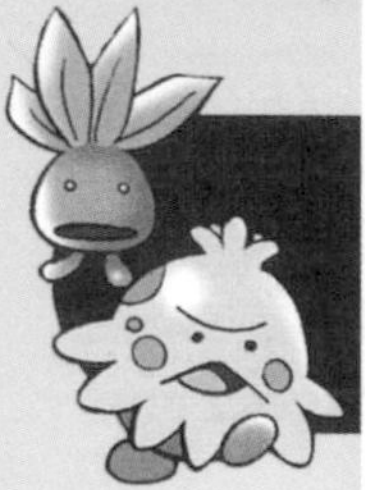

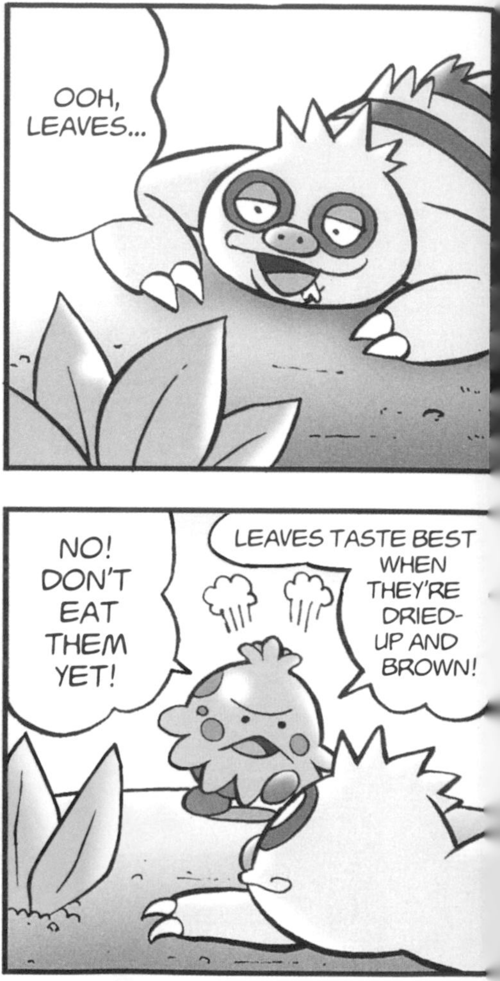
OOH, LEAVES...
NO! DON'T EAT THEM YET!
LEAVES TASTE BEST WHEN THEY'RE DRIED-UP AND BROWN!

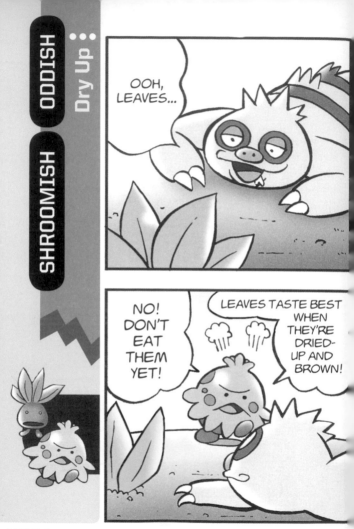

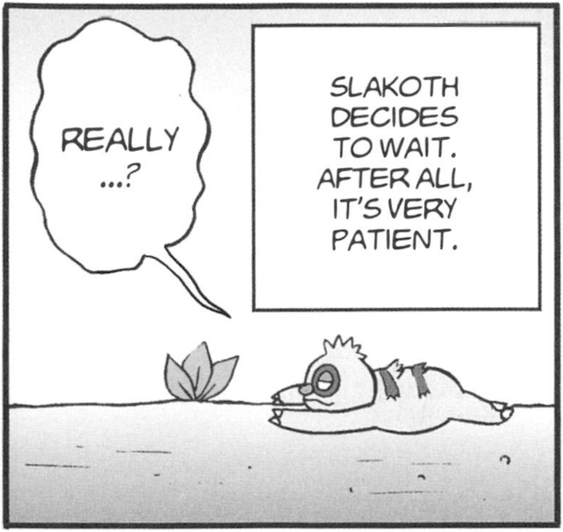
REALLY ...?
SLAKOTH DECIDES TO WAIT. AFTER ALL, IT'S VERY PATIENT.

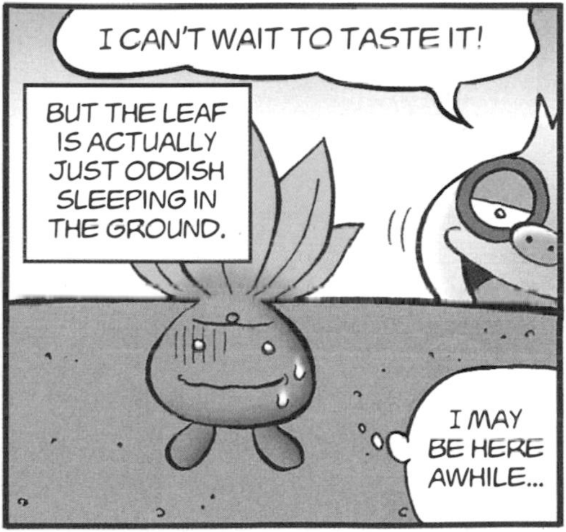
I CAN'T WAIT TO TASTE IT!
BUT THE LEAF IS ACTUALLY JUST ODDISH SLEEPING IN THE GROUND.
I MAY BE HERE AWHILE...

SHROOMISH

It loves to eat damp, composted soils in forests. If you enter a forest after a long rain, you can see many Shroomish feasting on the dirt.

ODDISH

During the day, it keeps its face buried in the ground. At night, it wanders around sowing its seeds. Its scientific name is *Oddium wanderus*.

HERACROSS
I've Fallen And...

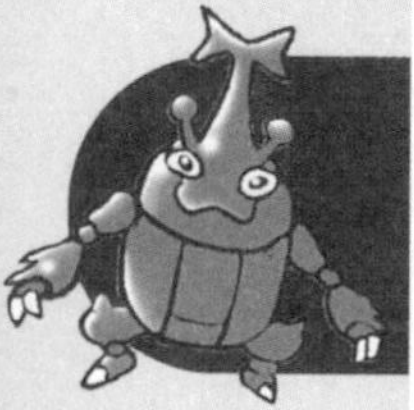

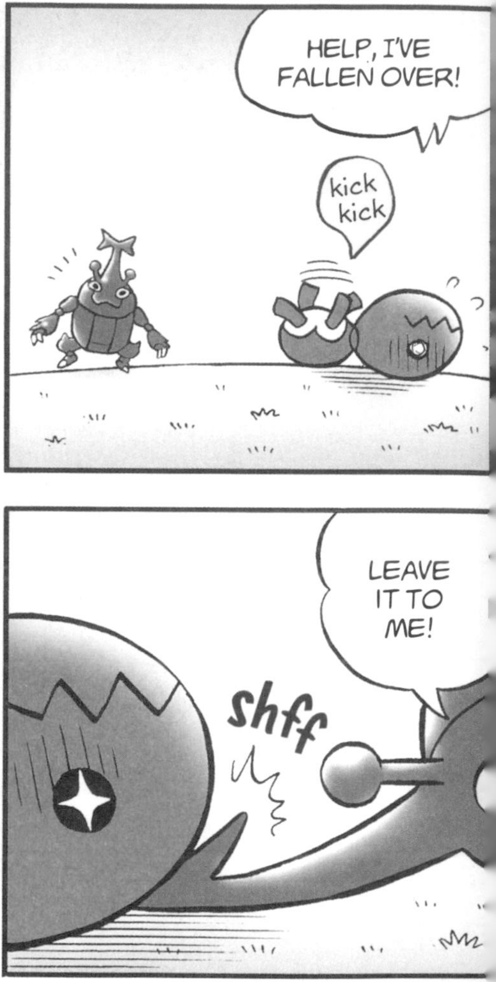
HELP, I'VE FALLEN OVER!
kick kick
LEAVE IT TO ME!
shff

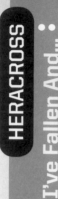

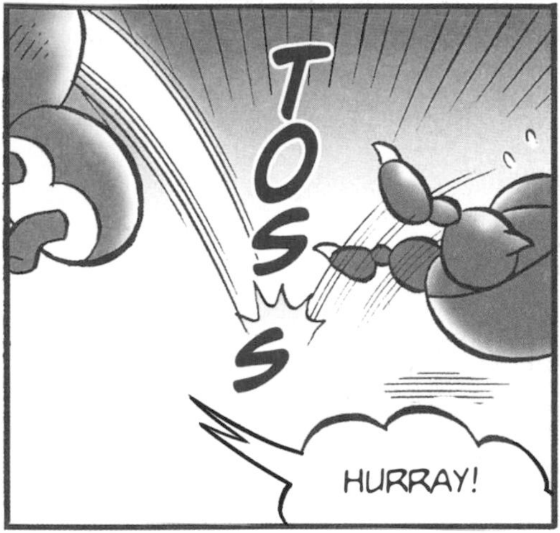
TOSS
HURRAY!

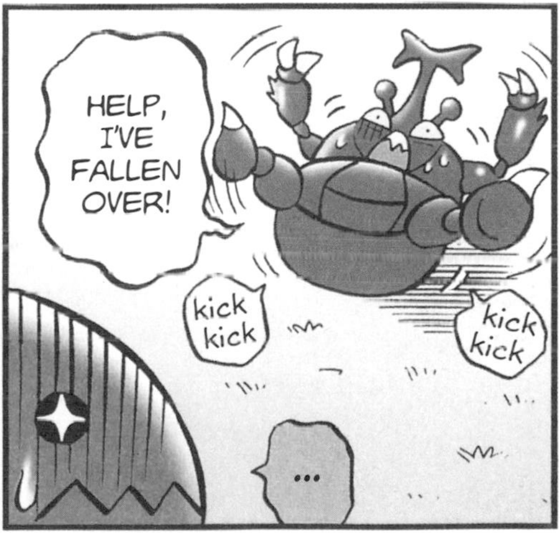
HELP, I'VE FALLEN OVER!
kick kick
kick kick
...

HERACROSS

They gather in forests seeking the sweet sap of trees. It is completely clad in a steel-hard shell.
It is usually docile, but if disturbed while sipping honey, it chases off the intruders with its horn, thrusts its prized horn under its enemies' bellies, then lifts and throws them.

SEE **PAGE 124** TOO!

SCIZOR MAWILE

By Any Other Name

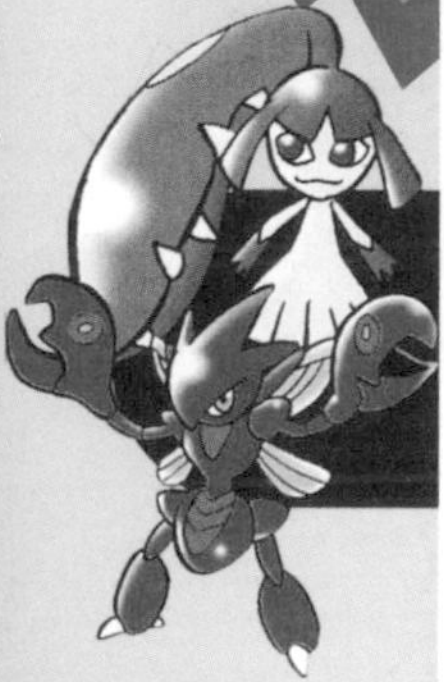

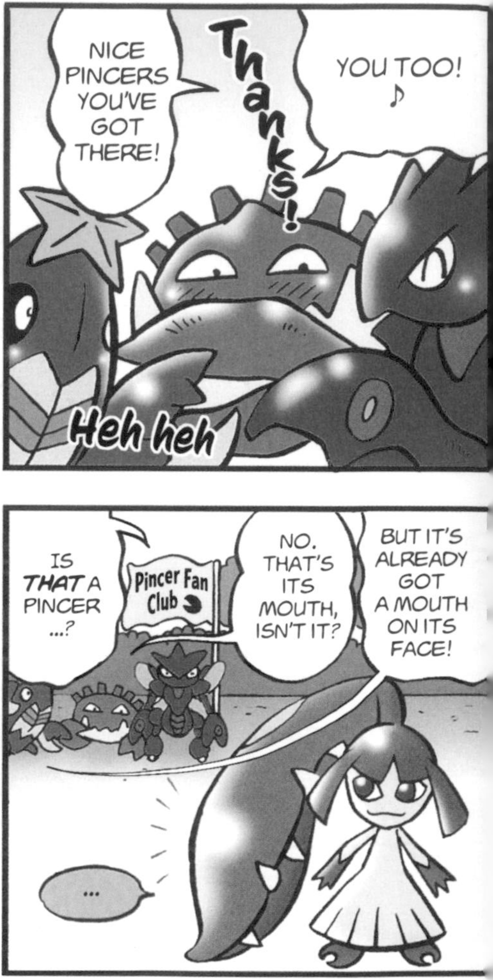
NICE PINCERS YOU'VE GOT THERE!
Thanks!
YOU TOO! ♪
Heh heh
IS *THAT* A PINCER ...?
Pincer Fan Club
NO. THAT'S ITS MOUTH, ISN'T IT?
BUT IT'S ALREADY GOT A MOUTH ON ITS FACE!
...

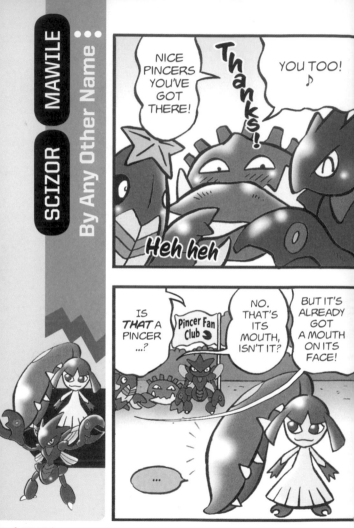

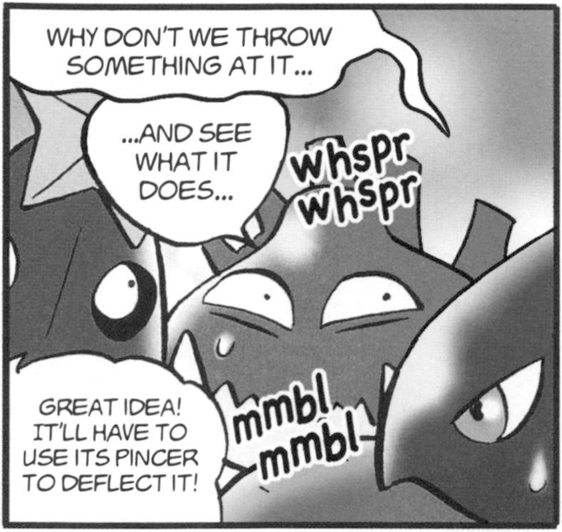
WHY DON'T WE THROW SOMETHING AT IT...
...AND SEE WHAT IT DOES...
whspr whspr
GREAT IDEA! IT'LL HAVE TO USE ITS PINCER TO DEFLECT IT!
mmbl mmbl

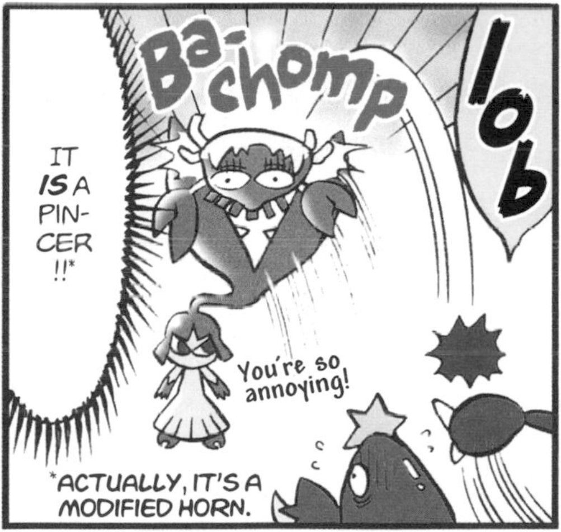
IT *IS* A PIN-CER !!*
Ba-chomp
lob
You're so annoying!
*ACTUALLY, IT'S A MODIFIED HORN.

SCIZOR

It swings its eye-patterned pincers up to scare its foes.

MAWILE

Its huge jaws are actually steel horns that have been transformed. It fools the foe into letting down its guard, then chomps down with its massive jaws.

MAGNEMITE: Bad Reception

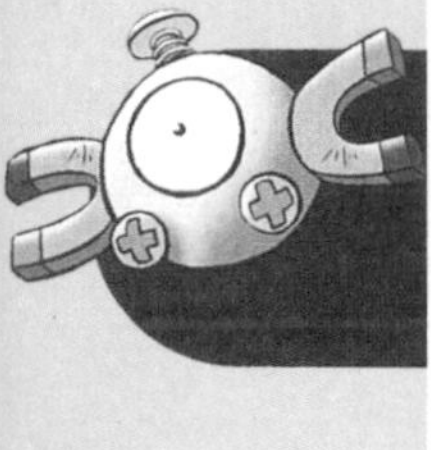

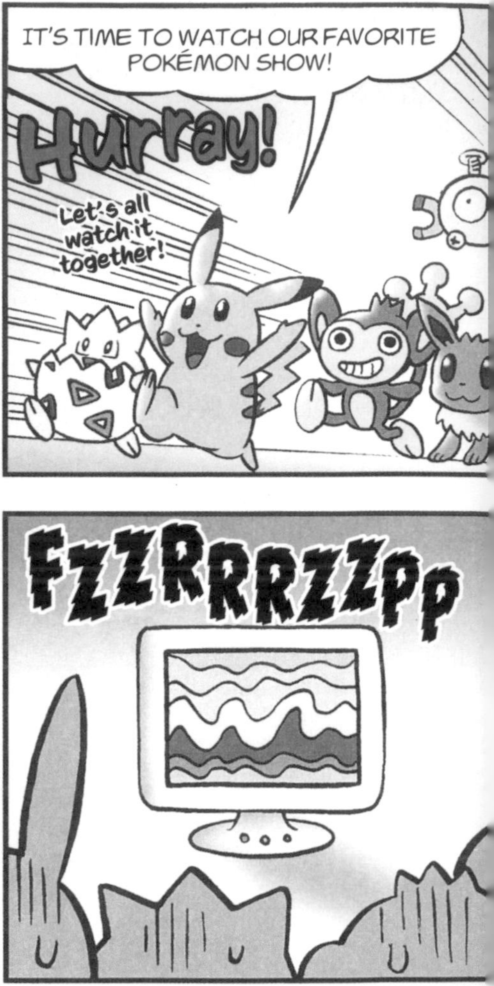
IT'S TIME TO WATCH OUR FAVORITE POKÉMON SHOW!
Hurray!
Let's all watch it together!
FZZRRRZZPP

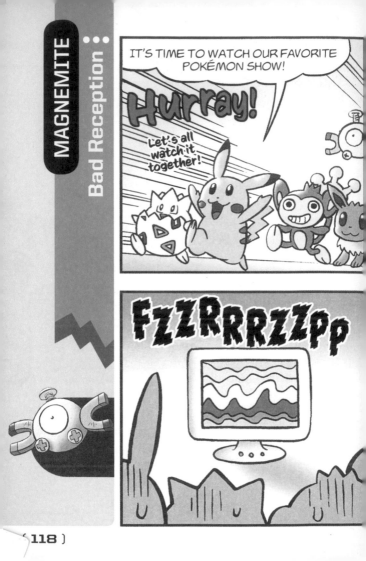

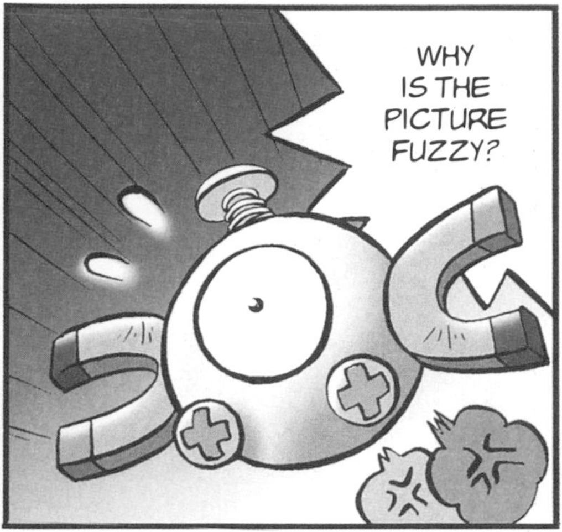
WHY IS THE PICTURE FUZZY?

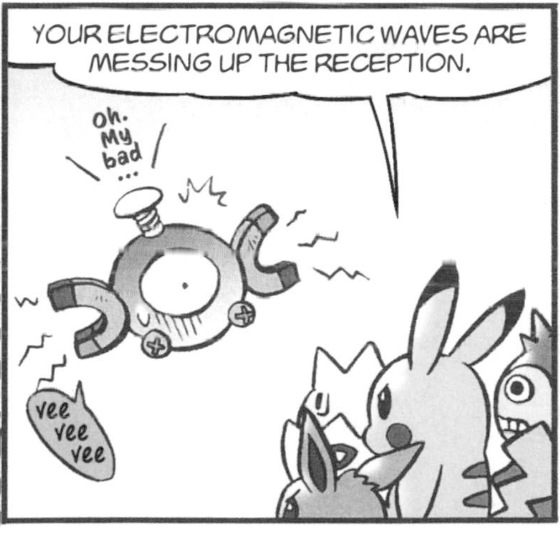
YOUR ELECTROMAGNETIC WAVES ARE MESSING UP THE RECEPTION.
Oh. My bad...
vee vee vee

MAGNEMITE

The units at its sides are extremely powerful magnets. They generate enough magnetism to draw in iron objects from over 300 feet away. The electromagnetic waves it emits expel antigravity, which allows it to float. It attaches itself to power lines to feed on electricity. It becomes incapable of flight if its internal electrical supply is depleted.

DEOXYS

Show-Off

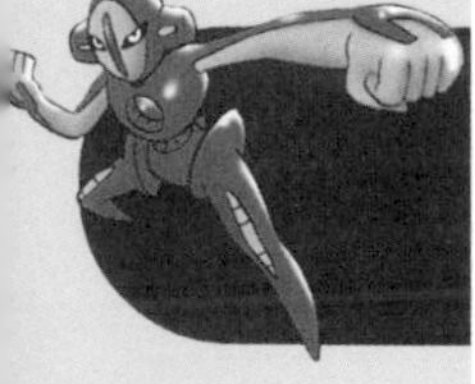

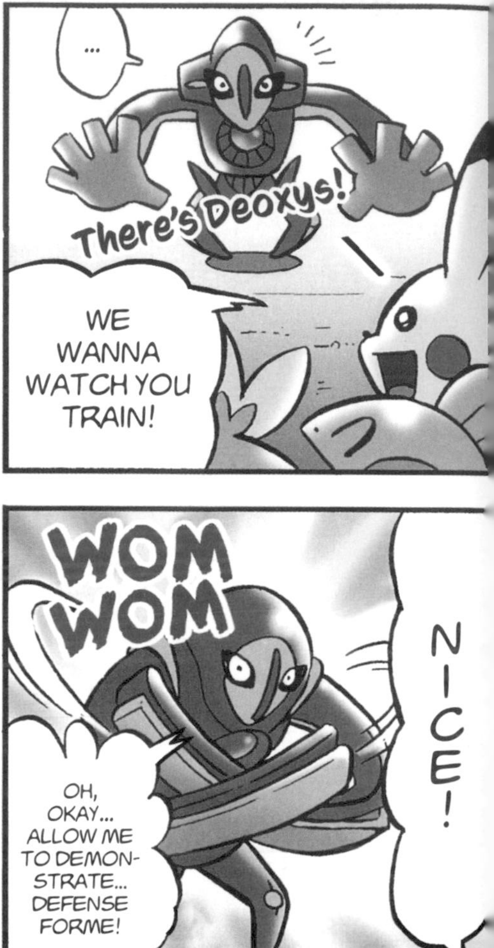
...
There's Deoxys!
WE WANNA WATCH YOU TRAIN!
WOM WOM
OH, OKAY... ALLOW ME TO DEMON-STRATE... DEFENSE FORME!
NICE!

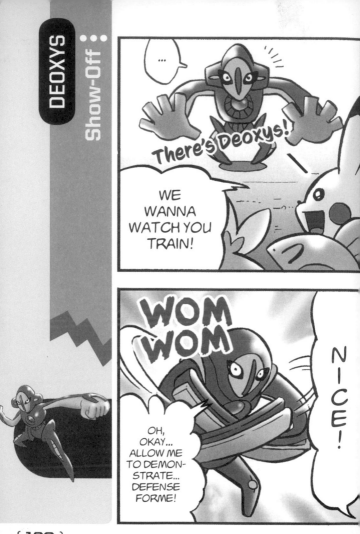

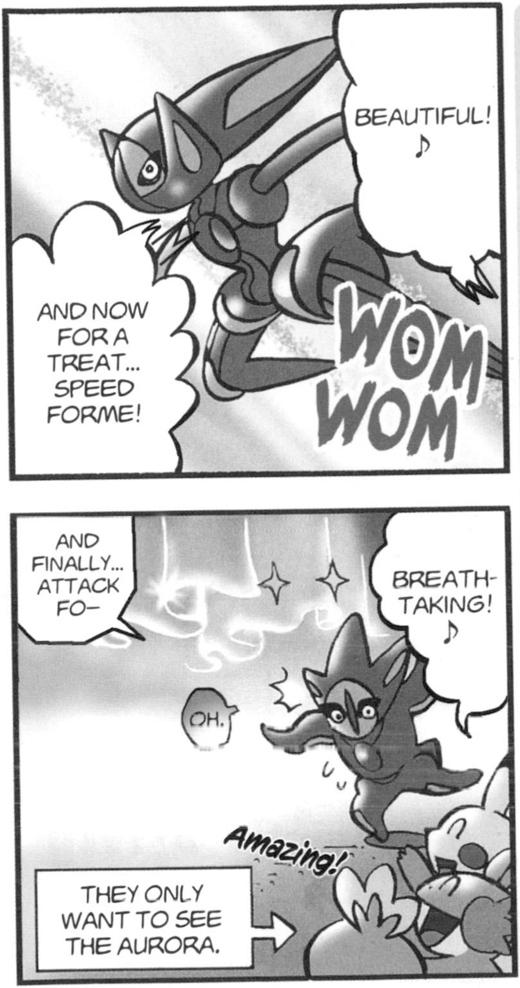
AND NOW FOR A TREAT... SPEED FORME!
BEAUTIFUL! ♪
WOM WOM
AND FINALLY... ATTACK FO–
BREATH-TAKING! ♪
OH.
Amazing!
THEY ONLY WANT TO SEE THE AURORA.

DEOXYS

A DNA Pokémon born from a space virus. It is usually in its Normal Forme, but it can change into its Defense Forme, Speed Forme and Attack Forme. When it changes, an aurora appears.

WALREIN SEEL

A Chill in the Air...

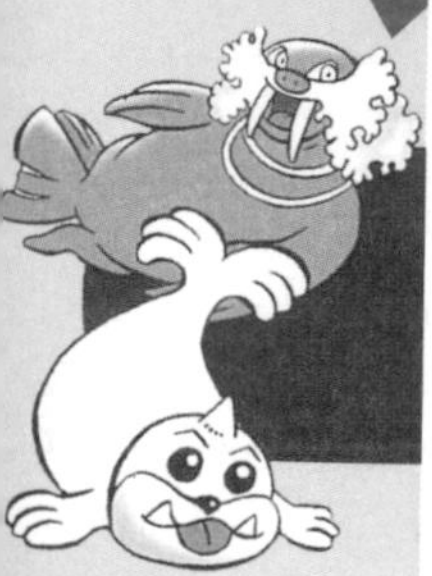

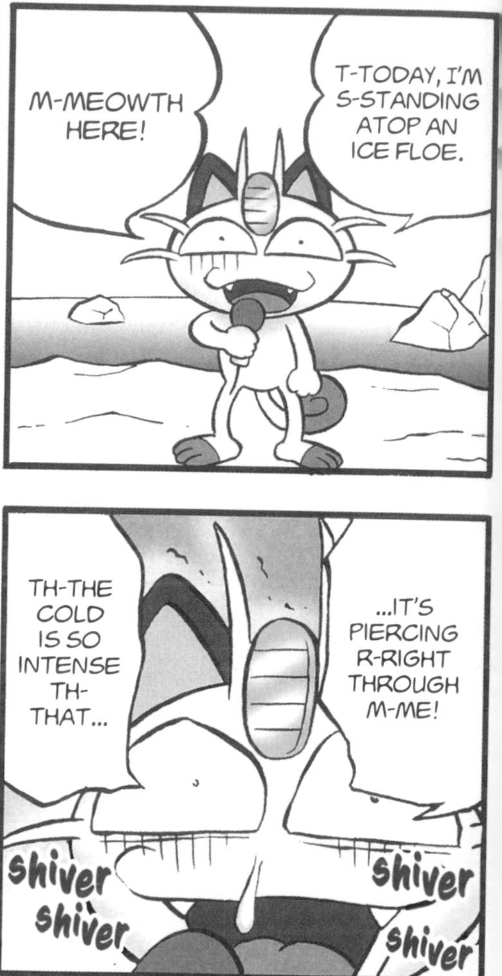
M-MEOWTH HERE!
T-TODAY, I'M S-STANDING ATOP AN ICE FLOE.
TH-THE COLD IS SO INTENSE TH-THAT...
...IT'S PIERCING R-RIGHT THROUGH M-ME!
shiver shiver
shiver shiver

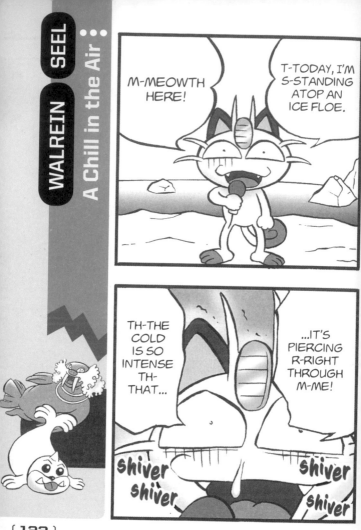

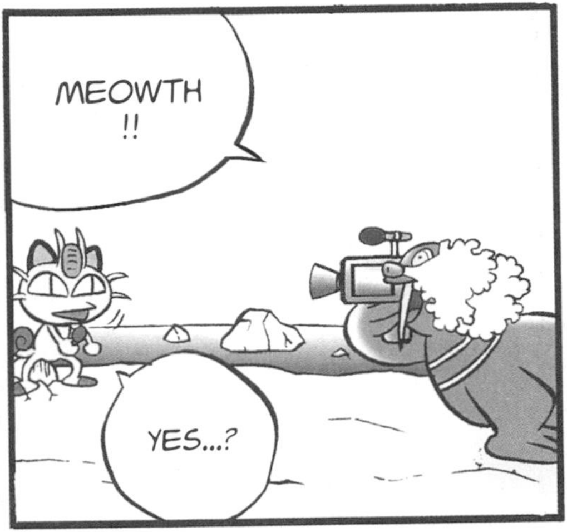
MEOWTH !!
YES...?

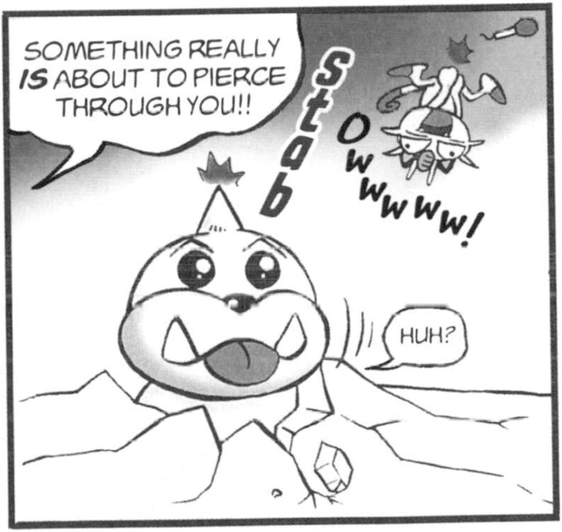
SOMETHING REALLY *IS* ABOUT TO PIERCE THROUGH YOU!!
Stab
OWWWWW!
HUH?

WALREIN

To protect its herd, the leader battles anything that invades its territory, even at the cost of its life. Its tusks may snap off in battle.

SEEL

It loves freezing cold conditions. When it needs to breathe, it punches a hole through the ice with the sharply protruding section of its head.

PINSIR

...I Can't Get Up!

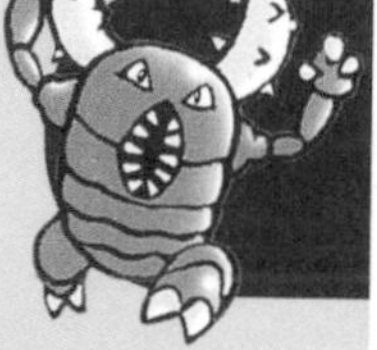

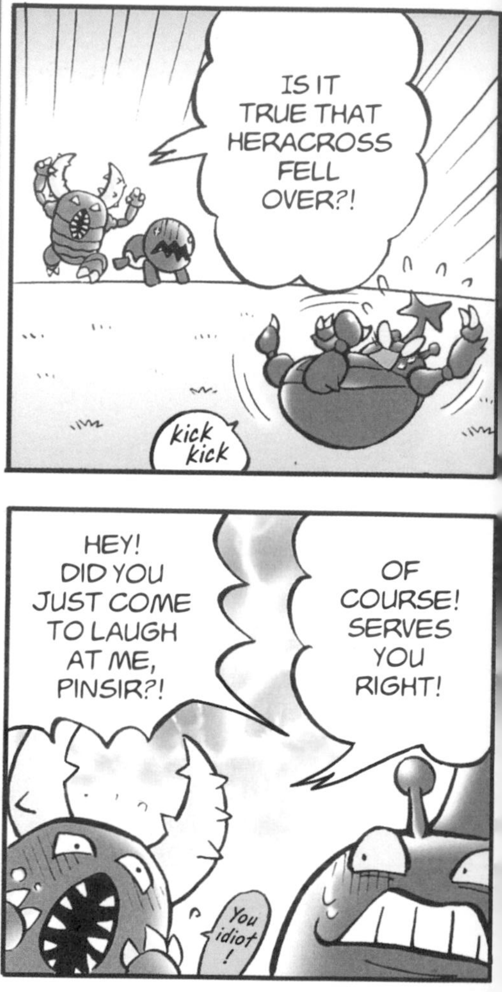

IS IT TRUE THAT HERACROSS FELL OVER?!
kick kick
HEY! DID YOU JUST COME TO LAUGH AT ME, PINSIR?!
OF COURSE! SERVES YOU RIGHT!
You idiot!

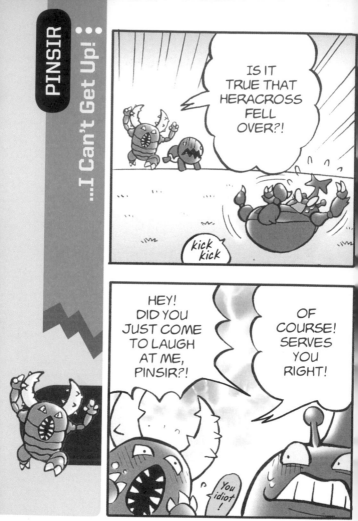

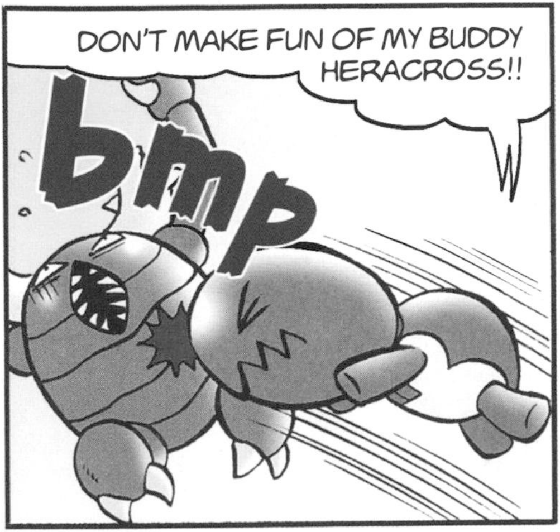
DON'T MAKE FUN OF MY BUDDY HERACROSS!!
bmp

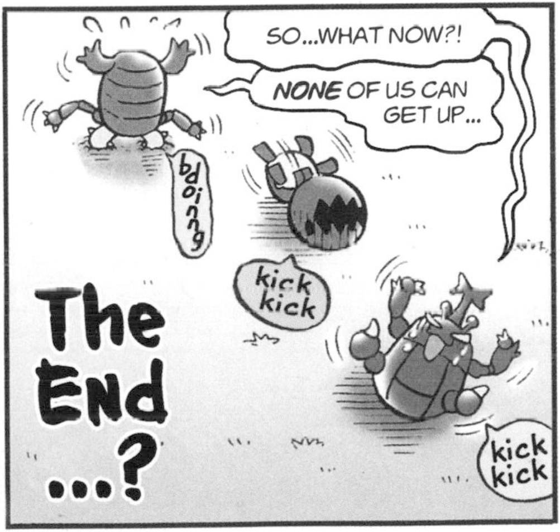
SO...WHAT NOW?!
NONE OF US CAN GET UP...
bdoinng
kick kick
kick kick
The End ...?

PINSIR

Its two long pincer horns are powerful and strong enough to shatter thick logs. Once it grips an enemy, it won't release it. If it fails to crush its foe in its pincers, it will swing around and toss the opponent. Because it dislikes cold, Pinsir burrows and sleeps under the ground on chilly nights.

LUGIA WAILORD

Hold Your Breath

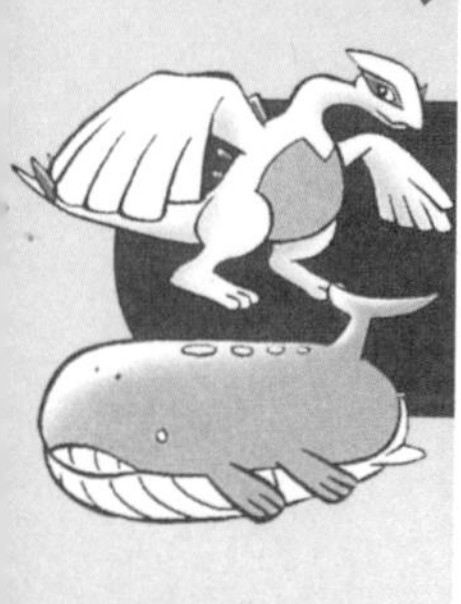

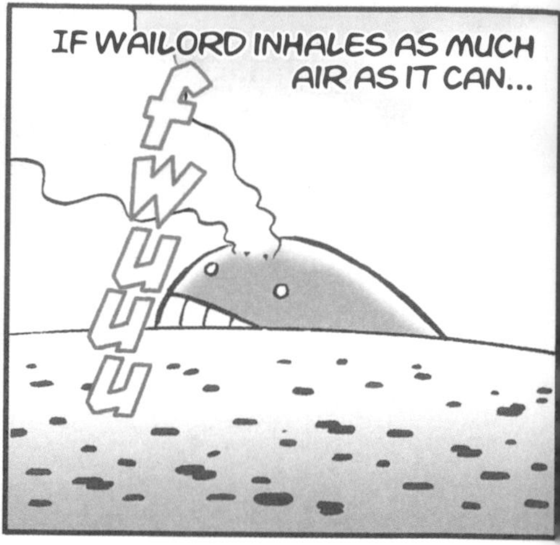
IF WAILORD INHALES AS MUCH AIR AS IT CAN...

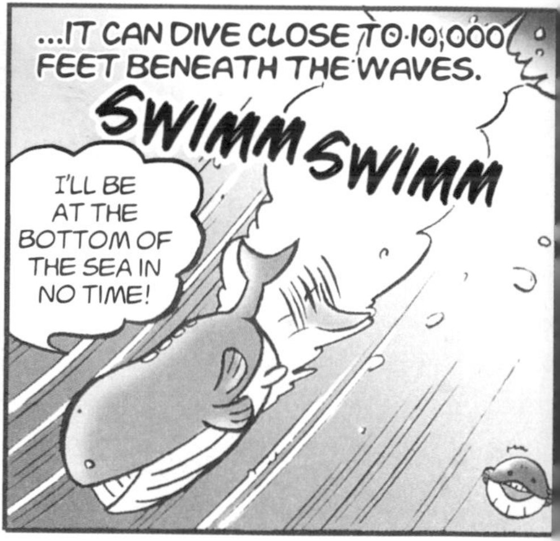
...IT CAN DIVE CLOSE TO 10,000 FEET BENEATH THE WAVES.
SWIMM SWIMM
I'LL BE AT THE BOTTOM OF THE SEA IN NO TIME!

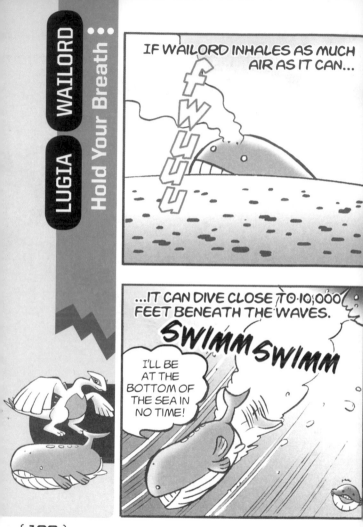

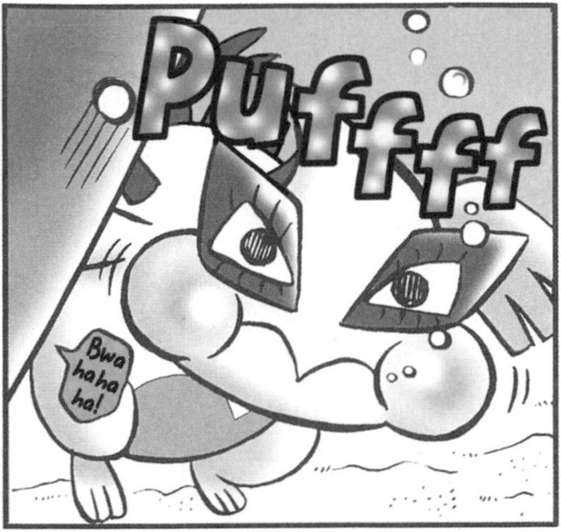
Pufff
Bwa ha ha ha!

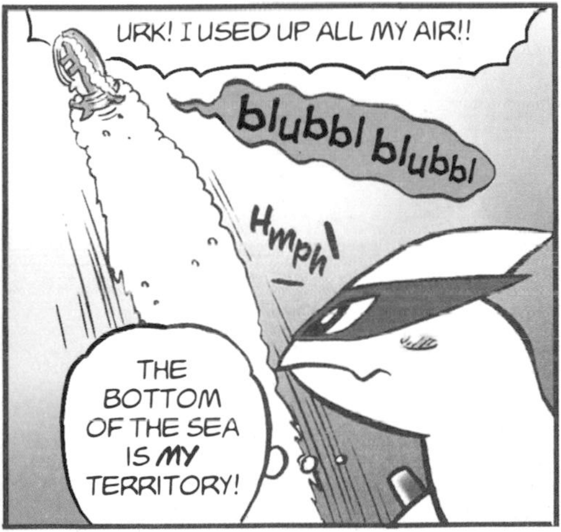
URK! I USED UP ALL MY AIR!!
blubbl blubbl
Hmph!
THE BOTTOM OF THE SEA IS *MY* TERRITORY!

LUGIA

It is said to be the guardian of the seas. It quietly spends its time deep at the bottom of the sea.

WAILORD

It is among the largest of all Pokémon. It breathes through nostrils that it raises above the sea. This giant Pokémon swims languorously in the vast open sea, eating massive amounts of food at once with its enormous mouth.

VULPIX CHARMANDER

Good Wishes

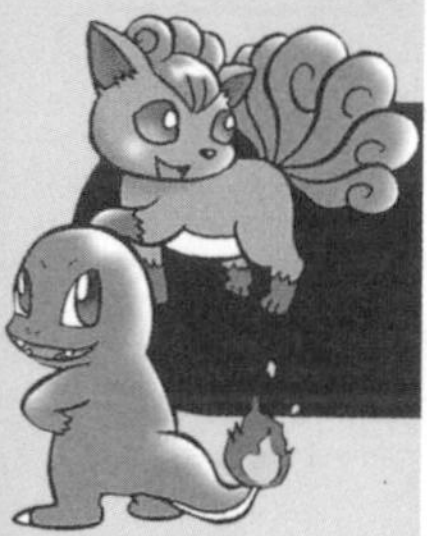

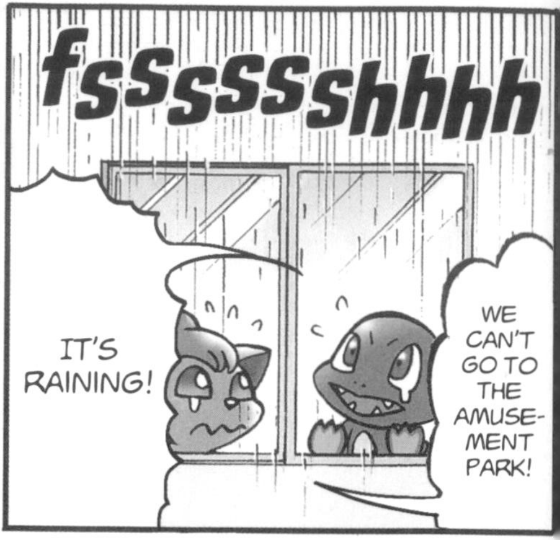
fsssssshhhh
IT'S RAINING!
WE CAN'T GO TO THE AMUSE-MENT PARK!

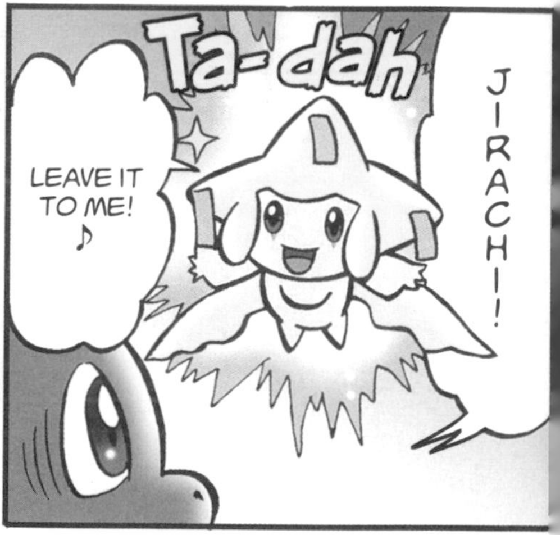
Ta-dah
LEAVE IT TO ME! ♪
JIRACHI!

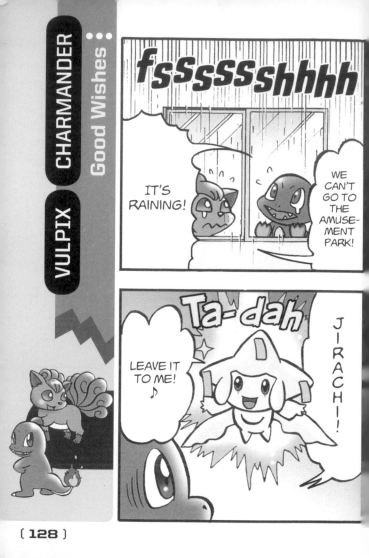

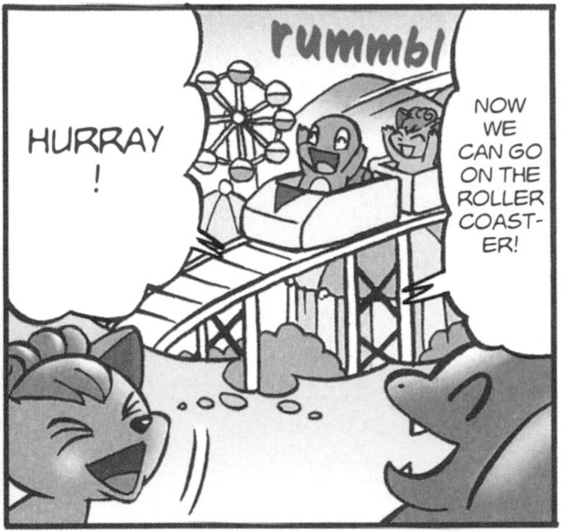
rummbl
HURRAY !
NOW WE CAN GO ON THE ROLLER COAST-ER!

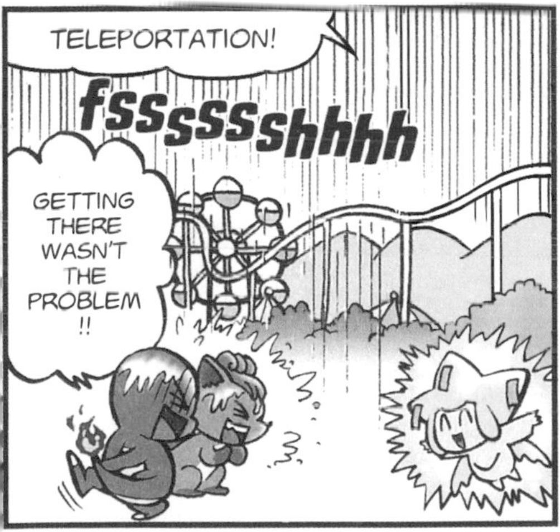
TELEPORTATION!
fsssssshhhh
GETTING THERE WASN'T THE PROBLEM !!

VULPIX

It can freely control fire, making fiery orbs like will-o'-the-wisps. Just before it evolves, its six tails grow hot as if on fire.

CHARMANDER

From the time it is born, a flame burns at the tip of its tail. Its life would end if the flame were to go out.

GROUDON NOCTOWL

Young at Heart

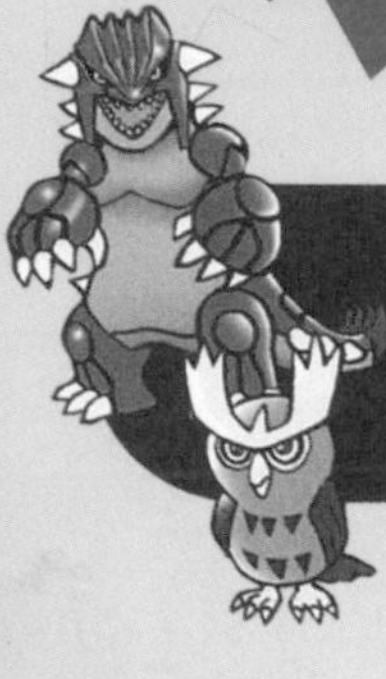

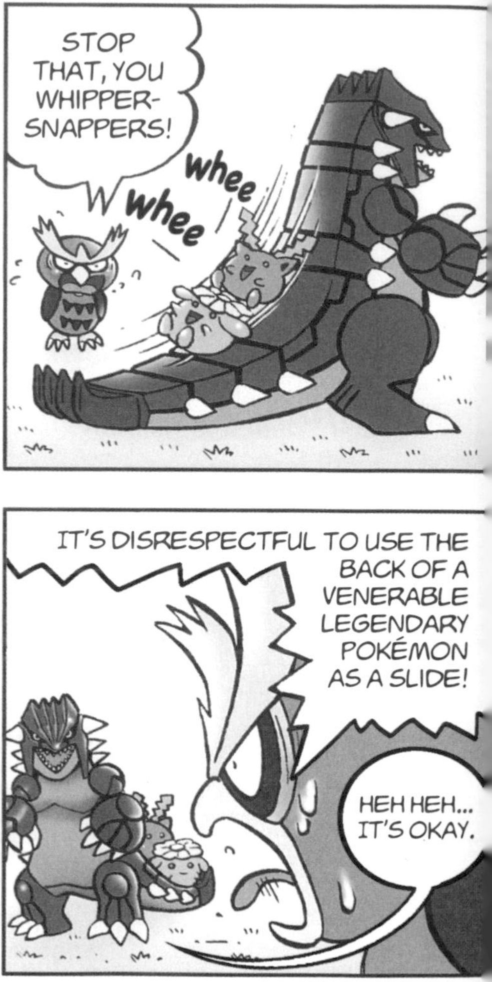

STOP THAT, YOU WHIPPER-SNAPPERS!
whee
whee
IT'S DISRESPECTFUL TO USE THE BACK OF A VENERABLE LEGENDARY POKÉMON AS A SLIDE!
HEH HEH... IT'S OKAY.

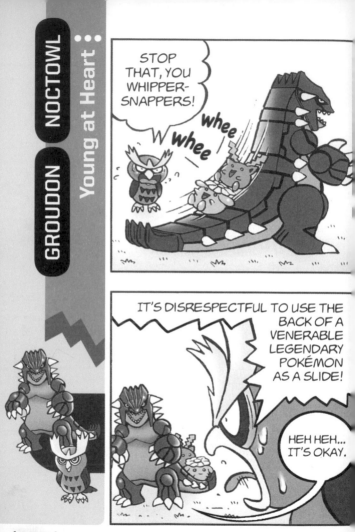

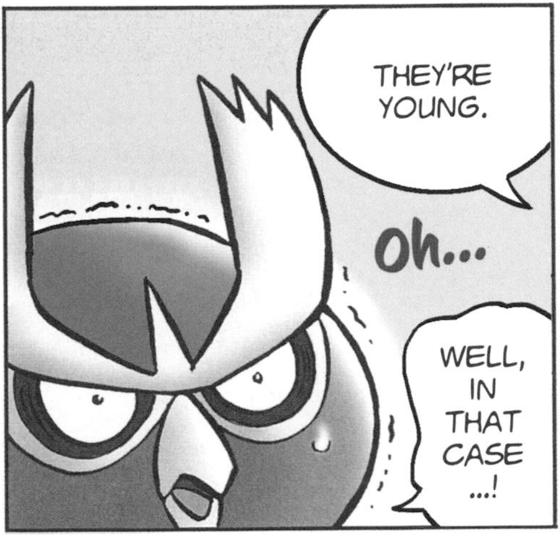
THEY'RE YOUNG.
Oh...
WELL, IN THAT CASE ...!

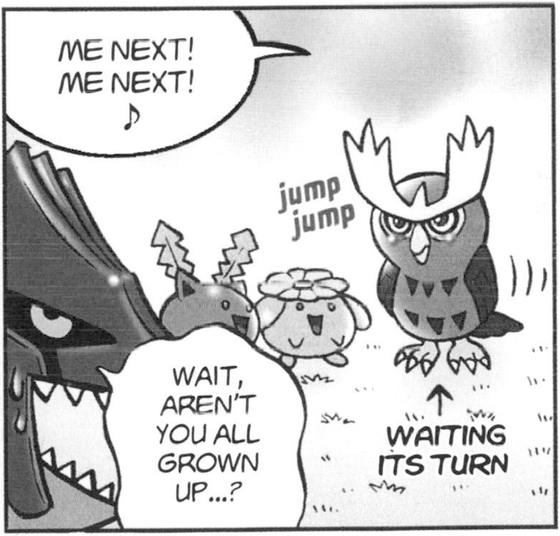
ME NEXT! ME NEXT! ♪
jump jump
WAIT, AREN'T YOU ALL GROWN UP...?
WAITING ITS TURN

GROUDON

It has long been described in mythology as the Pokémon that raised lands and expanded continents. It sleeps in magma underground and is said to make volcanoes erupt upon awakening.

NOCTOWL

When it needs to think, it rotates its head 180 degrees to sharpen its intellectual power. Its eyes are specially developed to enable it to see clearly even in murky darkness and minimal light.

TEDDIURSA

Fleeting Treasure

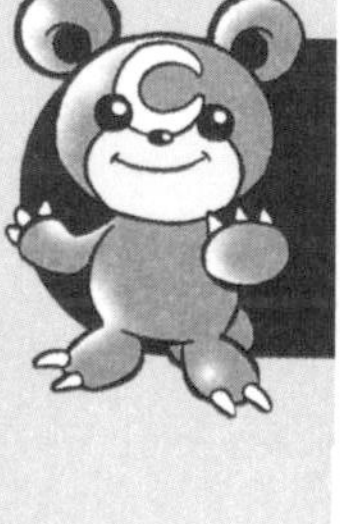

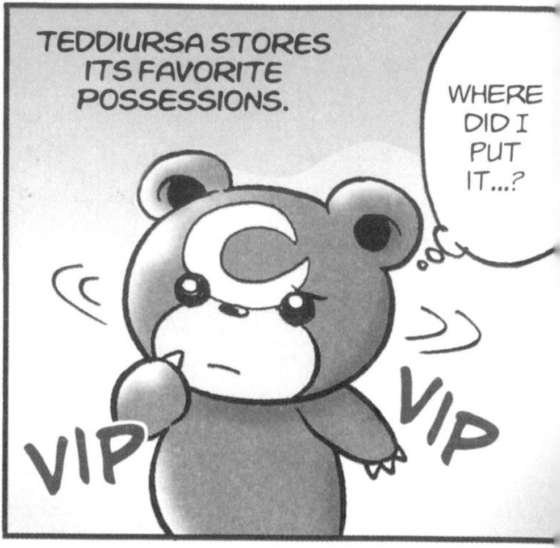
TEDDIURSA STORES ITS FAVORITE POSSESSIONS.
WHERE DID I PUT IT...?
VIP
VIP

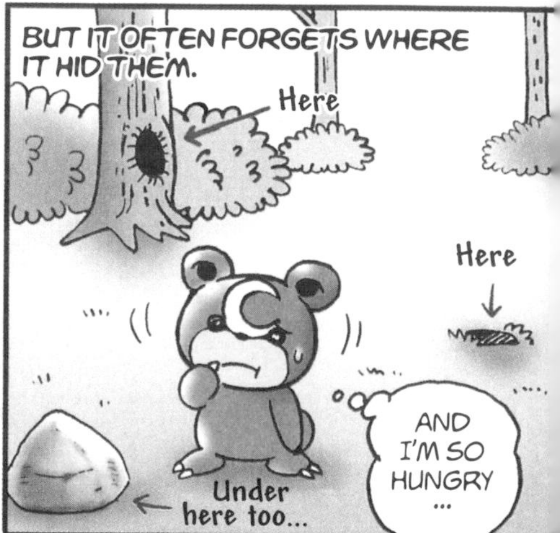
BUT IT OFTEN FORGETS WHERE IT HID THEM.
Here
Here
Under here too...
AND I'M SO HUNGRY ...

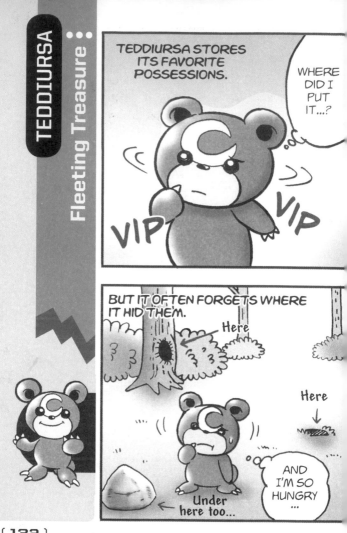

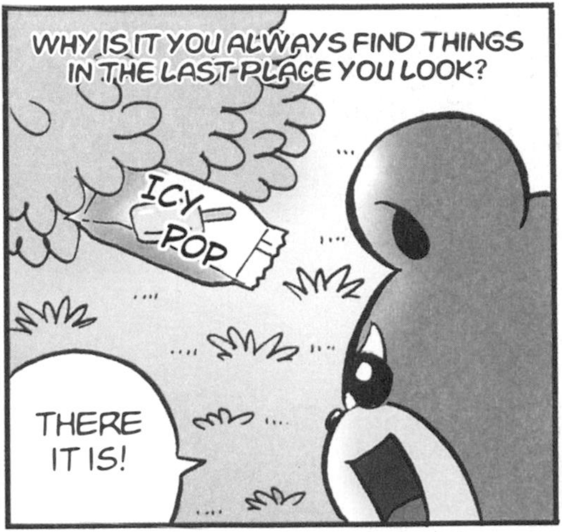
WHY IS IT YOU ALWAYS FIND THINGS IN THE LAST PLACE YOU LOOK?
ICY POP
THERE IT IS!

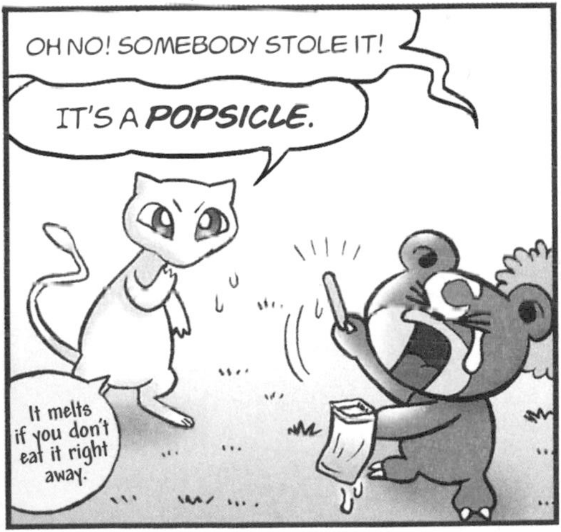
OH NO! SOMEBODY STOLE IT!
IT'S A ***POPSICLE***.
It melts if you don't eat it right away.

TEDDIURSA

Before food becomes scarce in wintertime, its habit is to hoard food in many hidden locations. If it finds honey, its crescent mark glows. It always licks its paws because they are soaked with honey. Teddiursa makes its own honey by blending fruits and pollen collected by Beedrill.

HITMONCHAN

A Solid Shadow

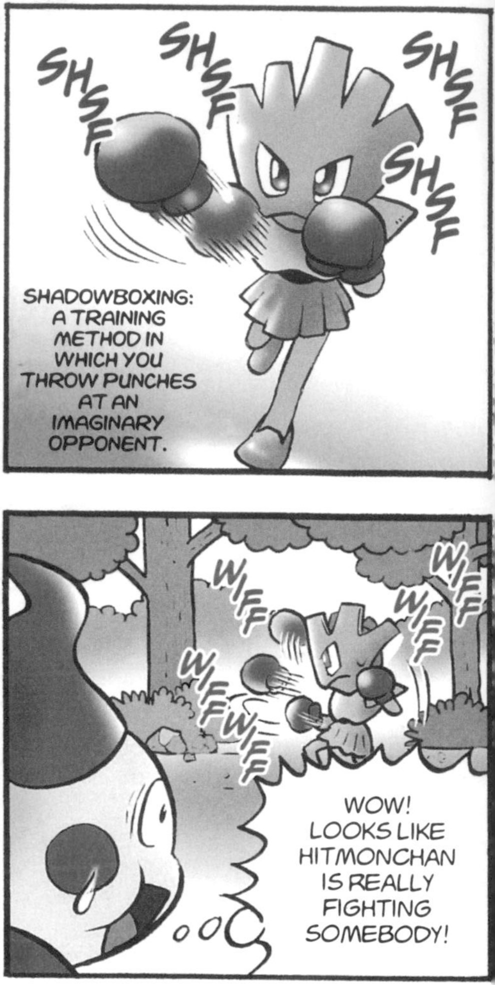

SHSF
SHSF
SHSF
SHSF
SHADOWBOXING: A TRAINING METHOD IN WHICH YOU THROW PUNCHES AT AN IMAGINARY OPPONENT.
WIFF
WIFF
WIFF
WIFF
WIFF
WOW! LOOKS LIKE HITMONCHAN IS REALLY FIGHTING SOMEBODY!

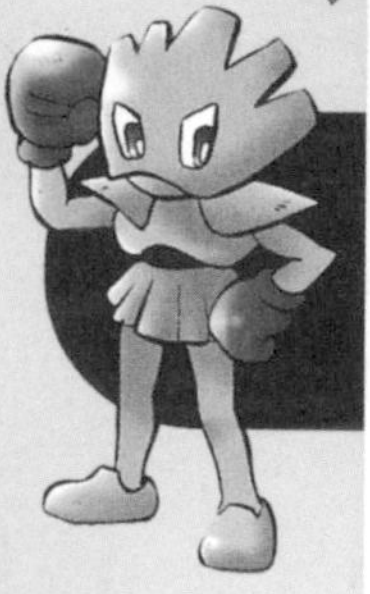

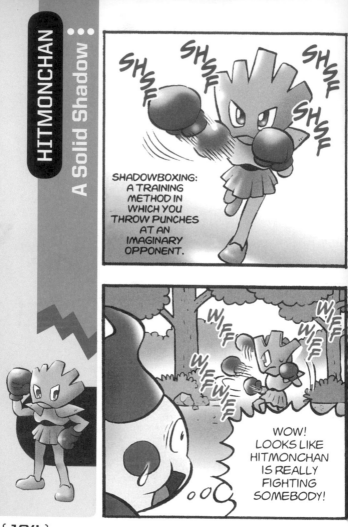

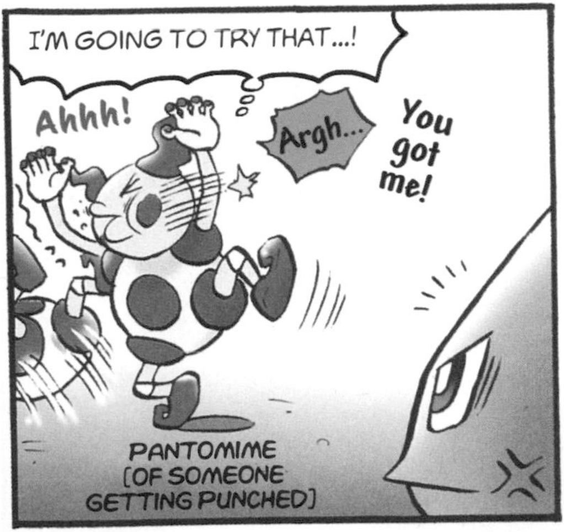
I'M GOING TO TRY THAT...!
Ahhh!
Argh...
You got me!
PANTOMIME [OF SOMEONE GETTING PUNCHED]

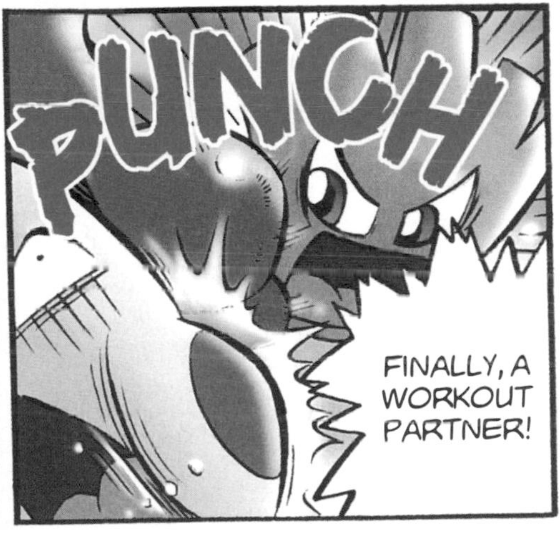
PUNCH
FINALLY, A WORKOUT PARTNER!

HITMONCHAN

It is said to possess the spirit of a boxer who has been working towards a world championship. While apparently doing nothing, it fires punches in lighting-fast volleys that are impossible to see. It punches in corkscrew fashion. It can punch its way through a concrete wall in the same way as a drill.

KANGASKHAN
Pouch of Dreams

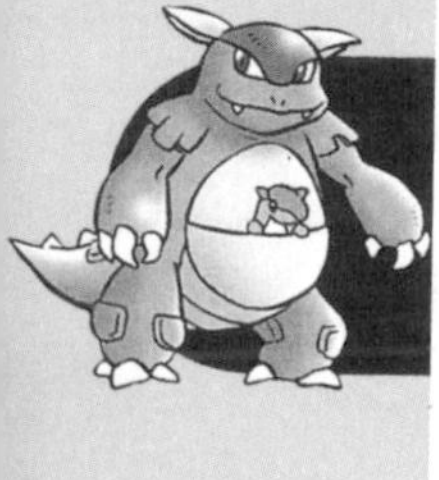

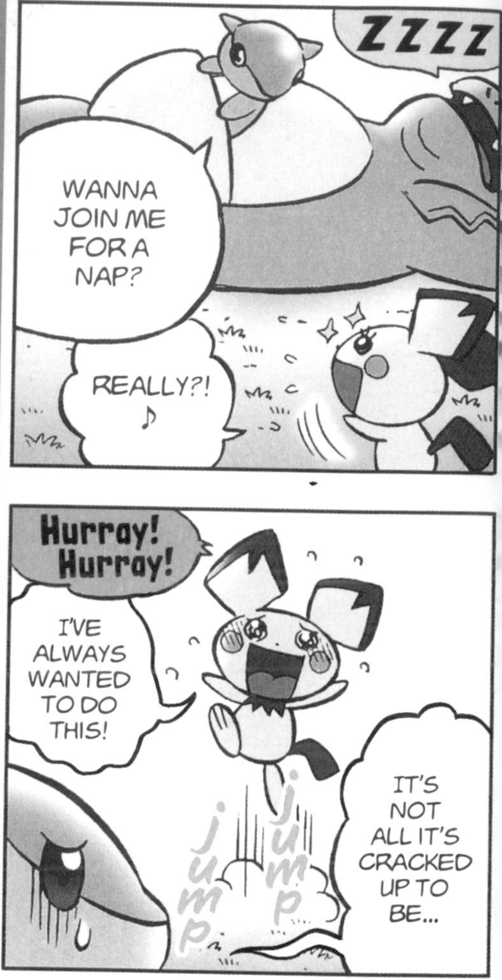
ZZZZ
WANNA JOIN ME FOR A NAP?
REALLY?! ♪
Hurray! Hurray!
I'VE ALWAYS WANTED TO DO THIS!
jump
jump
IT'S NOT ALL IT'S CRACKED UP TO BE...

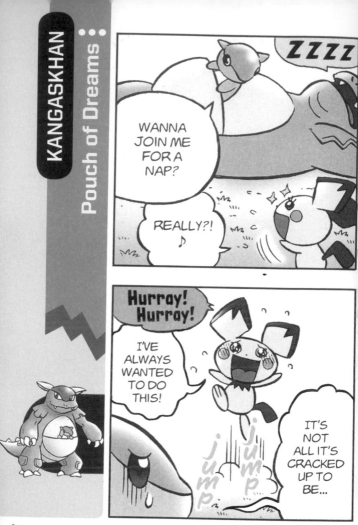

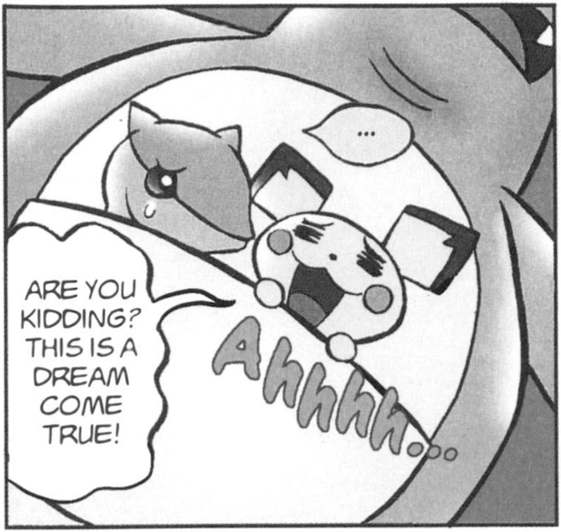
...
ARE YOU KIDDING? THIS IS A DREAM COME TRUE!
Ahhhh...

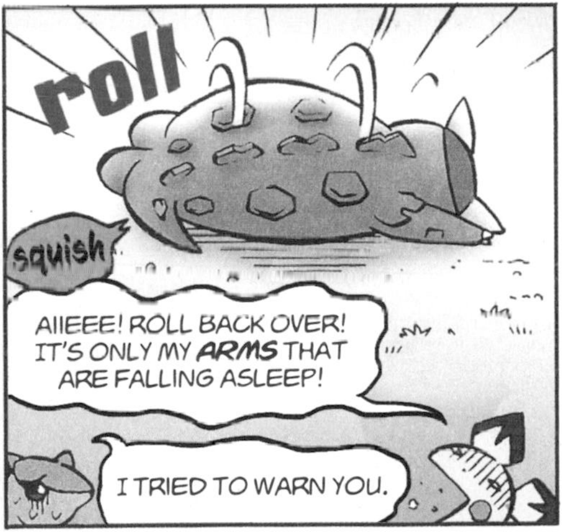
roll
squish
AIIEEE! ROLL BACK OVER! IT'S ONLY MY ***ARMS*** THAT ARE FALLING ASLEEP!
I TRIED TO WARN YOU.

KANGASKHAN

The female raises its offspring in a pouch on its belly. To protect its young, it will never give up during battle, no matter how badly wounded it is. The infant rarely ventures out of its mother's protective pouch until it is three years old.

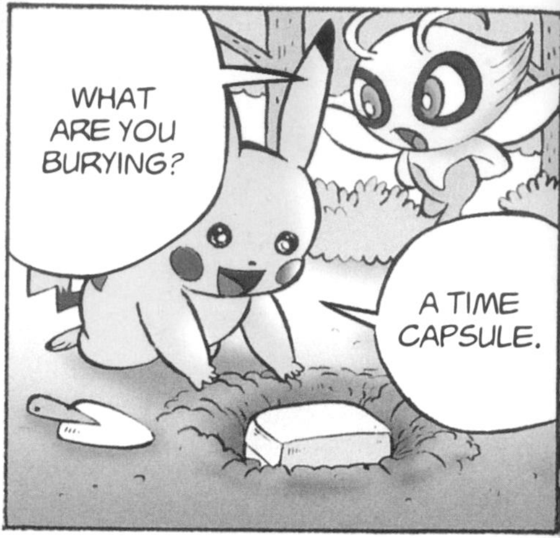
WHAT ARE YOU BURYING?
A TIME CAPSULE.

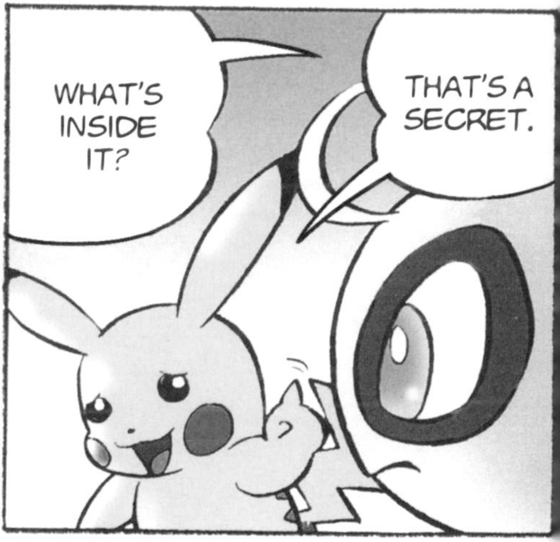
WHAT'S INSIDE IT?
THAT'S A SECRET.

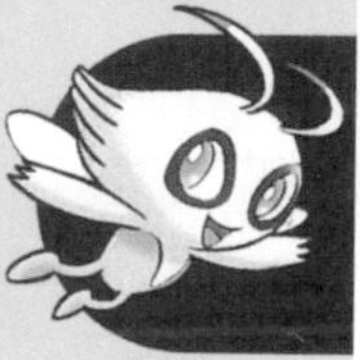

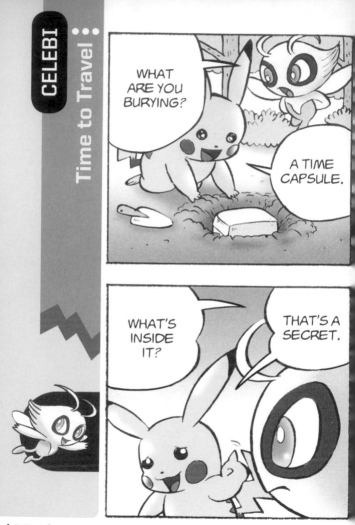

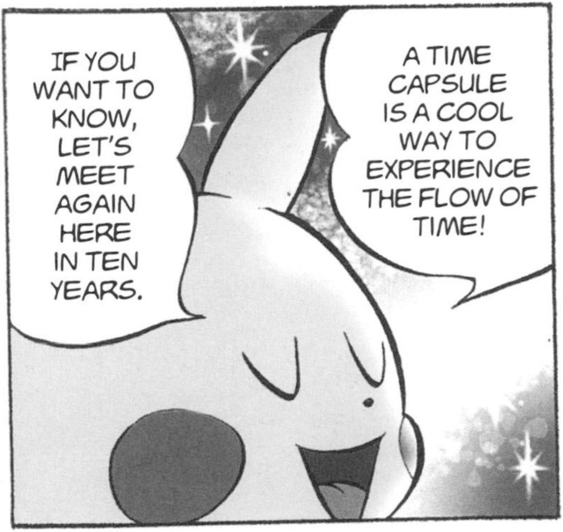
IF YOU WANT TO KNOW, LET'S MEET AGAIN HERE IN TEN YEARS.
A TIME CAPSULE IS A COOL WAY TO EXPERIENCE THE FLOW OF TIME!

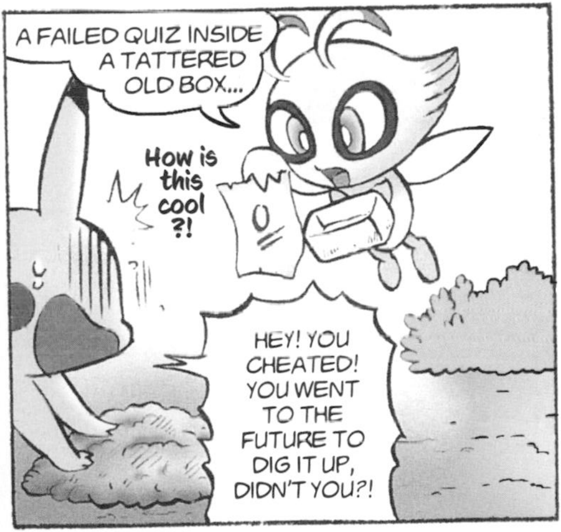
A FAILED QUIZ INSIDE A TATTERED OLD BOX...
How is this cool ?!
HEY! YOU CHEATED! YOU WENT TO THE FUTURE TO DIG IT UP, DIDN'T YOU?!

CELEBI

It wanders through time. Grass and trees flourish in the forests in which it has appeared. It is thought that so long as Celebi appears, a bright and shining future awaits us.

SHUPPET BANETTE
Curses, Foiled Again!

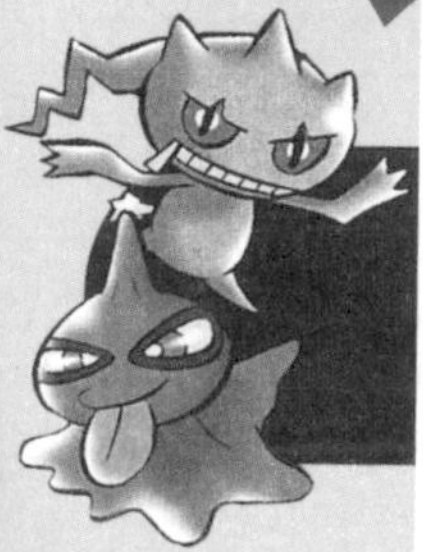

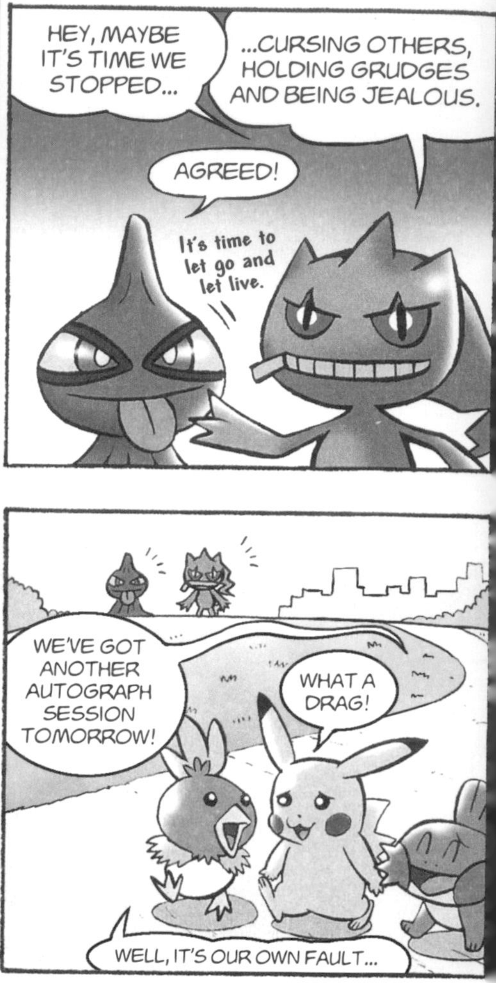
HEY, MAYBE IT'S TIME WE STOPPED...
...CURSING OTHERS, HOLDING GRUDGES AND BEING JEALOUS.
AGREED!
It's time to let go and let live.
WE'VE GOT ANOTHER AUTOGRAPH SESSION TOMORROW!
WHAT A DRAG!
WELL, IT'S OUR OWN FAULT...

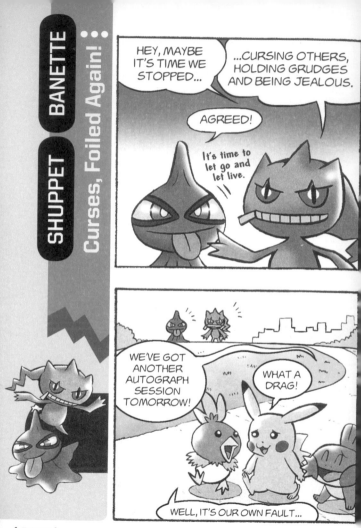

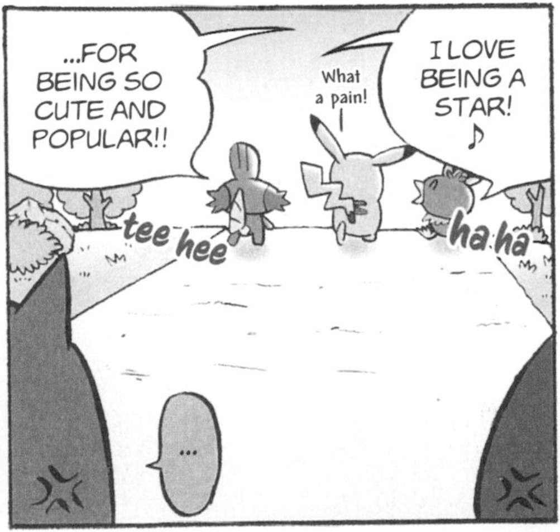
...FOR BEING SO CUTE AND POPULAR!!
What a pain!
I LOVE BEING A STAR! ♪
tee hee
ha ha
...

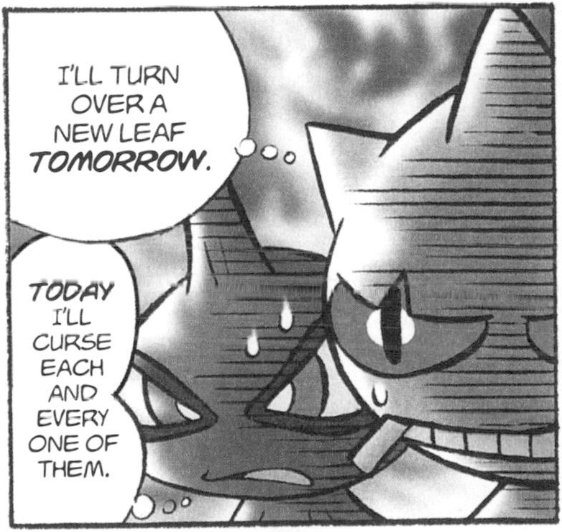
I'LL TURN OVER A NEW LEAF TOMORROW.
TODAY I'LL CURSE EACH AND EVERY ONE OF THEM.

SHUPPET

It roams about deep in the night seeking such negative emotions as grudges and envy. It retreats to its nest when the sun begins to rise.

BANETTE

It was originally a pitiful plush doll that was thrown away. It is said to live in garbage dumps and wander about in search of the children that threw it away.

PELIPPER
Cleared for Flight

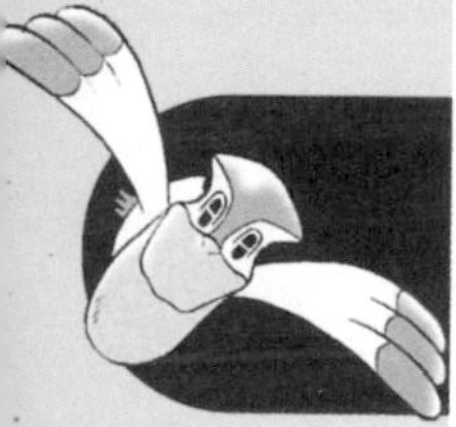

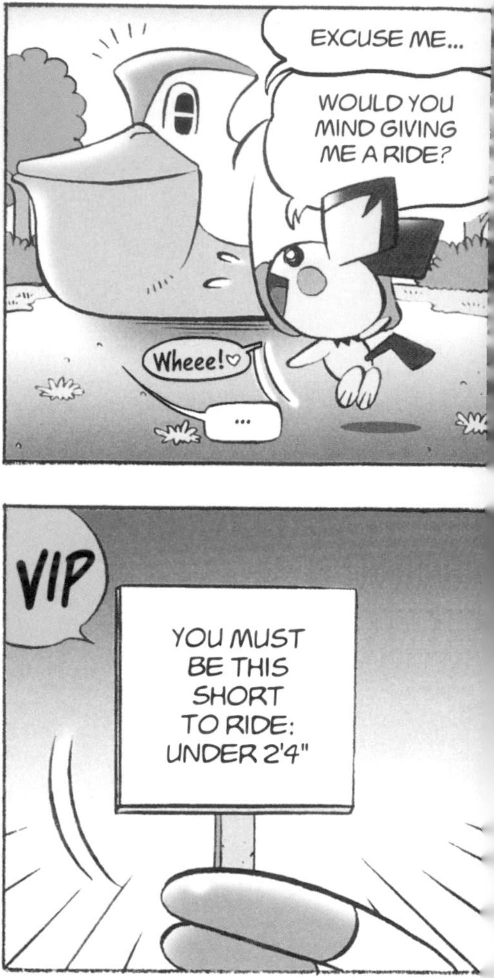
EXCUSE ME...
WOULD YOU MIND GIVING ME A RIDE?
Wheee!♡
...
VIP
YOU MUST BE THIS SHORT TO RIDE: UNDER 2'4"

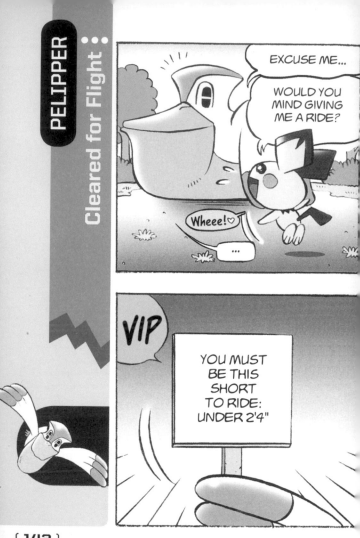

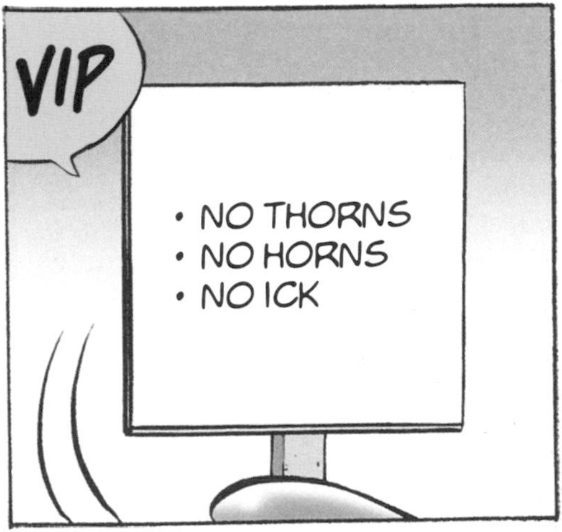
VIP
• NO THORNS
• NO HORNS
• NO ICK

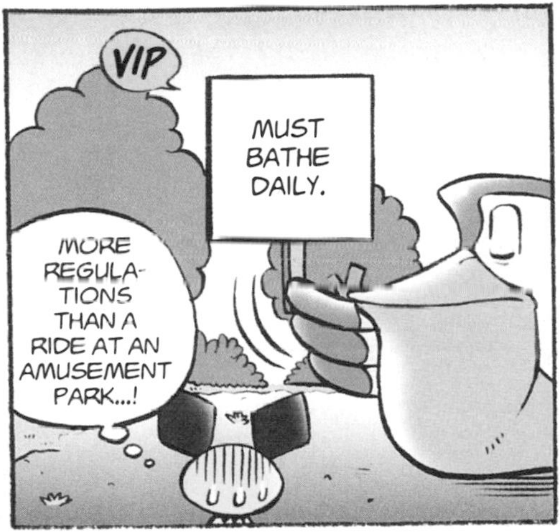
VIP
MUST BATHE DAILY.
MORE REGULATIONS THAN A RIDE AT AN AMUSEMENT PARK...!

PELIPPER

It is a flying transporter that carries small Pokémon and eggs inside its massive bill. It skims the top of waves as it flies. When it spots prey, it uses its large beak to scoop up the victim with water. It builds its nest on steep cliffs facing the sea and protects its eggs in its beak.

PORYGON

Karaoke Tournament

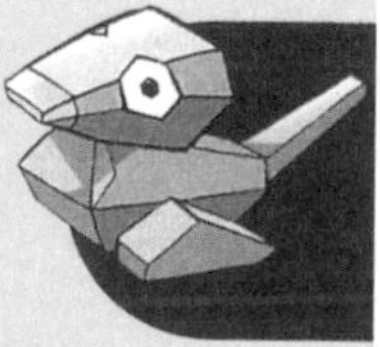

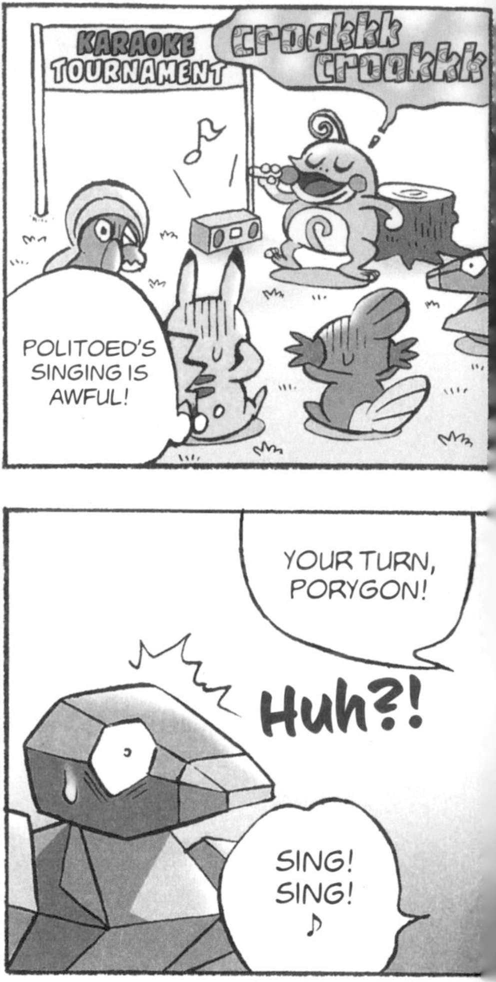
KARAOKE TOURNAMENT
Croakkk croakkk
POLITOED'S SINGING IS AWFUL!
YOUR TURN, PORYGON!
Huh?!
SING! SING! ♪

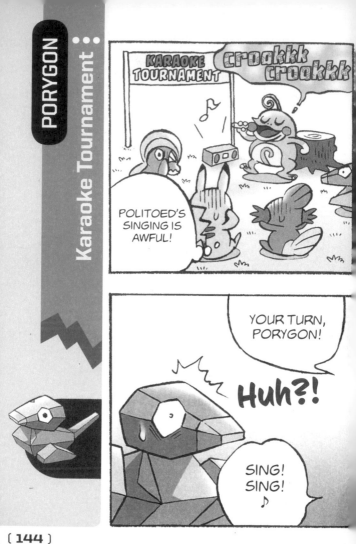

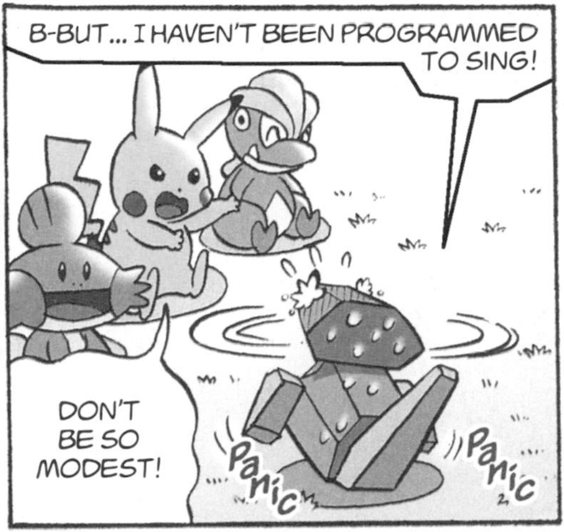
B-BUT... I HAVEN'T BEEN PROGRAMMED TO SING!
DON'T BE SO MODEST!
Panic
Panic

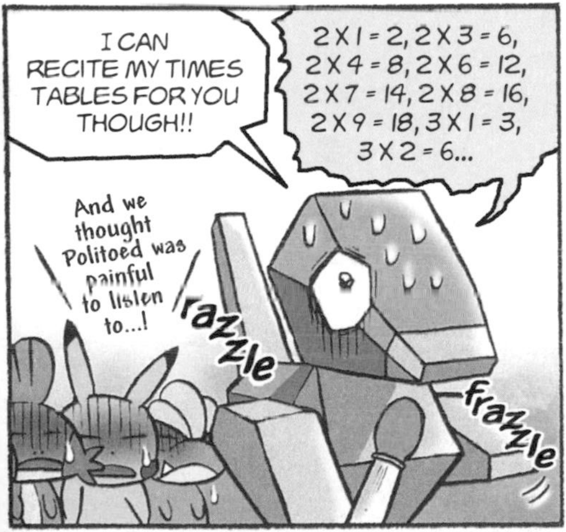
I CAN RECITE MY TIMES TABLES FOR YOU THOUGH!!
2X1 = 2, 2X3 = 6, 2X4 = 8, 2X6 = 12, 2X7 = 14, 2X8 = 16, 2X9 = 18, 3X1 = 3, 3X2 = 6...
And we thought Politoed was painful to listen to...!
razzle
frazzle

PORYGON

It is capable of reverting itself back to program data and entering cyberspace. This Pokémon is copy protected, so it cannot be duplicated by copying. Since it doesn't breathe, people are eager to try it in any environment. It is a man-made Pokémon created using advanced scientific means.

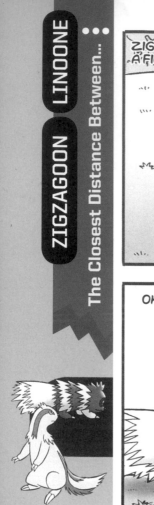

ZIGZAGOON LINOONE

The Closest Distance Between...

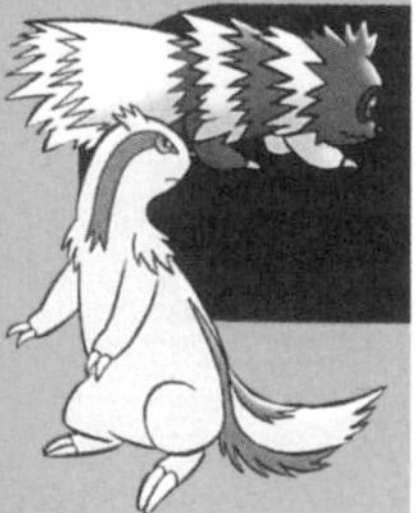

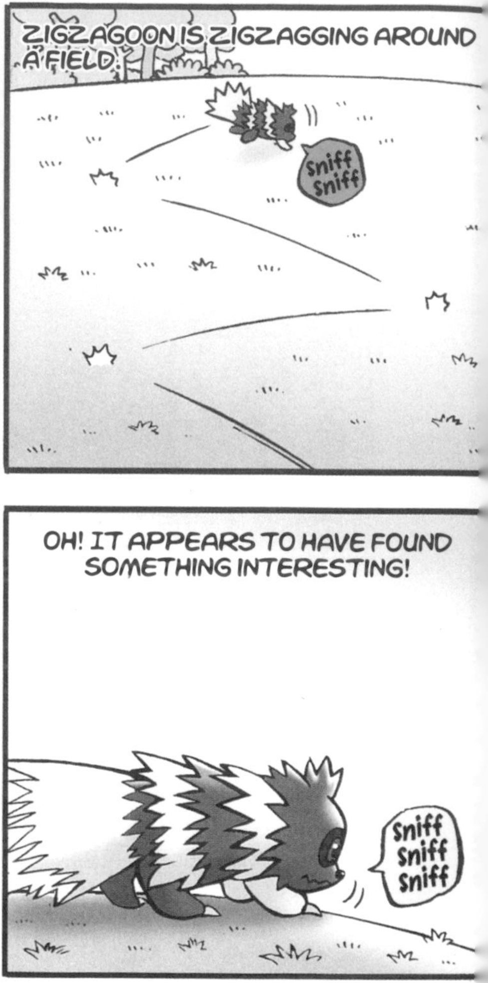

ZIGZAGOON IS ZIGZAGGING AROUND A FIELD.
Sniff sniff
OH! IT APPEARS TO HAVE FOUND SOMETHING INTERESTING!
Sniff Sniff Sniff

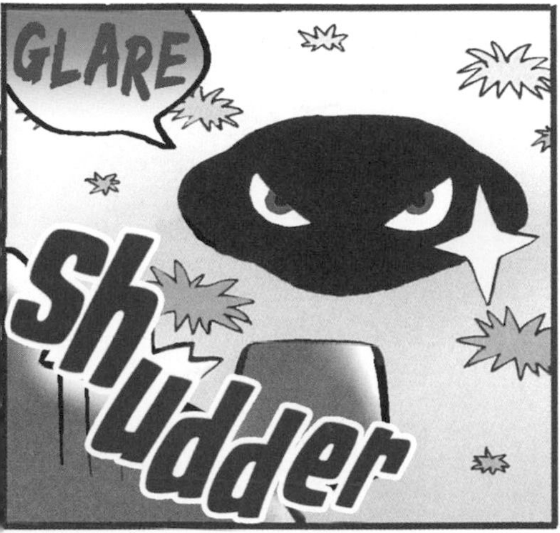
GLARE
Shudder

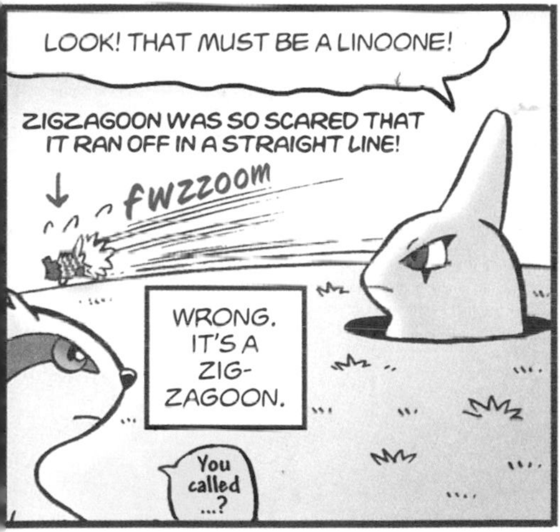
LOOK! THAT MUST BE A LINOONE!
ZIGZAGOON WAS SO SCARED THAT IT RAN OFF IN A STRAIGHT LINE!
FWZZOOM
WRONG. IT'S A ZIG-ZAGOON.
You called ...?

ZIGZAGOON

A Pokémon with abundant curiosity. It shows an interest in everything, so it always zigs and zags.

LINOONE

When running in a straight line, it can easily top 60 miles an hour. It has a tough time with curved roads.

CROCONAW

Shower Time...

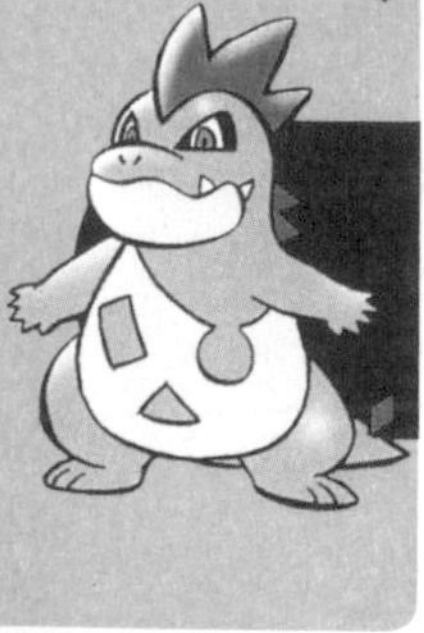

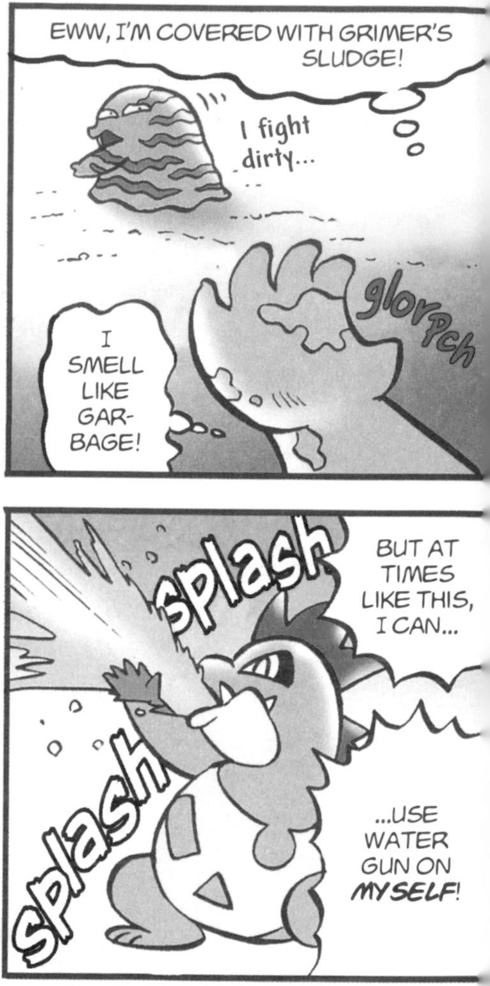
EWW, I'M COVERED WITH GRIMER'S SLUDGE!
I fight dirty...
glorpch
I SMELL LIKE GAR-BAGE!
splash
BUT AT TIMES LIKE THIS, I CAN...
splash
...USE WATER GUN ON MYSELF!

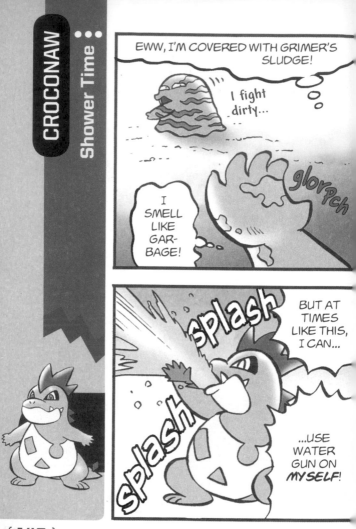

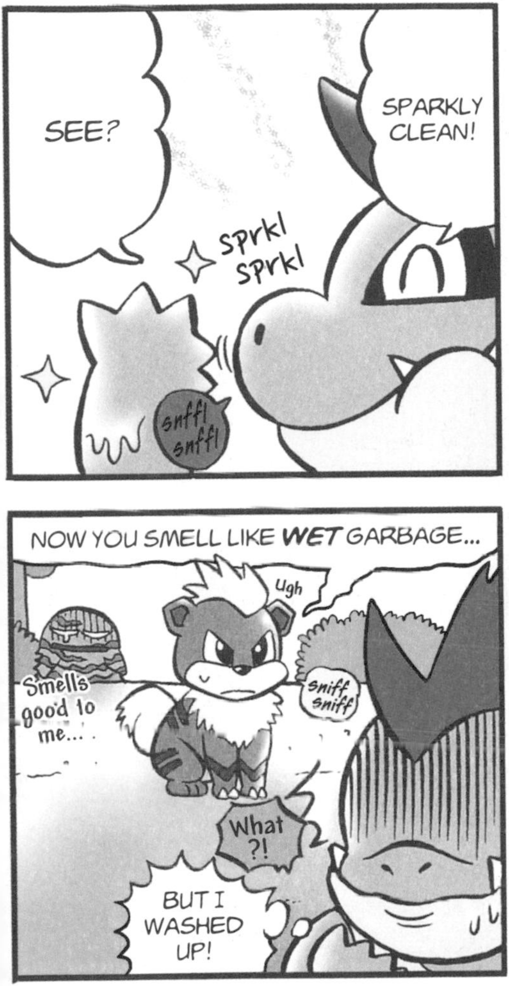
SEE?
SPARKLY CLEAN!
sprkl sprkl
snffl snffl
NOW YOU SMELL LIKE ***WET*** GARBAGE...
Ugh
Smells good to me...
sniff sniff
What ?!
BUT I WASHED UP!

CROCONAW

Once it has clamped its jaws on its foe, it will absolutely not let go. Because the tips of its fangs are forked back like barbed fishhooks, they become impossible to remove when they have sunk in. If it loses a fang, a new one grows back in its place. There are always 48 fangs lining its mouth.

MAGIKARP LUDICOLO

Bath Time...

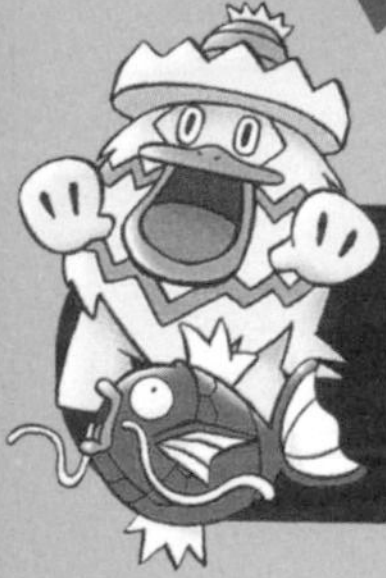

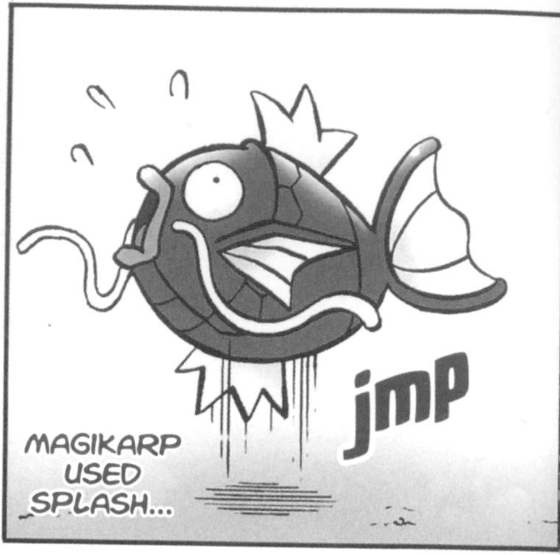
jmp
MAGIKARP USED SPLASH...

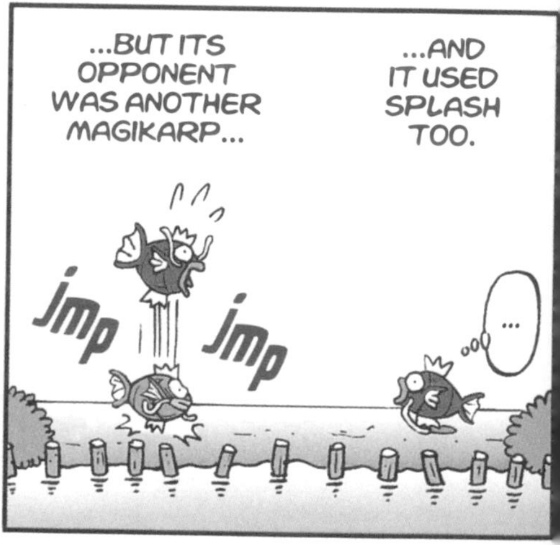
...BUT ITS OPPONENT WAS ANOTHER MAGIKARP...
...AND IT USED SPLASH TOO.
jmp
jmp
...

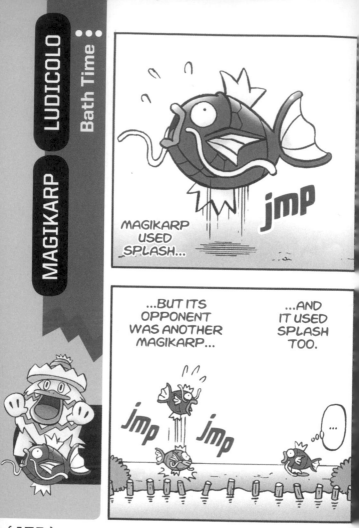

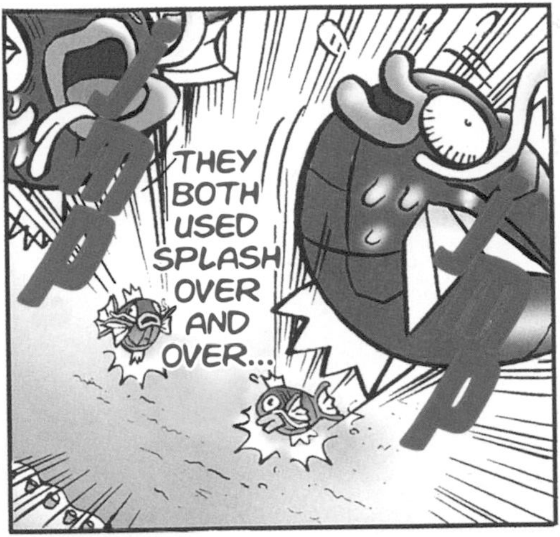
THEY BOTH USED SPLASH OVER AND OVER...

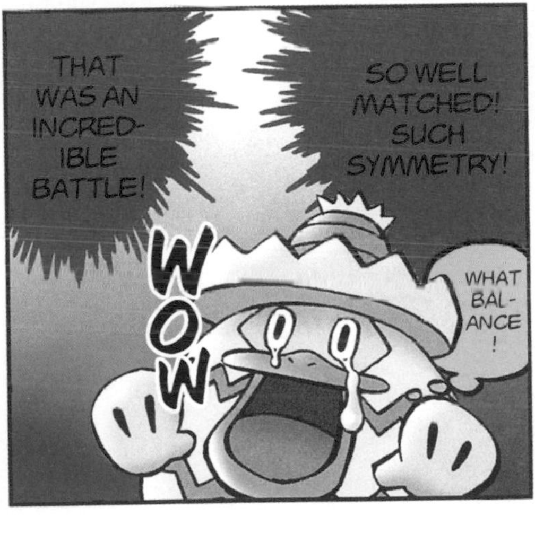
THAT WAS AN INCRED-IBLE BATTLE!
SO WELL MATCHED! SUCH SYMMETRY!
WOW
WHAT BAL-ANCE!

MAGIKARP

It is a pathetic excuse for a Pokémon that is only capable of flopping and splashing.

LUDICOLO

Upon hearing an upbeat and cheerful rhythm, the cells in Ludicolo's body become very energetic and active. It does not quail even when it faces a tough opponent.

PORYGON2 ••• Better Than Ever

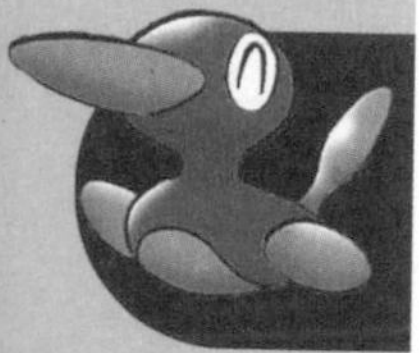

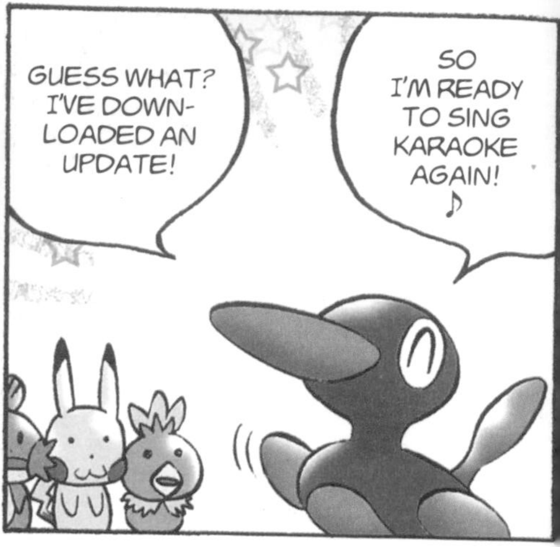
GUESS WHAT? I'VE DOWN-LOADED AN UPDATE!
SO I'M READY TO SING KARAOKE AGAIN! ♪

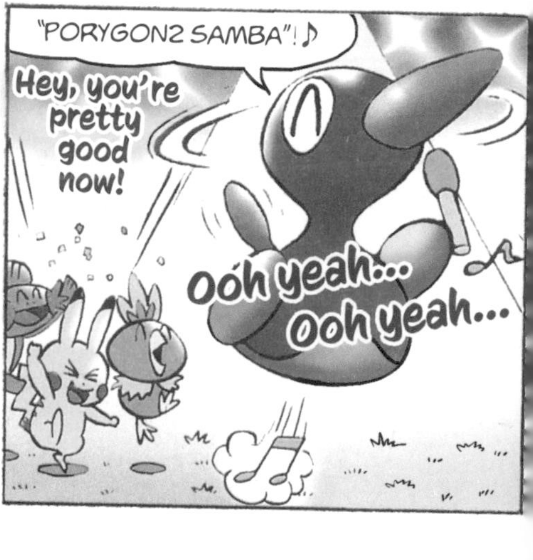
"PORYGON2 SAMBA"! ♪
Hey, you're pretty good now!
Ooh yeah... Ooh yeah...

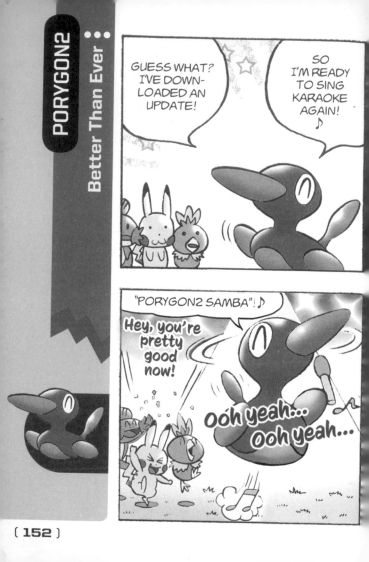

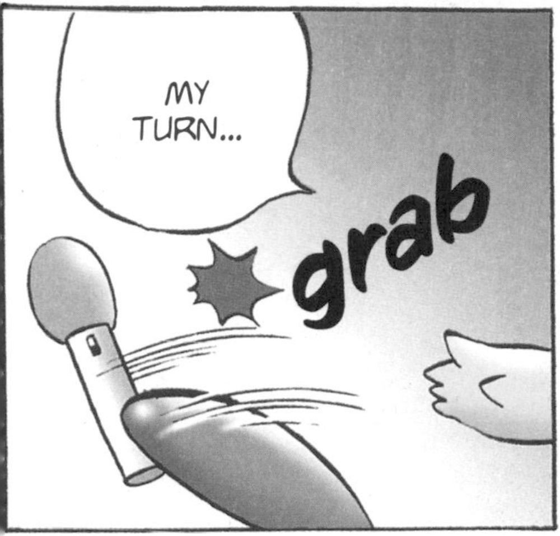
MY TURN...
grab

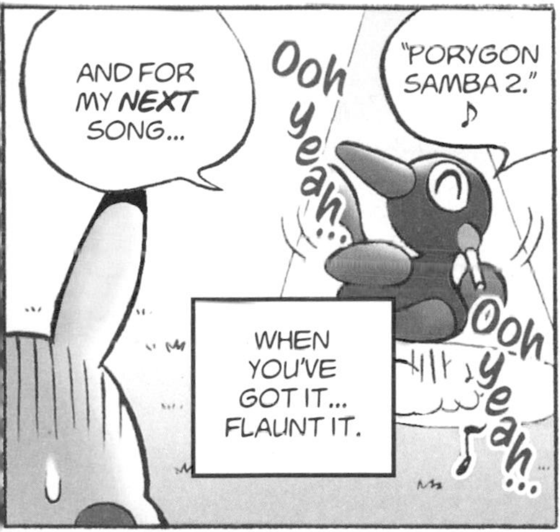
AND FOR MY ***NEXT*** SONG...
Ooh yeah!..
"PORYGON SAMBA 2." ♪
WHEN YOU'VE GOT IT... FLAUNT IT.
Ooh yeah..

PORYGON2

It was created by humans using the power of science. This upgraded version of Porygon is designed for space exploration. However, it can't fly. It has been given artificial intelligence that enables it to learn new gestures and emotions on its own.

TORCHIC

To Every Season

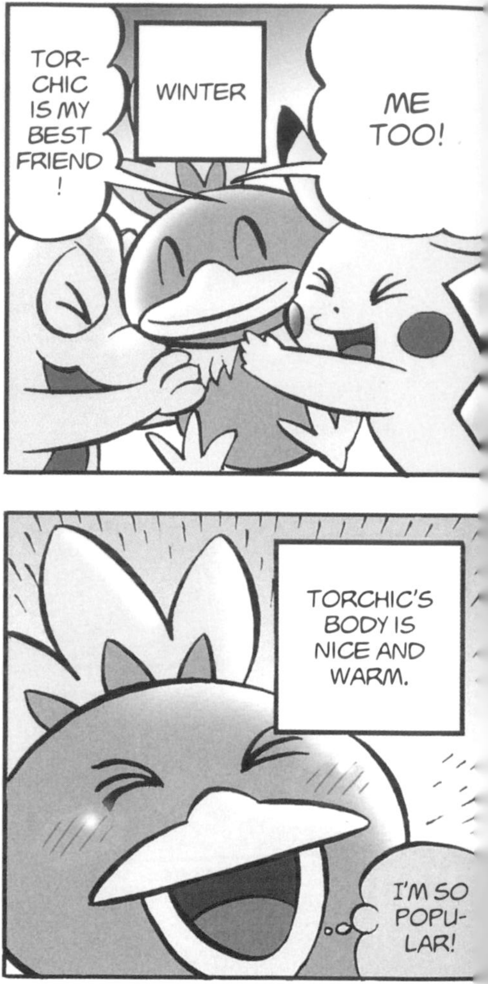
TOR-CHIC IS MY BEST FRIEND!
WINTER
ME TOO!
TORCHIC'S BODY IS NICE AND WARM.
I'M SO POPU-LAR!

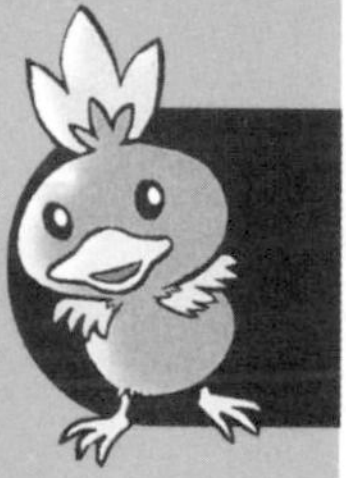

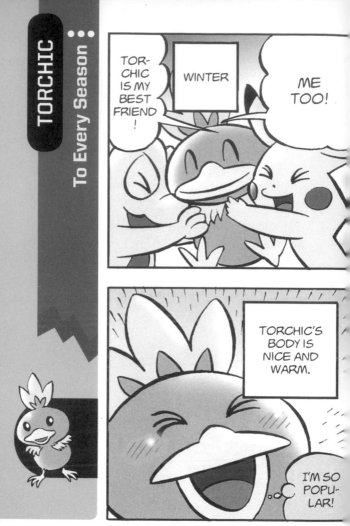

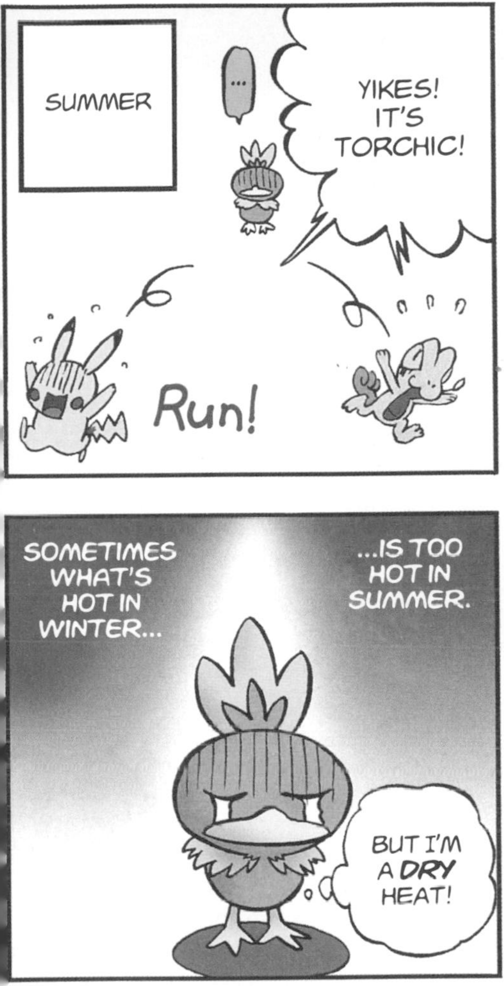
SUMMER
...
YIKES! IT'S TORCHIC!
Run!
SOMETIMES WHAT'S HOT IN WINTER...
...IS TOO HOT IN SUMMER.
BUT I'M A **DRY** HEAT!

TORCHIC

It has a flame sac inside its belly that perpetually burns. It feels warm if it is hugged. This Pokémon breathes fire of over 1,800 degrees Fahrenheit, including fireballs that leave the foe scorched black. Torchic dislikes darkness because it can't see its surroundings.

BELDUM METANG METAGROSS

King of Something

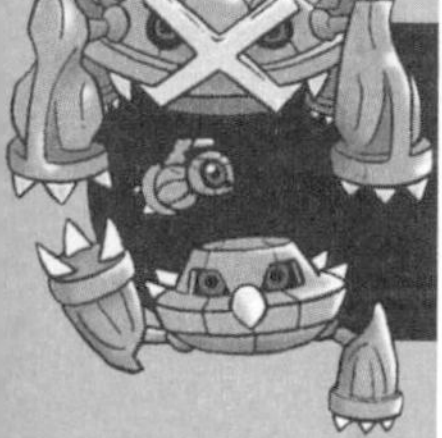

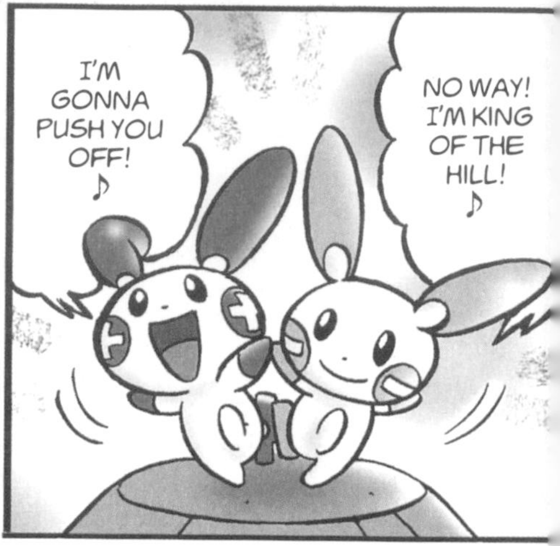
I'M GONNA PUSH YOU OFF! ♪
NO WAY! I'M KING OF THE HILL! ♪

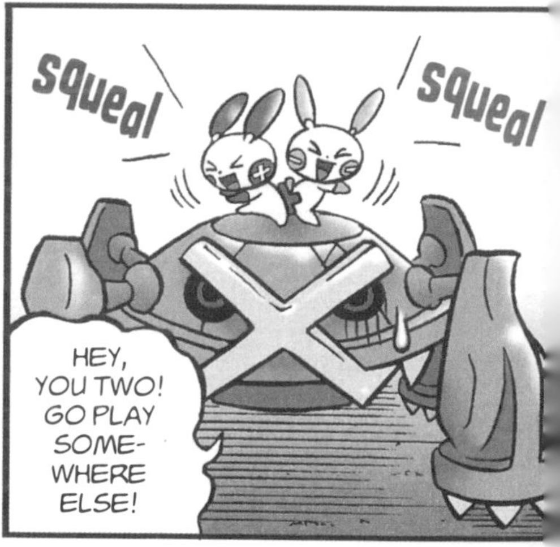
squeal
squeal
HEY, YOU TWO! GO PLAY SOME-WHERE ELSE!

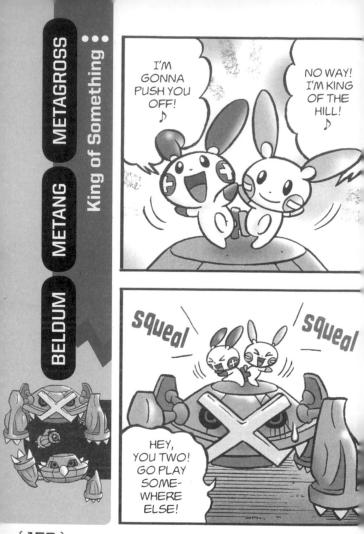

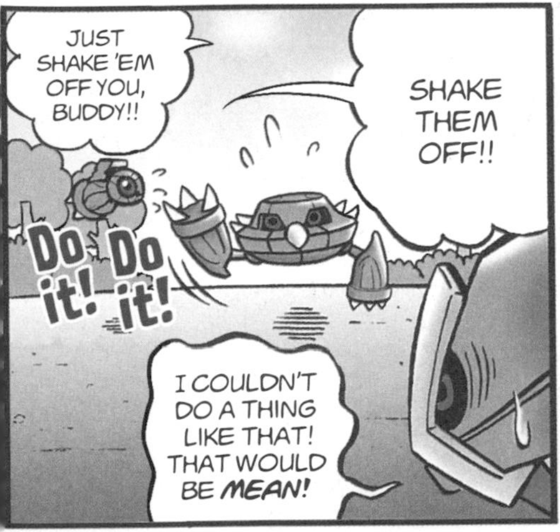
JUST SHAKE 'EM OFF YOU, BUDDY!!
SHAKE THEM OFF!!
Do it! Do it!
I COULDN'T DO A THING LIKE THAT! THAT WOULD BE MEAN!

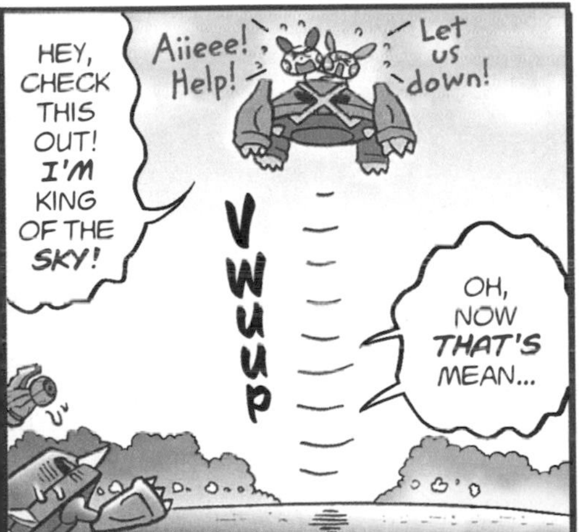
HEY, CHECK THIS OUT! I'M KING OF THE SKY!
Aiieee! Help!
Let us down!
VWUUP
OH, NOW THAT'S MEAN...

BELDUM

It keeps itself floating by generating a magnetic force that repels the world's natural magnetism.

METANG

When two Beldum fuse together, Metang is formed. It flies at over 60 miles per hour.

METAGROSS

It is formed by two Metang fusing. Its four brains are said to be superior to a supercomputer.

CHARMELEON URSARING

Hot Foot...

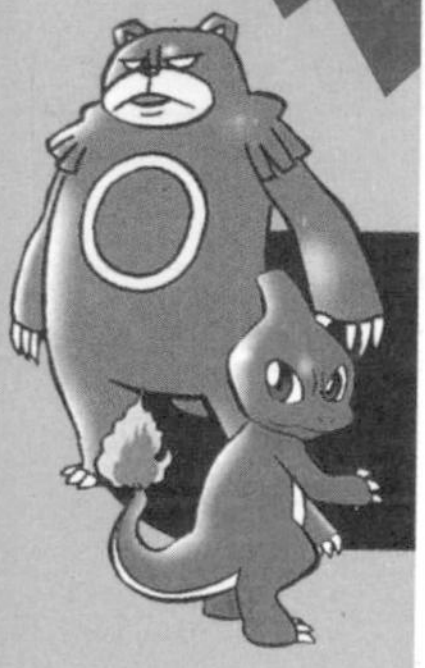

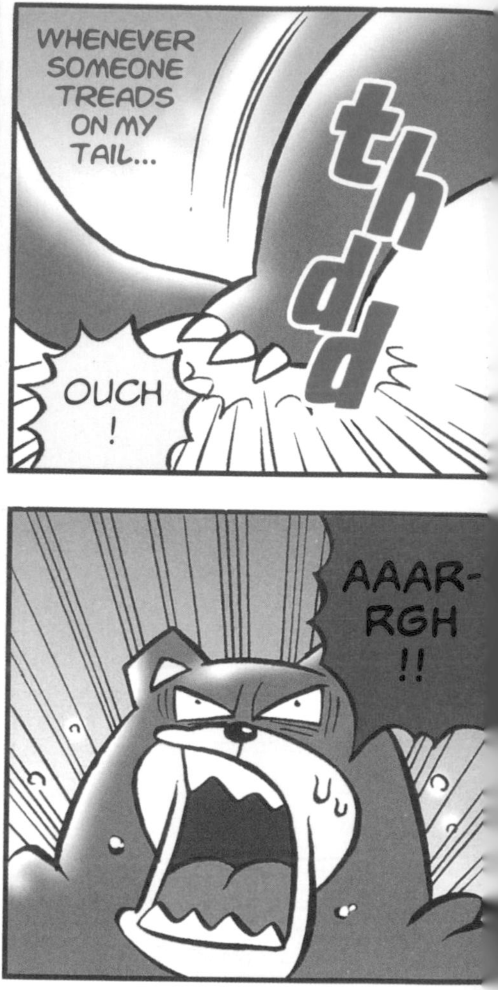
WHENEVER SOMEONE TREADS ON MY TAIL...
thdd
OUCH!
AAAR-RGH!!

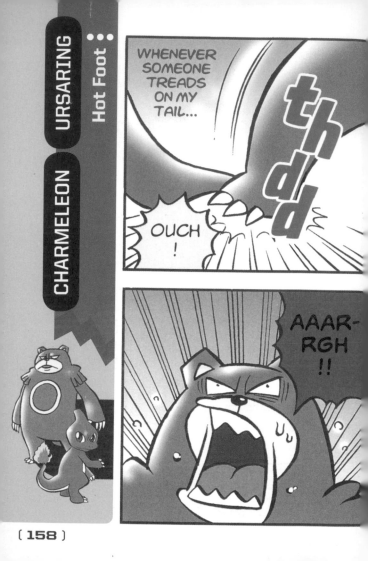

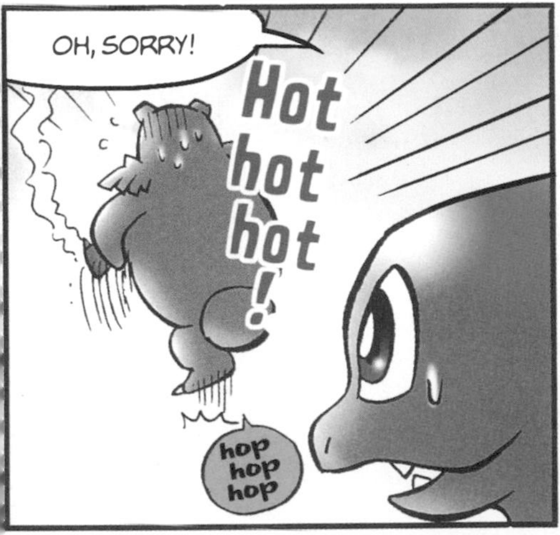
OH, SORRY!
Hot hot hot!
hop hop hop

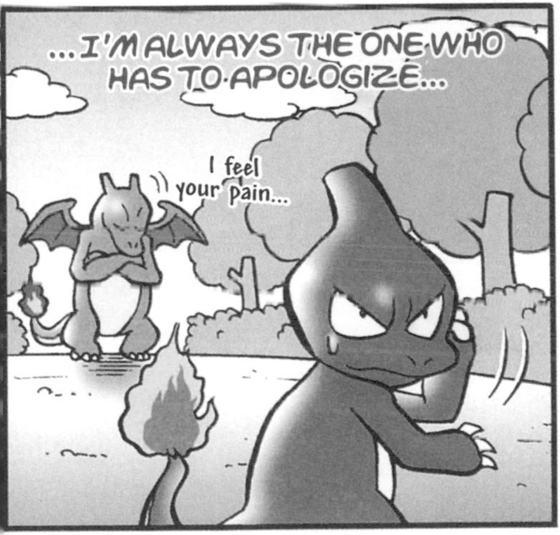
...I'M ALWAYS THE ONE WHO HAS TO APOLOGIZE...
I feel your pain...

CHARMELEON

It lashes about with its tail to knock down its foe. If it encounters a strong enemy, it becomes agitated, and the flame on its tail flares with a bluish-white color.

URSARING

In the forests inhabited by Ursaring, it is said that there are many streams and towering trees where they gather food. This Pokémon walks through its forest gathering food every day.

VILEPLUME

Use Your Head...

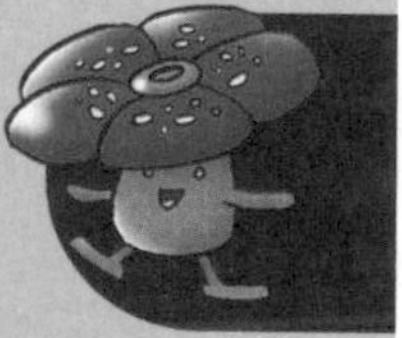

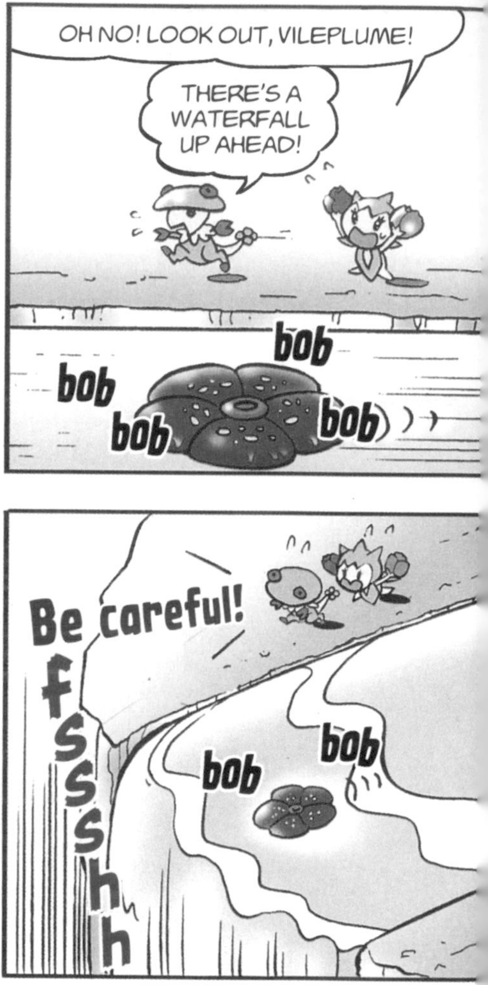
OH NO! LOOK OUT, VILEPLUME!
THERE'S A WATERFALL UP AHEAD!
bob
bob
bob
bob
Be careful!
fssshh
bob
bob

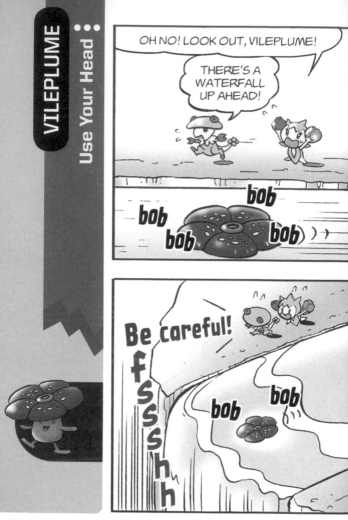

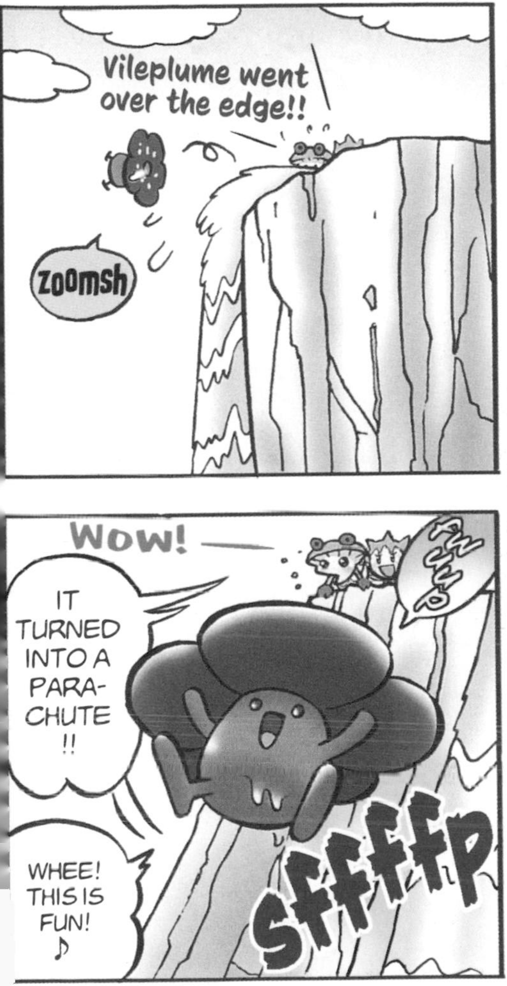

Vileplume went over the edge!!
ZOOMSH
WOW!
IT TURNED INTO A PARA-CHUTE!!
FWUUP
WHEE! THIS IS FUN! ♪
SFFFFP

VILEPLUME

Its petals are the largest in the world. It fiendishly scatters allergy-causing pollen from its petals. In seasons when it produces more pollen, the air around a Vileplume turns yellow with the powder as it walks. The larger its petals, the more pollen is scattered. The pollen is highly toxic and causes paralysis.

GROWLITHE TAILLOW

Common Scents

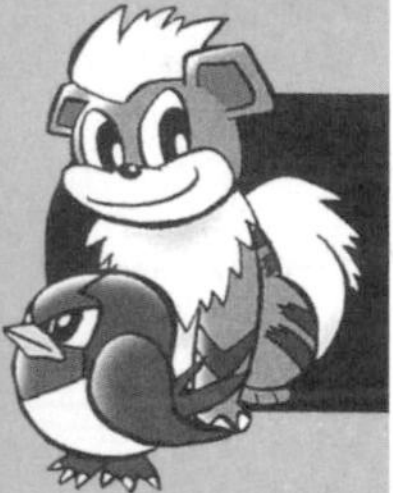

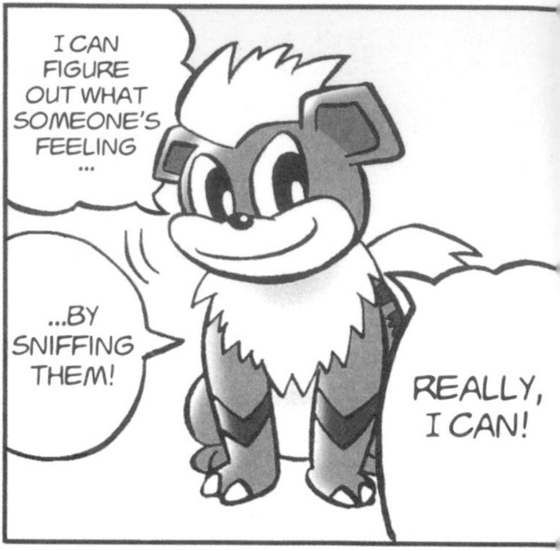
I CAN FIGURE OUT WHAT SOMEONE'S FEELING ...
...BY SNIFFING THEM!
REALLY, I CAN!

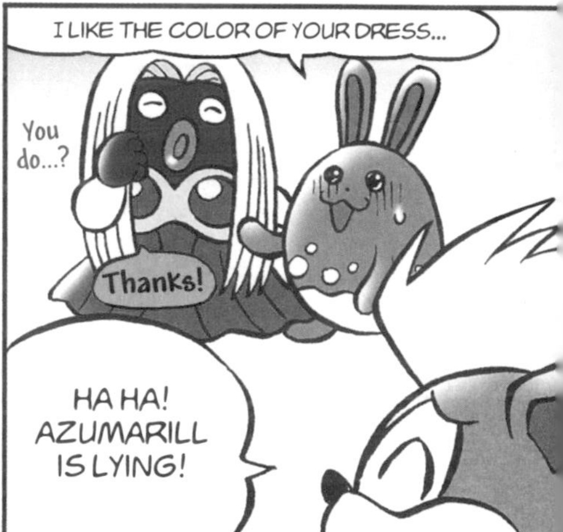
I LIKE THE COLOR OF YOUR DRESS...
You do...?
Thanks!
HA HA! AZUMARILL IS LYING!

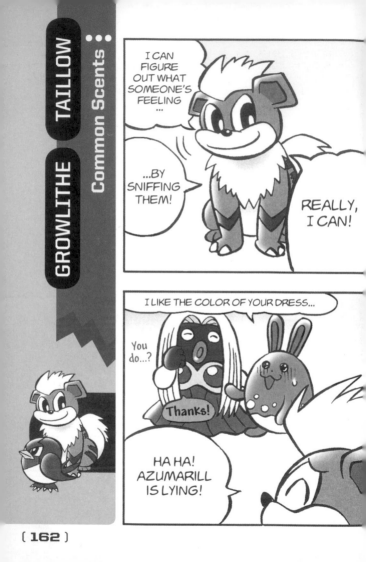

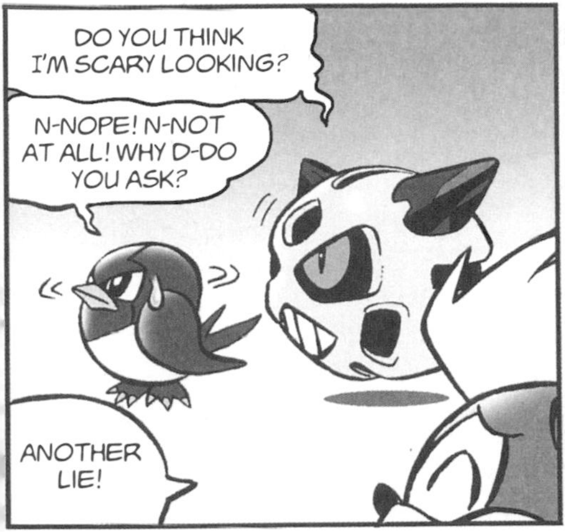
DO YOU THINK I'M SCARY LOOKING?
N-NOPE! N-NOT AT ALL! WHY D-DO YOU ASK?
ANOTHER LIE!

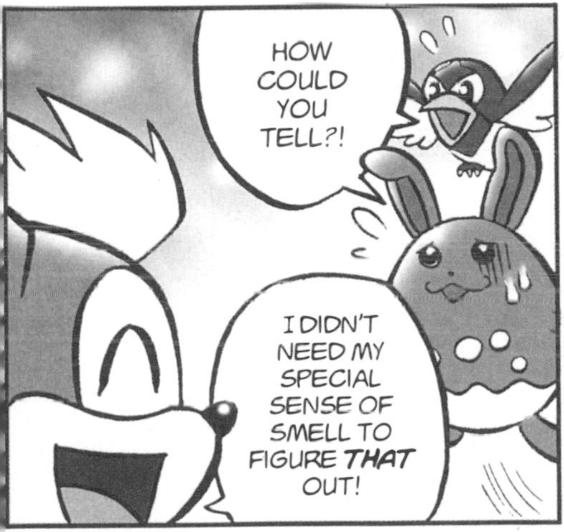
HOW COULD YOU TELL?!
I DIDN'T NEED MY SPECIAL SENSE OF SMELL TO FIGURE *THAT* OUT!

GROWLITHE

Very friendly and faithful to people. It uses its advanced olfactory sense to determine the emotions of other living things.

TAILLOW

Although it is small, it is very courageous. This gutsy Pokémon will remain defiant even after a loss. However, its will weakens if it becomes hungry.

POOCHYENA SKITTY

Listen Closely...

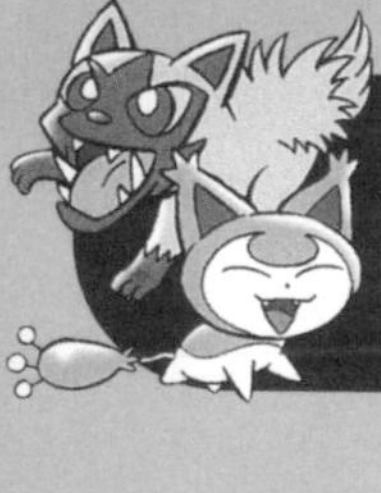

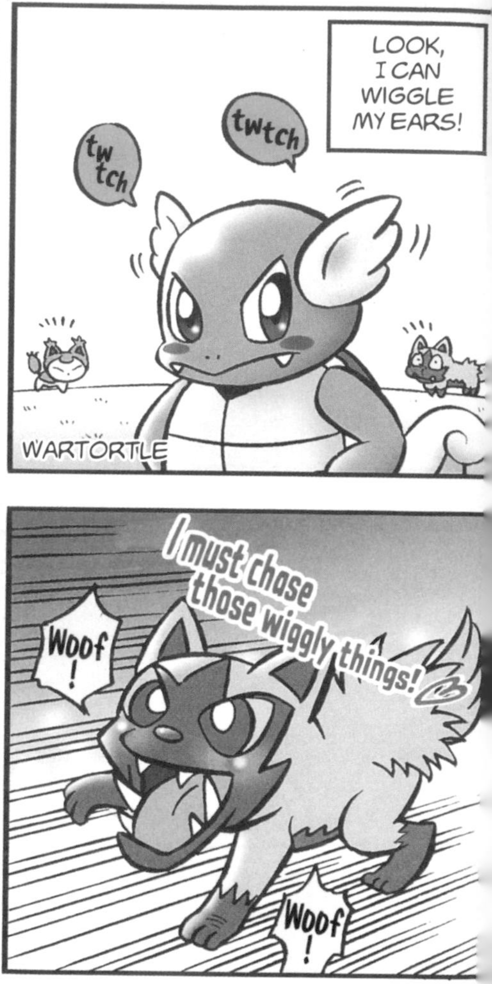
LOOK, I CAN WIGGLE MY EARS!
twtch
tw tch
WARTORTLE
I must chase those wiggly things!
Woof!
Woof!

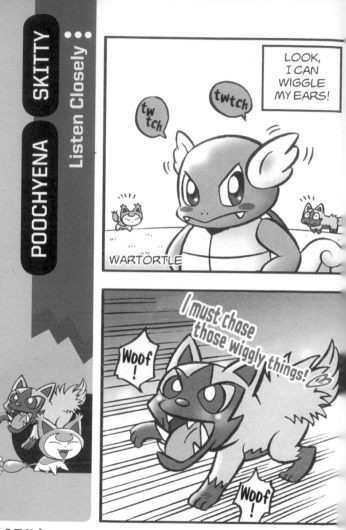

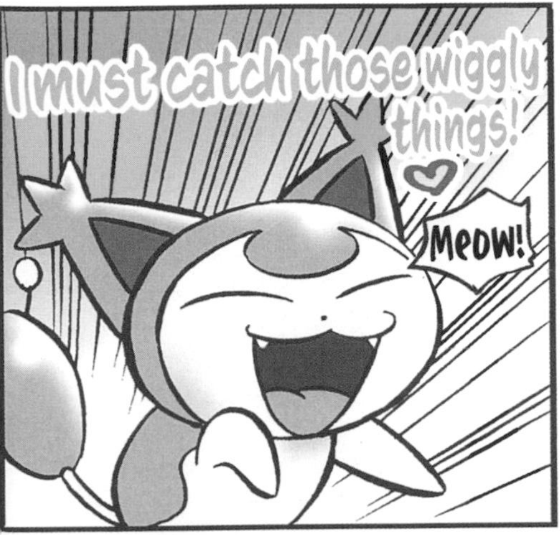
I must catch those wiggly things!
MEOW!

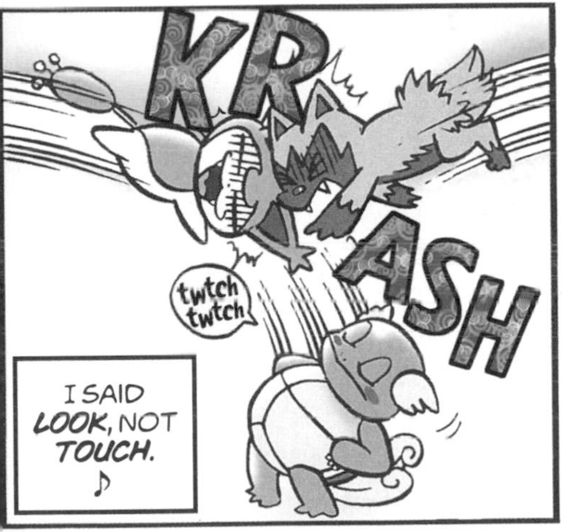
KRASH
twtch twtch
I SAID LOOK, NOT TOUCH. ♪

POOCHYENA

It takes a bite at anything that moves. It chases after fleeing targets tenaciously. It savagely threatens foes with bared fangs.

SKITTY

It has a habit of becoming fascinated by moving objects and chasing them around. This Pokémon is known to chase after its own tail and become dizzy. In the wild, it lives in the holes of trees in forests.

LATIAS LATIOS

Armchair Traveler

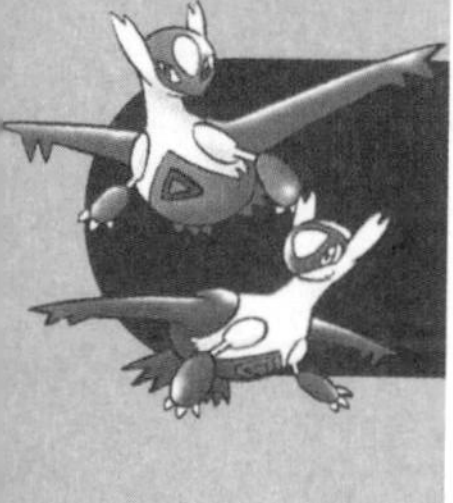

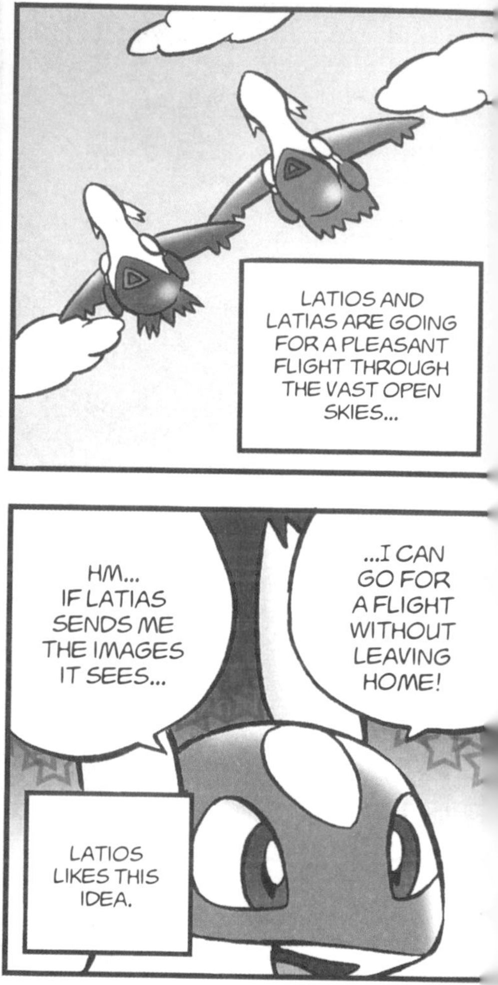
LATIOS AND LATIAS ARE GOING FOR A PLEASANT FLIGHT THROUGH THE VAST OPEN SKIES...
HM... IF LATIAS SENDS ME THE IMAGES IT SEES...
...I CAN GO FOR A FLIGHT WITHOUT LEAVING HOME!
LATIOS LIKES THIS IDEA.

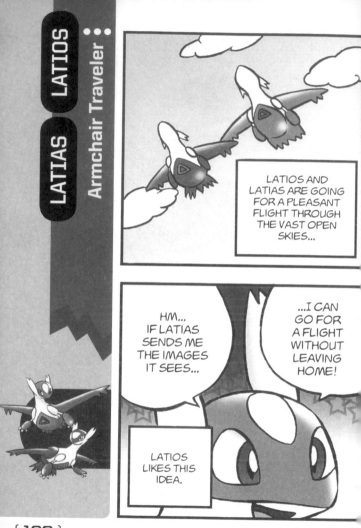

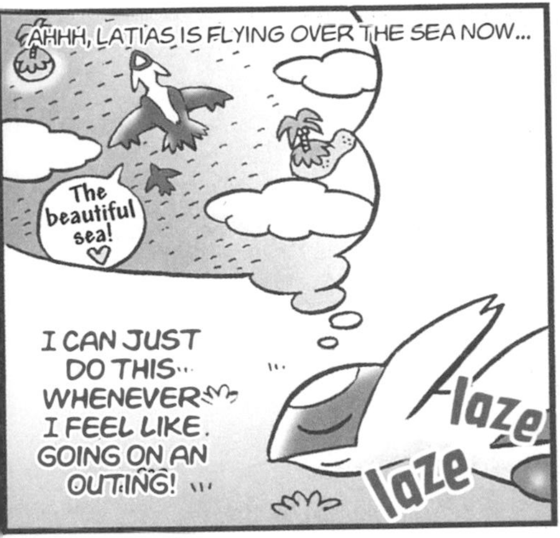
AHHH, LATIAS IS FLYING OVER THE SEA NOW...
The beautiful sea! ♡
I CAN JUST DO THIS... WHENEVER I FEEL LIKE GOING ON AN OUTING!
laze
laze

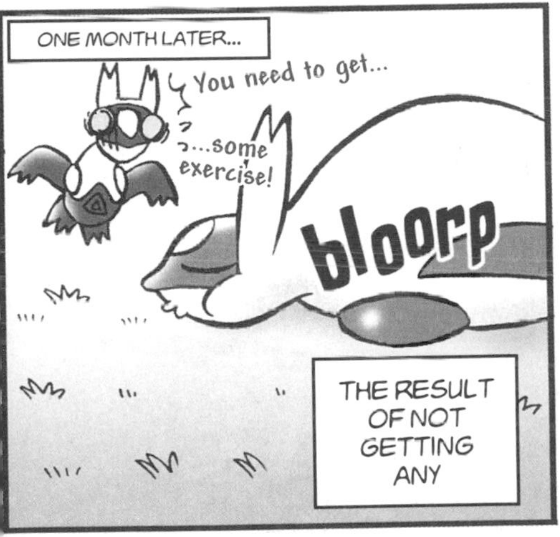
ONE MONTH LATER...
You need to get...
...some exercise!
bloorp
THE RESULT OF NOT GETTING ANY

LATIAS

It can telepathically communicate with people. It changes its appearance using its down that refracts light.

LATIOS

It has a docile temperament and dislikes fighting. Tucking in its forelegs, it can fly faster than a jet plane.

SENTRET FURRET Point of View

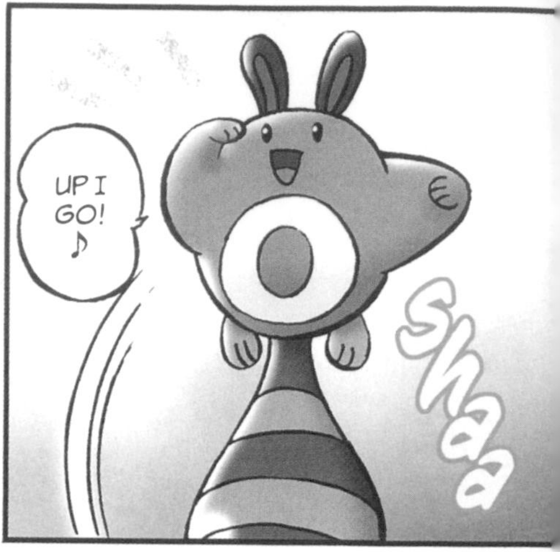

UP I GO! ♪
shaa

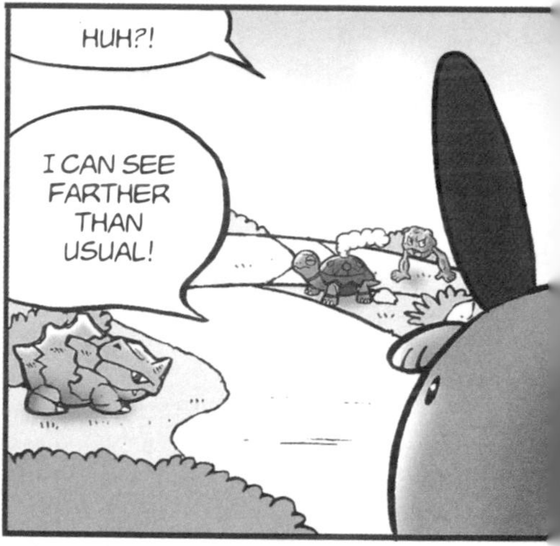

HUH?!
I CAN SEE FARTHER THAN USUAL!

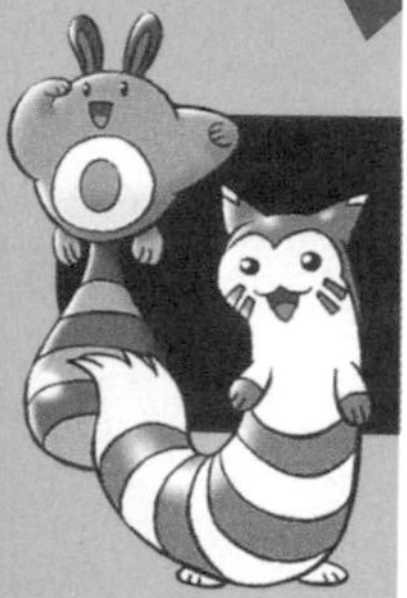

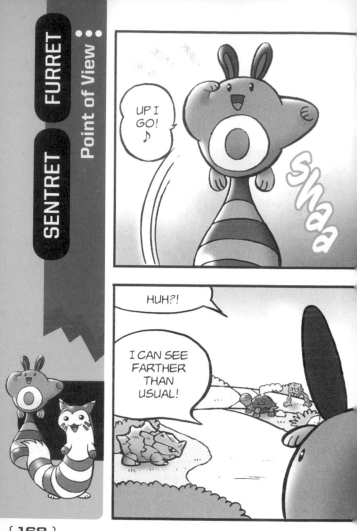

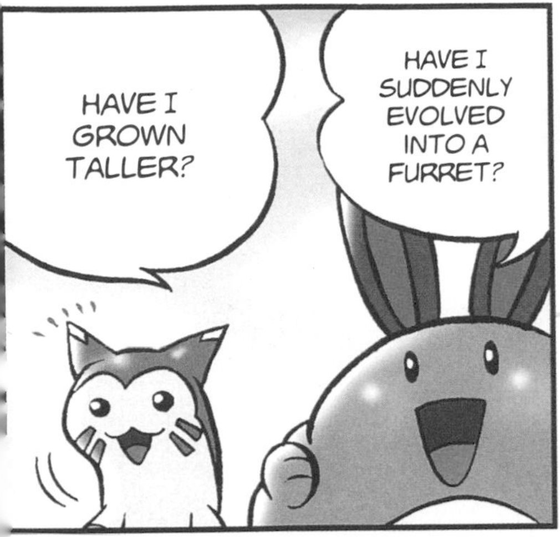
HAVE I GROWN TALLER?
HAVE I SUDDENLY EVOLVED INTO A FURRET?

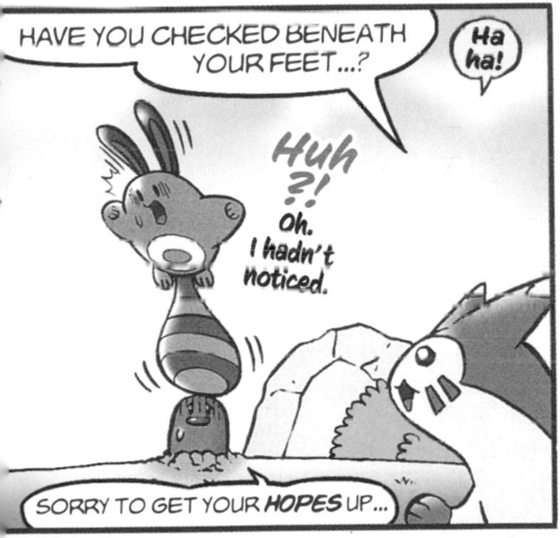
HAVE YOU CHECKED BENEATH YOUR FEET...?
Ha ha!
Huh ?!
Oh. I hadn't noticed.
SORRY TO GET YOUR **HOPES** UP...

SENTRET

A very cautious Pokémon, it raises itself up using its tail to get a better view of its surroundings. When this Pokémon becomes separated from its pack, it becomes incapable of sleep due to fear.

FURRET

In spite of its short limbs, this Pokémon is very nimble and fleet of foot. It makes a nest to suit its long, skinny body.

ENTEI

Hard to Please...

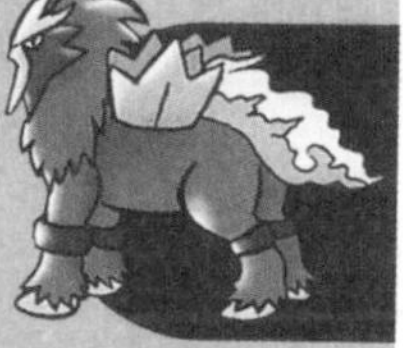

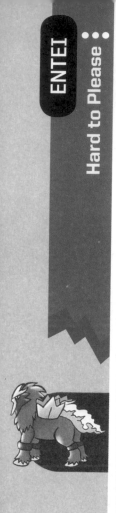

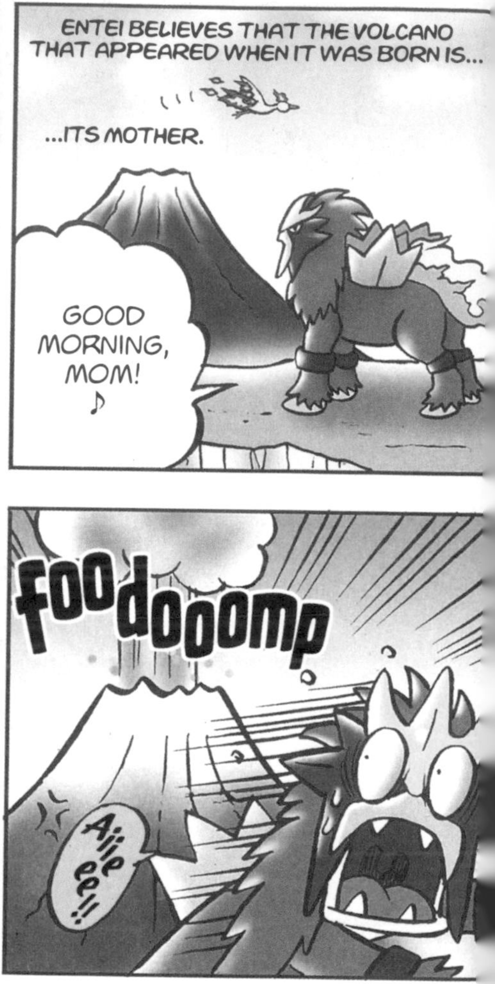
ENTEI BELIEVES THAT THE VOLCANO THAT APPEARED WHEN IT WAS BORN IS...
...ITS MOTHER.
GOOD MORNING, MOM! ♪
FOODOOOOMP
Aiiiee!!

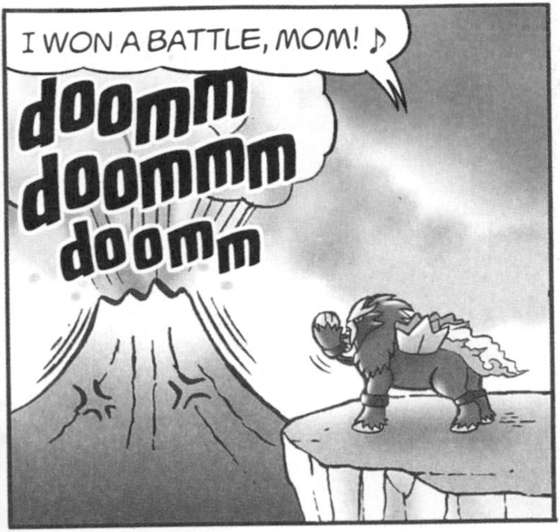
I WON A BATTLE, MOM! ♪
doomm
doommm
doomm

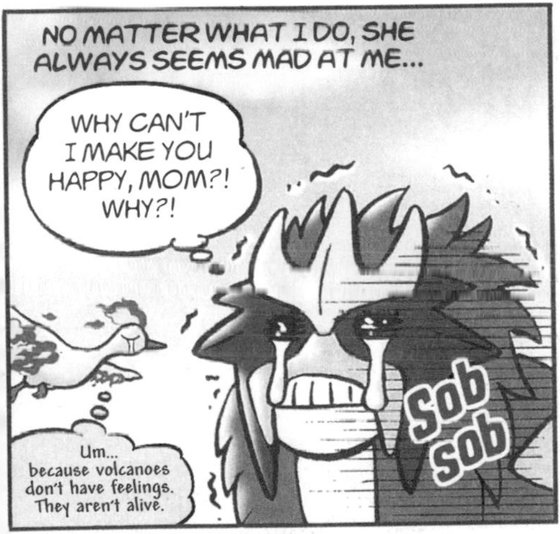
NO MATTER WHAT I DO, SHE ALWAYS SEEMS MAD AT ME...
WHY CAN'T I MAKE YOU HAPPY, MOM?! WHY?!
Sob sob
Um... because volcanoes don't have feelings. They aren't alive.

ENTEI

It is said that one is born every time a new volcano appears. Entei embodies the passion of magma. This brawny Pokémon wanders the world, spouting flames hotter than a volcano's magma.

WOOPER

It's Not Nice to Tease...

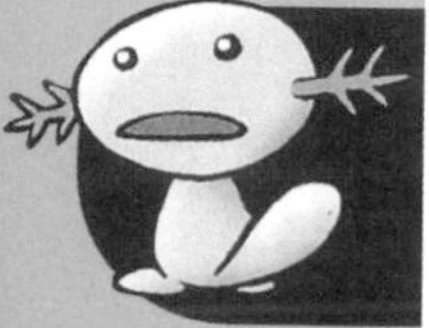

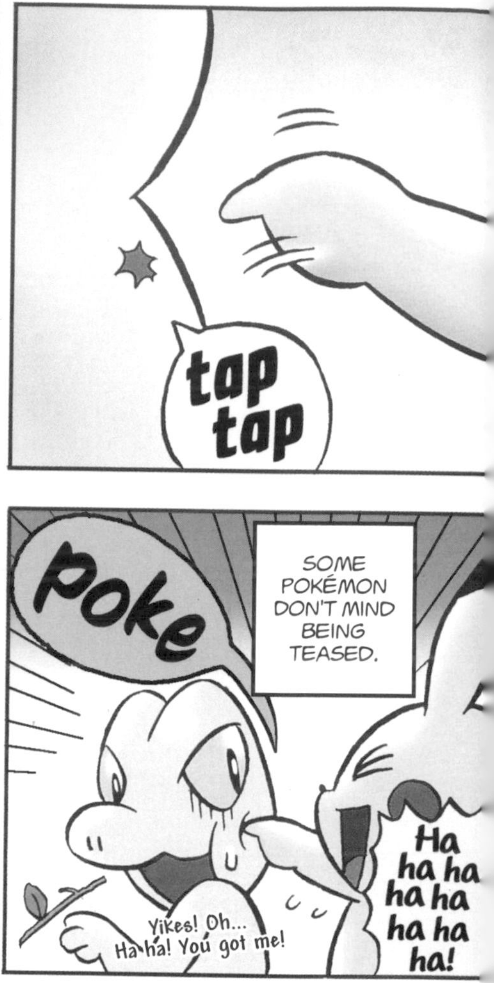
tap tap
Poke
SOME POKÉMON DON'T MIND BEING TEASED.
Yikes! Oh... Ha ha! You got me!
Ha ha ha ha ha ha ha ha ha!

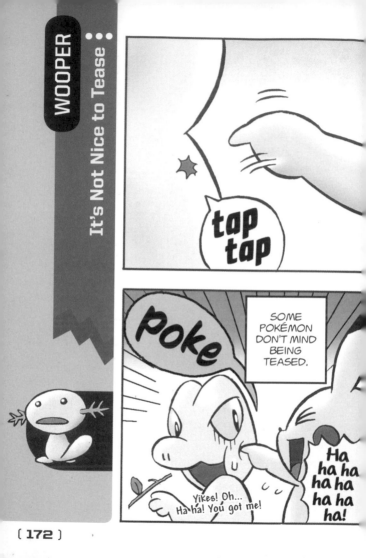

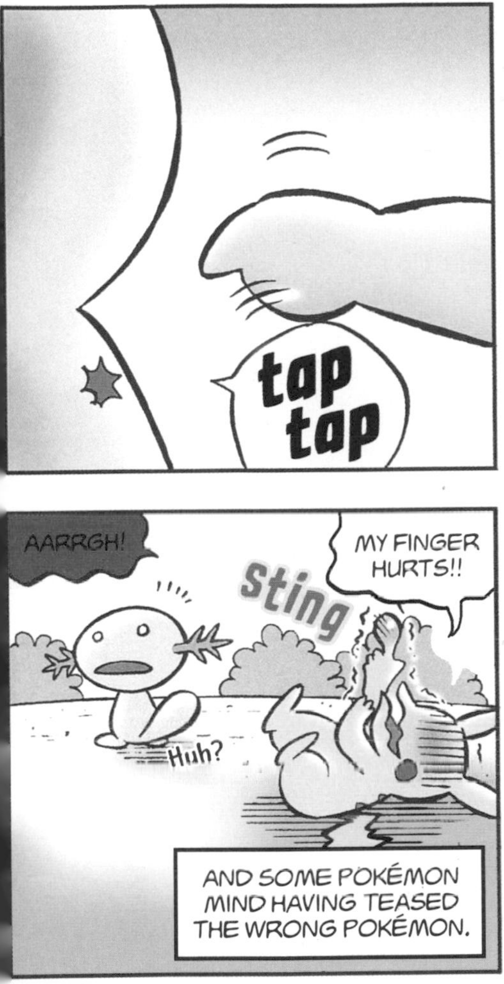
tap
tap
AARRGH!
MY FINGER HURTS!!
Sting
Huh?
AND SOME POKÉMON MIND HAVING TEASED THE WRONG POKÉMON.

WOOPER

It usually lives in cold water. However, it occasionally comes out onto land in search of food. On land, it coats its body with a gooey, toxic film that causes a shooting pain in anyone that touches it.

KYOGRE MARSHTOMP

Needs Waterproofing...

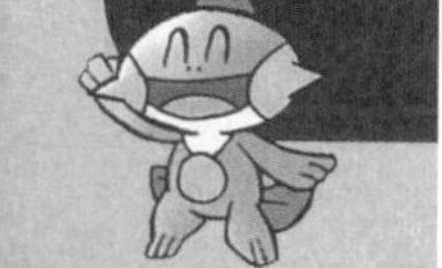

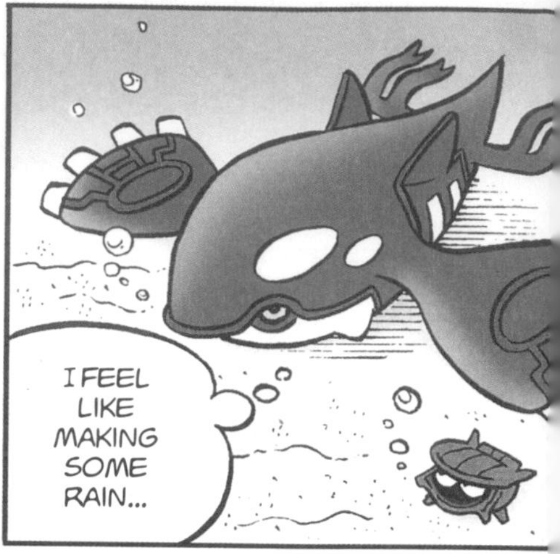
I FEEL LIKE MAKING SOME RAIN...

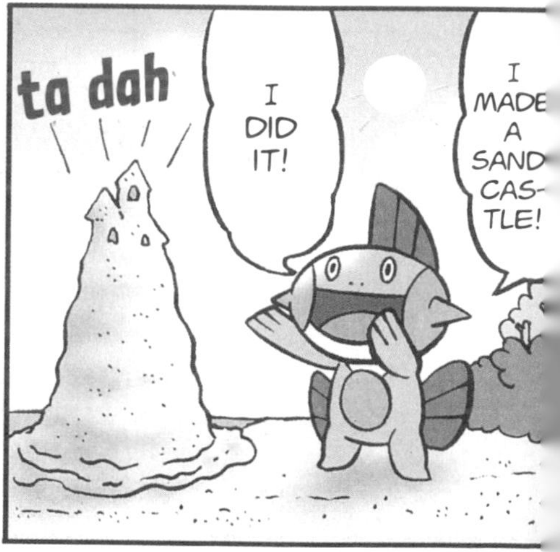
ta dah
I DID IT!
I MADE A SAND CAS-TLE!

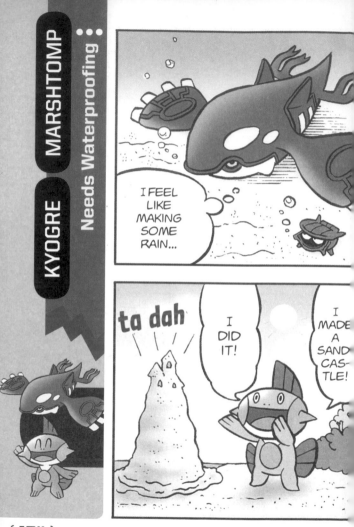

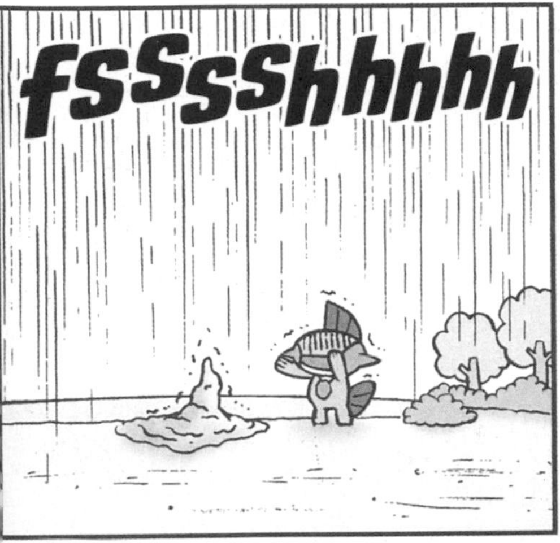
fsSsShhhhh

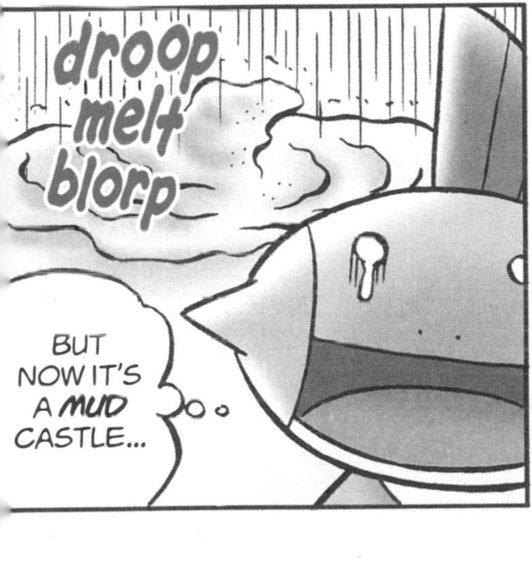
droop
melt
blorp
BUT NOW IT'S A *MUD* CASTLE...

KYOGRE

This Pokémon is said to have expanded the sea by bringing heavy rains. It has the power to control water. It saves people who are suffering from droughts.

MARSHTOMP

Because it weakens if its skin dries out, it replenishes its fluids by playing in mud. It excels at traveling quickly through mud.

SHARPEDO OMASTAR

Targeted Attack

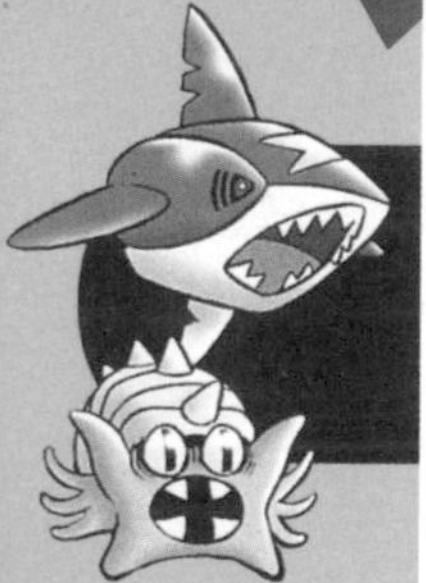

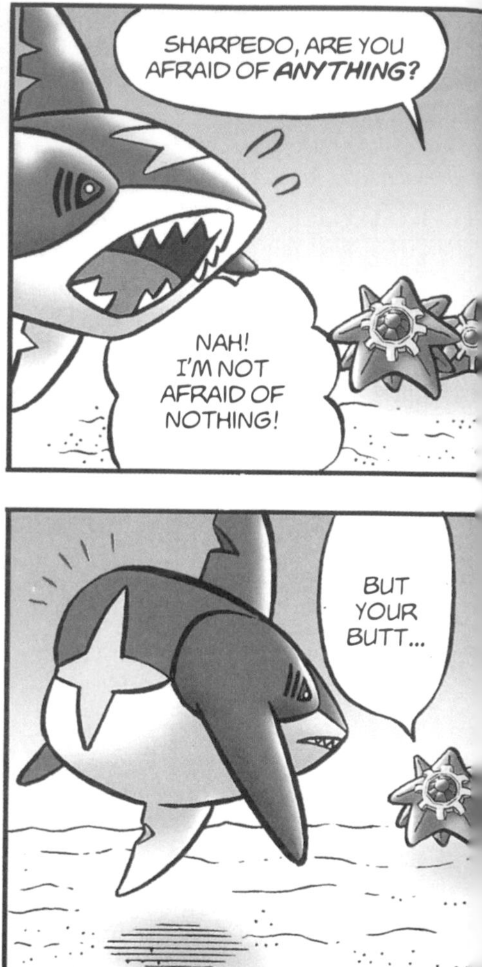

SHARPEDO, ARE YOU AFRAID OF *ANYTHING?*
NAH! I'M NOT AFRAID OF NOTHING!
BUT YOUR BUTT...

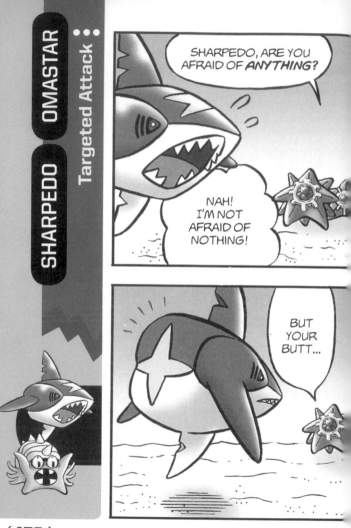

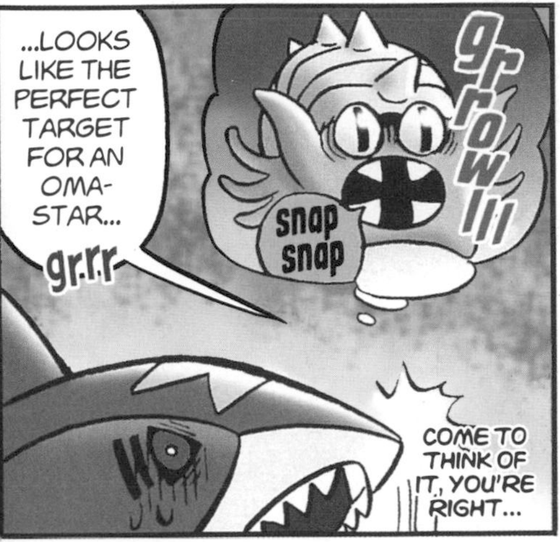
...LOOKS LIKE THE PERFECT TARGET FOR AN OMA-STAR...
grrowl!!
snap snap
gr.r.r
COME TO THINK OF IT, YOU'RE RIGHT...

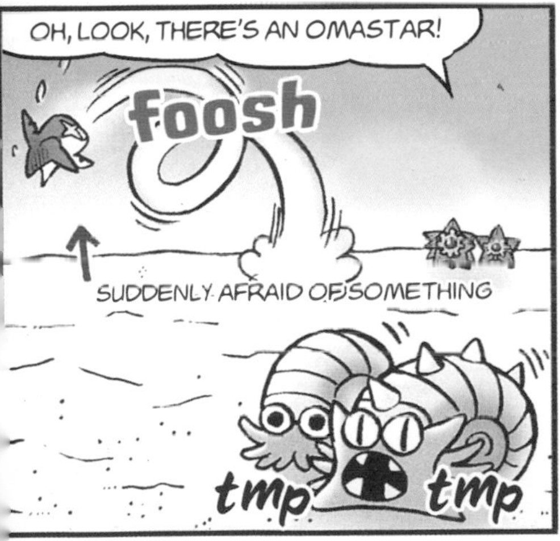
OH, LOOK, THERE'S AN OMASTAR!
foosh
SUDDENLY AFRAID OF SOMETHING
tmp
tmp

SHARPEDO

The vicious and sly thug of the sea. Sharpedo can swim at speeds of up to 75 mph by jetting seawater out of its backside.

OMASTAR

Its tentacles are as highly developed as hands and feet. As soon as it ensnares its prey, it bites.

GIRAFARIG WOBBUFFET

Tail Tale

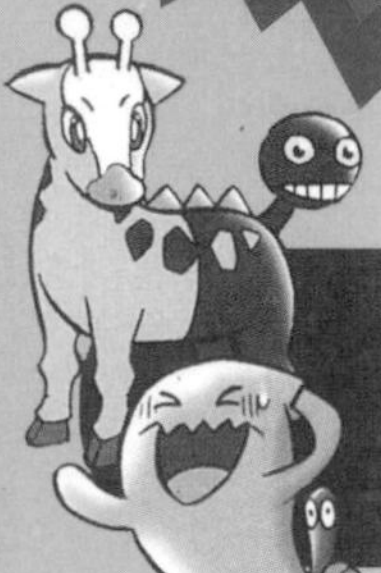

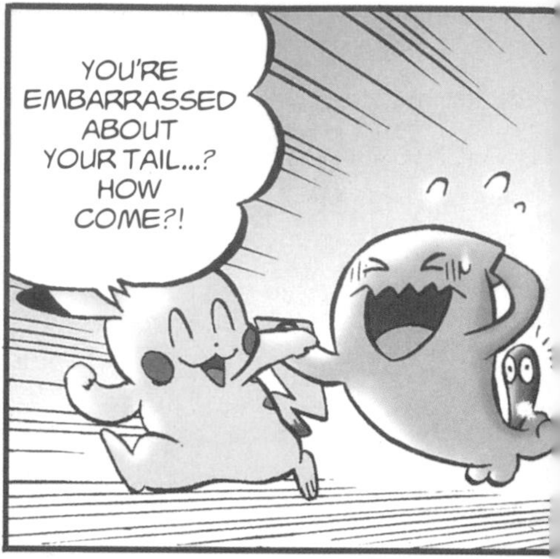
YOU'RE EMBARRASSED ABOUT YOUR TAIL...? HOW COME?!

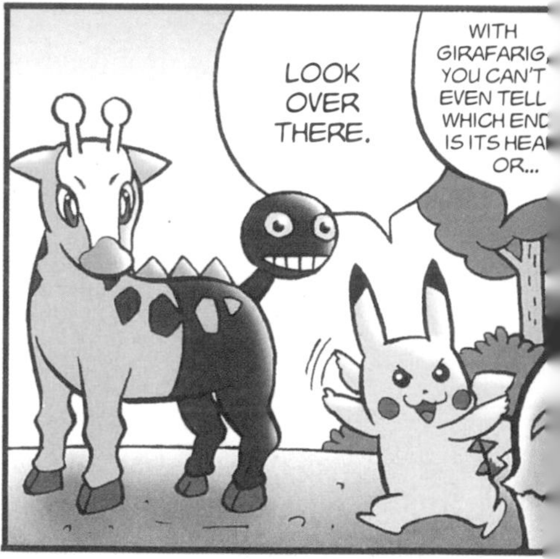
LOOK OVER THERE.
WITH GIRAFARIG, YOU CAN'T EVEN TELL WHICH EN IS ITS HEA OR...

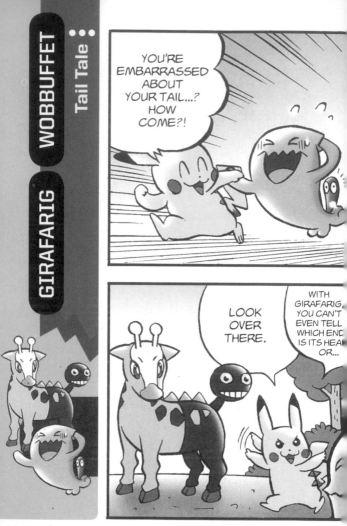

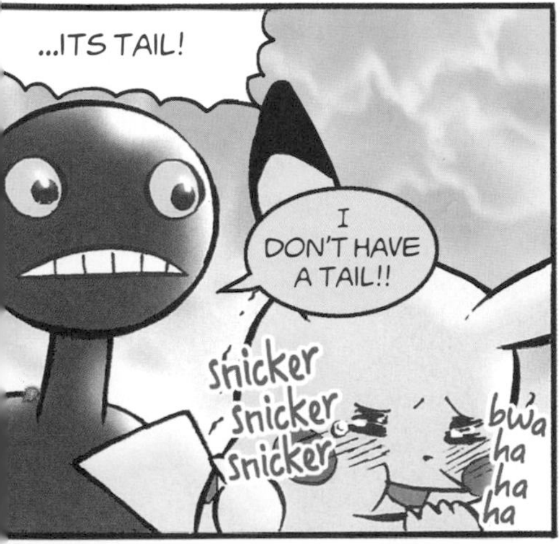
...ITS TAIL!
I DON'T HAVE A TAIL!!
snicker snicker snicker
bwa ha ha ha

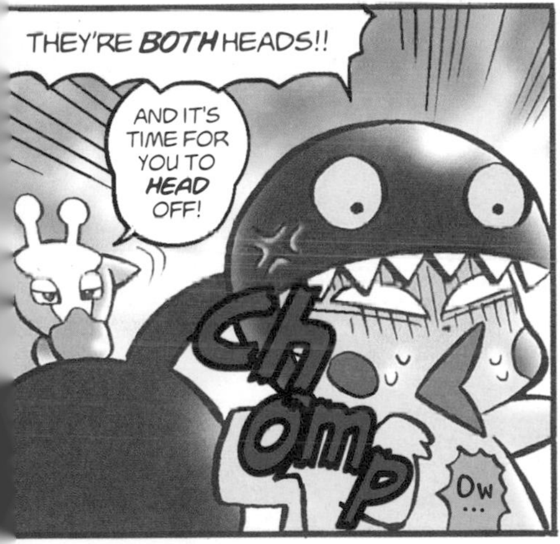
THEY'RE **BOTH** HEADS!!
AND IT'S TIME FOR YOU TO **HEAD** OFF!
Chomp
Ow...

GIRAFARIG

Its tail has a small brain of its own. Beware! If you get close, it may react to your scent and bite.

WOBBUFFET

To keep its pitch-black tail hidden, it lives quietly in the darkness. Usually docile, a Wobbuffet strikes back ferociously if its black tail is attacked.

PSYDUCK

Super Migraine...

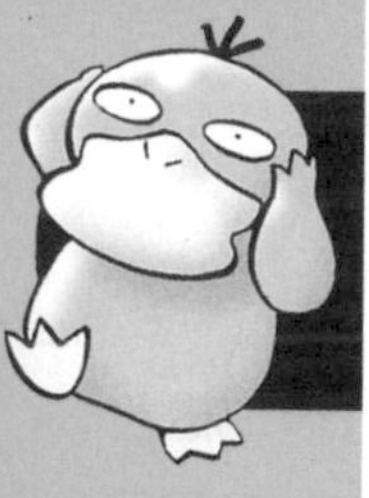

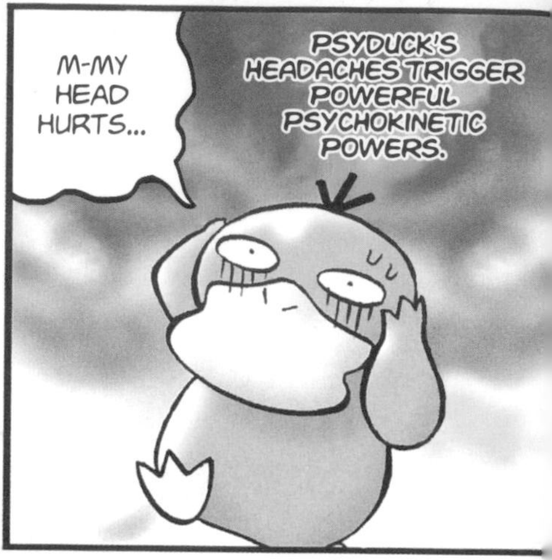
PSYDUCK'S HEADACHES TRIGGER POWERFUL PSYCHOKINETIC POWERS.
M-MY HEAD HURTS...

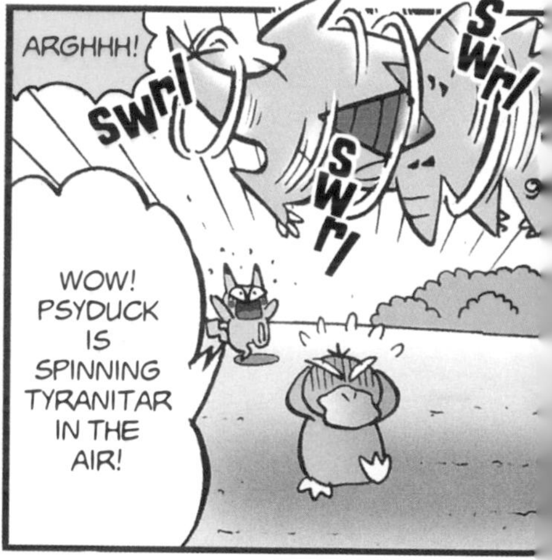
Swrl
ARGHHH!
Swrl
Swrl
WOW! PSYDUCK IS SPINNING TYRANITAR IN THE AIR!

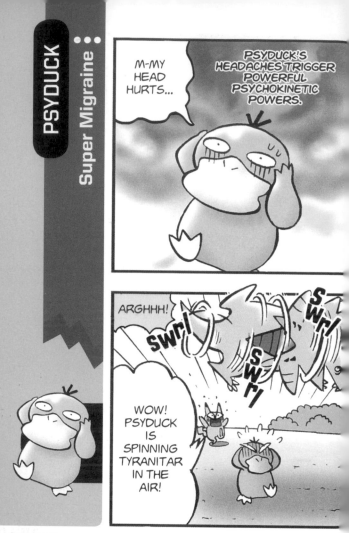

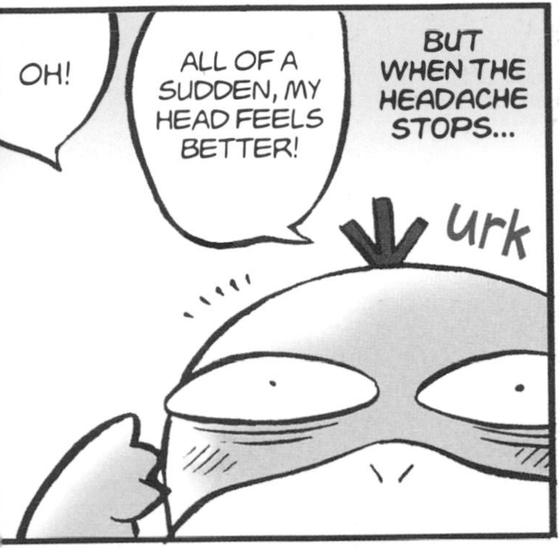
OH!
ALL OF A SUDDEN, MY HEAD FEELS BETTER!
BUT WHEN THE HEADACHE STOPS...
urk

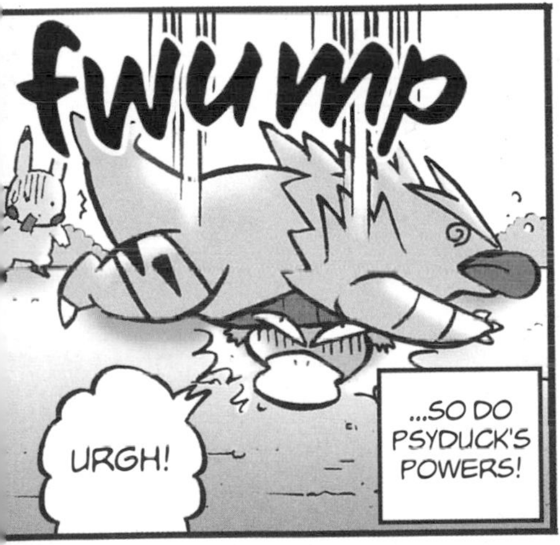
fwump
URGH!
...SO DO PSYDUCK'S POWERS!

PSYDUCK

It is constantly racked by a headache. When the headache turns intense, it begins using mysterious powers. However, it has no recollection of its powers, so it always looks befuddled and bewildered. It apparently can't form a memory of such an event because it goes into an altered state that is much like deep sleep.

AZURILL

Basic Physics

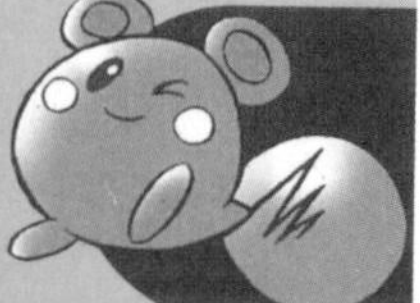

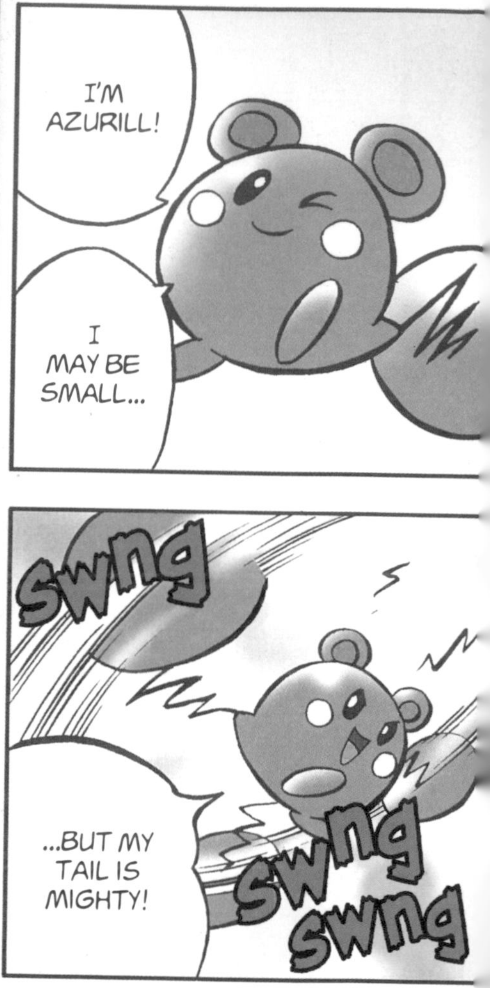

I'M AZURILL!
I MAY BE SMALL...
swng
...BUT MY TAIL IS MIGHTY!
swng
swng

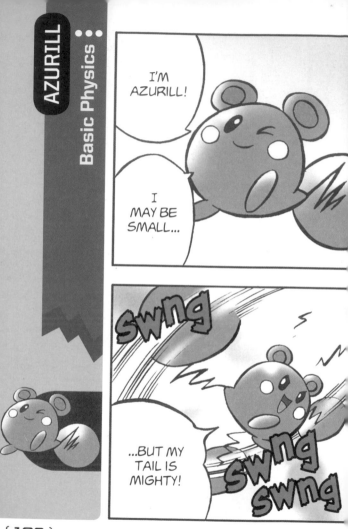

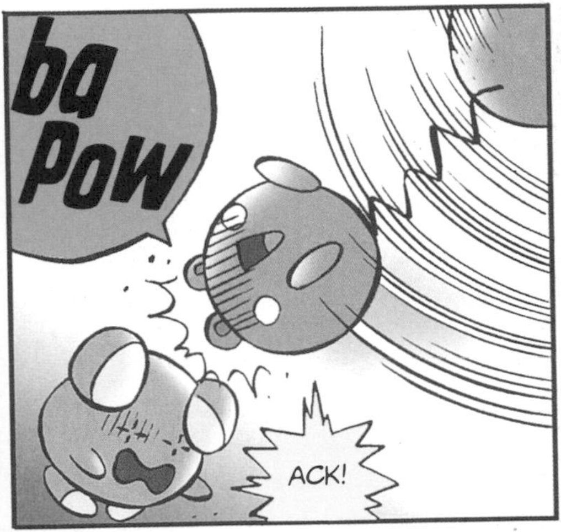
ba Pow
ACK!

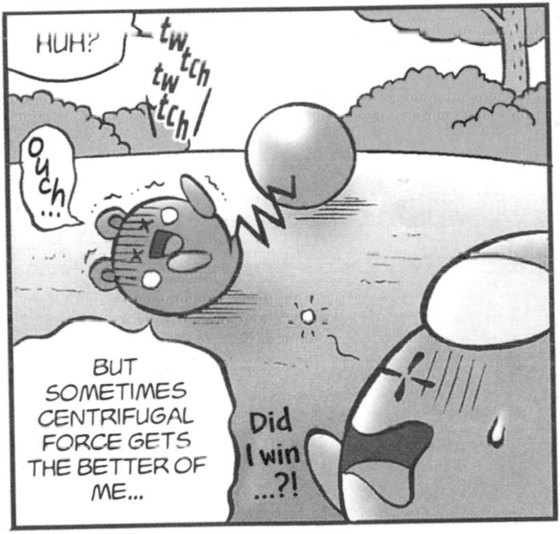
HUH?
twtch twtch
Ouch...
BUT SOMETIMES CENTRIFUGAL FORCE GETS THE BETTER OF ME...
Did I win ...?!

AZURILL

It battles by flinging around its tail, which is bigger than its body. It spins its tail as if it were a lasso, then hurls it far. The momentum of the throw sends its body flying, too. Its tail is very bouncy, like a rubber ball. On sunny days it has fun splashing about in water.

SANDSHREW NUMEL
Treasure Map

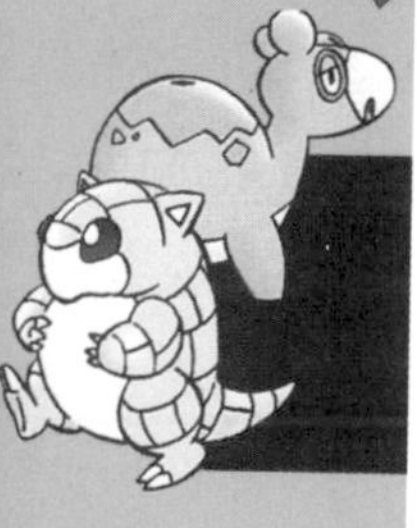

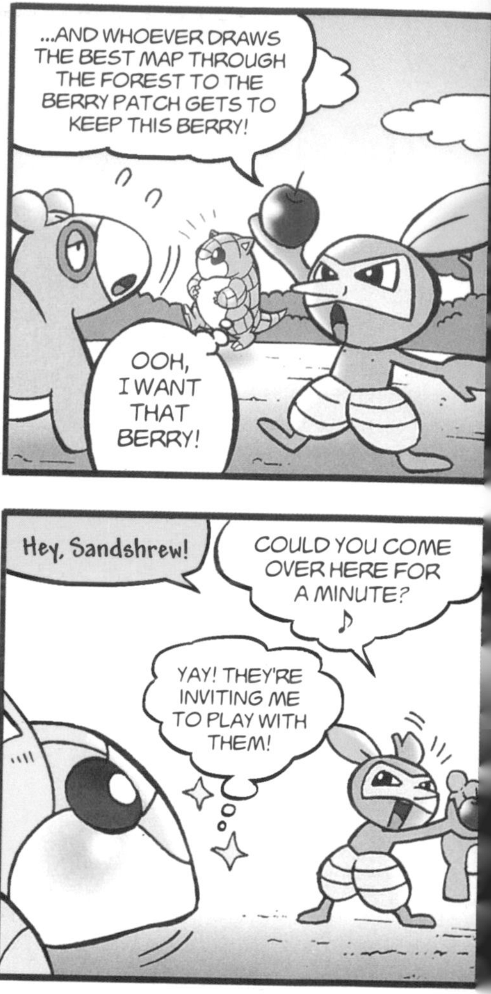
...AND WHOEVER DRAWS THE BEST MAP THROUGH THE FOREST TO THE BERRY PATCH GETS TO KEEP THIS BERRY!
OOH, I WANT THAT BERRY!
Hey, Sandshrew!
COULD YOU COME OVER HERE FOR A MINUTE? ♪
YAY! THEY'RE INVITING ME TO PLAY WITH THEM!

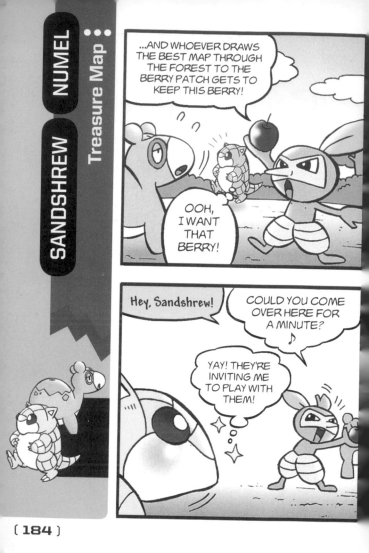

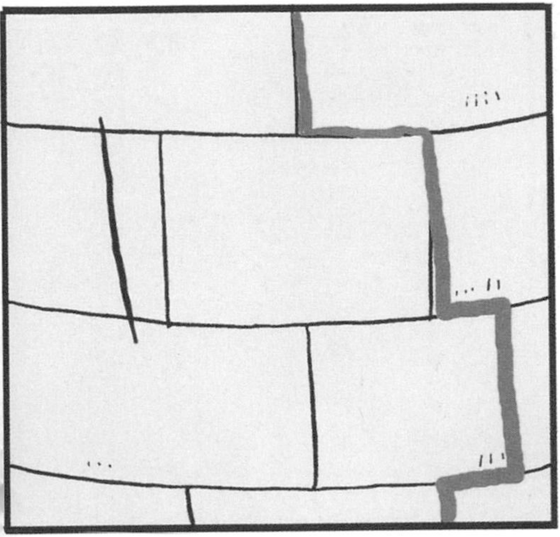

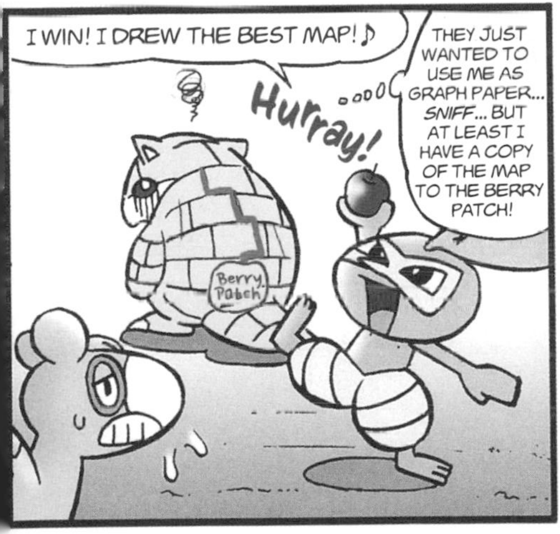
I WIN! I DREW THE BEST MAP! ♪
Hurray!
THEY JUST WANTED TO USE ME AS GRAPH PAPER... SNIFF... BUT AT LEAST I HAVE A COPY OF THE MAP TO THE BERRY PATCH!
Berry Patch

SANDSHREW

Its hide has turned tough and solid as a result of living in the desert. At night, it burrows into the desert sand to sleep.

NUMEL

It stores boiling magma in the hump on its back. It is a hardy Pokémon that can transport a 220-pound load.

RELICANTH HUNTAIL

Respect Your Elders

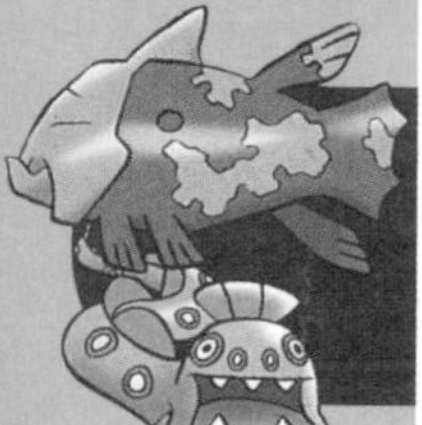

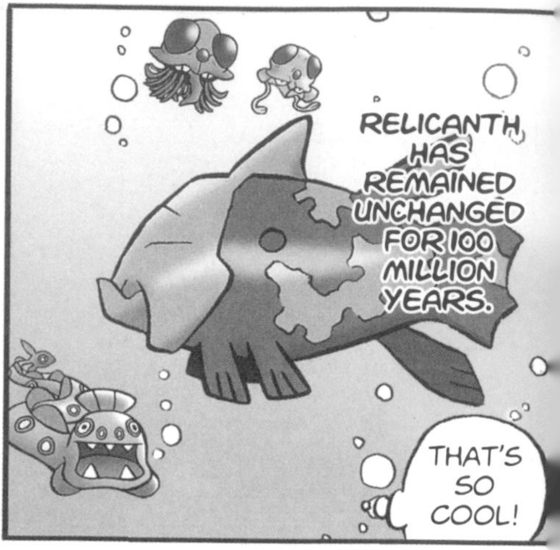
RELICANTH HAS REMAINED UNCHANGED FOR 100 MILLION YEARS.
THAT'S SO COOL!

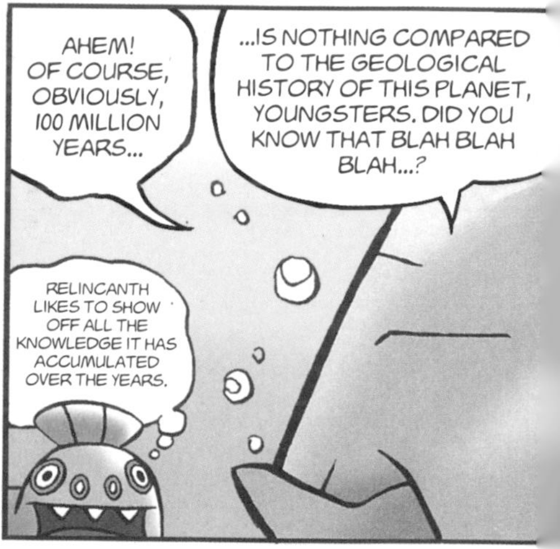
AHEM! OF COURSE, OBVIOUSLY, 100 MILLION YEARS...
...IS NOTHING COMPARED TO THE GEOLOGICAL HISTORY OF THIS PLANET, YOUNGSTERS. DID YOU KNOW THAT BLAH BLAH BLAH...?
RELINCANTH LIKES TO SHOW OFF ALL THE KNOWLEDGE IT HAS ACCUMULATED OVER THE YEARS.

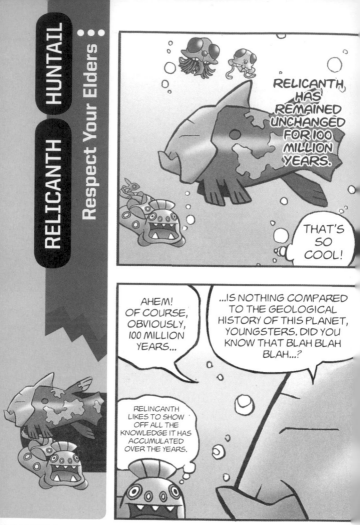

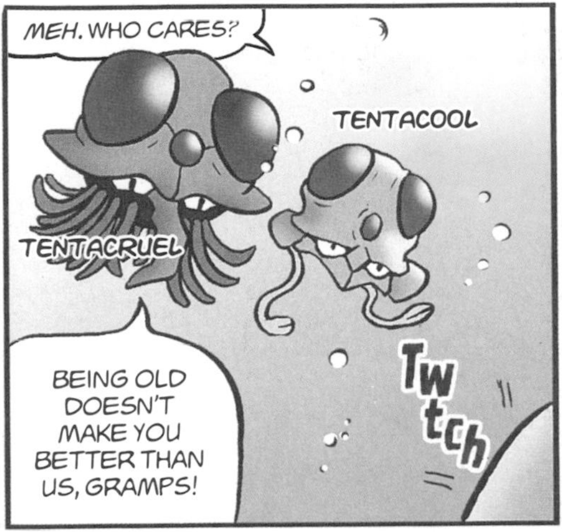
MEH. WHO CARES?
TENTACOOL
TENTACRUEL
BEING OLD DOESN'T MAKE YOU BETTER THAN US, GRAMPS!
Twtch

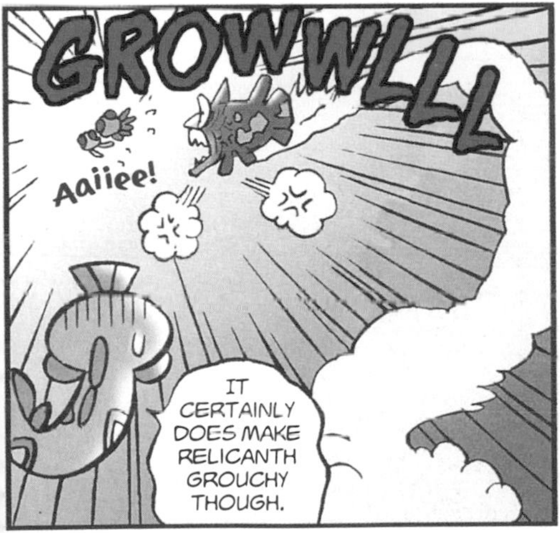
GROWWLLL
Aaiiee!
IT CERTAINLY DOES MAKE RELICANTH GROUCHY THOUGH.

RELICANTH

It has existed for a hundred million years without ever changing its form. It walks on the seafloor using its pectoral fins. This ancient Pokémon feeds on microscopic organisms with its toothless mouth.

HUNTAIL

It lives deep in the sea where no light ever filters down. It lights up its small fishlike tail to attract prey, then swallows the prey whole with its large, gaping mouth.

MISDREAVUS PICHU

An Electrifying Experience

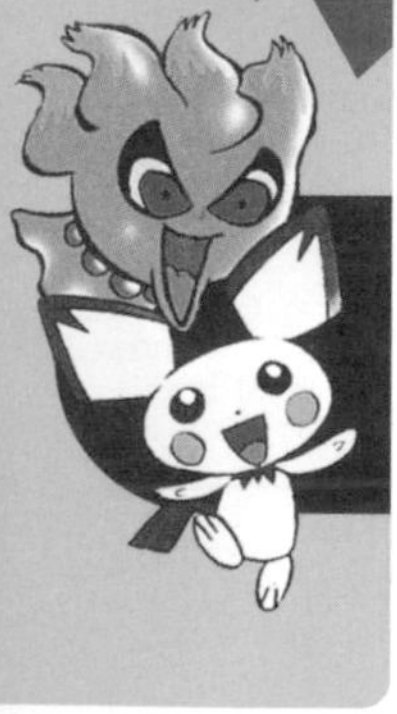

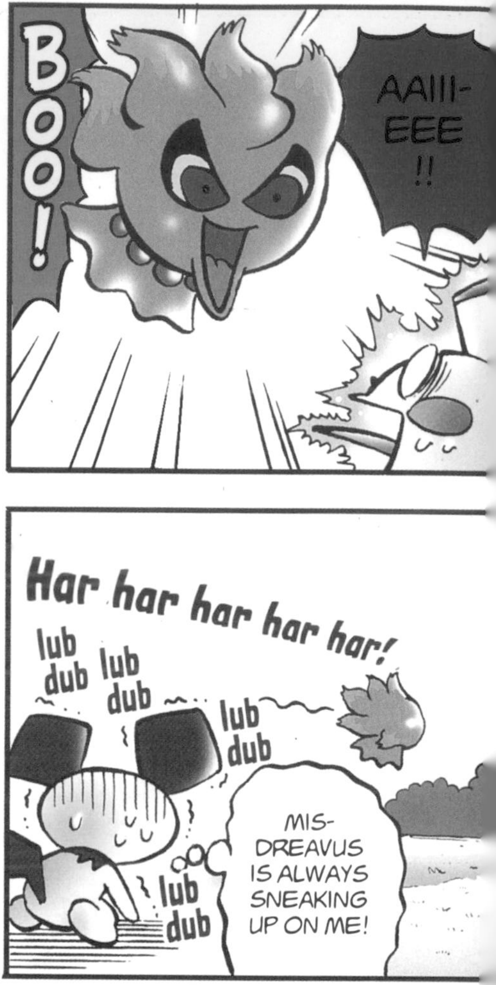
BOO!
AAIII-EEE!!
Har har har har har!
lub dub lub dub
lub dub
lub dub
MIS-DREAVUS IS ALWAYS SNEAKING UP ON ME!

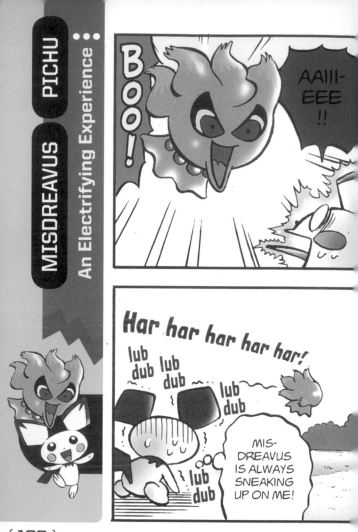

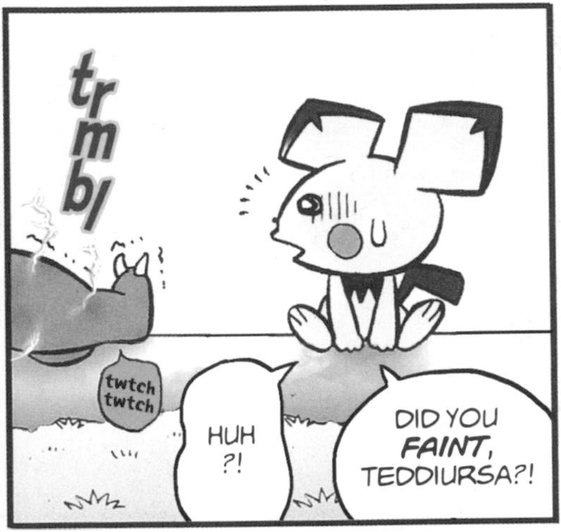
trmbl
twtch twtch
HUH ?!
DID YOU *FAINT*, TEDDIURSA?!

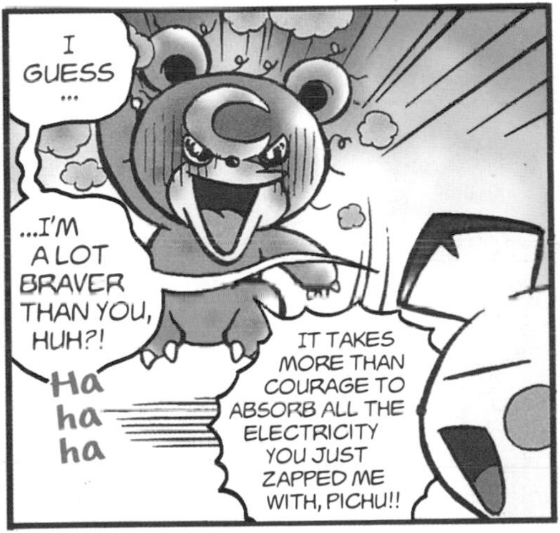
I GUESS ...
...I'M A LOT BRAVER THAN YOU, HUH?!
Ha ha ha
IT TAKES MORE THAN COURAGE TO ABSORB ALL THE ELECTRICITY YOU JUST ZAPPED ME WITH, PICHU!!

MISDREAVUS

It frightens people with a creepy, sobbing cry. It apparently uses its red spheres to absorb the fear of foes as its food.

PICHU

It is not yet skilled at storing electricity. It may send out a jolt if amused or startled.

ZANGOOSE SEVIPER

A Sorry Pair

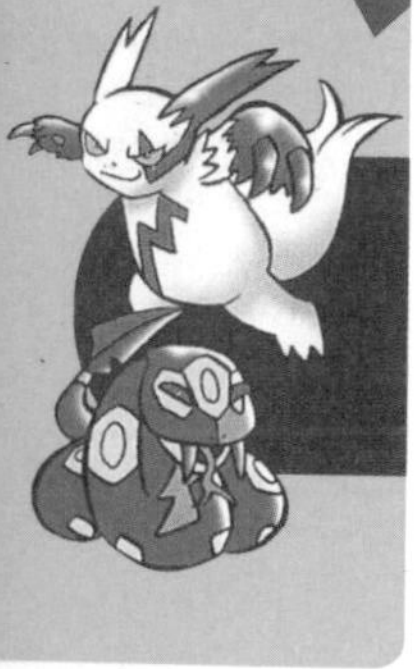

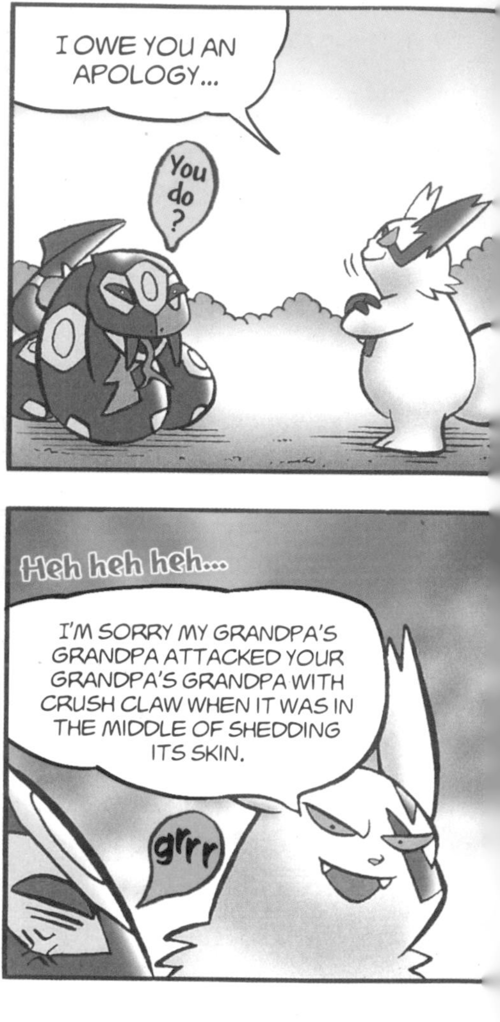
I OWE YOU AN APOLOGY...
You do?
Heh heh heh...
I'M SORRY MY GRANDPA'S GRANDPA ATTACKED YOUR GRANDPA'S GRANDPA WITH CRUSH CLAW WHEN IT WAS IN THE MIDDLE OF SHEDDING ITS SKIN.
grrr

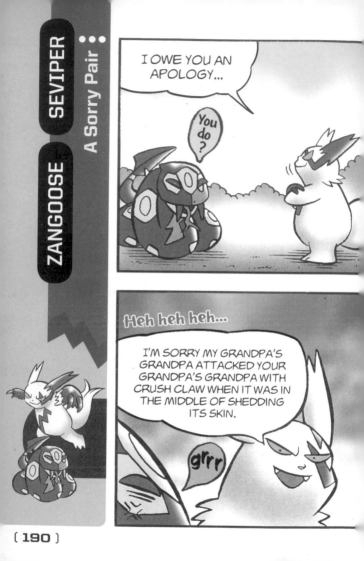

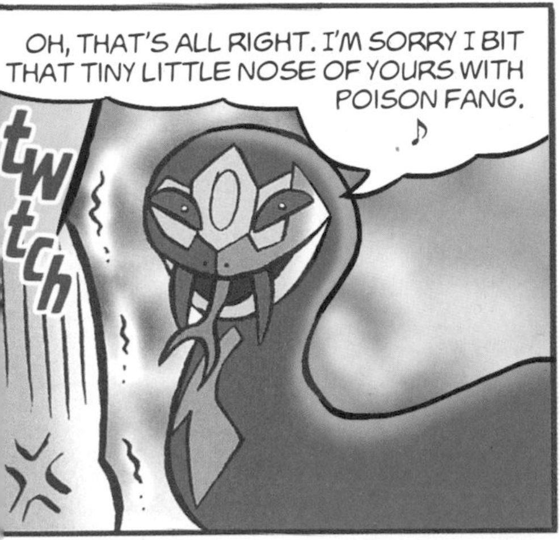
OH, THAT'S ALL RIGHT. I'M SORRY I BIT THAT TINY LITTLE NOSE OF YOURS WITH POISON FANG. ♪
twtch

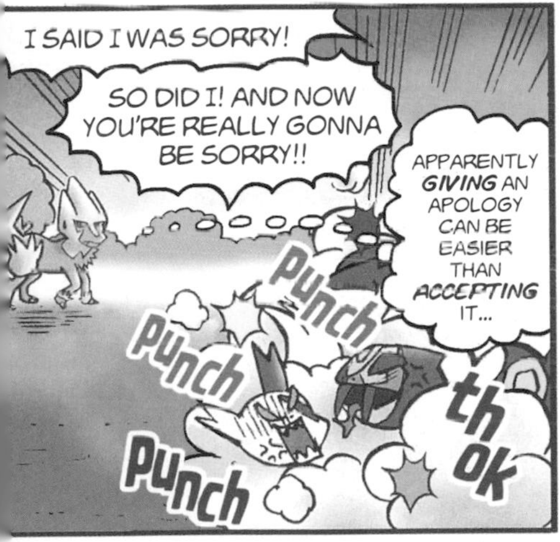
I SAID I WAS SORRY!
SO DID I! AND NOW YOU'RE REALLY GONNA BE SORRY!!
APPARENTLY *GIVING* AN APOLOGY CAN BE EASIER THAN *ACCEPTING* IT...
Punch
Punch
Punch
thok

ZANGOOSE

When it battles, it stands on its hind legs and attacks with its sharply clawed forelegs. Its fur bristles if it encounters any Seviper.

SEVIPER

Seviper and Zangoose are eternal rivals. Seviper counters a Zangoose's dazzling agility with its swordlike tail, which also oozes with a horrible poison.

AZURILL MARILL AZUMARILL

Having a Ball...

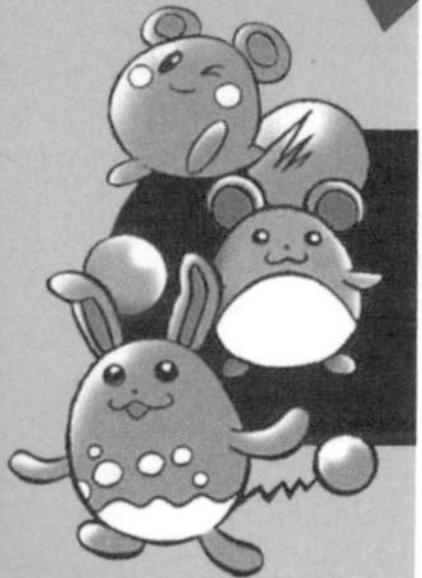

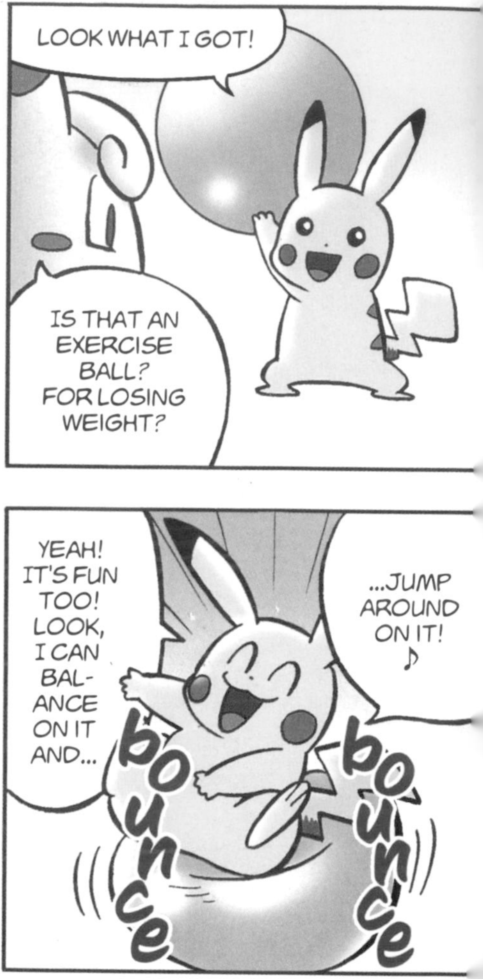

LOOK WHAT I GOT!
IS THAT AN EXERCISE BALL? FOR LOSING WEIGHT?
YEAH! IT'S FUN TOO! LOOK, I CAN BAL-ANCE ON IT AND...
...JUMP AROUND ON IT! ♪
bounce
bounce

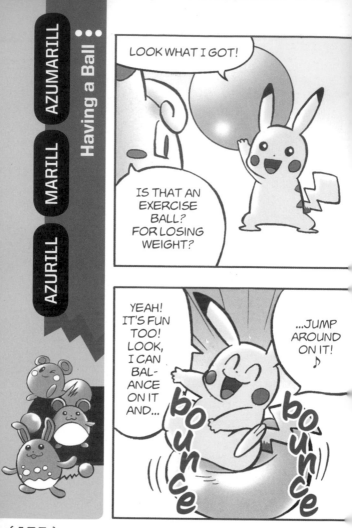

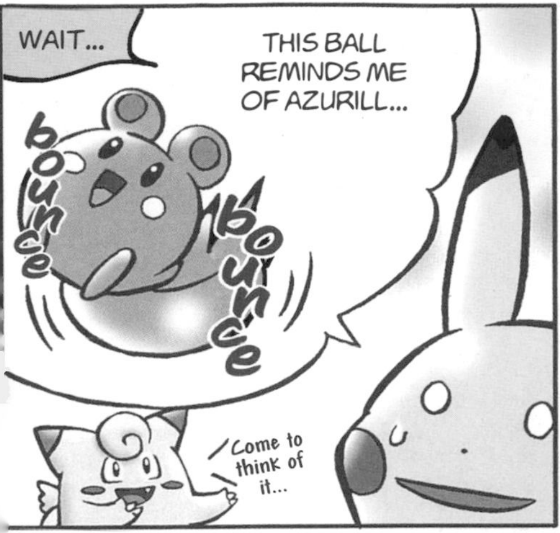
WAIT...
THIS BALL REMINDS ME OF AZURILL...
bounce
bounce
Come to think of it...

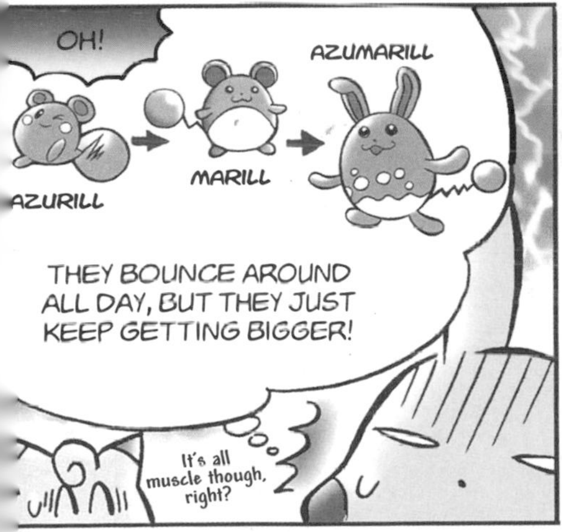
OH!
AZUMARILL
AZURILL
MARILL
THEY BOUNCE AROUND ALL DAY, BUT THEY JUST KEEP GETTING BIGGER!
It's all muscle though, right?

AZURILL

It can be seen bouncing and playing on its big, rubbery tail.

MARILL

Its body is covered with water-repellent fur. Because of the fur, it can swim through water at high speeds without being slowed by the water's resistance.

AZUMARILL

The bubble-like pattern on its stomach helps it camouflage itself when it's in the water.

ABSOL… Impending Doom

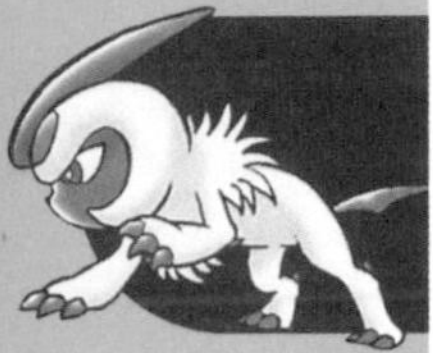

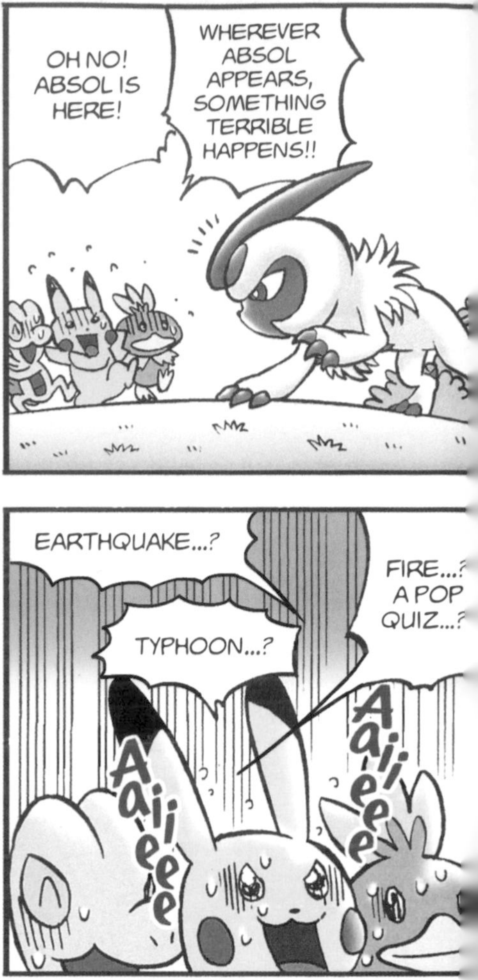
OH NO! ABSOL IS HERE!
WHEREVER ABSOL APPEARS, SOMETHING TERRIBLE HAPPENS!!
EARTHQUAKE...?
TYPHOON...?
FIRE...? A POP QUIZ...?
Aaiieee
Aaiieee

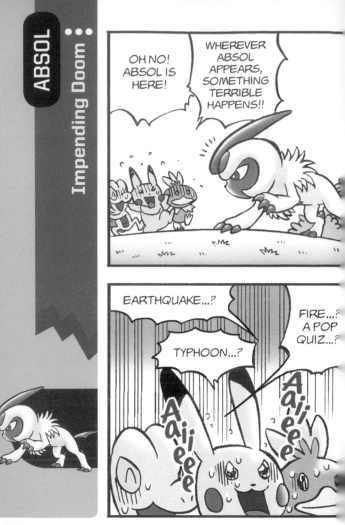

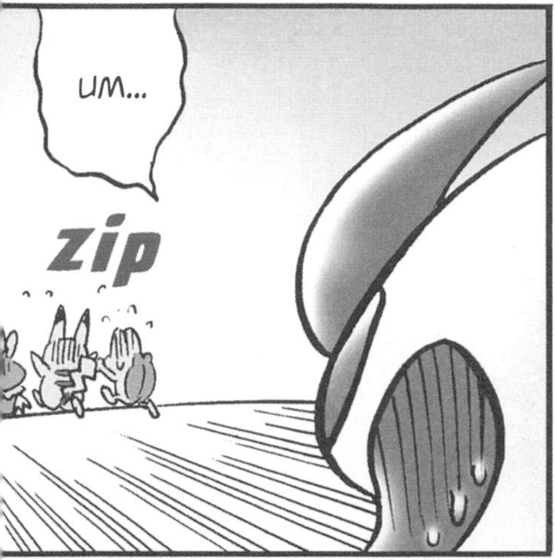
UM...
zip

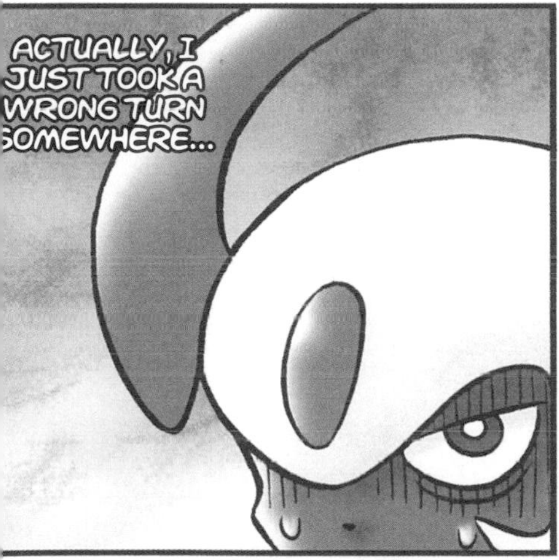
ACTUALLY, I JUST TOOK A WRONG TURN SOMEWHERE...

ABSOL

It sharply senses even subtle changes in the sky and the land to predict natural disasters. It lives in a harsh, rugged mountain environment. It appears when it senses an impending natural disaster. As a result, it has come to be known as the "Disaster Pokémon." It is a long-lived Pokémon that has a life span of 100 years.

RAYQUAZA DEOXYS

It's Not Really Nice to Tease

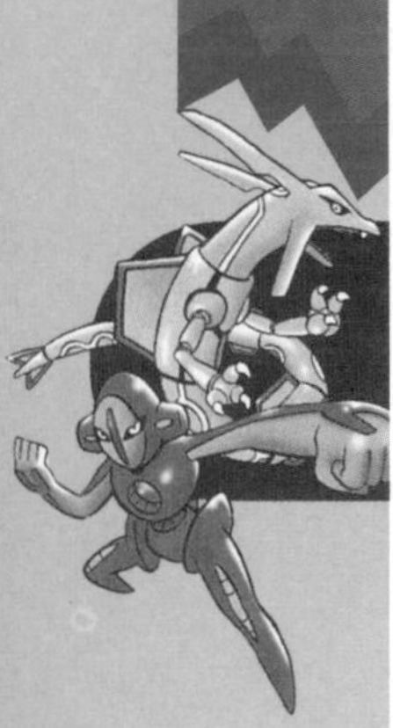

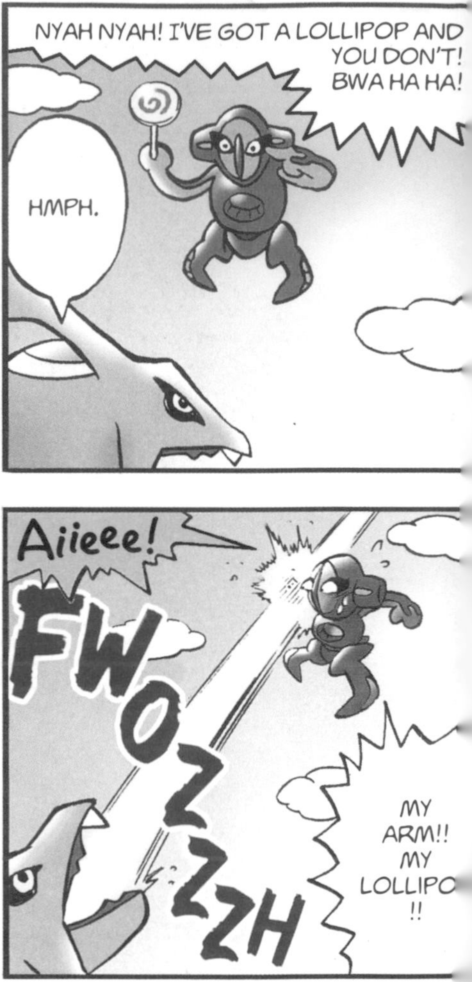
NYAH NYAH! I'VE GOT A LOLLIPOP AND YOU DON'T! BWA HA HA!
HMPH.
Aiieee!
FWOZZZH
MY ARM!! MY LOLLIPO !!

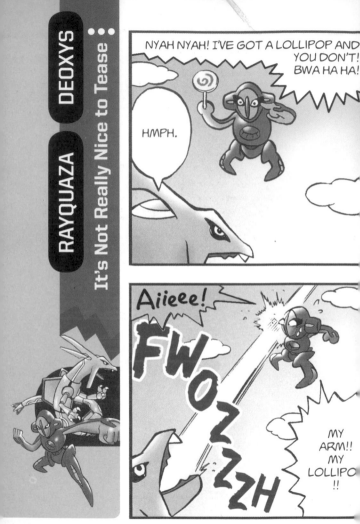

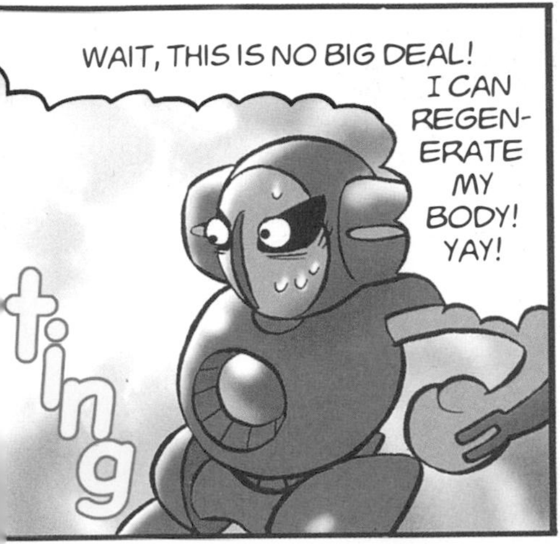
WAIT, THIS IS NO BIG DEAL!
I CAN REGEN-ERATE MY BODY! YAY!
ting

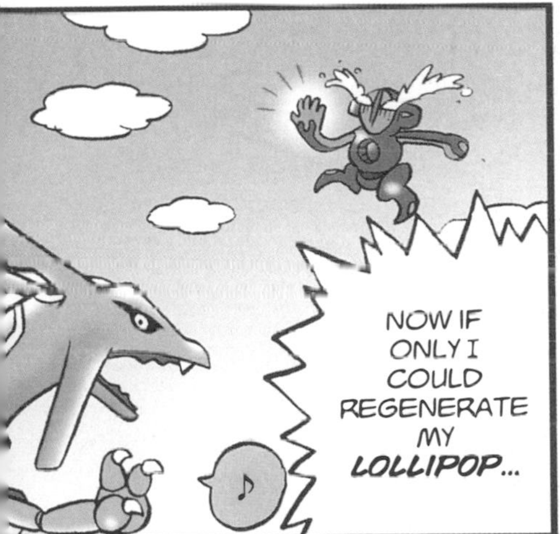
NOW IF ONLY I COULD REGENERATE MY *LOLLIPOP*...
♪

RAYQUAZA

It is said to have lived for hundreds of millions of years in the ozone layer, never descending to the ground. It appears to feed on water and particles in the atmosphere.

DEOXYS

The crystalline organ on this Pokémon's chest appears to be its brain. It is capable of regenerating its body when damaged.

REGIROCK REGICE REGISTEEL

Tough Talk

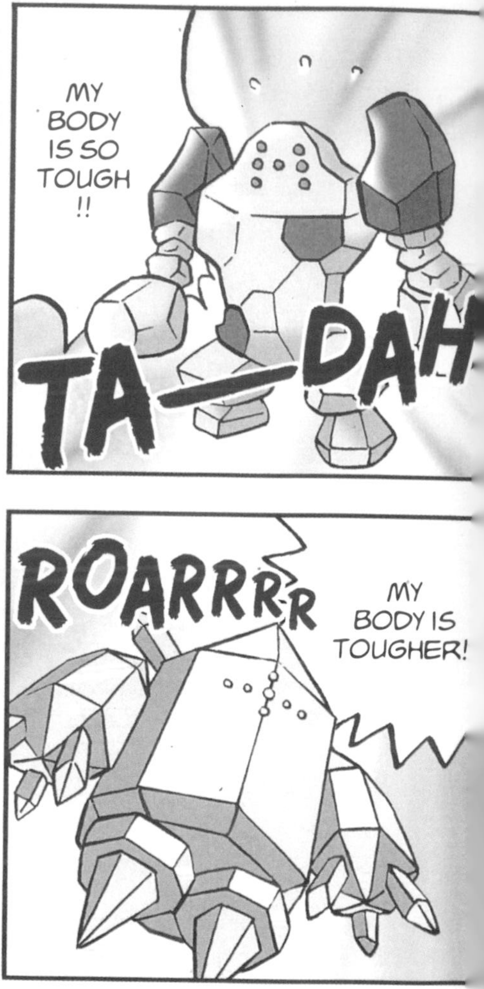

MY BODY IS SO TOUGH !!
TA—DAH
ROARRRR
MY BODY IS TOUGHER!

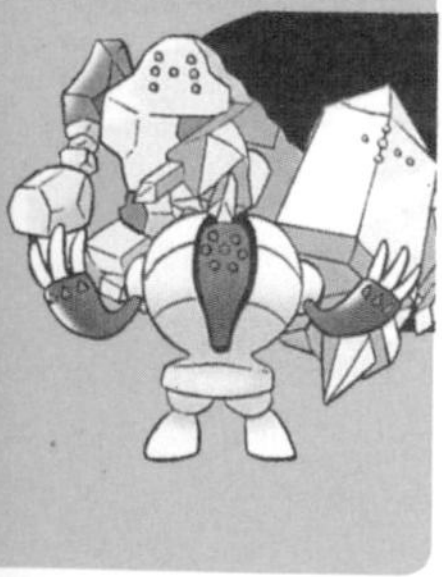

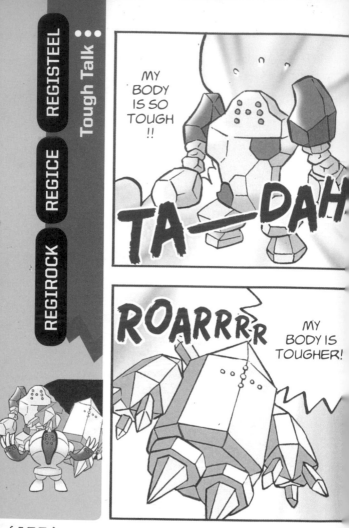

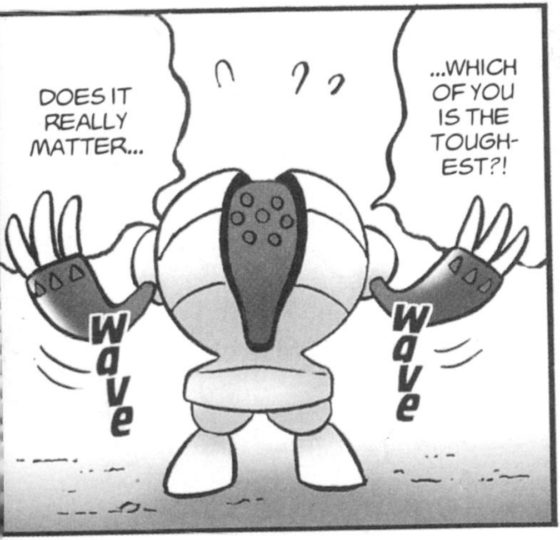
DOES IT REALLY MATTER...
...WHICH OF YOU IS THE TOUGH-EST?!
wave
wave

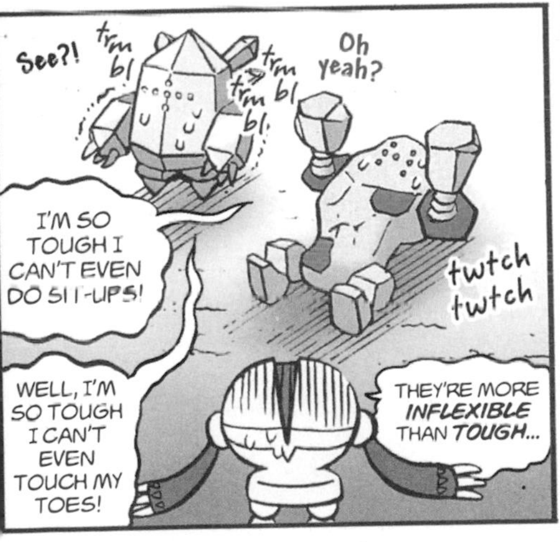
See?!
trm bl
trm bl
trm bl
Oh yeah?
I'M SO TOUGH I CAN'T EVEN DO SIT-UPS!
twtch twtch
WELL, I'M SO TOUGH I CAN'T EVEN TOUCH MY TOES!
THEY'RE MORE *INFLEXIBLE* THAN *TOUGH*...

REGIROCK

Its body is composed entirely of rocks. If part of its body chips off in battle, it repairs itself by adding new rocks.

REGICE

Its entire body is made of Antarctic ice. Regice cloaks itself with frigid air of negative 328 degrees Fahrenheit.

REGISTEEL

It is sturdier than any kind of metal. It hardened due to pressure underground over tens of thousands of years.

DITTO

So Close and Yet...

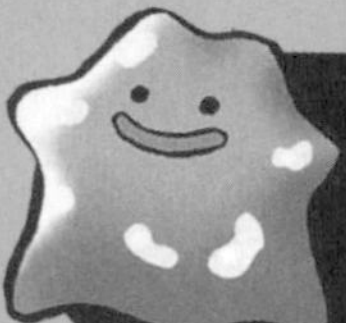

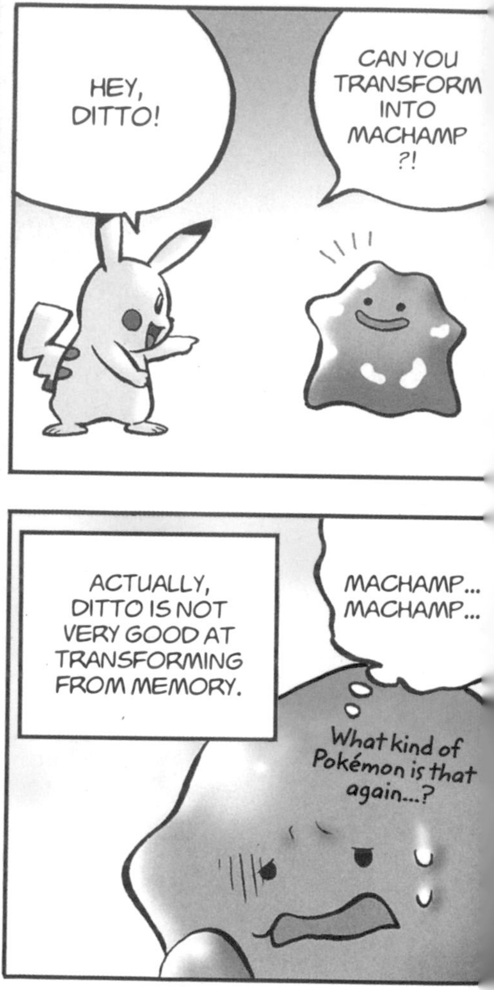
HEY, DITTO!
CAN YOU TRANSFORM INTO MACHAMP ?!
ACTUALLY, DITTO IS NOT VERY GOOD AT TRANSFORMING FROM MEMORY.
MACHAMP... MACHAMP...
What kind of Pokémon is that again...?

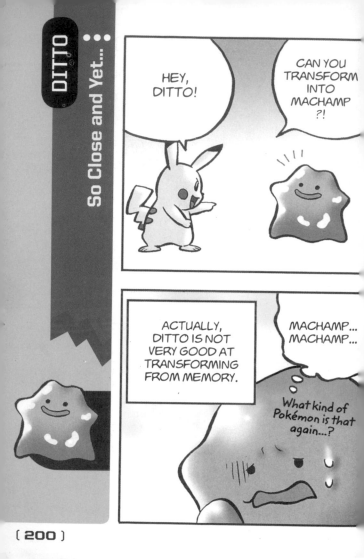

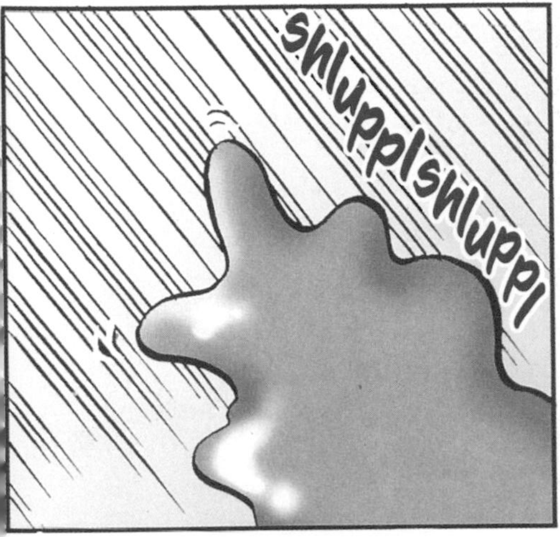
shlupplshluppl

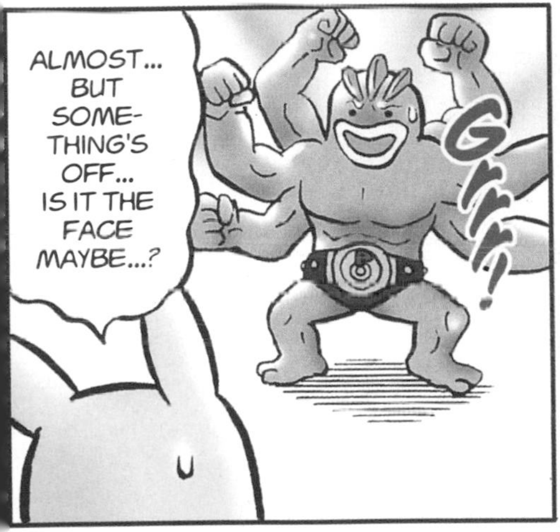
ALMOST... BUT SOME-THING'S OFF... IS IT THE FACE MAYBE...?
Grrrr!

DITTO

It is capable of copying another's genetic code to instantly transform itself into a duplicate. However, if it tries to change based on its memory, it gets details wrong. When it sleeps, it changes into a stone to avoid being attacked.

SLOWPOKE
Better Late Than Never

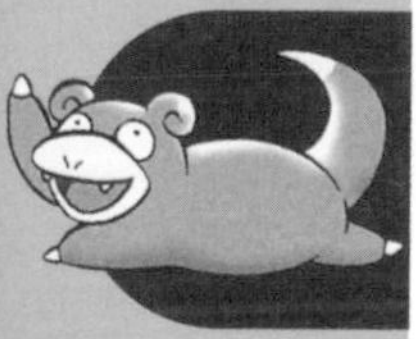

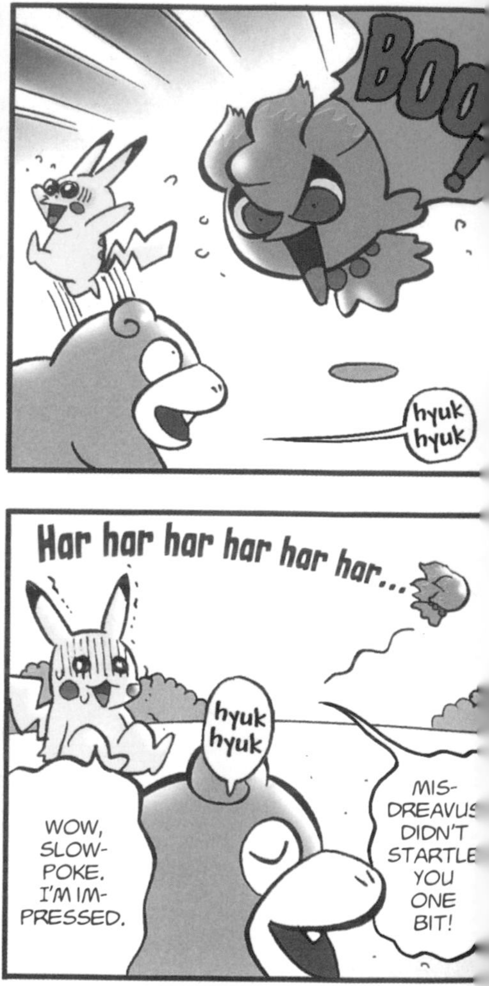
BOO!
hyuk hyuk
Har har har har har har...
hyuk hyuk
WOW, SLOW-POKE. I'M IM-PRESSED.
MIS-DREAVUS DIDN'T STARTLE YOU ONE BIT!

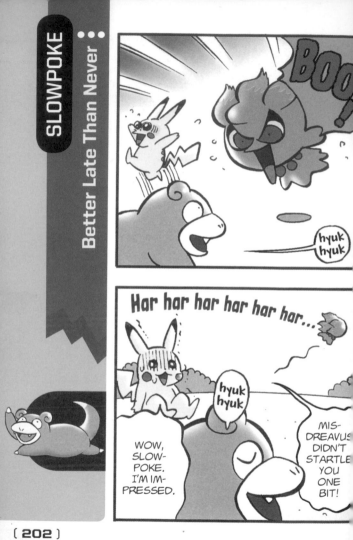

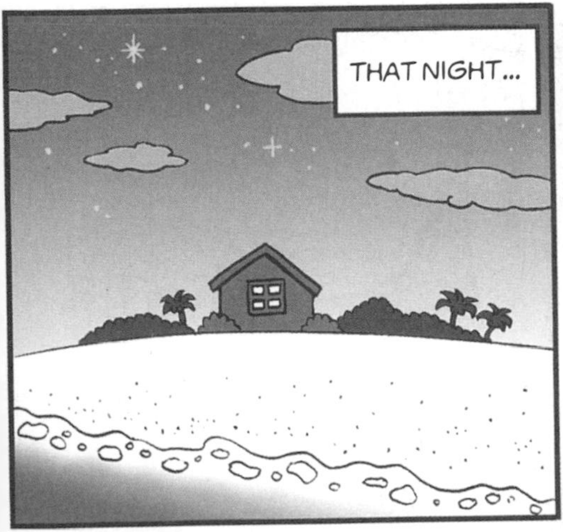
THAT NIGHT...

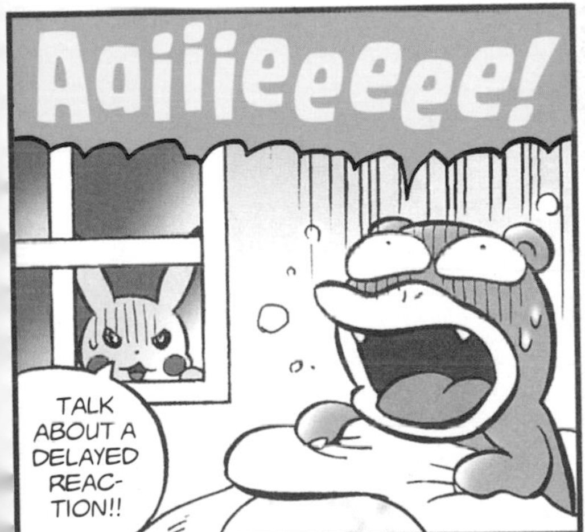
Aaiieeeee!
TALK ABOUT A DELAYED REAC-TION!!

SLOWPOKE

It uses its tail to catch prey by dipping it in water at the side of a river. However, this Pokémon often forgets what it's doing and spends entire days just loafing at the water's edge. It is incredibly slow and dopey. It takes five seconds for it to feel pain when under attack.

FEEBAS MILOTIC HORSEA

Inner Beauty Doesn't Change

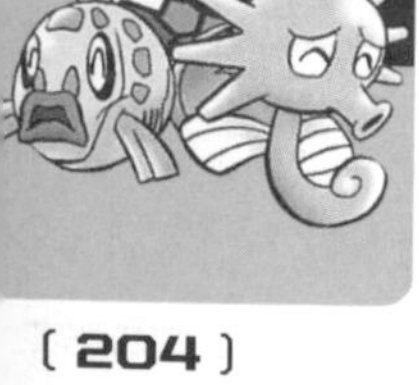

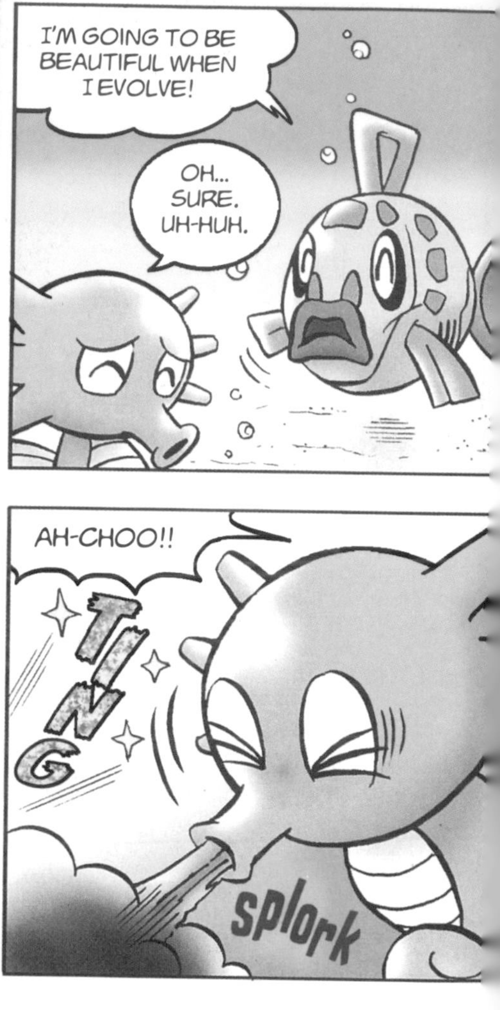
I'M GOING TO BE BEAUTIFUL WHEN I EVOLVE!
OH... SURE. UH-HUH.
AH-CHOO!!
TING
splork

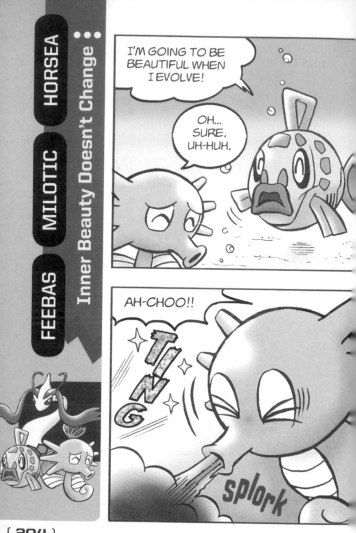

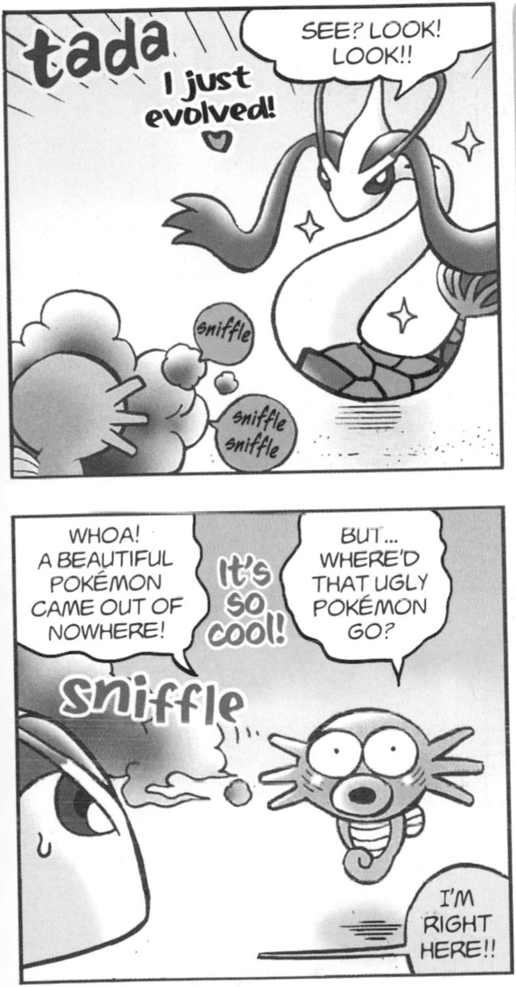
tada
I just evolved!
SEE? LOOK! LOOK!!
sniffle
sniffle sniffle
WHOA! A BEAUTIFUL POKÉMON CAME OUT OF NOWHERE!
It's so cool!
BUT... WHERE'D THAT UGLY POKÉMON GO?
sniffle
I'M RIGHT HERE!!

FEEBAS

While its body is in tatters, it has a hardy and tenacious life force that enables it to live anywhere.

MILOTIC

The evolved form of Feebas. It is said to be the world's most beautiful Pokémon.

HORSEA

By cleverly flicking the fins on its back from side to side, it moves in any direction while facing forward. It spits ink to escape if it senses danger.

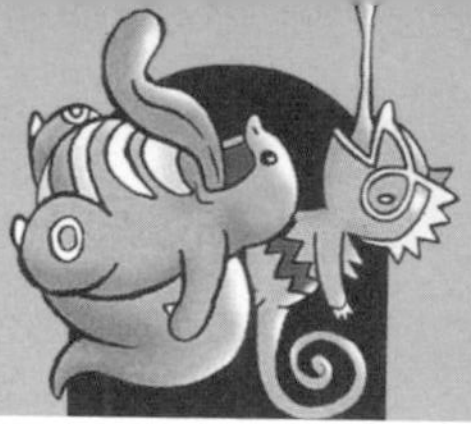

KECLEON LICKITUNG

Hold Your Tongue

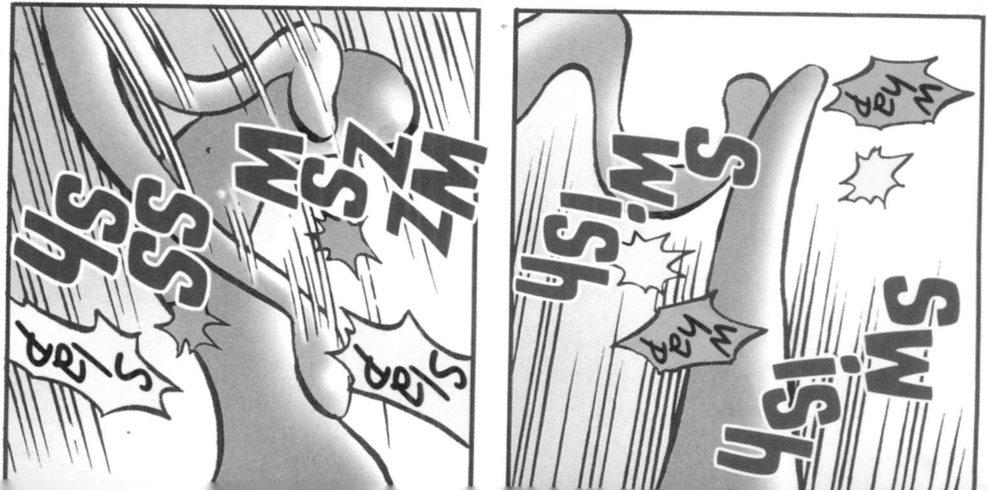
Swish
whap
Swish
whap
WZZSW
SSSh
Slap
Slap

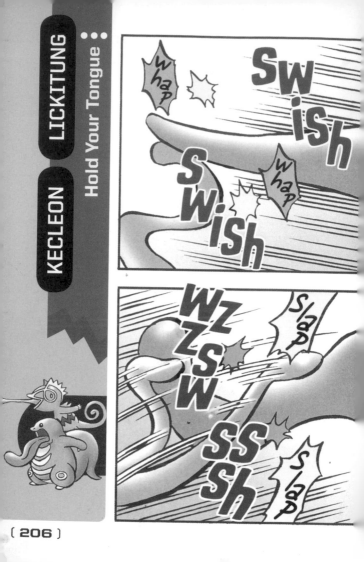

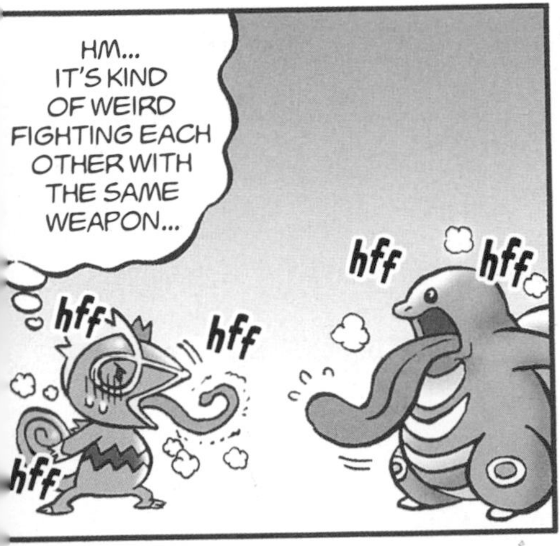
HM... IT'S KIND OF WEIRD FIGHTING EACH OTHER WITH THE SAME WEAPON...
hff
hff
hff
hff
hff
hff

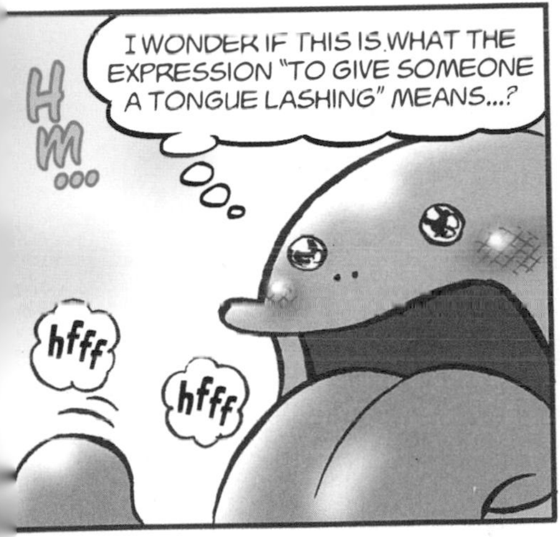
I WONDER IF THIS IS WHAT THE EXPRESSION "TO GIVE SOMEONE A TONGUE LASHING" MEANS...?
HMooo
hfff
hfff

KECLEON

It is capable of changing its body colors at will to blend in with its surroundings. There is one exception—this Pokémon can't change the zigzag pattern on its belly.

LICKITUNG

Its tongue is twice the length of its body. It can be moved like an arm to grab food and attack.

BAGON PIKACHU

Just an Expression

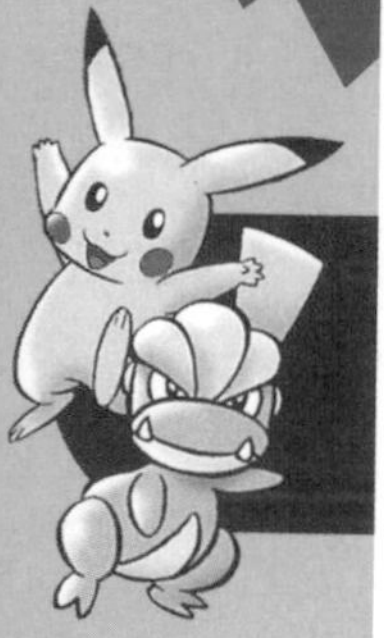

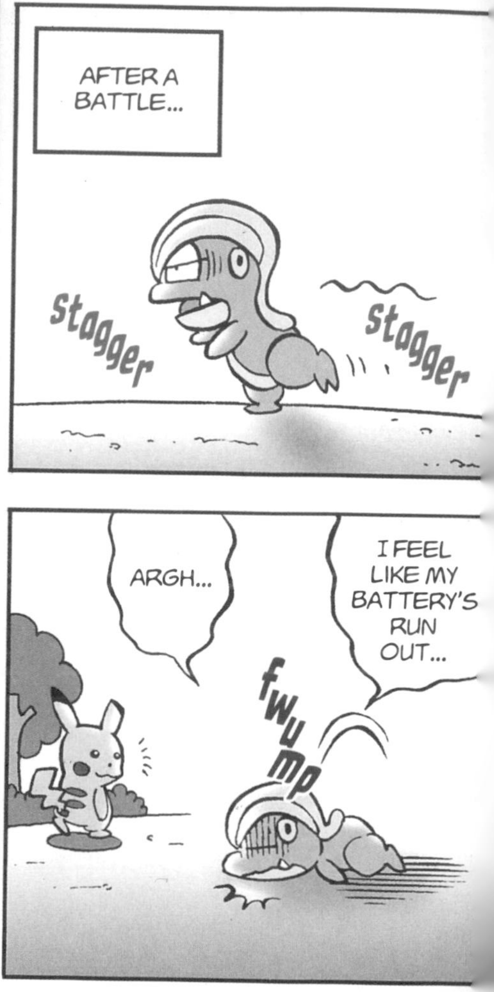
AFTER A BATTLE...
Stagger
Stagger
ARGH...
I FEEL LIKE MY BATTERY'S RUN OUT...
fwump

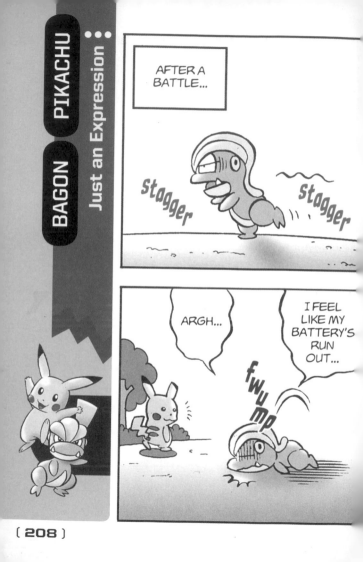

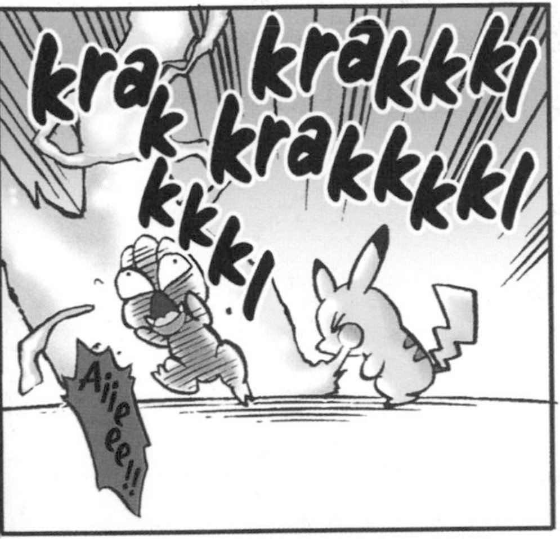
krak
krakkkl
krakkkkl
kkkl
Aiieee!!

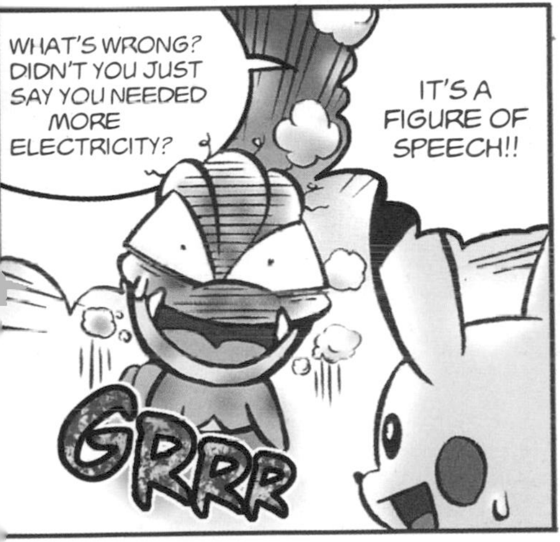
WHAT'S WRONG? DIDN'T YOU JUST SAY YOU NEEDED MORE ELECTRICITY?
IT'S A FIGURE OF SPEECH!!
GRRR

BAGON

Although it is small, this Pokémon is very powerful because its body is a bundle of muscles. It launches headbutts with its ironlike skull.

PIKACHU

This Pokémon has electricity-storing pouches on its cheeks. These appear to become electrically charged during the night when Pikachu sleeps. It occasionally discharges electricity when it is groggy after waking up.

SPINDA
At the Pun Tournament

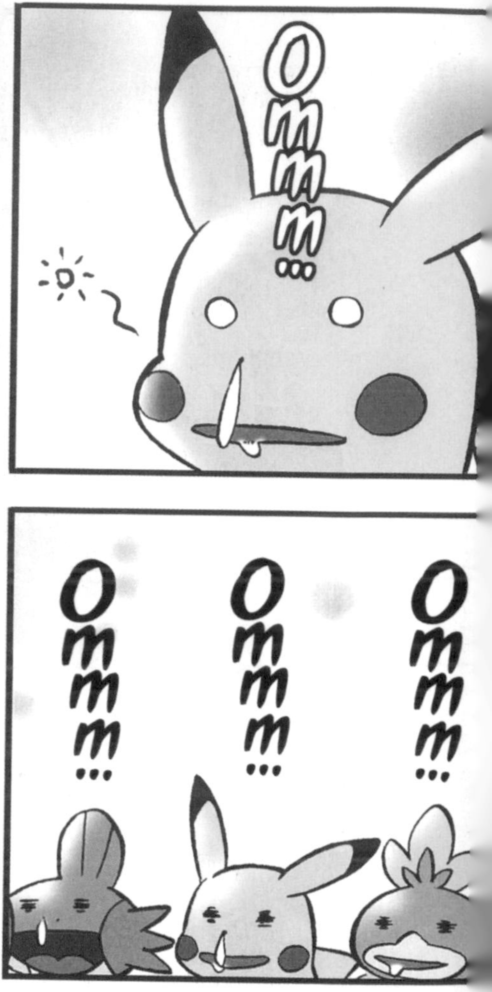
Ommm!!...
Ommm!!...
Ommm!!...
Ommm!!...

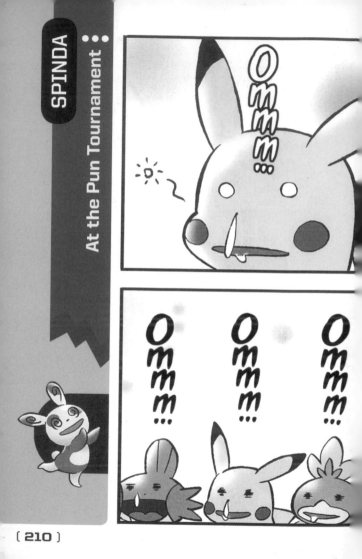

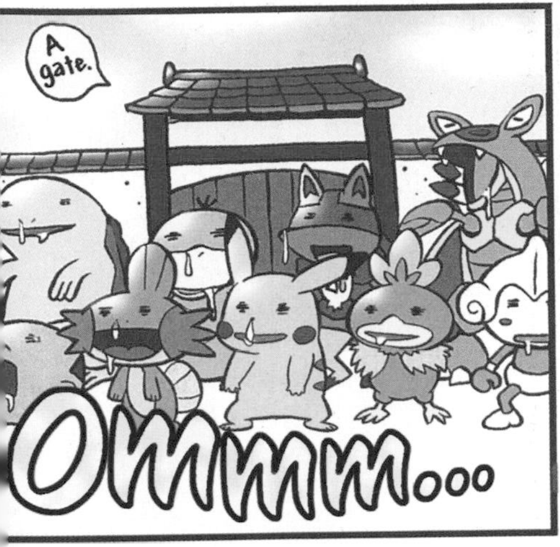
A gate.
OMMM...

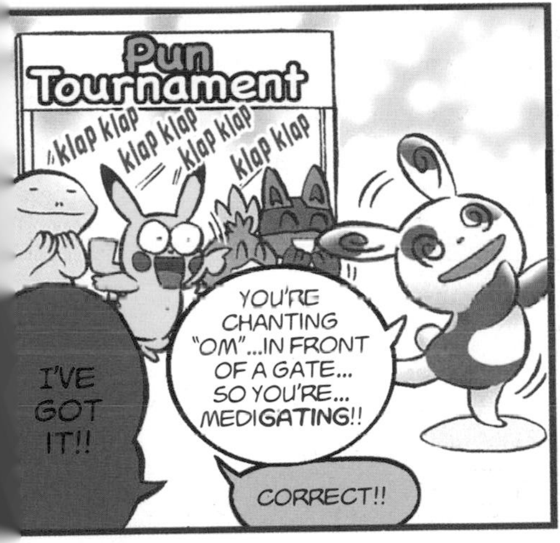
Pun Tournament
klap klap
klap klap
klap klap
klap klap
I'VE GOT IT!!
YOU'RE CHANTING "OM"...IN FRONT OF A GATE... SO YOU'RE... MEDIGATING!!
CORRECT!!

SPINDA

It is distinguished by a pattern of spots that is always different. Its unsteady, tottering walk has the effect of spoiling its foe's aim.

LUCARIO CYNDAQUIL

Surprise Attack!!

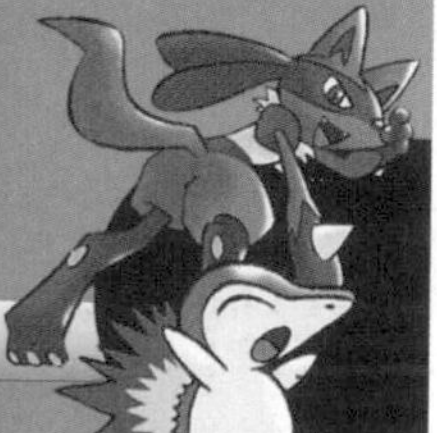

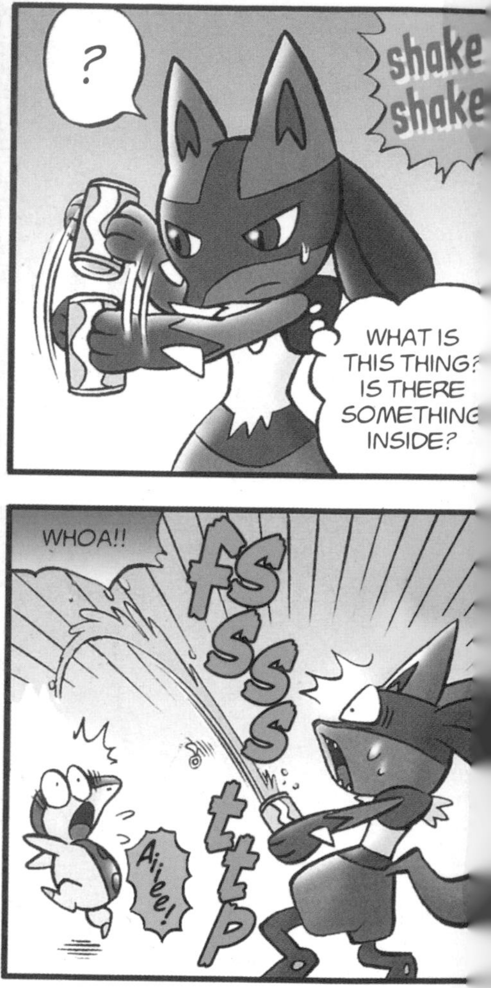
?
shake
shake
WHAT IS THIS THING? IS THERE SOMETHING INSIDE?
WHOA!!
fsssttp
Aiiee!

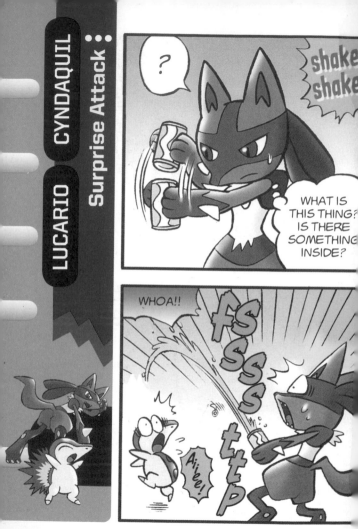

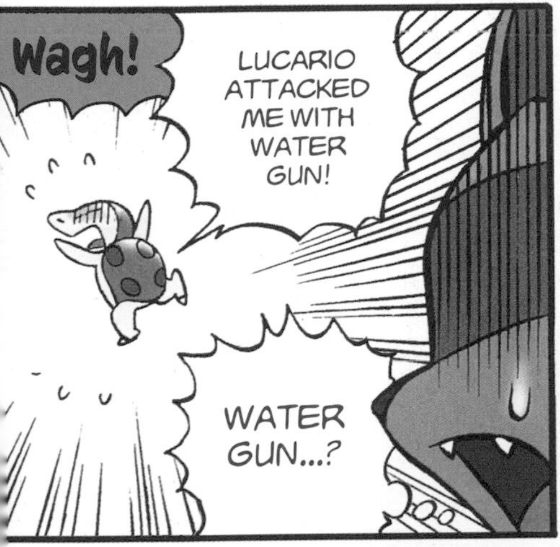
Wagh!
LUCARIO ATTACKED ME WITH WATER GUN!
WATER GUN...?

LUCARIO

This Steel- and Fighting-type Pokémon is known as the "Aura Pokémon."

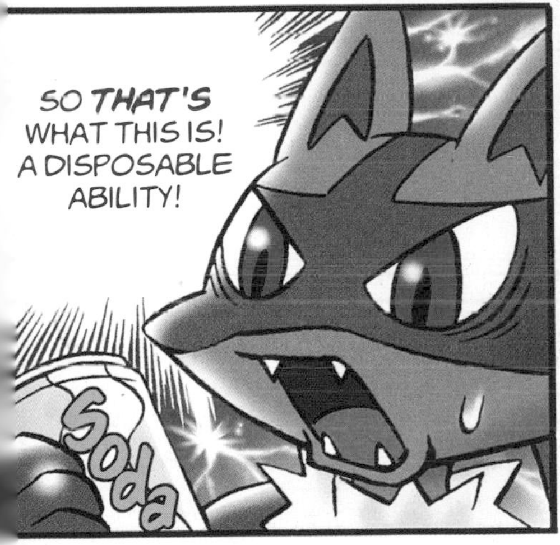
SO *THAT'S* WHAT THIS IS! A DISPOSABLE ABILITY!
Soda

CYNDAQUIL

It is timid and always curls itself up into a ball. If attacked, it flares up its back for protection. The flames are vigorous if the Pokémon is angry. However, if it is tired, the flames sputter fitfully with incomplete combustion.

WEAVILE WHISMUR
Getting an Earful

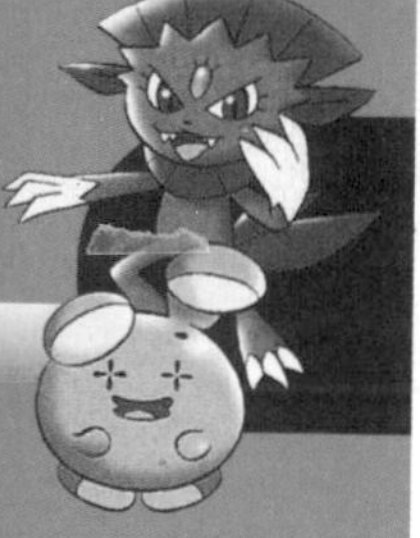

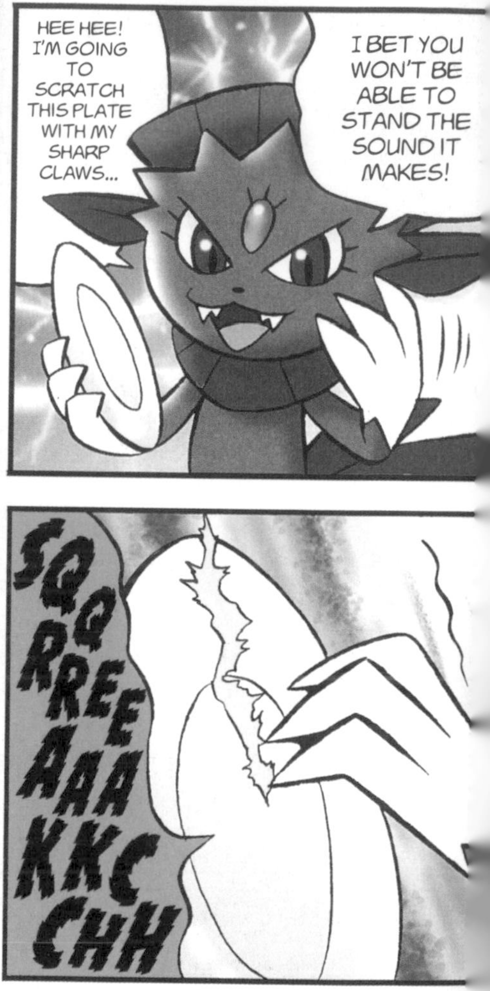
HEE HEE! I'M GOING TO SCRATCH THIS PLATE WITH MY SHARP CLAWS...
I BET YOU WON'T BE ABLE TO STAND THE SOUND IT MAKES!
SQQRREEAAAKKCCHH

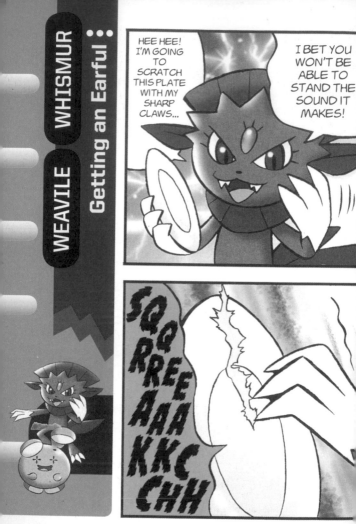

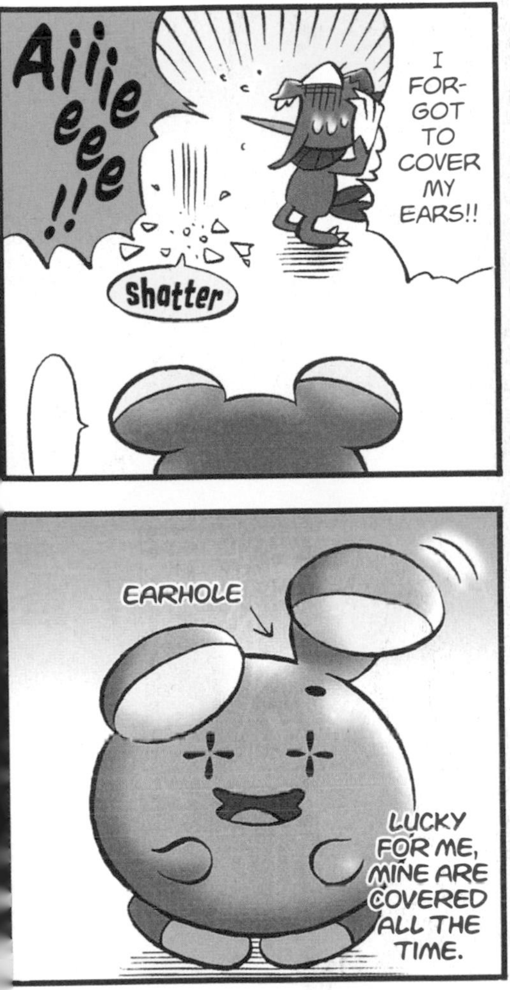
Aiiieeee!!
I FOR-GOT TO COVER MY EARS!!
Shatter
EARHOLE
LUCKY FOR ME, MINE ARE COVERED ALL THE TIME.

WEAVILE

This Dark- and Ice-type Pokémon is known as the "Sharp Claw Pokémon."

WHISMUR

If this Pokémon senses danger, it starts crying at an earsplitting volume. It inhales through its ear canals. Because of this system, it can cry continuously without having to catch its breath.

BONSLY SURSKIT
A Cry for Help

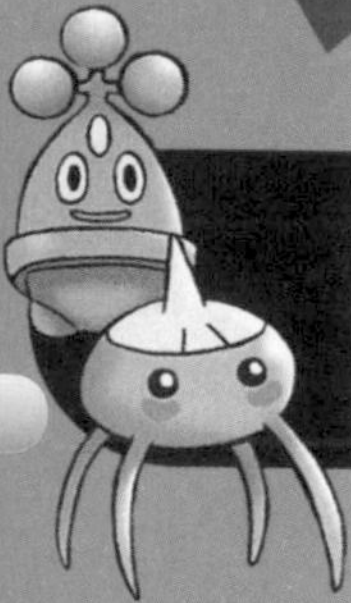

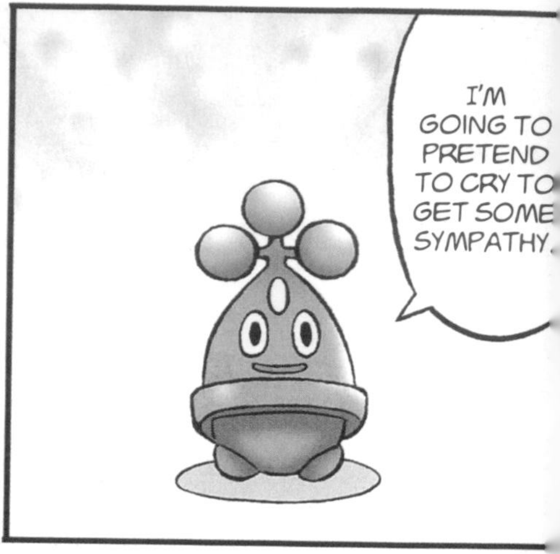
I'M GOING TO PRETEND TO CRY TO GET SOME SYMPATHY.

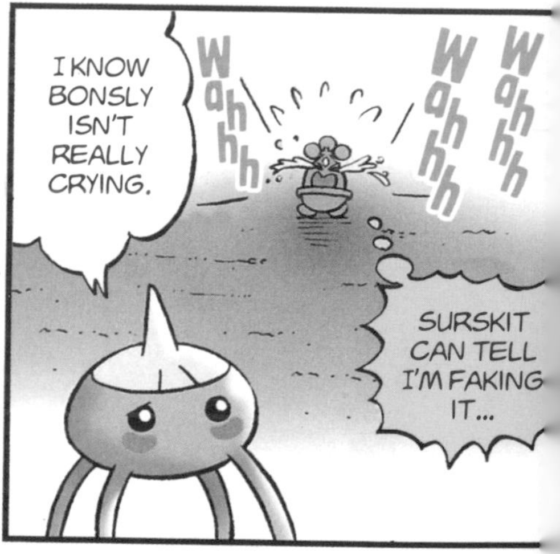
I KNOW BONSLY ISN'T REALLY CRYING.
Wahhh
Wahhh
Wahhh
SURSKIT CAN TELL I'M FAKING IT...

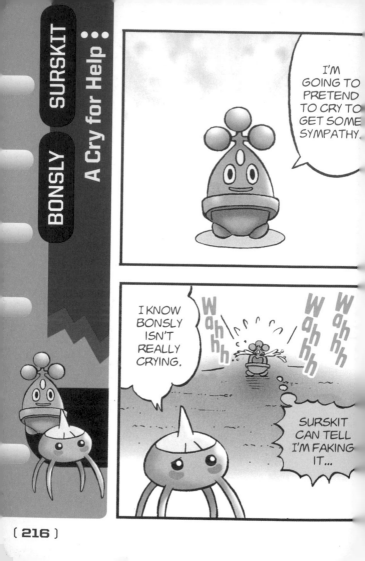

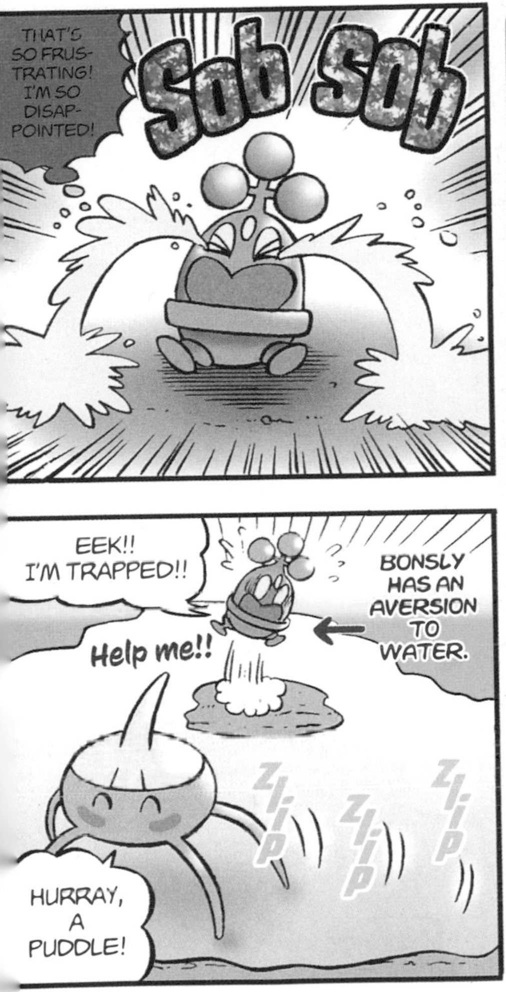
THAT'S SO FRUS-TRATING! I'M SO DISAP-POINTED!
Sob Sob
EEK!! I'M TRAPPED!!
Help me!!
BONSLY HAS AN AVERSION TO WATER.
HURRAY, A PUDDLE!
Zlip
Zlip
Zlip

BONSLY

This Rock-type Pokémon is known as the "Bonsai Pokémon."

SURSKIT

From the tip of its feet, it secretes an oil that enables it to walk on water as if it were skating. Surskit usually lives on ponds, but after an evening shower, it may appear on puddles in towns. If it senses danger, it secretes a thick, sugary syrup from the tip of its head.

MIME JR. MR. MIME

Commit to Your Art

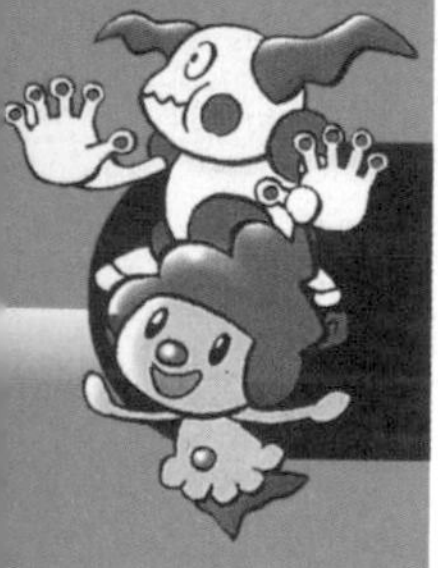

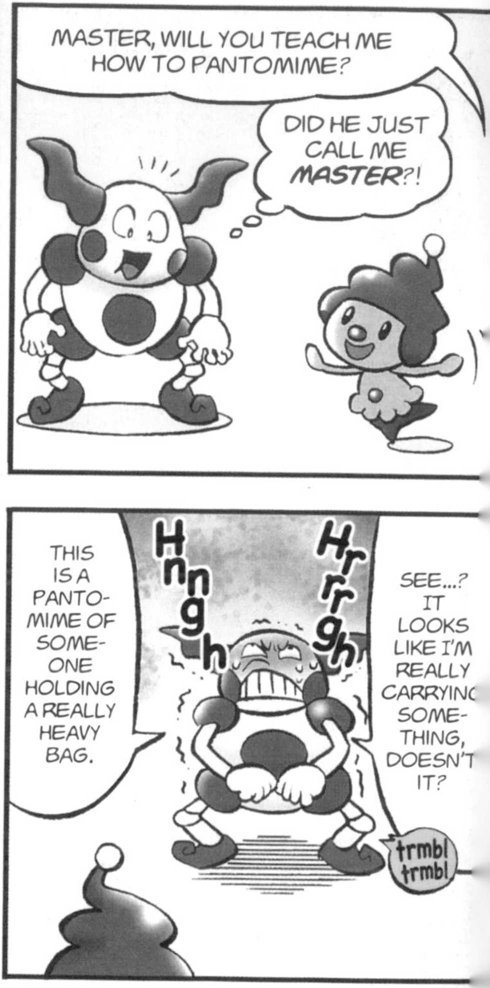
MASTER, WILL YOU TEACH ME HOW TO PANTOMIME?
DID HE JUST CALL ME *MASTER*?!
THIS IS A PANTO-MIME OF SOME-ONE HOLDING A REALLY HEAVY BAG.
Hnngh
Hrrrgh
SEE...? IT LOOKS LIKE I'M REALLY CARRYING SOME-THING, DOESN'T IT?
trmbl trmbl

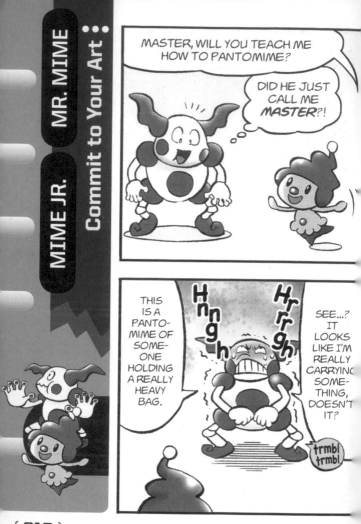

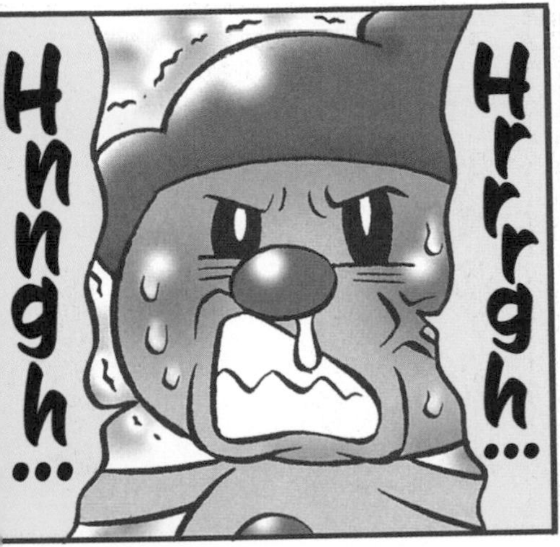
Hnngh...
Hrrrgh...

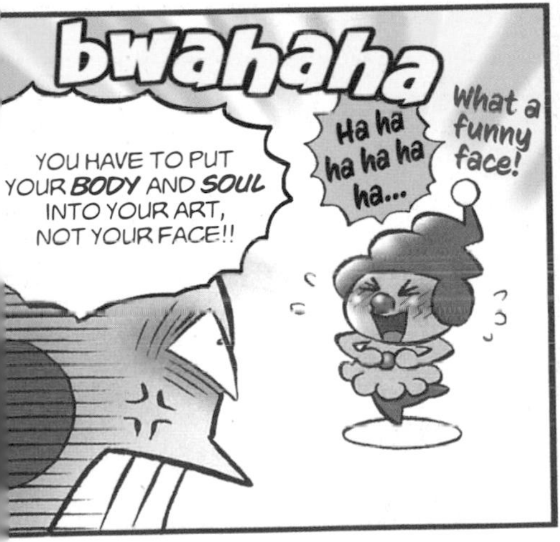
bwahaha
YOU HAVE TO PUT YOUR BODY AND SOUL INTO YOUR ART, NOT YOUR FACE!!
Ha ha ha ha ha ha...
What a funny face!

MIME JR.

The "Mime Pokémon."

MR. MIME

It is a master of pantomime. Its gestures and motions convince observers that something unseeable actually exists. Once observers believe in it, it exists as if it were a real thing. If Mr. Mime is interrupted while miming, it will suddenly Double Slap the offender with its broad hands.

MUNCHLAX MAGCARGO
A Nice Hot Meal

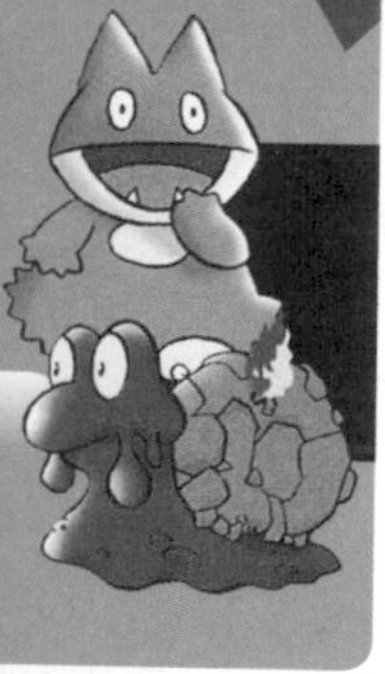

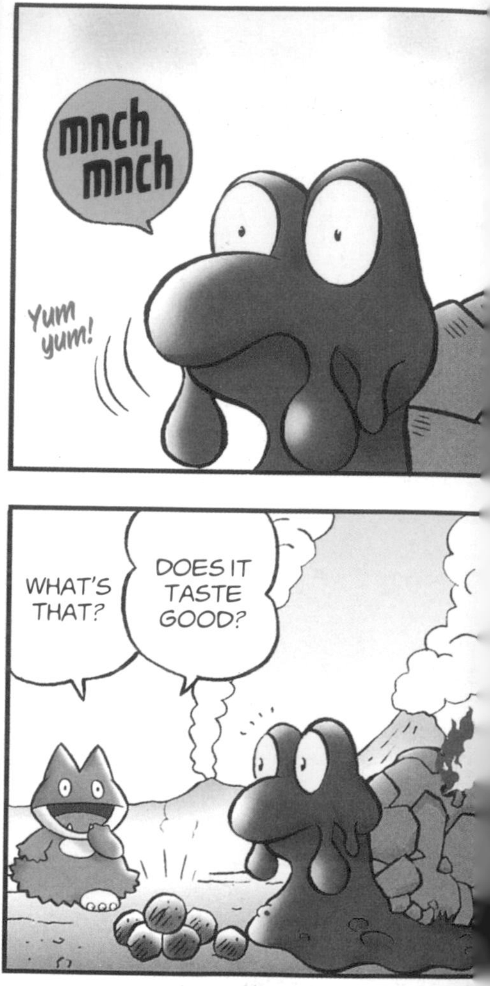
mnch mnch
Yum yum!
WHAT'S THAT?
DOES IT TASTE GOOD?

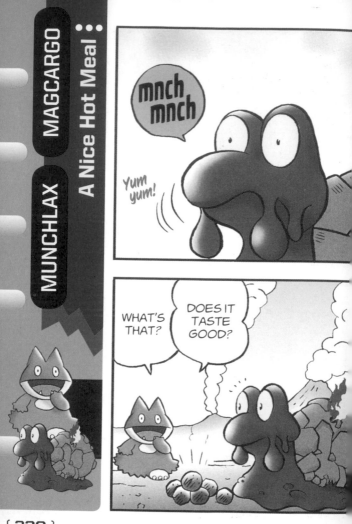

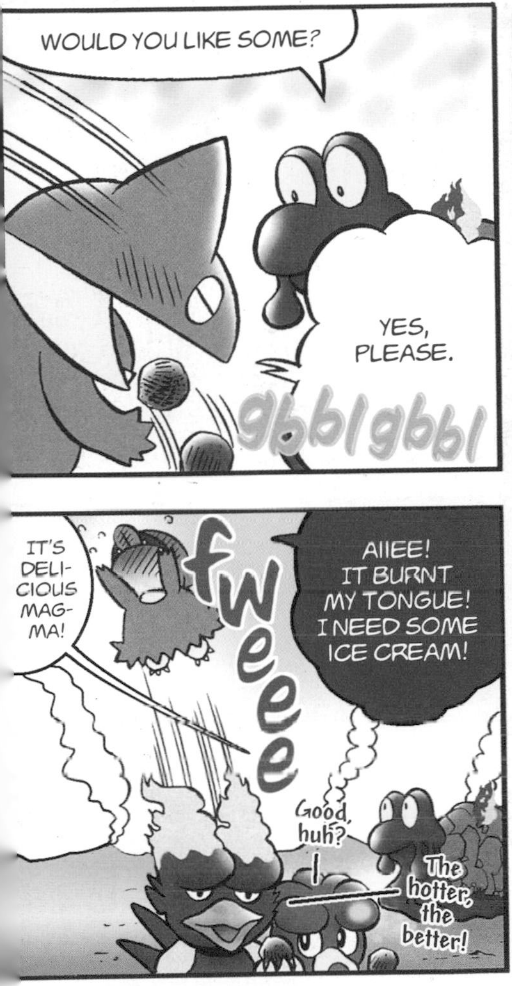
WOULD YOU LIKE SOME?
YES, PLEASE.
gbbl gbbl
IT'S DELI-CIOUS MAG-MA!
fweee
AIIEE! IT BURNT MY TONGUE! I NEED SOME ICE CREAM!
Good, huh?
The hotter, the better!

MUNCHLAX

This "Big Eater Pokémon" is a Normal type and the preevolved form of Snorlax. A carefree Pokémon who is always sleeping. It eats a lot with its large mouth.

MAGCARGO

The shell on its back is made of hardened magma. Tens of thousands of years spent living in volcanic craters have turned Magcargo's body into magma.

Use this alphabetical list to find the pages with comics and information about your favorite Pokémon!

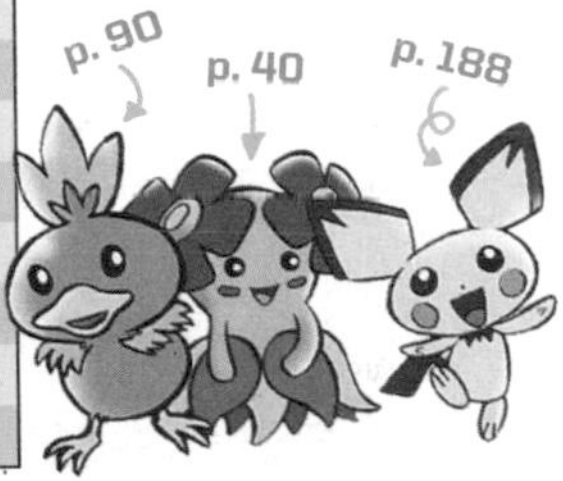

p. 90
p. 40
p. 188

Pokémon Pocket Comics Classic
VIZ Media Edition

Story & Art by SANTA HARUKAZE

©2018 The Pokémon Company International.
©1995–2006 Nintendo / Creatures Inc. / GAME FREAK inc.
TM, ®, and character names are trademarks of Nintendo.

ALL COLOR BAN POKÉMON 4KOMA MANGA ZENSHU
by Santa HARUKAZE
© 2006 Santa HARUKAZE
All rights reserved.
Original Japanese edition published by SHOGAKUKAN.
English translation rights in the United States of America, Canada, the United Kingdom,
Ireland, Australia and New Zealand arranged with SHOGAKUKAN.

Original Japanese Edition
With the Cooperation of / Shogakukan-Shueisha Productions Co., Ltd.
Editor / Jun SAKATA (Jungle Factory)
Designer / Tariji SASAKI

English Adaptation/Bryant Turnage, Annette Roman
Translation/Tetsuichiro Miyaki
Touch-up & Lettering/Susan Daigle-Leach
Design/Shawn Carrico
Editor/Annette Roman

The stories, characters and incidents mentioned in this publication are entirely fictional.

Printed in China

Published by VIZ Media, LLC
P.O. Box 77010
San Francisco, CA 94107

10 9 8 7 6 5 4 3 2 1
First printing, November 2018

PARENTAL ADVISORY
POKÉMON POCKET COMICS
CLASSIC is rated A and is suitable
for readers of all ages.

viz.com